Pra

"Eric Brown's *Helix* is a classic concept—a built world to dwarf Rama and Ringworld—a setting for a hugely imaginative adventure. *Helix* is the very DNA of true SF. This is the rediscovery of wonder."
Stephen Baxter

"Eric Brown is *the* name to watch in SF."
Peter F. Hamilton

"Eric Brown joins the ranks of Graham Joyce, Christopher Priest and Robert Holdstock as a master fabulist."
Paul di Filippo

"*Kéthani*'s beauty is in its simplicity—by never attempting to aim above its height, it attains a kind of self-contained allure that is almost impossible to ignore. This is surely one of Brown's breakthrough stories, an achievement that highlights the extensive talents of an author destined, like his characters, for something far greater."
SciFi Now

"There is always something strikingly probable about the futures that Eric Brown writes... No matter how dark the future that Eric Brown imagines, the hope of redemption is always present. No matter how alien the world he describes, there is always something hauntingly familiar about the situations that unfold there."
Tony Ballantyne

well is balance the big concepts with the character drama... Brown's prose is very readable... You'll have a good time with it."
Deathray Magazine

"Brown concentrates on stunning landscapes and in the way he conveys the conflicting points of view between races... No matter how familiar each character becomes, they continue to appear completely alien when viewed through the opposing set of eyes. Brown has a casual and unpretentious style and... the accessibility, the tenderness between characters and more importantly the scale of wonder involved are what makes this highly enjoyable escapism."
Interzone

"Eric Brown is a masterful storyteller. *Helix* is put together extraordinarily well, jumping between the POVs of Hendry and Ehrin, holding back on key bits of information and delaying inevitable moments with leaps of perspective timed precisely to make us want to read to the end. It's a fun read... the action is all worked through with great finesse... All the elements are here for something great: a massive construct, first contact with an alien species, an autocratic government... Eric Brown is often lauded as the next big thing in science fiction and you can see why..."
Strange Horizons

ALSO BY ERIC BROWN

Novels
Xenopath
Necropath
Kéthani
Helix
New York Dreams
New York Blues
New York Nights
Penumbra
Engineman
Meridian Days

Novellas
Starship Fall
Starship Summer
Revenge
The Extraordinary Voyage of Jules Verne
Approaching Omega
A Writer's Life

Collections
Threshold Shift
The Fall of Tartarus
Deep Future
Parallax View (with Keith Brooke)
Blue Shifting
The Time-Lapsed Man

As Editor
The Mammoth Book of New Jules
Verne Adventures
(with Mike Ashley)

COSMOPATH

A BENGAL STATION NOVEL

ERIC BROWN

SOLARIS

First published 2009 by Solaris
an imprint of Rebellion Publishing Ltd.
Riversde House
Osney Mead
Oxford
OX2 0ES
UK

www.solarisbooks.com

ISBN-13: 978-1-84416-833-0

10 9 8 7 6 5 4 3 2 1

A CIP catalogue record for this book is available from the
British Library.

Designed & typeset by Rebellion.

Printed and bound in the US.

This novel is for the Pickerel Regulars; Chris Beckett, Una McCormack, Philip Vine and Ian Whates

ONE

THE KORTH ASSASSIN

Vaughan was three days into a routine murder investigation when the assassin came after him with a pulse-gun.

The monsoon rains were late this year and it was another sultry day on Bengal Station. Soon the seasonal downpour would drop unannounced from the heavens, deluging the top level and sluicing away the accumulated filth of months. Until then the heat would remain intolerable and the mood of the citizens increasingly fraught. The humidity incubated anger, and hair-trigger tempers tripped at the slightest provocation. Vaughan had been working for the Kapinsky Agency long enough to know that the crime rate spiked in the weeks leading up to the first rains. It was never his favourite time of year.

He sat at a table on the terrace of the Kit-Kat Bar overlooking Silom Road, a glass of ice-cold Blue Mountain beer before him. He tapped the keys of the handset on his left wrist, enabling his tele-ability, and instantly the minds of those around him flared into life.

Four days ago a high-class prostitute had been stabbed to death in an alley off Silom Road. The death of another working girl would have passed unnoticed, and uninvestigated, had she not been the favourite of someone high up in the government. The Kapinsky Agency had been called in to bring the killer to justice, and Lin had dropped the case in Vaughan's lap.

The other telepaths in the agency had ragged him about the job, but Lin had known what she was doing. Six years ago Vaughan's wife Sukara had left Thailand, where she had been a working girl in a Bangkok brothel, and now she taught English to the girls who worked the escort agencies around Silom Road. She had known the murdered woman, and put Vaughan into contact with the woman's friends who might otherwise have been suspicious of an official investigator.

He'd talked to the women, and scanned them, but come up with nothing.

Now he scanned at random, on the off chance that he might happen upon some stray thought, conscious or subconscious, that might lead him in the right direction. He flitted through minds close by, dipping for memories of the dead woman. She was known in the bar, but no one working or drinking here today knew anything about her death. The escort agency had its base next door, in the polycarbon high-rise that soared like a scimitar into the cloudless blue sky. Vaughan moved through the minds of the women there, quickly, not wanting to mire himself in the short-term memories of working prostitutes: some had known the murder victim, and many were grieving. In the penthouse suite, Vaughan came across the pulsing collective signature of an orgy: four respected Indian politicians and a dozen Thai and Indian women were working up a sweat in the air-conditioned, mattress-lined room reserved for gold-chip customers. One of the men had been the dead girl's patron, now sublimating his grief with the energetic assistance of his next favourite.

Vaughan withdrew his probe, despite the first stirrings of arousal – or perhaps because of them. These situations were common in his line of work, and he felt like a voyeur.

He touched a control on his handset and mind-silence sealed over him. He wondered if it were guilt that moved him to dial Sukara's code.

"Jeff!" She beamed up from his metacarpal screen. "How's it going?"

"Slowly. Are you at the hospital yet?"

"Daddy!" Li's round face pushed Sukara from the frame and giggled at him. She looked better than she had for days, the waxy pallor gone from her cheeks. "We going to see doctor!"

Sukara appeared again. "I'm just in the grounds. I'll call you when we've seen Dr Chang." She peered past him. "Are you in a bar, Mr Vaughan?"

He smiled. "All in the line of work."

She laughed. "Love you, Jeff. Bye."

It's nothing, he told himself for the hundredth time that day. Li had been sick for a week, listless and lacking appetite. He'd put it down to the time of year, but Sukara had taken Li to see their local medic who'd recommended a specialist, just to be on the safe side. Vaughan wished he'd been present at the examination, in order to discern the truth behind the medic's bland platitudes.

He'd reassured Sukara that there was nothing to worry about, and wished he could convince himself.

"Mr Vaughan?"

He looked up. A gamin Thai street-kid, about fourteen, bandy-legged and flat-chested, squinted at him in the blazing sun.

Vaughan was taken back years, to the time he'd first met Sukara's sister, Tiger. This kid was her double.

He smiled. "How can I help?"

The girl made a nervous knot of her fingers. "Ah, you Sukara's husband, no?"

"That's right."

"You investigate murder of Kia, no?"

Vaughan sat up. "Right again. Why don't you sit down and I'll get you a drink?"

The kid winced as a flier screamed overhead, violating airspace. She slipped into the seat opposite and Vaughan ordered a mango lassi from a passing waiter. Her face was slick with sweat.

If the girl knew Sukara, then that meant she was a prostitute. Surreptitiously, below the level of the table, he enabled his tele-ability. The girl's psyche swamped him. He fielded the emanation, damped it down, and was surprised to learn that the kid was eighteen.

"You knew Kia, right?" he asked.

Her grief leapt at him. Images of Kia and the kid – her name was Lula – strolling through in the park were uppermost in her mind; deeper, and Vaughan saw the images of her everyday work, the abuse she had suffered recently. He shut them out.

"Kia and me, we good friends. Like sisters. She knew man, regular customer. He frightened her, said he was going to kill her…"

He probed. The first thing he came across was the fact that she knew he was a telepath; she had debated coming to him with this information, at once not wanting him reading her secrets, but compelled to tell him what she knew.

And what pitiful secrets… She'd stolen a necklace from the market last week, when she had no money; she'd enjoyed sex with a young man who treated her well… Vaughan felt a sudden upwelling of emotion and incipient tears stung his eyes.

She also knew what Sukara had told her: that she, Sukara, had once been a working girl, and now she was married to the finest man in the world. The kid thought it a fairy story, hardly believed it could be true, and Vaughan read in her juvenile mind the doubt that any relationship between a man and a woman could be as good as Sukara claimed.

"This man…?" he prompted.

He captured the image of the guy as it surfaced in her mind: a well-dressed Indian business-man.

"His name is Mr Narayan…" she began, but Vaughan had already read that, and more.

Narayan owned a bar off Silom Road, a plush sex club catering for the half a dozen alien races which stopped off at the Station spaceport. Narayan had hired Kia's services once a week, then tried to lure her into working for him. When she'd refused, saying she didn't want to work with Ee-tees, he'd beaten her and threatened her life.

The kid recounted all this to Vaughan between

sips of lassi, and he nodded and let her go on. Whether Narayan was her killer remained to be seen, but it was his first lead in three days.

She faltered, then said, "Mr Vaughan...?"

He reached across the table and laid a hand on hers. "Kia wasn't in pain. It happened so quickly. She didn't even know she'd been attacked."

The girl's wide eyes leaked big tears and she bit her lip, nodding.

He was aware of her next question forming, and pre-empted it, "Of course I love Sukara. She's a very special person. We... we went through a lot together."

"Sukara, she say, you saved her life."

He smiled. In reality, Sukara had saved his life. He said, "We saved each other, Lula."

She said, "Maybe I'll find someone, one day, no?"

Vaughan nodded. "I think the boy you know, Ajay – he's a good person."

She beamed. "You think so? So do I!"

He read her joy as she stood up, making to go. Vaughan stopped her. He took out his wallet and offered her a hundred baht note.

She stared at the money, then murmured, "I don't want paying for telling you about Mr Narayan. I did it for Kia—"

"I think Kia would like you to buy the dress you were looking at the other day. Didn't she always say you suited red?"

Lula smiled and took the note, then waved and slipped from the terrace. Seconds later she was lost in the crowd surging along the street.

He sipped his drink, leaving his tele-ability enabled. He was aware that the orgy next door had played itself out; the politicians returning to the senate while the girls took showers or counted their earnings.

He spoke into his handset and got through to a female-voiced computer program at the agency. "What can you tell me about a Mr Narayan, the owner of the Blue World Bar, Silom Road?"

"One moment, please."

The reply came a second later. "Rajeesh Narayan, forty-five, Indian national, resident of Bengal Station. Criminal record for illegal transference of cash, illicit narcotic substances. Address: Penthouse suit, Blue World Bar, Silom Road, Trat Mai sector."

"Anything else?" he asked.

"Negative."

He cut the link and looked along the street. The crowd surged down the thoroughfare like some multiheaded Chinese dragon, accompanied by a miasma of conflicting emotions. He was about to deactivate when he sensed something: a hundred metres to his left, he came across an area of mind-static, which indicated a citizen wearing a mind-shield. He glanced up and caught a quick glimpse of someone staring at him. Seconds later the fluid movement of the crowd concealed the watcher.

He'd seen enough, though, to recognise the alien: a tall, jade-green humanoid from Tau Ceti III. What did they call themselves? The Korth.

He wondered at an Ee-tee wearing a mind-shield. The fact was that the workings of alien minds were so abstruse as to be unreadable by human telepaths. He wondered if this one was taking no chances – or if he, Vaughan, was being paranoid. Had the alien actually been looking at him?

He scanned, but found no evidence of the mind-static, and told himself not to be so uptight. The alien had evidently moved off, out of range.

He deactivated, relaxed into the resultant silence, and finished his drink.

Two minutes later he quit the terrace and slipped into the crowded street, making for the alley and Narayan's sex club.

Silom Road stretched from one corner of the Station to the other, a main arterial through-way connecting the rich Thai suburbs of the north-eastern sector to the spaceport. The raised railway ran parallel, along which white trains strobed like torpedoes; overhead, the din of the crowd was frequently drowned out by the scream of fliers crisscrossing the Station at five times the speed of sound.

He reckoned he had another half-kilometre to walk when his handset chimed. He accessed the call, assuming it was Sukara.

Instead, Lin Kapinsky's thin face stared up from the screen. "Jeff, where are you?"

"Checking a lead on the Kia murder case. What's wrong?" He paused beneath the awning of a body-sculpting parlour, aware of the stench of cauterised flesh that seeped from the entrance.

"Maybe nothing. It's just that... You know Patel, the telepath you worked with years back at the 'port?"

"Sure. What about him?"

"He was found dead earlier today. His throat cut. Police suspect a professional assassin."

Vaughan nodded, feeling suddenly numb. He'd liked Patel, a cheery Bengali who'd never let the stress of the job sour his amiability.

Something clicked. He said, "You're linking it with the other deaths, right?"

"Look at it this way, that's the third telepath murdered this week. I could put them down to coincidence, but then I got the police report on Connors—"

"And?"

"The work of a professional. Shot through the head at close range. The first was Travers, and he was taken out by a car-bomb, again the work of a pro. And now Patel."

He nodded. "Any thoughts?"

"I've got no goddamned idea at all, Vaughan."

He grunted, "You don't know how reassuring that sounds."

"Okay, wise-guy, what do you think?"

He glanced across the street, at a snake charmer using an electric oboe to coax a Lyran silver eel from its basket. "They all worked for different agencies, right?"

"Go on."

"So chances are they weren't working on the same case. Therefore, the killer, or killers, aren't trying to protect themselves, or whoever."

"There is one link," Kapinsky said. "Travers, Connors, and Patel, they were each the very best telepath working for their respective agency."

Vaughan shrugged. "Coincidence?"

"Might be, but I'm taking no chances. I've always thought you were up there in the top four…"

"What are you trying to say, Lin?" he asked, knowing full well what she was about to lay on him.

"You're the best I've got, Vaughan–"

"And you want to protect your investment, right?"

"Shades of the cynical Vaughan of old."

He smiled. "No. I just know the way your mind works. So... what do you suggest?"

"Take a week off, hole up in some expensive hotel. Lay low and we'll take it from there."

"A week off on full pay? You're turning into an altruist, Lin."

"Like you said, just trying to protect my investment."

"Okay, I'll just get something out of the way. Five o'clock tonight I'll take off with Su and the girls."

"I'd rather you quit now and get the hell out. The Kia case can wait."

"Lin, I've just got the first real lead in three days. I'll be through in an hour."

She hesitated, then nodded. "Okay, but by five tonight you're out of here, okay? I'll keep you posted."

He cut the connection. Three telepaths killed within a week looked like more than just coincidence. And if Kapinsky was spooked enough to subsidise a short vacation, he wasn't about to complain.

He left the reek of singed flesh behind and elbowed his way through the crowd. He was tall, even for a Westerner, and therefore a good head and shoulders taller than the Indians and Thais around him. He could see over the heads of the milling crowd to the near horizon, where skyscrapers and towerpiles bristled like the brandished weapons of a charging army. In the distance a dozen voidliners, great bulging behemoths painted in the various liveries of their lines, moved with gargantuan grace over the spaceport, coming in to land after long voyages across the Expansion or setting forth on trips to the many far-flung colony worlds.

He came to the alley and pushed his way through the crowd, then instinctively pressed himself against the crumbling wall and enabled his tele-ability.

He scanned, searching for the distinctive signature of mind-shield static. He thought he caught a brief signal – then it was gone, swept away in the surging pedestrian flow. He peered around the corner, looking for the tall jade-green Tau Cetian: all he saw were the smiling faces of Thais and Indians going about their endless daily business. Reassured, but still wary enough to keep his program enabled, he moved off down the alley.

The Blue World Bar was a discreet two-storey establishment – one floor on the top level of the Station, and the lower one on the level below – which fronted for an expensive and exclusive brothel.

As he flashed his ID at the surly doorman and pushed his way inside, Vaughan couldn't help being aware of the hundred or so minds within the bar. Half of them were human, and in less than ten seconds he read everything from revulsion at the acts some of them were required to perform, to vicarious ecstasy at being made love to by the supernumerary phalluses of a Capellan amphibian.

Then there were the alien minds, which communicated themselves to Vaughan as great abstract swirls of emotion, fragmented images he had no hope of decoding. He guessed it was something like being blind and having to make sense of an oil painting by dint of touch alone.

He steered his probes away from the alien miasma and looked for evidence of the bar's owner, Mr Narayan.

In the mind of a bar-girl he gleaned the information that Narayan would be returning at four. It was now just after three.

Vaughan ordered a beer and looked around the low-lit room. The floor-space was divided into booths and areas of sunken sofas, where men and women entertained aliens with drinks and drugs before retiring to private rooms on the lower level. The walls were adorned with moving images of various worlds: he recognised the spaceport at Mars, the blue jungles of Jharu, Acrab II, and the famous floating cities of Gharab, Procyon VI. The entire ceiling was given over to what at first he thought was a work of abstract art. A pulsing orange oval took up much of the space, within which was a spinning blue disc; dotted about the oval were perhaps a hundred bright white lights, like stars.

Seconds later, Vaughan realised that he'd seen something similar before, and the image resolved itself.

It was a stylised representation of the human Expansion. The blue disc was Earth, the orange oval the extent of human territory, and the hundred or so white lights the planets to date discovered and colonised. Only then did he make out the dozen duller red points, which denoted the homeworlds of the sentient aliens discovered during humankind's ever outward push. He knew that the Expansion extended some eight hundred light years from Earth in every direction, and as he sipped his beer he wondered idly what marvels might be contained in the infinite reaches beyond humanity's current, infinitesimal diaspora.

Then his attention was snatched away by a new arrival in the entrance lobby to his left. He sensed the scratchy static of the mind-shield, then turned and saw the Tau Cetian slip into the room and move to a distant booth.

He counselled caution. There was no evidence, yet, to jump to the conclusion that the alien was following him. The bar was a legitimate destination for Ee-tees, after all.

In the mind of the bar-girl he located the position of the stairs that led down to Level Two. He finished his beer, pushed himself from the bar, and made his way casually towards the exit.

Steps led down a stairwell. He descended, keeping tabs on the area of static in the bar above his head. He came to a second, smaller bar, around the perimeter of which were doors leading to bedrooms, group chambers, and sex pools. Ahead was the sliding door of the exit, and beyond that the artificial daylight of Level Two.

Vaughan hurried towards the exit, pulse racing. Seconds later the static high above him shifted as the alien made its move.

He told himself that it could still be coincidence, but at the same time he knew he was kidding himself. The static moved towards him as the alien took the stairwell.

He left the bar and crossed the concourse; the esplanades and outdoor bars were busy with citizens drawn to this level's air-conditioning after the heat of the top level, and the mind-noise was correspondingly loud. Vaughan crossed towards the entrance of a municipal park, which called itself the Australasian Arboretum. Gum trees and eucalyptus extended for a kilometre in every direction, providing adequate cover from the pursuing Korth.

He entered the park and hurried along a path, rounded a bend, then ensuring he was unobserved stepped from the path and ducked through a stand of gum trees. He doubled back on himself, moving towards the concourse.

The Korth was on the second level now, pacing through the bar towards the exit. The hiss of static became louder in Vaughan's head as he came to the perimeter fence. He knelt, concealed himself behind a fan of ferns, and peered back towards the Blue World Bar.

The alien emerged from the bar. Vaughan expected it to pause, assess its options before moving on. To his alarm, the Korth paced across the concourse towards the park's entrance. How the hell did it know? Unless, of course, it was guessing.

It wore a thick winter jacket – its homeworld was a sultry desert that made the Sahara seem like the north pole – and Vaughan knew that the bulky padding might easily conceal a weapon.

He considered his options, made a decision, and moved. He ran through the vegetation that fringed the arboretum. There was another exit half a kay away; he'd take that and jump aboard a downchute to a crowded lower level, then attempt to lose himself there.

He probed. The alien was moving along the path. A second later it left the path and entered the shrubbery, heading towards him.

As Vaughan ran, he accessed his handset. Kapinsky answered immediately.

"Lin. I'm being followed. A Korth. Can you track me?"

Kapinsky leaned to her right for a second, tapping a console. "I've got you on-screen."

"Get some security down here. I don't know how the bastard's doing it, but it knows where I am."

"You armed?"

"A laser. But if the Korth's a professional assassin—"

"Shit. I said you should have got the hell out right away. Okay…" She spoke into a throat-mic, summoning security, and Vaughan cut the connection.

He probed. The floating static was perhaps fifty metres to his right, moving straight through the undergrowth as the alien attempted to cut him off.

He pulled the laser from beneath his shirt and thumbed off the safety control. He knew better than to bed down and enter into a shoot-out with the Korth. It was a pro, and it probably packed more efficient fire-power than his standard-issue laser.

His only hope was to outrun the bastard until security caught up with him.

He heard what sounded like the roar of a flame-thrower, and a nano-second later a wall of vegetation to his right vaporised in an instant. His heart kicked. Reflex self-protection threw him to the ground as the broad-pulse beam slashed through the air where his torso had been. He rolled, fired instinctively, and saw the alien duck behind the shattered bole of a eucalyptus tree.

Vaughan dived for cover and crawled through a bed of loam, shouldering aside green bamboo shots. He heard a second roar, heard foliage ignite behind him. He rolled onto his back and fired six times, hoping to buy himself time. He was about ten metres from the gate and the crowds that surged beyond. If he could lose himself in the press, make it to the downchute…

Then the alien called to him, and the sound sent fear tearing through Vaughan as the pulse beam had failed to do.

"Vaughan." It was a high-pitched hiss, totally alien, sounding unlike any rendition of his name he'd heard before.

How in Christ's name was the bastard tracking him? He knew that none of the extraterrestrial races discovered so far had such a highly developed sense of smell. But what about some other alien sense?

Unless, of course, it was itself a telepath and was following the static of his own mind-shield.

If so, then once he made it to the crowd he could switch off his shield and his thoughts would be relatively indistinguishable among those of the citizens around him, especially as his pursuer was an Ee-tee.

The idea gave him a kick of hope as he pulled himself through the last of the shrubbery before arriving at the gate.

He reckoned the Korth was around thirty metres behind him. He crouched, turned, and laid down a burst of fire, then surged from the border and sprinted for the gate. A beam lashed after him, reducing the concrete gate-post to rubble.

He barged through the crowd, earning insults in

three languages. He ducked his head and elbowed his way across the street, disabling his mind-shield and running a mantra he'd learned on a training course for just such a situation. The old Buddhist line, *Om mani padme hum...* Empty one's mind. Think of a flame, alone in the universe, then extinguish the flame, and think of nothing...

Which, with an alien assassin bent on slicing him into slivers, was easier said than done.

He probed. The Korth, signified by the area of static, had paused by the gate. The pause lasted three seconds, and then the alien was after him.

Vaughan was bigger than the Indians and Thais around him and, propelled by fear, he made rapid progress through the crush to the gates of the downchute station. He sprinted towards the closing mesh gate of a carriage and barged his way in. The gate clanked shut behind him. He looked back through the diamond lattice as the carriage dropped ponderously. The signature static was ten metres away, though the alien itself was not visible through the press of humanity on the station concourse.

The carriage dropped, leaving the second level behind, and Vaughan rationed himself to a small dose of relief.

He called Kapinsky. "Where the hell is security, Lin?"

"On their way. You're dropping from the second, right? The Korth is following in the next carriage. I have a team on the fourth-level station. Get out there and lose yourself in the crowds."

"You got it."

He got through to the agency computer and said, "Korth, from Tau Ceti III. Are any of them telepathic?"

A fraction of a second later the soft female voice answered, "Not telepathic. Empathetic. They cannot read thoughts, merely emotions."

"They can read the emotions of other species?"

"Affirmative," came the reply.

"And human mind-shields? Are they effective against the Korth?"

"Negative."

Which was how the Korth had tracked him so far, not by tracing the static given off by his integral mind-shield, but by identifying his emotional signature and locking onto it. Which was bad news, he thought, as he wouldn't be safe concealing himself in a crowd...

He cut the connection.

He was pressed up against a fat Sikh and a bony sadhu, both eyeing the tall, sweating Westerner with bovine suspicion. The overcrowded carriage was hot and stank of rank body odour, but at least he was safe until he reached the fourth level.

He thought of Sukara, wondering why the sudden vision of her should enter his head now. She was smiling at him, giggling over a glass of wine.

A minute later the carriage slowed and bobbed to a halt. The mesh gate rattled open and Vaughan popped himself from the press.

He hurried through the station, attempting to work out who among the loitering citizens were members of the security team. He scanned, detected half a dozen mind-shields in the vicinity, and hoped they wouldn't stand on ceremony when the Korth emerged. He'd never before believed in summary execution, but there was nothing like the threat of death to encourage a shift of opinion.

He exited, looked left and right, and headed for an alleyway packed with Indians who were leaving a cinema.

Above him, the Korth was dropping towards Level Four. He kept probing as he was carried along in the flow of humanity. The static ceased its fall, was held in place – obviously as the carriage came to a halt and the gates opened – then it moved again, on a horizontal plane this time.

Seconds later the other mind-shields in the vicinity converged.

Even a hundred metres away Vaughan heard the shouts and screams, and the roar of the incendiary pulse beam.

Sickened, he slid his probe around the area. Five of the six mind-shields belonging to security were still, unmoving. One was mobile, but had slowed significantly, and Vaughan guessed the man was injured and rolling in agony.

One area of mind-static had exited the station and was heading down the alley towards him.

The Korth, presumably.

If he could outrun the bastard, put about a half kilometre between him and his pursuer and get himself out of range of the alien's mind-probes, then he was home free... The problem was, how to do that among the press of humanity on this level? The rub was, he needed the crowd to give him some measure of cover, but he needed relatively open space if he were to make a run for it...

Then he remembered the Aquaworld habitat on this level, and allowed himself a second small ration of hope.

He squeezed from the crowd, sprinted along a relatively depopulated boulevard, then cut across a plaza towards the beckoning logo of a leaping dolphin, above which arced the legend: Aquaworld.

A week back, after bringing Li and Pham here to sample the water-wonders of Aquaworld, he'd vowed never again to be suckered into the crass black hole of corporate merchandising. Now he approached the gates as if they were the pearly portals of heaven itself.

He probed. The alien was in the alley, turning into the boulevard. About a hundred metres away, Vaughan estimated.

He ran through the entrance, throwing a wad of baht at a startled clerk, and headed towards the Antares IV waterworld concession.

Families lined up before the airlocks that gave access to the variously sized submersibles, but the lock for the one-man subs was vacant. He overpaid another clerk and slipped into the airlock. Seconds later he inserted himself feet-first into the sub, dogged the hatch, and familiarised himself with the controls. He steered through the irising portal, easing the sub from the airlock and into the facsimile of the aqueous habitat of Antares IV.

Last week he'd taken the girls on a leisurely tour of everything the vast tank had to offer, taking in the coral habitats of the squid-analogues and the great shoals of the planet's sentient natives, the diaphanous cetaceans who communicated via a complex sequencing of their polychromatic internal organs. Now he made straight for the diametrically opposite airlock down on the fifth level. The tank was, he guessed, about a kilometre square; with luck he'd be able to outrun the limit of the Korth's mind-probe and lose himself on Level Five when he exited.

He sent out a probe. The patch of static was dimming as he drew away from the airlock. He gripped the controls and shot between a shoal of tiny silver fish, like a million coins moving as one: these were the unique Sarth, he recalled, a sub-sentient hive-mind in control of a myriad separate bodies.

His handset buzzed. He accessed the call.

"Jeff," Kapinsky said. "Good thinking. We have teams on Levels Four and Five and tracking the Korth."

"Tell 'em to take care. You saw what the bastard did to the first team?"

"They're taking appropriate measures, Jeff. See you soon."

"Let's hope so," Vaughan replied, but Kapinsky had cut the link.

He probed again, and to his relief failed to locate the signature static. All he picked up was the mind-noise of the families flitting through the water in their subs. He looked ahead; he could see the vast wall of the tank, camouflaged with a multicoloured coral effect, before which flitted shoals of alien fish. He sighted the circular hatch of an airlock and headed for it.

A minute later he slipped his sub into the hatch. The vehicle rang as mechanical grabs made it fast and water sluiced from the lock. Seconds later a green light indicated that it was safe for Vaughan to alight. He pushed himself from the sub and hurried to the outer hatch, shallow breathing to mitigate the stench of Antares brine and seaweed.

Seconds later he was through the hatch and striding towards the Aquaworld exit. He probed. There was no evidence of the Korth's mind-shield static in the vicinity.

This sector of Level Five was a business district, and the three-storey offices crammed between the level's floor and ceiling were emptying of tired citizens after a day's shift. Vaughan joined them, inserting himself into a flow of Tata drones as they made for the nearest downchute station.

He continued past it and a few hundred metres further on slipped into a bar and ordered a Blue Mountain beer.

He regained his breath, and along with it his composure. Now he allowed himself to feel the fear that his adrenaline had so far kept at bay. With the delayed fear came the intellectual fall-out: for whatever reason, someone had set an alien assassin on his trail, the same someone who had already brought about the deaths of three other telepaths.

His thoughts were interrupted by the summons of his handset. That would be Kapinsky, to tell him that security had got the Korth and he was free to show his face.

He accessed the call.

"Sukara?"

She stared out at him. She looked, he thought, shocked. It came to him that she somehow knew what had happened to him. Then she spoke, and began weeping.

He listened to what she had to say, and it was as if something inside him had turned to ice.

He shook his head and asked her to tell him again, and she repeated herself. She said she'd see him back at the apartment in an hour and cut the connection.

Vaughan stared at the blank screen, his heartbeat thudding.

When he looked up, he saw the Korth standing in the entrance to the bar and scanning the drinkers in the bar's dim interior.

He should never have let Sukara's call divert his attention from probing for the mind-shield static. Then, he might have done something about the approach of the alien assassin. Now he was cornered, and instead of feeling fear, all he did feel was a sadness for Sukara and the girls if he failed to best the alien in the ensuing shoot-out.

He went for his laser, at the same time wondering why the Korth hadn't singled him out and attacked immediately. As he surreptitiously thumbed off the safety control, it came to him. The Korth was an empath, and had been locked on to his earlier emotional signature.

The fact was that Sukara's call had, briefly, disrupted that default signature, submerging it with his shock...

No sooner had this thought formulated than the alien turned, easing its laser from the folds of its padded jacket.

Something moved behind the Korth, and before either the alien or Vaughan had time to discharge their respective weapons, a woman in combat fatigues yelled something Vaughan didn't catch.

The alien pirouetted, levelling its laser. The woman fired. The flash blinded Vaughan and he dropped to the floor. When he next looked, the Korth was swaying in the entrance, headless, before falling in stages on its multi-jointed legs and scattering tables and chairs.

Watched by petrified customers, the woman stepped over the alien's corpse, holstering her pistol, and strode over to Vaughan while the rest of her team moved in on the alien. She gave him a hostile look.

"Vaughan?"

He climbed to his feet.

"You're one lucky son of a bitch, man," she said.

"Lucky?" he whispered to himself as the woman rejoined her team.

He raised his wrist and activated his handset, replaying Sukara's message.

"Jeff," she had wept. "Jeff, I've just seen Dr Chang, and he said, he said…" She broke down, then managed, "Jeff, Li has leukaemia!"

TWO

IN TWO MINDS

Parveen Das shut down her softscreen and smiled at the three seminar students. "Right. That's it for today, and for the term. Enjoy your holidays."

"Are you going away?" Rukshana asked her. She was Das's favourite student, a Dalit plucked from the slums by Kolkata University's Uniquely Gifted programme. The girl reminded Das of herself at seventeen, bright and eager to learn and innocent. How things had changed in just twenty years.

"Would you believe I'm taking a voidliner out to the Expansion's farthest limit and visiting a relatively unexplored colony world?"

"No!" her students said as one.

Das nodded. "No lie. In a few days I'll be hurtling through the void. I'll tell you all about it when I get back."

Their disbelief was to be expected; she reminded herself that most of her students had never left Bengal State, never mind the Communist States of

India. The stars were a destination beyond their wildest dreams.

When her students left the room, she turned to the window and stared out. From the fourth floor of the university's west wing, she had a bird's-eye view down College Street and across the sprawl of Kolkata. Pedestrians filled the wide conduit between ancient, flaking buildings like ants in a formicary. The flow was never-ending, and Das found the sight of so many citizens mind-numbingly depressing: they represented so much mind-noise, which thanks to her latest implants she was able to switch off altogether, unlike in the early days when the constant migraine of brain-noise had almost driven her mad. Now, the mere sight of packed humanity was enough to trigger a surge of retrospective pain.

How she longed for the wide open spaces of the Deccan, or the empty wilderness of some of the colony worlds she'd visited, where she had taken a car and driven for hundreds of kilometres, parked up and stood out in the open and turned on her tele-ability.

Silence. Absolute silence. Not a human mind in any direction...

She had an hour to kill before she made her way to the labs. She locked her room and passed the Senior Commons Room. She considered popping in for a coffee, but decided against it. Bhandra haunted the SCR and he'd hit on her as usual with his overweening assumption that, because she was single and in her late thirties, she was desperate and available. She'd once probed him and read his desires towards her. That had been enough to ensure she was never alone in the same room with him; she had no wish to be bound and sodomised and stabbed with burning incense sticks, even by a distinguished professor of twenty-first century English.

She bought a coffee at the university's outdoor café and sat on the terrace, staring through the railings at the passing tide of pedestrians. There were no beggars on the streets these days, unemployment was low, and India was enjoying its greatest period of prosperity for a century. From the main building of the university, a great Indian flag flapped in the sultry breeze: an orange, white, and green tricolour with a red hammer and sickle at its centre.

She wondered how great a part in the country's prosperity people like her had played, the millions of citizens the party had plucked from poverty and educated so that they might one day pay-back and serve the motherland in countless ways. How had she come to work for the government, and did she resent the gentle coercion a suited official had applied to her conscience shortly after her graduation? It was still a question she wrestled with daily.

She knew that her colleagues, and many of her students, wondered about her: the brilliant xenologist, with a dozen books to her name, internationally famous and feted by politicians and research institutes, who lived alone and had never – at least since she had taught the university, which was ten years – had a boyfriend, or a girlfriend, come to that.

How could she tell them that her ability militated against finding that perfect someone whom she might trust and love? Always, on meeting seemingly pleasant and charming men, she had succumbed to the temptation of ascertaining whether their psyches were as pristine as their outward personas – and always she had been disappointed. It was easier to absorb herself in her work, in her students – in her occasional government duties – and keep a tight rein on her emotions.

And then, a month ago, she had met Rabindranath Chandrasakar at a party at the Chinese embassy; a colleague had introduced the billionaire voidline owner, and they'd chatted for an hour. He'd surprised her on two counts: for a filthy capitalist exploiter of his workers, he was a gracious, charming and intelligent man – and he seemed genuinely interested both in her work and in her as a person. She judged he was more than thirty years her senior, but he'd kept himself in good condition and could easily pass for fifty.

He'd surprise her again a day later when he invited her to dine at an exclusive French restaurant in the city's international quarter. They'd discussed her work, his experiences on various planets around the Expansion, and had parted with a chaste kiss.

They'd met regularly after that, and two weeks ago he'd asked her to stay the night in his insultingly opulent penthouse suite, and she had willingly agreed. She'd surprised herself again, and enjoyed the experience of sexual intimacy. Earlier, over dinner, she'd been tempted to probe him, but decided instead to tell him about her ability, about her desire to read his mind.

Chandrasakar had smiled and said that he was shielded with the latest Rio technology – for security reasons, of course. But, perhaps, one day when he knew her better...

She'd wondered if she truly wanted to disappoint herself with access to his secret thoughts and memories... but she was gladdened that he was willing to consider opening himself to her inspection, one day.

The last time they'd met, a few days ago, he'd said that he'd like her to accompany him on an expedition to an unexplored star.

What could be more romantic than that?

A tall Chinese guy slipped into a seat at a nearby table and accessed his handset. He glanced up at Parveen and smiled, and she looked away quickly. She wondered if she were exuding more confidence since Chandrasakar's attentions; she'd noticed men looking at her more often recently. The thought disturbed her, oddly; she liked the idea of being unnoticed, of blending into the background.

He looked at her again. She thought he was about to say something, but she glanced at her handset and saw that it was time to be heading off. She finished her coffee, pushed through the crowded street and hailed a cab to take her south to the government labs in the Taltala district.

Five minutes later the car eased itself through the lab checkpoint; she paid the driver and stepped out, into the blazing summer heat, and hurried towards the guarded entrance. She showed her pass and the security woman nodded her through. After a series of further checks she found herself in a plush waiting room equipped with softscreens showing news programmes from around the world, and even from off-world. She watched an item on the building of a new dam on Mars until a receptionist called her name.

An elevator carried her to a secure underground lab, where she underwent another security scan and at last was admitted into Dr Prakesh's hallowed inner sanctum. She had expected a sanitised, scrubbed-clean technical lab when she'd first been summoned here, five years ago, staffed by technicians in white coats and rubber gloves and disposable galoshes. The reality was more like some holo-movie director's idea of a tech-geek teenager's garage, staffed by scientists whose dress code was sub-casual.

Dr Prakesh wore his hair long and gathered in a bunch. He was seated at a desk, peering through a magnifying visor. He didn't look up.

"Another upgrade, Ajay?" she asked as she shoved a pile of hardware from a swivel chair and sat down.

"The latest, and a new implant."

She suspected Ajay Prakesh suffered from autism, or at least Asperger's; at home with AIs and drone-bots, he found interaction with human beings difficult, and eye contact an impossibility.

In his company, Parveen felt almost normal.

"A new implant? What else do they want you to shove into my brain?"

He shook his head. "Not into your head. In fact, we're taking your old rig out."

"Out?"

"Ah-cha. Upstairs wants you fitted with the very latest. It'll be sourced in your handset and routed up your arm into your cerebellum. We're also upgrading your viral capabilities."

"When do I have the surgery?"

He blinked, and almost brought himself to look at her. "No surgery. We'll do it here."

She looked around at the hi-tech chaos, discarded curry trays, and crumpled plastic lassi bottles. "Hardly the most hygienic surroundings, Ajay."

He shrugged and blinked. Through the mag-visor, his bloodshot eyes looked as vast as moons. "Just following orders."

"Okay, let's have it."

He opened a wide, flat drawer and pulled out a shrink-wrapped package containing wires and coils of something like microfilaments. "The latest from the Hooghli lab. Bit more powerful than the one you've got, and the shield is foolproof."

"But why scrap the occipital?" she asked. The occipital rig was what made her telepathic, amplifying the effects of the operation she'd undergone in her late twenties.

He blinked. "Word from upstairs is that this is what will be fitted to all subjects – I mean undercover operatives – from now on."

Subjects, she thought, just about summed up what Prakesh thought of her and the other telepaths. Just the boring meat end of much more interesting soft- and hardware.

"Security," Prakesh went on. "After the op, no one will be able to tell you have tele-ability. No occipital give-away, see?"

She nodded. "So what do I do?"

"Wait while I call in a nurse, and then I'll yank out the old rig and insert the implant."

"You make it sound... industrial," she said.

"Industrial?" He blinked, the joke beyond him. "No, it's just technical."

He buzzed, and two minutes later a professional-looking nurse – professional in that at least he wore a white coat and surgical gloves – entered the lab and readied her for the procedure.

He swabbed the back of her neck around the golden inlay of her occipital rig, and Prakesh inserted some wires and probes. Parveen felt something moving around just under the skin at the base of her skull – imagine a gecko trapped in there, as she'd once tried to explain the sensation to her controller – and a second later something else clunked into her skull. Prakesh yanked, as if trying to pull her brain out through too small a hole, and from the corner of her eye she caught sight of wires and filaments dripping goo. She didn't ask.

The nurse slapped some synthi-flesh over the wound and said it'd heal in no time.

Prakesh was already working on her handset.

He opened the unit, exposing chips, and eased one end of a red filament into a port. The nurse said, "Don't be alarmed. You'll feel an odd sensation crawling up your arm. In fact, if you look closely enough you'll see the working end moving sub-dermally…"

Prakesh touched a pin to a control mechanism in her handset, and the spooled filament unwound as it was fed up the length of her arm.

"Hey," she said, as a burning sensation shot from her wrist to her shoulder, along with a tiny subcutaneous ripple. She felt something move across the outside of her skull and dock with whatever mechanism remained in her occipital region.

Prakesh ran a diagnostic and read something from a screen. "All done. Care to check it?"

"You mean, probe someone?"

Prakesh took his shield, on a chain around his

neck, and handed it to the nurse. "Just leave the room for a second."

Parveen looked at him. "You sure?"

"*Chalo!*" He shooed the nurse from the room and turned to read something from a com-screen; as far as he was concerned, he'd done his duty so far as Parveen Das was concerned and he was moving on to the next problem.

"Ah-cha, I'm enabling now, Ajay."

He nodded absently, and she tapped the code into her handset and sent out a probe towards the technician.

Shiva... She was right. Autism. There was a serious lack of anything like emotion going on in there, and even empathy was absent, but she did pick up a maelstrom of concern about... codes and programs and wetware paradigms that meant nothing to her at all. She killed the link and gave thanks that she was who she was.

"Works like a dream, Ajay," she said.

"Mmm..." he murmured.

She moved to the door.

"Oh," Prakesh said as she was about to leave. "Message from Anish – he wants you upstairs as soon as you've done here."

"I'm on my way."

If Prakesh were autistic, then Anish Lahore was the opposite, whatever the term for that might be.

He was a fat man whom Parveen had never seen stand up. In fact, she'd never seen him out of the bucket chair that cupped his three hundred pounds of solid fat; without its confines, she feared he might overflow and take up most of the floor-space in his roomy office.

He was an effusive, over-emotive Bengali in his sixties who habitually greeted Parveen by clutching her hands and hanging on for long seconds.

Anish had been her controller for three years now, and he was more like an uncle to her than some conniving party spymaster.

Or, rather, that was the image he liked to project.

He was shielded, of course, so Parveen had never had the opportunity to read him.

"Par-veen!" He gripped her hands like a solicitous grandmother and beamed into her face. "Are they treating you well at the university? I read your last paper. Ex-cellent. A gem." He had the odd linguistic habit of breaking up his words as if to add emphasis.

She managed to regain possession of her hands and sit down across the desk from him.

"Professor Ranjit Khan behaving himself?" Anish asked.

This was part of her job she didn't like. Anish Lahore wouldn't have called it snooping on her colleagues, in so many words, but that's what it amounted to. Khan was a party member, but someone high up suspected him of bourgeois sympathies. Anish had asked Parveen to keep an eye on him, report back to him any meeting the professor might have with foreign academics or politicos.

Parveen rather liked the dashing professor of applied linguistics, and made sure that what she did dish on him was innocuous.

"Khan's on his best behaviour, Anish. Anyway, what did you want to see me about?"

"How are things... *progressing* with your tame tycoon, Parveen?" Anish asked with the merest hint of a lascivious glint in his fat-slitted eyes. "I've heard that he might be travelling off planet...?"

Nothing, but nothing, escaped the attention of the party. The day after her third, and amorous, meeting with Chandrasakar, Anish called her in and asked her all about it – like a girlfriend wanting the low-down.

"Of course," he'd said, "Chandrasakar is a very powerful and influential figure. His interests, by their very nature, are opposed to those of the State. It would help if you were able to become a... confidant, shall we say, of the man."

So that was clear, then; she would be allowed to conduct an affair with Chandrasakar, but at the same time she must remember that she worked for India, and that anything she learned of potential use to the State would be very helpful indeed.

A couple of days ago Chandrasakar had zipped a message to her handset: *That trip to the stars, Parveen... are you still interested?*

She said now, "He suggested I come along."

"And will you take up this most generous invitation?"

She smiled. "What do you think?"

He beamed. "Wonderful. I'm sure the trip will be more than worthwhile, on many levels."

She laughed at her controller's lack of tact. "What do you want, Anish?"

"Mr Chandrasakar is embarking upon an expedition to Delta Cephei VII," he said. "It isn't an established colony." He produced a data-pin from his desk. "There's more about the background of the planet in here. Digest and destroy, Parveen. Among his team, so far, are a pair called…" He leaned forwards and peered at the screen on his desk. "Dr Kiki Namura and Dr David McIntosh, a biologist and a geologist respectively. Now, Mr Chandrasakar doesn't know this – his security is shamefully lax – but they're both embedded spies, working for the Federated Northern States of America. I'd like you to keep an eye on them – you know the routine. Also, Chandrasakar is in the process of hiring the services of another telepath, one Jeff Vaughan. He has no affiliations. He is what they call in the business a loose cannon, and they can be dangerous, Parveen. If you could ascertain his loyalties and the like…" he beamed, "that would be splen-did."

She nodded. "I'll do my best, Anish," she said.

He went on, "We have a cloaked voidship in the vicinity. I want you to report to the ship with whatever you find on Delta Cephei VII. Also, if things become difficult down there, and your cover is compromised, then the same ship will be on hand to effect your evacuation. The data-pin contains the ship's code."

She took the pin and slipped it into an inner pocket.

"And," he finished, "I wish you every enjoyment in your… assignations with your bourgeois paramour. I can rely on you not to allow your heart to overrule that considerable intellect, can't I?"

"Anish, how long have I been working for the party?"

"Ex-cellent!" He clapped his hands before his bulging belly and beamed at her as she rose.

"I shall be in touch, my dear," he said. "Bon voyage, as they say."

She smiled and took her leave, dropped to the street and decided to walk home rather than hail a taxi.

On the way through avenues crowded with street-vendors and performers – snake charmers with extraterrestrial eels, the latest fad – she considered Anish, and how she might handle the mission he'd handed her. For years she'd managed to walk the tightrope between party loyalty and her own interests, and she didn't want to fall off the high-wire now. She knew what she felt for the party, and for Chandrasakar... and recently she'd woken in the early hours, sweating, caught on the horns of what she considered an ethical dilemma.

So far, she'd let her heart rule her head – pushing aside her objections to her lover's politics – but how long might that be able to continue before she allowed her position to be compromised?

She felt sick at the thought and pushed it to the back of her mind.

Later, she would come to the realisation that she owed her life to the fact that her handset pinged as she was passing her favourite restaurant, the Montaz. She subscribed to a channel that filtered news stories dealing with telepaths to her handset. She glanced at the screen – read that a third telepath had been murdered on Bengal Station – saw that she was passing the Montaz and decided rather than go to the bother of cooking for herself she'd have an aloo dhal and a beer while reading about the latest killing.

She found a table beside the window, ordered, and called up the story on her screen.

A telepath called Patel had been killed while investigating a murder case for the Lewis–MacBride Agency. There were no witnesses and the police had little to go on, though they did say that they thought it likely the murder was linked to the killings of two other telepaths that week.

She'd taken an interest in the case not just because it involved her line of work: she'd known one of the victims, Connors, when he'd worked for the Police Department in Kolkata before moving to Bengal Station.

The killings so far, she knew, involved telepaths working on different cases for three different agencies... which made it hard to pin a motive on the killer. The only thing that linked the three dead men was their psi-ability.

She knew that, rationally, she had no reason to worry – but she worried.

Her aloo dhal arrived and she ate hungrily while watching the kaleidoscopic flow of citizens in the street outside.

Her handset pinged with an incoming call. The sender's name – Chandrasakar – flashed up, and she accepted it with a fluttery sense of excitement.

His well-fed face smiled out at her.

"My dear, delighted you can come along!"

She laughed. "Try keeping me away, Rab."

"I'll be on Bengal Station for a few days from tomorrow, overseeing the refit of a liner. Would you be able to get across? You can stay on the ship with me."

"Term's just ended. I'm a free agent..." She tried not to smile at the terrible pun.

"That's wonderful. I'll be in touch tomorrow. Everything okay with you?"

She considered mentioning the murders and telling him not to worry, in case he'd heard about the killings, but decided against it. "I'm fine. Relieved that the term's over for summer. No more lectures to prepare and dull papers to mark."

"And a vacation to look forward to," he finished. "I must rush. See you soon."

She smiled. "Bye, Rab."

She finished the dhal. She thought about the mission to Delta Cephei VII, and then her thoughts returned to the killings. She was telling herself that she had nothing at all to worry about when she looked up and saw, striding past the restaurant, the tall Chinese guy she'd noticed in the café earlier.

She thought it best to err on the side of caution. She paid for her meal and slipped from the restaurant through the rear entrance.

She was in a narrow alley packed with citizens. If, in the unlikely event that the guy was an assassin, he would be unlikely to strike in the crowded streets of downtown Kolkata.

His natural course of action, she reasoned, would be to make his way to her apartment, wait there, and strike when she returned.

Her apartment was in a tenement block half a kay from here. She reckoned she could get there, do what she had to do, and get out again in minutes. She took a shortcut through the back alleys and reached her apartment five minutes later. She was sweating, and it had nothing to do with the stifling humidity that suffocated the city.

She activated her security cams, both inside her rooms and out, circuited the signal through to her handset, then slipped out through the back entrance and down the fire-escape.

A minute later she was sitting in a bar across the street, sipping a Blue Mountain beer and watching the streets for any sign of the Chinese guy.

She was being paranoid, she told herself; and yet, mixed with the fear, she had to admit to feeling a frisson of excitement.

She'd been recruited to the party in her early twenties, tested psi-positive, and given the cut five years later. At the time, she'd hoped that the augmentation would prove to be a way out of the cloistered groves of academia; she'd dreamed of thrilling missions and derring-do, especially after being sent on training courses to hone her self-defence... But her expectations had been based on too many sensational holo-movies as a kid. The work she'd been given had been routine surveillance, snooping and snitching, as she liked to call it.

Her academic work had continued as before and she'd visited colony worlds friendly to the Indian cause, where reality was just another version of that on Earth, despite some interesting local variations and some genuinely bizarre aliens.

Her life, for so long, had been uneventful... and then she'd found a lover, and now she was being followed by an assassin.

Except, she told herself, she was imagining things.

She drank her beer and thought about visiting Rab on Bengal Station.

And then she saw the Chinese guy, and her heart juddered.

He eased himself through the press in the street, stood on the sidewalk looking up at her apartment, and then pushed through the revolving door and disappeared inside.

She activated her screen and stared at the revealed picture. It showed an empty landing, the top of the stairwell, and the elevator door opposite her apartment.

Holding her breath, she waited... Ten seconds later the man appeared on the landing.

The camera looked down on him from above the door of her apartment: it showed a lean-faced man in his early thirties. He looked fit, agile, but something in his dark eyes was dead.

The eyes of an assassin, she thought.

He took something from the pocket of his jacket, applied it to the lock, and a second later slipped into her apartment.

She tapped her handset and the image on the screen flickered and switched to one showing her lounge. The man moved quickly, stepping through to her bedroom to check for her in there, and then into the bathroom. He returned to the lounge, checked the sliding door to the fire-escape, ensured that it was locked, then drew the drapes and looked around the lounge. He selected a reclining chair, dragged it to the centre of the room and positioned it facing the door. He sat down, drew a slim pistol from his jacket, and waited for her to arrive home and meet her death.

She raised the bottle to her lips. She was shaking so much that she dribbled beer down her chin. She replaced the bottle on the table and stared at the screen. She had a sidewise view of the killer, sitting calmly in her chair, and she wondered at the psyche of someone who could willingly accept the commission to end another's life.

She smiled to herself. She had the guy where she wanted him; she was angry, and she wanted to know why she was being targeted. She also wanted him to know that he had failed, that she had been equal to him; that the hunted had become the hunter.

The assassin knew that she was a telepath, so he would be shielded. She wouldn't be able to approach the building, send out a probe and read his motives. She would have to take him alive, rip out his shield – wherever that might be – and then read him.

But how to go about that?

She finished her beer and left the bar, shouldering her way across the crowded street to the tenement. She stepped through the revolving door and came to the stairs. She decided to climb them rather than take the lift.

On the first landing she checked her handset. The guy was still seated, silent, impassive. She hurried up to the fourth floor and stepped lightly across the landing, leaning against the wall to the left of her door and drawing her laser.

She watched the killer on the screen, then hunkered down to wait.

There were three other apartments on this, the top level; one was owned by a businessman who she knew was out of town at the moment, one by a cop who worked till midnight, and the third was vacant. She wouldn't be disturbed by neighbours asking what on earth she was doing squatting outside her own apartment.

She watched the screen and settled down for a long wait. She knew she had the advantage; sooner or later he would move, slip to the loo, or decide to help himself to a snack. She'd be ready when he returned.

The man had obviously done his homework. He knew she arrived home between six and six-thirty weekdays, without variation. Even when going out with Rab, she always arrived home, changed and left around seven. He must have known that she never brought home friends, or Rab, at this time… She wondered how long he'd been watching her, and the thought filled her with fear and rage.

She shifted slightly, to ease the cramp in her left calf, but never took her eyes off the screen.

It was a long wait, but eventually, as she knew he would, he stood and moved to the kitchen.

She patched the image from the kitchen through to her handset and watched the guy. He was hauling open the door of her cooler, squatting to select a beer… He gripped his pistol in his right hand.

She moved fast. She stood, slipped her card into the lock, and eased open the door without making a sound.

She stepped into the lounge, watching the screen.

He made his choice – a Blue Mountain, so the bastard had good taste – stood and looked around for an opener. He found it, screwed into the wall, and eased the cap from the beer.

She cat-stepped across to the open door and looked through. The guy had his back to her, still gripping his pistol. He hadn't yet taken a chug from the bottle. Her heart was thudding. She felt, she would admit later, elated.

She raised her pistol and shot the assassin through the small of the back. He fell with more noise and commotion than she'd expected; a high cry of pain, a thrashing of arms and legs; the crash of the beer bottle. On his belly on the floor, he tried to turn and fire. She stepped over him and lasered his weapon from his hand, removing three fingers in the process. She kicked the pistol across the floor.

She knelt, patted him down for weapons, and found a small, oval bulge in the inner pocket of his jacket.

She hauled him onto his back, not only to get at his shield, but so that he could see that it was her, his intended target, who'd got to him first.

His eyes were wide with pain, or it might have been shock at seeing her, and she smiled.

She reached into his pocket, pulled out the shield, and tossed it through the door into the lounge. She activated her tele-ability, aimed the pistol at his face, and probed.

She didn't remain in his head for very long, not liking the images of the dead he had racked up in ten years of hiring himself out as an assassin. She scanned for what he knew about her – which was surprisingly little. She did learn that his paymaster was Chinese, and that he suspected he'd been hired by the government in Beijing. She also learned one other very interesting fact.

A week ago the killer had been fitted with a program – and not just your run-of-the-mill psi-program.

The assassin was a necropath.

She read his instructions, sent to him via a soft-softscreen needle. He was to assassinate one

Parveen Das and read in her dead or dying mind any information pertaining to the Chandrasakar Organisation's imminent mission to Delta Cephei VII...

She quit the cloaca of his mind and killed her program.

She looked at the guy's injuries, the neat hole to the left of his spine, the bleeding stubs of his fingers... It was touch and go whether he'd live.

She stepped over him, retrieved the bottle of beer from the floor. A third of its contents remained. She moved to the lounge, dragged the recliner into the kitchen and sat down.

She got through to Anish and reported the situation, then sat back and tipped the remaining beer into her mouth as she watched the killer squirming on the floor. He looked up at her, something almost beseeching in his eyes. She stared at him without saying a word, without the slightest expression on her face.

She tried to assess what she felt, now. The anger was gone, the rage at the thought that he had intended to take her life.

She felt...

After the elation, after the rage, she felt not so much avenged at what she had done, but almost ashamed.

The man might die, and she had done this.

The party had turned her into a very efficient killer, and as with so many aspects of her life at the moment she was in two minds about the fact.

THREE

COVER EVERY ANGLE

Sukara clutched Li's hand and stepped from the elevator into the busy foyer of the St Theresa Hospital, Level Two.

The little girl toddled alongside her, chattering away about puppy dogs and kittens and grasping the certificate of bravery awarded her by the medic. Sukara heard nothing, lagged in a layer of insulation that numbed her to sensory impressions from the outside world. All around her people came and went, citizens absorbed in their own illnesses, staff intent on their duties, but Sukara felt as if she were locked into a wrap-around holodrama that meant nothing to her.

Dr Chang, a fat Chinese man in his sixties, had told Sukara his findings after examining Li. He had gone over the facts, and then again, accustomed to having to repeat himself to patients and loved ones in shock. Li had leukaemia, Dr Chang had told Sukara; but with the latest medical techniques available there was a seventy per cent chance of Li making a full recovery in a matter of weeks.

Then Dr Chang had handed her on to an admin clerk, who had gone through a lot of facts and figures about the various treatments and their respective costs. What it boiled down to, though the clerk had not said this in so many words, was that the higher the grade of hospital care Sukara's insurance cover could pay for, the greater Li's chance of survival. Her daughter's life would only be assured if she had the requisite funds to pay for her treatment.

Numbed, Sukara had allowed the clerk to download all the literature into her handset, and told the woman that she'd contact the health authorities when she'd discussed things with her husband.

The first thing she'd done on leaving the specialist's office had been to contact Jeff, but she'd been able only to blurt a few words before breaking down and cutting the connection. Now she wished she hadn't bothered him. He was working on a murder case, and for all she knew he might have been scanning when she called. She wondered if that might be why he hadn't called back yet.

Li tugged her hand. "Pet shop now?" she piped.

Sukara smiled, fighting back tears. She nodded. "Just for a short while. We've got to pick Pham up from school in an hour."

"Soon I go to school like a big girl," Li said with all the pride of a four-year-old.

Sukara nodded, biting her lip to stop the sob that welled in her throat.

They left the hospital and entered the vast cavernous space that advertised itself as Level Two's recreation area, a square kilometre of sculptured parkland, lakes and forests. To the west, the entire outer bulkhead of the station had been removed to allow a free circulation of air and sunlight – except that, with the monsoon late this year, the air here was as cloying and sultry as a sauna-bath.

Next to the hospital was an arcade of kiosks and shops. Li dragged Sukara to her favourite: a tacky emporium selling all manner of furry creatures, and some not so furry, from the many colony worlds of the Expansion. Li had badgered her parents to be allowed an alien pet, but Jeff was having none of it.

Sukara agreed. She didn't agree with keeping Terran animals, even cats and dogs, and the latest fad for extraterrestrial pets she considered sick.

Li squealed with delight and ran off down the aisle, pressing her nose up against the glass enclosure, which housed, Sukara read, a Merk from Sigma Draconis IX. Li laughed and pointed at the creature, a snowball with six legs and four eyestalks. She moved on to the next animal, and the next, and Sukara stared down at a gallery of weird and improbable creatures. She wondered how they felt, captured and ferried across the light years to end up in the home of some pampered office worker on Bengal Station.

Her friends had just laughed at her concern, saying that the animals were no more intelligent than rats or mice, but even so Sukara thought that their imprisonment was wrong.

She remembered when she was little more than a prisoner, shackled to the Bangkok brothels she had worked in; she was sure that some of her customers had thought of her as less than an animal back then, and had proved it by treating her like one.

She shut her mind to memories of the past. She had a great life here...

Then she saw Li, skipping with delight from animal to animal, and fear clutched at her heart.

She wanted nothing more than to be in Jeff's arms, to hear his reassuring words. She thought of calling him again, apologising for hanging up so abruptly, and telling him that she was fine now, that Li would be okay... But she knew that she couldn't trust herself not to break down again, and anyway Jeff was obviously busy.

She lured Li from the alien pet shop with the promise of a Vitamilk, and she bought two ice-cold bottles from a street-vendor's stall. They walked to Pham's school on the far side of the rolling parkland, sucking at the straws.

The school was a tubular building surrounded by lawns dotted with play areas, climbing frames and sandpits. A noisy posse of children milled behind the perimeter fence, while mothers, fathers, and even in one or two cases spider drones, waited for their children to be processed. Sukara inserted her pin into the gate's sensor unit and the school's guardian drone responded and led Pham to the gate, which slid open at her approach.

Pham ran into Sukara's arms, kissing her cheeks.

"Hi, Li!" Pham laughed. Then she remembered and looked at Sukara. "What did the doctor say about Li, Mum?"

Sukara put on a brave smile. "She'll be fine. She needs some pills, and a short stay in hospital, then she'll be as good as new."

Li danced in front of Pham, holding the carton of Vitamilk before her grinning face. "Look what I've got!"

"I'll get you one on the way home, Pham," Sukara said.

"Can we walk today?"

Sukara smiled and nodded. They usually took the train home, but Sukara couldn't face the thought of the crowds today. Their ocean-view apartment was beyond the park about a kilometre from here.

She bought another round of Vitamilk from a kiosk and set off home.

She watched her daughters race ahead across the grass, two slim jet-black haired, beautiful girls who to all outward appearances were biological sisters. Four years ago they had adopted Pham, an orphan runaway from a factory on Level Twenty whose ambition had been to see the sky for the first time; her other dream, though she knew it wouldn't be achieved as easily as seeing the sky, had been to belong to a real family, with a mother and father who loved her.

Sukara loved her like her own. Pham was a bright kid with a great sense of humour and a serious side that belied her age; her sophistication was, Sukara thought, quite natural considering what she'd gone through to reach the top level, where she had at last seen the sky.

When Li was born, Pham was beside herself with joy: not only did she have a real mother and father, but now she had a little sister, too.

They ran after each other across the grass, spilling milk and giggling, and Sukara felt like crying again.

Her handset chimed, and more than anything she wanted it to be Jeff.

She beamed when his face filled the screen. "Jeff! I'm sorry about... I shouldn't have–"

"Su, don't worry, okay. I've looked into things. Li'll be fine, okay?"

Lips pursed, Sukara nodded. "I know, Jeff. It's just..."

He said, "Su, will you do something? As soon as you get home, pack a few bags. We're going away for a while."

She stared at his face on the screen. "Away?"

He hesitated, then said, "A holiday. A short break. We all need a rest."

"A holiday? Not away from the Station? Li needs–"

He interrupted. "No, not away from the Station. A luxury hotel on Level One, west side."

She just laughed and shook her head, knowing better than to ask him where he'd get the money to pay for it.

"I have a couple of things I need to clear up here. But I'll get back in about an hour. Be ready to leave then, okay?"

She nodded, wanting to ask him what all the hurry was about.

"I'd better get off. See you soon, Su. Love you."

"Love you too, Jeff. See you."

Pham danced towards her, pulling Li after her like a rag-doll. "Was that Dad?"

Sukara nodded. "We're going on holiday, kids. A big hotel."

"Will it have a pool?" Pham asked.

"I think it probably will," Sukara said.

"And pets?" Li chipped in. "Pets from the stars? We went to the pet shop, Pham. I saw ice-mice! Ice-mice, ice-mice!"

"Well, probably not alien pets. But you never know, it might have aliens staying."

"Aliens with ice-mice!" Li cried, and they ran off laughing and yelling again.

They arrived at the apartment thirty minutes later, and while Pham fixed herself and Li a quick meal, Sukara filled two cases with clothes and toiletries. While she packed, she wondered about what Jeff had said about a break. It was unlike him to act on impulse like this; he usually discussed holidays with her and the girls.

She finished packing and sat on the bed. She could hear the girls, crashing about in the kitchen. Soon the smell of toast and tomato soup drifted through the apartment.

She tried not to think about the future and Li, and told herself to be brave when Jeff arrived; but when she heard the outer door slide open, and he called her name, she broke down and ran into the lounge, sobbing.

She hit him in a rush and he caught her, reassuringly solid. He held her to him, stroking her hair, repeating soothing words while she cried. "The doctor said it was leukaemia, Jeff. He said Li had a seventy per cent chance of getting better."

"That's good odds, Su," he said softly, stroking her hair. "She's going to be fine." He looked around the room. "All packed?"

She nodded.

"Fetch the girls. I'll get the insurance details. Where's the pin?"

"In the bedroom, the unit on my side, top drawer."

He was gone two minutes while Sukara rounded up Pham and Li. They were sitting at the breakfast bar in the kitchen, munching sopping toast, clown's smiles of tomato soup expanding their mouths.

"Come on, you two. Eat up. We're going on holiday."

They crammed toast into their mouths and jumped from the high stools.

Jeff called from the bedroom, "There's a flier waiting. Let's get a move on."

"Hear that, girls? We're going in a flier."

Jeff emerged from the bedroom, tucking the insurance policy pin into the breast pocket of his imitation leather jacket. Li yelled when she saw him and launched herself. He picked her up, hugged her to him and kissed the top of her head. Pham nuzzled against his legs.

Sukara leaned against the kitchen door, watching them. She felt a hit of emotion in her chest, swelling. She wanted to cry out loud that she loved them so much.

Jeff smiled across at her. "C'mon, let's get a shuffle on, girls."

He led the way from the apartment, Li on his hip and Pham clutching his hand. Sukara hurried after them.

They took the upchute to Level One. A flier was waiting outside the chute station, from the taxi firm Sukara knew the Kapinsky Agency used. They climbed aboard and the driver took off and banked south-west without waiting for instructions.

Li bounced about on Jeff's knee, peering out excitedly. Pham looked up at Sukara and smiled uncertainly. She wondered if the girl had picked up on her uneasiness: she had an almost preternatural ability to second-guess her mother's feelings in times of stress.

Sukara glanced across at Jeff; he was staring out of the side window. He saw her watching him, smiled and squeezed her hand.

She knew, then, that something was wrong – more than just Li's illness. It wasn't like Jeff to suggest taking off like this. She wanted to ask him what was happening; but now, with the girls so excited, was not the right time.

On cue, with an empathy that came from so long together, Jeff caught her eye and mimed a shushing gesture.

Heart thudding, she gazed forwards as the flier decelerated, banked swiftly, and came down with amazing delicacy on the cantilevered landing-pad of the Ashok Hilton, a ziggurat of reflective silver glass overlooking the Bay of Bengal.

Jeff grabbed the cases while Sukara took the girls, and they rode an elevator to the penthouse suite. "The penthouse?" Sukara said, amazed.

"I'll tell you when we're settled, Su."

The suite consisted of two big bedrooms, a bathroom the size of a skyball court, and a lounge as big as their apartment; the lounge had floor-to-ceiling windows on two sides, with spectacular views over the hotel's stepped gardens and the open sea.

The girls screamed in delight and ran around the suite. Jeff took Sukara's hand and pulled her out onto the balcony. They stood side by side, watching a distant starship phase in from the void.

"Jeff, will you please tell me what's going on?"

He licked his lips, gazing out to sea. "Su, there's no danger, but Lin decided on this merely as a precaution—"

"Jeff!"

He ran a strong hand down her spine. "Three telepaths have been killed in the past week. The cops don't have a clue. There seems to be no connection between the dead men, other than they're telepaths. Anyway, Lin's taking no chances. She's paying for her staff to lie low for a week or so."

She looked up at him. "Jeff, is that all? Tell me truthfully. You don't seem…"

"Su, I've just found out Li has a serious illness. Of course I don't seem myself."

She looked at him. "There's more, Jeff. Tell me."

He hesitated. "Okay. When you called yesterday… an assassin was coming after me—"

She stared. "What? What happened?"

"Security got him before he reached me."

She shook her head. "And you've no idea why this assassin…?" She thought about it. "Were you all working on the same case?"

He smiled. "You'd make a good cop. That's the first thing we thought of. But no. There's no seeming connection at all."

She stroked his hand. "But will you be okay here? Others won't come after you?"

"Su, chances are I'd be fine back at the apartment. But you know Lin. She covers every angle."

They held each other for a while, then Sukara said, "I'll get them to bed, then we can talk, okay?"

He helped with the ritual of washing faces and cleaning teeth, and gave them each a goodnight kiss before Sukara whisked them to bed, told them a made-up story, and promised a trip to the zoo in the morning.

When she returned to the lounge, Jeff had opened a couple of beers from the bar. "I'll order food from room service. Thai or Indian?"

"I don't feel that hungry." She saw his expression. "Okay, then. Indian."

He dialled two meals, carried them from the service unit, and sat down beside her on the squishy divan. They ate in silence, then read the details of their daughter's disease.

"Okay, let's look on the bright side," he said. "At least the disease can be treated."

She stroked his thigh, feeling bulky muscle beneath the material. Unshed tears made her eyes ache. "But... but look at the cost, Jeff!"

He whistled. "For the full treatment... two hundred thousand dollars, US. Okay, that's a lot. But we can do it."

She looked at him. "You sure?"

He smiled, grimly. "I'm not going for second best, Su."

"I know," she said. "But how...?"

He slipped the insurance data-pin into his handset and scrolled through the details. He frowned.

"What?" Sukara said.

"We'll be lucky if it covers thirty per cent of the cost."

"So that means... we have to find around a hundred and forty thousand dollars, right?"

He nodded. "In the region of."

She felt close to despair, then. "But how, Jeff? How the hell can we..."

He pulled her to him and kissed her head. "We

have around thirty thousand saved from the Breitenbach case, yes?"

She sniffed and nodded. "Okay, thirty thousand. That still leaves over a hundred to find."

"Su, there's no problem. Listen, Lin's been going on at me for a long time to work more shifts. I do... what... three days a week at the moment? And I'm taking scut work. There are some big cases I'm passing up."

"So if you worked more hours, on bigger cases..." She felt guilty saying it: how would she feel if she had to read criminal minds all day long, week after week? It was bad enough Jeff having to work three days a week.

He laughed and shook her. "Hey, why so glum? Do you know how much I'll rake in a week if I do six days on some of the big cases Lin's been trying to offload?"

She shook her head, watching him.

"Around five thousand a week. US. With that kind of earning power I can get a loan for a hundred thousand no problem."

"But six days a week, Jeff? And you'll be working murder cases, won't you?" She looked at him, and realised how much she loved this man, and that made her feel even more guilty. The fact was, she wanted him to do all that work, read all those evil minds, even though it'd be painful for him to do so.

But she felt she had to put in a token protest. She knew it. And he knew it... and that made her feel even more guilt-stricken.

He saw this and laughed, pulled her to him and kissed her.

"I'll get on to Lin in the morning, sort something out."

"But the assassin...?"

"Once all this has blown over, I'll up the shifts."

She nodded. "Oh, Jeff... Everything was going so well, wasn't it? I was so happy. We had everything. Two lovely girls. I had you..."

"Hey, we've still got those things. Everything'll work out fine, believe me. And seventy per cent are good odds, Su."

She looked at him. He was smiling down at her, radiating strength and confidence. She felt something melt within her, despair and at the same time relief that she had this man at the centre of her life.

Later, around midnight, with the best part of six bottles of beer consumed between them, Sukara stopped off at the door to the girls' bedroom and leaned against the woodwork, staring in at the quietly sleeping figures. They were almost identical, embryonic shapes in their beds, jet hair dark against the pillows, breaths synchronised as they slept.

Wondering what the future might hold, she pushed herself away from the door and joined Jeff in bed. They came together in silence and held on to each other like the survivors of a shipwreck.

FOUR

AN IRRESISTIBLE OFFER

That morning, Vaughan had a lucid dream. It was a replay of the chase the day before, and its after-math. He was sitting in the bar, thinking he'd shaken the Korth, when Sukara called him with the news about Li. Then the jade-green alien was stand-ing on the threshold and this time, with the arbitrary revisionism of dreams, Vaughan watched as the Korth killed the security woman with a single burst of its pistol and turned to face him...

He cried out and sat up in bed, overwhelmed by the fact that had Sukara not called him last night then the Korth would undoubtedly have killed him.

He stared around the luxury hotel room, momen-tarily confused. The floor-to-ceiling window looked out over stepped gardens, and beyond them the vast expanse of the Bay of Bengal shimmered in the early morning sun.

Sukara stirred beside him. She rubbed her eyes and smiled, and Vaughan reached out and cupped her head. Even first thing in the morning, even with the scar that bisected her face, she was beautiful. They kissed.

"Jeff," she murmured. "Thanks for last night. I feel a lot better."

"We'll be fine," he said. "Li'll be fine."

"Jeff, after what happened yesterday..."

He nodded. The assassin, on top of the news about Li's condition, was a burden he could have done without. He was torn; part of him wanted to work on the case, find out what the hell was going on. Another part wanted nothing more than to hole up with Su and the kids and concentrate on getting Li cured. But how to pay for that without actively working, and so putting himself in danger?

Pham traipsed barefoot and sleep-fuddled into the bedroom. She climbed between them and snuggled in. "Li's still sleepy." She looked up at Vaughan with massive eyes wide below her pudding-bowl fringe. "She'll be okay, won't she, Daddy?"

He tweaked her nose. "She'll be fine in no time," he said.

A soft double-note chime announced they had a caller.

"Who the hell can that be?" Vaughan said, swivelling out of bed and dressing quickly.

"Maybe room service with a big breakfast," Pham said. She thought of little but her stomach these days.

He moved from the bedroom and crossed the plush suite.

A screen beside the door allowed the room's occupant to view the caller. Vaughan activated it and stared with disbelief at the revealed face.

"Mr Vaughan? It is your old friend and servant

come to offer his services in this, your time of need."

"How the hell did you find out where we were?" Vaughan asked.

The old man smiled, looking more than ever like a leathery old turtle. "I have my contacts, Mr Vaughan; there is little that does not come, in time, to my attention."

"Well, you'd better come in."

Vaughan opened the door and stepped aside as Dr Rao, diminutive in his impeccable Nehru suit, made a namaste gesture and slipped into the room.

"It's been a long time, Rao. Three years?"

The old man beamed. "Closer to four, during which, need I say, you have often been in my thoughts."

Vaughan smiled, wondering what the old rogue wanted this time. He gestured to the sofa before the plate-glass window, and Rao crossed the room and eased himself into its embrace.

"Su!" Vaughan called. "We have a visitor."

Seconds later Sukara entered the room, knotting her kimono and peering at their guest.

"Dr Rao?" she said.

Vaughan watched conflicting emotions pass across his wife's face. Six years ago, it was Rao who had informed Sukara of her sister's death; four years ago, the Brahmin Fagin had helped Vaughan locate Pham and save her life.

"Well, this is a big surprise, Dr Rao," she said.

"And before breakfast, too," Vaughan said. "We're just about to eat? Care to join us?"

"As ever," Rao said primly, "your generosity cannot be spurned. A salted lassi and idli, perhaps."

Vaughan dialled up coffee, idli, and toast from room service, and a minute later the wall unit chimed. He carried the tray across to the coffee table and set it down before Rao.

He considered enabling his tele-ability and reading Rao's motives for coming here. The memory of the last time he'd dipped into the doctor's mind, however, stilled his hand. He had no real desire to meld with Rao's cunning, sanctimonious psyche. And anyway, by scanning Rao he'd pick up the girls' thoughts too, and he'd promised himself that he'd never do that.

Pham joined them, snuggling in between Vaughan and Sukara on the sofa, while Dr Rao sipped his lassi and consumed the idli in three bites. He attended to his lips with a napkin, then sat back and laced his fingers across his stomach.

"Now," Vaughan said, sipping his coffee. "First off, how did you know we're here?"

"Simplicity itself, Mr Vaughan. I needed to contact you last night, and sent one of my children to your apartment. However, you were leaving, surrounded by guards, and so my child exercised her wit, hailed a taxi-flier and followed you here. By the time she returned, I deemed it too late to intrude upon your privacy."

"How can I help you?"

The doctor smiled. "Happily, it is I who am admirably positioned on this occasion to extend the hand of succour to you."

Vaughan suppressed the urge to smile at the man's arch formality. "And how might you do that?"

Rao removed his antique wire-rimmed spectacles and made an exhibition of polishing the lenses, all the while smiling with self-satisfaction. He replaced the glasses, blinked at Vaughan and said, "It has come to my attention that you are, if I might make so bold, in the position where, ah... extra finances might facilitate your desires?"

Vaughan turned to Sukara. "I think he means we need some extra cash," he said.

"Your economy with the language is succinct, if lacking in a certain elegance, if I might make the observation."

Sukara said, "How do you know?"

"My dear, I am an esteemed member of the medical profession. I have friends in elevated positions. I also know that to successfully discharge financial obligations in the matter of effecting a cure for your daughter's condition will demand a considerable sum. Now, it so happens that I am in the position to effectuate a situation whereby such sums are within your attainment."

"In plain English, if you don't mind, Rao."

"In unadorned parlance, as per your request, Mr Vaughan; I have a contact who is desirous of making your acquaintance so that he might put to you a certain business proposition–"

"I'm doing nothing illegal, Rao."

Rao pantomimed a gesture of shock. "Mr Vaughan! I assure you that my contact would be sorely discommoded at such an imputation."

"Who is it and what do they want?"

"My contact is none other than the feted businessman and voidship tycoon, Mr Rabindranath Chandrasakar." Rao sat back primly and smiled.

Vaughan shook his head. "So what does the multi-billionaire starship magnate with half the

Expansion in his pocket want with me, Rao?"

"That, Mr Vaughan, he did not disclose to me, his humble servant. Suffice to say, Mr Chandrasakar is confident that you will grant him an audience, as not only might doing so ease your financial situation, but also take you away from the Station at this time of... ah, shall we say... personal peril."

"What do you know about that, Rao?" Vaughan snapped.

Dr Rao raised both palms in a gesture of impugned innocence. "Merely what Mr Chandrasakar vouchsafed; to wit, that yesterday an attempt was made upon your life."

Vaughan looked at Sukara. He didn't like the sound of leaving the Station, and he had no doubt that the self-serving Dr Rao was revealing less than he knew, but at the same time he was intrigued by the offer of financial aid.

Sukara murmured, "You could always meet the guy, Jeff, see what he wants you to do."

Dr Rao beamed. "I can see that the passing years have done nothing to blunt your wife's perspicacity, Mr Vaughan."

"Okay, Rao. I'll see him. But I'm promising nothing."

Rao spread his hands wide and beamed. "In that case I will contact Mr Chandrasakar immediately and effect a meeting."

He stood, creakily, and moved towards the door, where he spoke in hushed tones into an ancient communicator.

Beside Vaughan, Pham whispered, "What did the man say, Daddy?"

Sukara squeezed her. "He said that he might have

work for Daddy, to pay for Li's medicine."

Pham looked at Vaughan, and he nodded.

Rao returned. "Mr Chandrasakar is more than delighted at the prospect of making your acquaintance, Mr Vaughan. He suggests that we make immediate tracks for the spaceport, where he is currently supervising the refitting of one of his liners."

Vaughan nodded. "Give me thirty minutes to get a shower, and I'll be with you."

Dr Rao smiled. "I shall await you in the coffee house in the plaza, Mr Vaughan." He made a gallant bow to Sukara. "It was, as ever, a delight to make your acquaintance."

Sukara smiled uncertainly and nodded as Rao hurried from the room.

Vaughan showered, changed, and then slipped into Li's bedroom. She lay on her tummy, mouth open. She looked, in sleep, the picture of vulnerability, and Vaughan wanted nothing more than to hug her.

He returned to the lounge, kissed Pham and embraced Sukara.

"Be careful, Jeff," she whispered.

"Always am," he said. "I'll tell you all about it when I get back."

He kissed her and hurried from the room.

He sat in the passenger seat and stared out.

The flier banked and came in low over the packed streets bordering the spaceport. The streets terminated seconds later and they were flying over the relatively barren expanse of the spaceport, the deck pocked with docking rings and populated by starships at rest. Vaughan had worked here six years ago, and starship technology had moved on in that time; many of the ships he'd worked on had long gone to the scrapyard, to be replaced by a new series of faster, more efficient voidships. He stared down at the sleek, insectile vessels decked out in the colours of the many starship lines.

The flier slowed abruptly, hovered, then lowered itself gently to the deck alongside the flank of a voidliner; Vaughan was put in mind of a minnow beside a vast basking whale as he climbed out and stared up at the curving mountainside of the Chandrasakar Line ship.

Dr Rao peered out at him from the back seat. "I will leave you here, Mr Vaughan, and wish you every success in your employment with Mr Chandrasakar."

"You presume much, Rao."

The doctor smiled and jogged his head from side to side. "I think you will find Mr Chandrasakar a persuasive gentleman, Mr Vaughan." He raised his cane in farewell. "Until next time."

The flier blasted its turbos, turned on its axis, and sped off.

A tall Indian woman in a trim crimson uniform appeared at his side. "Mr Vaughan? If you would care to accompany me to Mr Chandrasakar's quarters..."

Discreetly, Vaughan enabled his tele-ability and probed. The woman was shielded, as were most of the workers beyond the skin of the ship.

She led the way to a ramp, which climbed into a brightly lit interior; they passed through a concourse like a busy shopping mall. Wherever he looked, uniformed workers scurried back and forth, engineers attended open inspection panels and drones – spindly AIs like spiders – scuttled up the walls and across the great arched dome of the ceiling, pausing occasionally to insert needle probes into access ports.

The woman gestured towards a sliding door and Vaughan stepped onto an elevator plate. They rode the plate as it shot up a diaphanous column, and down below the frantic workers were quickly reduced to the aspect of ants.

The plate halted and the woman indicated a long corridor, which Vaughan guessed ran towards the nose cone of the liner.

Five minutes later they arrived at a pair of sliding doors. The woman said, "Apologies for the trek, Mr Vaughan." She indicated the opening doors with an elegant hand. "Mr Chandrasakar will see you now."

He sent forth a probe, and came up against a patch of static in the room before him. Not that he had expected Chandrasakar to have gone without a mind-shield.

Now was one of the times he wished he was equipped with the latest anti-shield viruses. He'd approached Lin just last month, requesting she at least think about investing in the programs. She'd reminded him that they were illegal, and that she wasn't prepared to stump up the hefty fines if her agency was discovered to be using the viruses. Vaughan had decided not to argue.

He stepped over the threshold and behind him the door hissed shut, leaving him alone with the billionaire voidship tycoon.

On the way to the port he'd accessed all the infor-

mation on the tycoon available to the agency's com
program, which was precious little. Chandrasakar
was a notoriously private person who kept a low
profile. He was also one of the richest men in the
Expansion and something of a philanthropist, subsi-
dising hospitals and children's homes on Earth and
on the many colony worlds under his financial aegis.

Vaughan had never seen an image of the tycoon,
and he was surprised by what he saw now. Perhaps
he'd been expecting someone who in the flesh might
be a match for all his mercantile achievement, more
of a film star than a captain of industry: someone tall
and thrusting, endowed with the armour of arrogance
that had earned him his current eminent position.

The opposite was true. Chandrasakar was short,
rubicund, and seemingly perpetually cheerful. He
had a full head of oiled hair and wore an old-fashioned black suit, opened to accommodate the thrust
of his ample belly.

He moved nimbly around a desk, hand extended
to take Vaughan's.

"It's good to meet you at last. Dr Rao has told me
much about you."

"I..." Vaughan hesitated, wondering whether
what he was about to say would be considered
undiplomatic. "I must say that I'm surprised you
know the good doctor."

Chandrasakar laughed as he made his way over
to a well-stocked bar. "The truth to tell, Rao and I
were schoolboys together over sixty years ago. Blue
Mountain, isn't it?"

Vaughan smiled his acceptance, wondering what
else the tycoon might know about him.

"We've kept in contact ever since. Rao, for all his

scheming, has a veritable heart of gold. There have been times when Rao has proved, shall we say, a useful contact."

"Such as now?" Vaughan suggested.

Chandrasakar gestured towards a semicircle of sofas positioned before the delta viewscreen over-looking the sloping nose of the starship. Vaughan sat, nursing his beer.

Chandrasakar sat down opposite, legs apart, so that the globe of his belly was ensconced upon his lap. "Dr Rao mentioned that you were the best telepath working on the Station."

"Dr Rao flatters me."

"He also mentioned your current... situation."

Vaughan smiled without humour. "Rao gets his nose into everything."

"I calculate that the cost of your daughter's treat-ment and aftercare should total in the region of a quarter of a million dollars. I hope you don't mind my observing that your current insurance might not cover such an expense, and that even a telepath of your renown might be working for a long time in order to meet the shortfall."

Vaughan said what he was thinking. "Rao said that you could help me. He also said that whatever you wanted would get me off the Station."

"Ah, yes, my people apprised me of yesterday's contretemps. You're not the first telepath to be tar-geted. You might be pleased to know that I have the best people working on the case."

Vaughan nodded. "How can I help you, Mr Chandrasakar?"

"Please, call me Rabindranath."

Despite his innate distrust of both those in power

and those with wealth – which often amounted to the same thing – Vaughan found it hard to dislike the tycoon. He wished, though, that he could have read what the man was thinking.

Chandrasakar sat back on the sofa with a little body-hop that left his feet dangling, comically, a few inches from the plush carpet. Vaughan wondered if it were a deliberate ploy to convince him of the tycoon's humanity.

"Mr Vaughan, I would like to employ you for approximately two weeks. In recompense, I will have your daughter treated here on the Station by the world's finest physicians; I will foot the bill for her treatment and aftercare and for your wife and your adopted daughter's accommodation throughout the period. I will also pay you a stipend of some one hundred thousand dollars, US, and compensate the Kapinsky agency for the duration you will be contracted to me."

Vaughan's immediate reaction was to ask why Chandrasakar had singled him out, from all the other telepaths working on Earth. Instead he said, "What do you want me to do?" He could not bring himself to call the tycoon by his first name.

"You will accompany me to a newly discovered planet in the Delta Cephei system, at the very edge of the human Expansion."

Vaughan inclined his head, considering the notion of being away from Sukara and the girls for two weeks – even in return for what the tycoon was offering. "If you don't mind me saying, that doesn't answer my question."

Chandrasakar nodded. "Let me begin by telling you something about what will take us to Delta

Cephei VII, Mr Vaughan."

Will take us... Vaughan thought. Already, in the mind of the billionaire, his acceptance of the job was a *fait accompli*.

Chandrasakar stood and moved to the delta screen, staring out across the spaceport. He looked, Vaughan thought, an almost comical figure, with his short legs, his protuberant gut, and mass of artificially darkened hair. If he'd schooled with Rao, then he was in his sixties or early seventies, though his wealth had gone a long way to disguise the fact.

"A little over a year ago," Chandrasakar said, turning to Vaughan, "one of my exploration ships was out beyond the limit of the Expansion, a thousand light years from Earth. You might know that one of my many business enterprises is that of stellar exploration. The discovery of new, Earth-like worlds, or of worlds whose resources might be utilised, is an essential component in the continued success of my business. To that end, my exploration ships are forever pushing out the limits of human expansion."

Vaughan sipped his beer and sat through the publicity spiel without comment.

The tycoon went on, "My ship, *The Pride of Mussoree*, was in the region of the yellow-white supergiant Delta Cephei when all contact with ship and crew was lost. Immediately I initiated a rescue mission, re-routing a ship to investigate. Three months ago, I heard from the captain of the rescue mission. They had discovered the *Mussoree*. It had come down near the equator of the seventh planet in the Delta Cephei system, a planet wholly covered by a strange fungal growth. The ship had not crash-landed, and appeared intact, its drives in perfect condition and its voidspace telemetry in full working order."

"And the crew?" Vaughan asked.

"Two of its crew of four were missing. One was found dead in the ship. The fourth member, the engineer, was in cryo-suspension–"

"What happened?" Vaughan asked.

Chandrasakar pursed his lips. "That we do not know, Mr Vaughan. The engineer made it into the cold sleep unit, with the help of the AI drones, but she died of her injuries shortly after."

Chandrasakar stopped there, and the silence stretched. He was watching Vaughan.

"And how," Vaughan asked, hoping that his hunch was not right, "might I be of any help?"

Chandrasakar nodded. "Mr Vaughan, I know something of your past."

Vaughan felt his pulse quicken. "And?"

"And... I know that you were seconded into the Toronto Police force at the age of twenty, specifically to the Homicide division. I know you underwent an operation to bring about your telepathic ability – not just any telepathic ability, but the ability to read the dwindling minds of the dead. You were made a necropath, Mr Vaughan."

He kept calm, took a long swallow of beer and nodded at the tycoon. No one on the Station, other than Sukara, should have known about his past in Canada.

"How did you find out?"

"I have my... I suppose you could call them spies, informants. That is of little concern, though. What matters—"

Vaughan interrupted. "I no longer read dead minds. I had the hardware removed years ago."

"I have the surgeons, and the technical experts, who can reinstall it."

"Why do you think I had it taken out in the first place?"

"No doubt you had your reasons—"

"Do you have any conception of the pain of reading dead minds, Mr Chandrasakar?"

"Candidly, I cannot begin to imagine the experience, but—"

"It's something I never wish to experience again."

Chandrasakar smiled. "Not even," he said, "for the sake of your daughter?"

You bastard, Vaughan thought.

The tycoon continued, "My surgeons will reinstall the hardware, an advanced version, with the latest programs. It is my hope that you will accompany me to Delta Cephei VII, where you will read the mind of the dead engineer and learn exactly what happened to the crew of the *Mussoree*. Needless to say, this information will be vital if we hope to utilise the full resources of the planet."

"You said the engineer died in cold sleep. How long ago was this? Months? In that case her thoughts might be..."

He stopped. Chandrasakar was shaking his head. "The cryo-suspension preserved her at the second of brain death, Mr Vaughan. When the suspension is reversed, you will have access to her dwindling mentation. You will be able to read what happened."

Vaughan hung his head. He knew, despite himself, that he would accede to the billionaire's wishes. His protests, he told himself, would be futile, a charade to persuade himself that he had at least put up some resistance.

"When you read a dead mind," he said slowly, "it's as if you're dying yourself. You are one with the dead subject, falling towards oblivion. All that the subject has ever known, ever experienced, is being extinguished, and they know it... and you share this, and the final terrible realisation that this life is all, that there's nothing beyond death but eternal oblivion. It... that awareness... it lives with you and makes the hours after reading the dead almost intolerable."

Chandrasakar allowed a few seconds to elapse, and when he spoke his tone was conciliatory. "I can only imagine the hell you so graphically describe, Jeff. But let me reassure you, I will have medics on hand to ease the aftermath of the reading, to prescribe sedatives..."

Vaughan looked up from his beer, ready to give in.

Chandrasakar said, "And immediately you have read the engineer, I will have the program removed. It will be a one-off reading, for which I will underwrite the complete care of your daughter."

Vaughan smiled, without the slightest trace of good humour. "I need to talk this over with my wife."

Chandrasakar inclined his head. "Perfectly understandable, Mr Vaughan."

"When does the ship leave?"

"Tomorrow. The journey will take approximately forty-eight hours. A return trip is scheduled for ten days after that."

From the breast pocket of his suit, the tycoon withdrew a red velveteen case and passed it across to Vaughan.

He opened it. Two silver data-pins sat in a nest of rucked silk. He looked up, inquiringly.

The tycoon said, "These will enable you and your wife to communicate with each other through the void. The technology is barely a month old."

Vaughan had heard rumour that communications through voidspace would soon be achievable. He whistled, despite himself.

Chandrasakar smiled. "Yes, it is phenomenally expensive, but in this case it would be churlish to deny you the facility."

Vaughan finished his beer. "If I do agree to your offer, I want the assurance of protection for my family while I'm away. I don't know what the bastard who's targeting us wants, but I'd feel better if Sukara and the girls were adequately guarded."

"That will be arranged. And if there's anything else you might require..." Chandrasakar stepped forwards and held out his hand. Vaughan hesitated, then took it. "I anticipate hearing from you by the end of the day, Mr Vaughan. You will find a flier outside to return you to your hotel."

Vaughan gripped the man's hand and looked into his brown eyes, resenting the smile on the Indian's face, which indicated the tycoon knew he had got what he wanted.

The same crimson-uniformed woman escorted him through the ship to the waiting flier, and he sat back in the padded seat and considered the meeting as the flier powered up. Chandrasakar stood for everything that Vaughan mistrusted about the modern world, and he was convinced the tycoon had told him only a partial story about the mission... but what he was offering was too great a reward to refuse.

The flier lifted, banked and carried him towards the Ashok Hilton.

FIVE

GUT FEAR

Every month Sukara took the girls to the Extraterrestrial Zoo on Level Two, watching them as they moved in wonder from one alien habitat to the next. Usually she was as excited as the girls, but today she was unable to summon the enthusiasm as the girls shrieked and pointed at one bizarre creature after another. She thought of Jeff, somewhere above her at the spaceport, meeting with the bigshot billionaire voidline owner. No doubt the tycoon could help them out financially, but what might the man want from Jeff that he was willing to pay to save the life of a girl he had never met?

The reappearance of Dr Rao after so many years had brought back a slew of painful memories. Six years ago Sukara had arrived on the Station looking for her sister, Tiger, who had left Thailand hoping to make a new life for herself. Instead she had fallen into the clutches of Dr Rao, who had amputated her left leg and sent her onto the streets to beg for a living. Rao lived with 200 kids on a crashed starship welded into position between Levels Twelve and Thirteen, and he liked to think of himself as an altruist, the benefactor without whom the streets kids would be subject to the jungle laws of the streets. Sukara still didn't know what to think of Dr Rao, even though Jeff bore the man a grudging respect. What Rao did might seem evil to some, but as Jeff had more than once pointed out Rao was the last chance many of these kids had, even if he profited by their servitude.

Her memories of six years ago were painful. Tiger had died of a drug overdose a week before Sukara reached the Station – but through Dr Rao she had met Jeff, and the meeting had changed her life.

If only Tiger could have lived to meet Li and Pham, she thought; if only they could have lived together on the Station like one big, happy family.

She wondered how Jeff was getting on with Chandrasakar. She trusted her husband's instincts. Being a telepath made him – even when he wasn't able to read someone – an astute judge of character; he was able to pick up on subliminal traits in someone's gestures and mannerisms, almost unconscious signals, which told him whether a person was to be trusted or not. She was sure that the billionaire wouldn't be able to put anything over on him.

She watched Li, jumping up and down in front of the glass enclosure which housed a Lyran octopoid, a hairy creature which looked like a cross between a spider and a squid.

Absently, Sukara read the caption on the enclosure while the girl listened, rapt.

As they walked to the next habitat, Pham said seriously, "When I'm older I want to travel to other planets and see all kinds of animals, just like Dad has."

Sukara smiled. "I'm sure you will, Pham."

"I'd like to be a xenologist."

Sukara stared at her daughter. There were times when Pham came out with things that amazed her. "A... *xenologist*?"

"Someone who studies alien races," Pham said matter-of-factly.

Sukara smiled. "That'd be great, wouldn't it?"

They came to the habitat of a Hathinar, from Acrab XII – a cetacean sentient basking in a cubic kilometre of almost-boiling water. As the girls pressed their noses against the glass tank, the creature came close and regarded them with a swivelling eyeball the size of a flier.

What Pham had just said reminded her of something Dr Rao had mentioned that morning: that what Chandrasakar wanted Jeff to do would take him away from Earth for a while.

Jeff would be away while Li was being treated, and the thought filled Sukara with despair. It was bad enough Li being ill while she and Jeff were together, but she wondered how she would cope without Jeff's support.

Her handset chimed and she accessed the call instantly. She beamed at Jeff, smiling up at her from the screen set into the back of her hand. "How did it go?"

"Fine, fine. I'll tell you all about it when we meet. You still at the zoo?"

She nodded. "We could meet you at the café in Himachal Park."

He blew her a kiss. "See you there in fifteen minutes." He cut the connection.

"Hey, girls. That was Daddy. We're meeting him in the café."

"Vitamilk!" Li cried.

"Can I have an ice-cake?" Pham asked.

"If we leave here now and no complaints, okay? I need to see Daddy about something important."

As they boarded a carriage at the upchute station, Pham said, "About Li's medicine, Mum?"

Sukara smiled. "Daddy's going to do some work to earn the money to pay for Li's treatment," she said. Well, she hoped so... and instantly she felt guilty at the presumption.

They stepped from the clanking carriage and moved with the crowd across the road towards the gates of the park. This was Sukara's favourite place on all the Station, an area of green calm amid the bustle that was the top level. The amazing thing was that the spacious lawns and peaceful coppices were never crowded, and the café overlooking the ocean was an oasis of sanity. Also, the coffee was the best in the area.

She found a table by the perimeter rail, ordered a coffee for herself and Vitamilk for the girls, and stared out across the ocean as Pham and Li played Spot the Starship Line: the spaceport was a kilometre to the north of here, and voidships were materialising over the sea every few minutes. Jeff had spent hours teaching the girls to recognise the various colours of the many starship companies that berthed at the station.

Five minutes later she made out a tall, striding figure cross the grass towards them, jacket slung casually over his shoulder.

He ordered a beer, kissed Sukara and the girls, and sat down.

Sukara stared, wide-eyed. "Well?"

He watched the girls as they moved off towards the railed enclosure, out of earshot. His expression gave nothing away. "Well, providing you agree, I'm the temporary employee of the Chandrasakar Organisation."

She looked at him, suspicious. "If I agree?"

"Well, I wasn't going to say yes without talking it over with you, was I?"

She felt her heart thumping. "What does he want you to do?"

"First, I'll tell you what he'll do for us. One, he'll underwrite Li's entire care and aftercare in the Station's best medical centre, with the best surgeons. Second, on top of that he'll pay me a hundred thousand dollars, US."

She pulled a frightened face. "But what does he want you to do?"

He took a mouthful of beer. "Read a mind."

She cocked her head. "Read a mind? Come on!"

"That's it. Read a mind. One mind–"

"So why doesn't he just hire a run-of-the-mill telepath who'd do it for a few thousand?"

"Well... it will mean being off-planet for a while. Two weeks."

"While Li undergoes treatment," she said in a small voice.

He shrugged. "I'm sorry, but that's how it is."

"So... what's the catch? And it can't be just that you'll be off-planet for a couple of weeks. What's so special about this mind?"

He hesitated for a second or two, then nodded and said, "It's dead."

She stared at him, her stomach turning. "Oh, Jeff! No! No way. You said, after what happened... You said you'd never do it again."

"That was before Li fell ill," he said, picking at the label on the beer bottle.

The terrible thing, the treacherous thing, was that she wanted him to take the job. "Tell me about it, Jeff..."

So he told her about a mission that had gone wrong out on the limits of the Expansion, some woman had gone and got herself killed, only she wasn't properly dead but in cold storage or something, and the rich-ass tycoon wanted Jeff to go in there and read her dying mind when they'd thawed the corpsicle out... and it would be hell, but it would save their daughter's life.

So how could she not agree to that?

She looked at him. He remained impassive, hard-faced.

"What do you think?" she murmured.

"I've got to do it, Su. How could I refuse? Just think, if I passed up the opportunity, and we bankrupted ourselves to buy the best we possibly could... and we knew we could afford a bit more if only we had it... and what if Li – what if she didn't make it? Christ, how would we feel then?"

She stared at him, tears filling her eyes.

"Chandrasakar will assure that she gets the very best treatment money can buy. We couldn't do that, even with the insurance policy. We'd get what we could afford, good treatment but not the best. And I'm not willing to take the risk."

She said, "I want the best for Li, Jeff, but I'm frightened for you."

"Hey…" He reached out and thumbed tears from her cheeks. "I can handle it. I'll think of you and Li and Pham, and it'll be all worthwhile, okay?"

She nodded, staring into her cold coffee. She looked up. "I'll miss you, Jeff," she whispered.

He pulled something from his pocket, what looked like a small velvet pen case. He opened it and withdrew two silver pins. He passed one across to her.

"What is it?"

"A com program. We'll be able to communicate through the void. I'll be able to tell you what's happening out there on Delta Cephei VII. You can keep me updated on Li's progress."

She held the pin up before her; it scintillated in the sunlight. "I never realised they could do that…"

Jeff smiled. "State of the art, newly released." He slipped the pins back into the case. "Anyway, I'll contact Chandrasakar and tell him I'll do it, okay?"

Mutely, avoiding his eyes, she nodded. "When do you leave, Jeff?"

"Tomorrow, just after midday. A shuttle up to an orbital station, and then aboard a voidship called *Kali's Revenge*. I'll be back in a little under two weeks."

"God, Jeff, I'll miss you. I know we'll be able to talk, but…"

He leaned forward and kissed her on the lips. "I'll soon be home and Li will be as good as new. Then everything will be back to normal again, okay?"

She forced a smile and nodded, and wondered why she had the gut fear that things wouldn't turn out quite so well.

SIX

A GOOD MAN

Parveen Das leaned to starboard in the cushioned seat as the flier banked on its approach run to Bengal Station. This was the first time she'd ever set eyes on the marvel of twenty-second-century design and technology, a foursquare, twenty-level hive that was home to over thirty million citizens. It was the size of ten cities, or even a medium-sized country, a military-industrial power in its own right and independent of Indian political influence and that of the China, Europe, and the Federated Northern States of America. Despite all it represented, Parveen could not deny that something about it – its sheer size for one thing, the teeming vitality of the place – inspired awe.

The flier levelled out and flew low over the Station's north-west sector, and what before had been nothing more than a colourful circuit-board seen from afar now resolved itself into a vast expanse of streets and avenues, buildings and parks; even from this height she could see that the place was packed with humanity; pedestrians filled many of the streets and fliers criss-crossed the sky, travelling along a complex skein of colour-coded air corridors.

Below, the spaceport came into view. This took up a good eighth of the Station's top level, a rectangle marked with docking rigs and a hundred starships at rest, and dozens more phasing in or out. Vehicles beetled their way between the behemoths and port personnel scurried like ants between the ships and terminal buildings.

Chandrasakar's new voidliner stood beside the perimeter rail overlooking the ocean. It dwarfed those ships nearby, a sturdily massive ship like a towerpile on its side. It was painted in the racing-green livery of the Chandrasakar Organisation, and bore an entwined CO in gold within a ring of stars.

The symbol gave Parveen a kick in the stomach at the thought that very soon she would be in Rab's arms.

The flier landed and she climbed out. Efficient as ever, Zonia, Chandrasakar's PA, was waiting to greet her and lead the way through the ship.

Ten minutes later – it took that long to negotiate the corridors, elevators, and vast chambers of the ship's capacious interior – Parveen hurried through the sliding door into Rab's private suite.

He was facing a wall-mounted softscreen, speaking with someone – but he ended the conversation as soon as he saw her and hurried across the room, arms outstretched.

"Parveen, it's been too long."

They kissed. He took her hand and escorted her into a lounge furnished with sunken sofas and a long bar, overlooking the margin of spaceport and the sea beyond. He poured her a beer and himself a scotch and soda, and they curled in a luxurious sofa and talked.

"You can't imagine my relief that you're here, Parveen. I've been having nightmares ever since your call."

She had contacted him that morning about the assassin, and he'd ordered her to take the first available flier to the Station.

"And the assassin?" he asked.

"He's alive. The police questioned him, but I can't imagine they'd learn anything more than what I read."

"And you said he was probably working for the Chinese?"

She shrugged. "That's what the assassin suspected, anyway."

"And he was a necropath?"

"The idea was he'd kill me and read what I knew about the Delta Cephei mission." She took a long swallow of icy beer.

Chandrasakar shook his head, worried. "Needless to say, the mission was supposed to be known only to myself, my security staff, and a few trusted technicians and scientists."

"One of them," she said, "is working for... whoever."

"The list is pretty long," he said. "Any of my competitors in business, the big Expansion-wide lines; the superpowers, Europe, China, America..." He looked at her. "I wouldn't rule out India, either."

She hated the duplicity, but she had to nod at his suggestion.

"Anyway, I have my security chiefs trying to worm out the traitor."

She looked at him. "And then? What'll happen to him, or her?"

As far as he knew, she was no more than an eminent professor of xenology, untainted by the tooth-and-claw machinations of the realpolitik arena. She had failed to mention that she'd dealt with the assassin herself, telling him instead that she'd called in the police when neighbours had seen someone entering her apartment, and had removed his shield and read his mind before they'd stretchered him from the apartment.

She wished she could open up to him, tell him the truth, but that was an impossibility.

He said, "What happens in that situation, when we find a spy in our midst... and it's only occurred once in my memory... is we mind-wipe the traitor to erase any knowledge of the Organisation's secrets and then return him, or her, to our competitor."

Which was a long-winded lie, she suspected: traitors would be summarily executed. It was exactly what her government would have done, and she couldn't blame Chandrasakar for protecting his interests.

"If they're employing necropathic killers to try to learn details about the Delta Cephei mission," she said, "it suggests that they don't know that much."

"And it also suggests," he said, taking her hand, "that the traitor is not someone I've entrusted with priority information, which is a relief."

He told her about the other telepaths murdered recently.

"Do you think the same people who came after me are responsible for the killings?" she asked.

He nodded. "The three were telepaths I'd targeted as suitable to have accompany me on the mission."

She stared at him. "Not so much a security leak as a deluge..."

"And don't I know it, Parveen? Anyway, since then I've hired the best telepath on the Station." He shrugged. "I'd rather not have an outsider along, but he's good–"

She stroked his cheek. "I could always replace him," she said. "It's not too late, Rab."

He laughed at this, surprising him. "Parveen, I wouldn't wish his ability on anyone..." And he told her what she'd already learned from the pin Anish Lahore had given her: that the only surviving crew member of the Chandrasakar exploration ship that had landed on Delta Cephei VII earlier this year was a woman who, though technically dead, was in cryogenic suspension awaiting a necropath's attention.

She asked him about the mission, but he seemed unwilling to tell her much more. "When we're aboard the *Kali*," he said, "and I can be certain of ultimate security."

"I can always help you with that," she said.

Chandrasakar laughed. "If you could keep tabs on Vaughan and the scientists... I'd like to think the latter can be trusted, but who knows?"

She nodded. "I'll do that."

"Vaughan's been around. I had my people do the usual checks. He's a very closed, reserved person. There's a phrase – a cold fish. Well, Vaughan's one of those."

"How did you buy him?"

"I exercised my altruistic nature," he said. "His youngest daughter is seriously ill, and I arranged for her treatment and care. It was an offer he couldn't refuse."

"I'm curious to meet this Mr Vaughan."

"Like I said, if you could keep him under observation… It's a delicate mission and the last thing I want is a maverick telepath pouring oil on smooth waters." He laughed and reached out for her. "But all this talk…" he said, slipping a hand through her hair.

She didn't really know if he was an expert lover, never having had many lovers, but she suspected that he was experienced, and he certainly knew how to make her happy. They made love in the sunken sofa as night fell and the ocean beyond the viewscreen glittered with the light of the full moon.

In his arms, she wondered not for the first time what he saw in her. She was scrawny and flat-chested, her face too round to be classically pretty, her nose too snub. She had considered cosmetic surgery, when she was younger, but when she'd become politicised she'd rejected the idea, dismissing stereotypical images of beauty as a bourgeois materialistic concept.

She had learned to be happy with what she'd got. Rab certainly enjoyed the sex, but she thought that what really attracted him was the conversation, their political arguments: she suspected that few women in his social circles dared argue the point with him on any subject, and certainly not politics. But that had been how their relationship started, in the ambassador's mansion, when they'd been introduced and Rab had said, "Ah, yes, I have read one of your papers, if I'm not mistaken. Thought-provoking, if politically naïve..."

She had caught the twinkle in his eye, and proceeded to argue her corner.

She'd come to know the tycoon over the following weeks. A lonely man surrounded by yes-men and women who were attracted only to his wealth, his wife had died ten years ago and he'd never remarried. The relationships he'd embarked upon since then, he'd told her, had been abject failures.

Now she lay in his arms, stroking his chest, and he reached out and touched a control unit, indicating the ceiling. "Look."

She laid her head next to his and together they watched the domed ceiling turn transparent. A thousand scintillating stars flung their light down around them. "And when we're on Delta Cephei VII, we'll make love beneath new and unfamiliar constellations..."

She propped herself on an elbow, sliding a leg across his loins. He reached up and slipped a hand around her neck. He frowned.

"Oh, I had an upgrade the other day," she told him. She indicated her handset. "It's all in here now. Less noticeable. Some of the people of the colony worlds I work on are a little on the conservative side and mistrust tele-heads, as they call them."

She'd told him that she was a telepath just before the first time they made love, explaining that although it was impossible for humans to read the thoughts of alien species, in her line of work as a xenologist the ability did help to occasionally gain impressions, however abstract, of a subject race's mental processes. It was a thin piece of reasoning, she knew, but Chandrasakar seemed to buy it.

Oh, how she hated having to lie, she thought, especially to the man she loved.

They made love again, for the last time on Earth.

She woke early the following morning, the intimacy of the night before a warm glow in her mind. Chandrasakar was already up, sitting in his dressing gown and conducting business via a wall-mounted softscreen. He brought her coffee and a croissant when he saw her stirring, and they sat on the bed and ate.

"We're all set to take the shuttle at ten," he told her. "I've staged a little reception at the spaceport before we go, just to allow people to get to know each other."

She stroked his hand. "I've never made love in the void."

He laughed. "Then it will be a first for both of us."

"Rab..." She felt a sudden explosion somewhere within her. "Love you..." she murmured, and she wondered if she had weakened her position by showing her hand.

He smiled, reached out, and touched her cheek.

They showered and dressed, Parveen slipping into a racing green Chandrasakar Organisation uniform and checking herself in the mirror. She liked what she saw. The uniform gave her an air of authority that her casual clothes had lacked. They left the ship and took a flier on the short hop across the port to a reception lounge.

Before they stepped from the flier, Parveen asked, "Rab, do... I mean, your team, the scientists and security... do they know about me and you?"

He shook his head, then squeezed her hand. "But they soon will."

His words, his reassuring smile, worked as an affirmation, and she was walking on air as she left the flier and entered the reception lounge.

There were perhaps fifty people milling about inside. Drone waiters and humans circulated with trays bearing drinks and snacks. People stood in small groups, chatting casually. Most of them wore the Organisation uniform, green denoting Chandrasakar's scientific staff, blue security, and red the ship's crew – the various pilots, co-pilots, engineers and catering staff. Parveen noted very little colour mix: each specialism preferring the company of their own.

"Come, I'll introduce you."

He led her across to the far side of the lounge where three groups of scientists were talking shop; when Chandrasakar arrived, they turned as one and merged to form a larger group, smiling at the tycoon and conferring the same, though tempered by curiosity, on Parveen.

Rab introduced her as one of the world's leading xenologists as they moved around the group. The scientists were unfailingly polite, but behind the amity, the smiles and witticisms, she noted a few raised eyebrows at the pairing of the world's richest businessman and a scientist from communist India.

She returned their pleasantries; she wanted to access her tele-ability and read what these people were really thinking about her. They would be shielded – being employees of the Chandrasakar Organisation – but she suspected that her viral software would be sufficient to overcome their guards. She decided that there would be plenty of time to probe during the coming days.

Chandrasakar introduced her to a loud, rangy Australian with a mop of red hair, David McIntosh, and a diminutive Japanese woman who could have passed as a twelve-year-old schoolgirl, Kiki Namura. Her interest piqued, Parveen fell into conversation with the pair. They were, if her controller Anish Lahore was correct, FNSA plants. She would probe them later, to see what their friendly, open personas were concealing.

She talked to them about their specialisms – McIntosh was a geologist, Namura a biologist – and guessed that they were more than just friends; something about their body language, the mirror gestures and the looks they gave each other when the other was talking, suggested recent intimacy. She wondered if she and Rab were so transparent.

"What are you hoping to find on Delta Cephei VII, Dr Das?" Namura asked, with the odd breathless intonation of her race. "According to the reports, the planet is uninhabited."

She nodded. "I'm along for the ride," she said. "More as an... observer, let's say. And you never know–" she twinkled a smile at the minuscule Japanese woman, "we might come across some little green men."

McIntosh boomed a laugh and raised his beer at her.

Chandrasakar took her elbow and moved her on. A group of a dozen blue-uniformed men and women moved to accommodate her and Rab into their midst. They were abstaining from alcohol and sipped juices instead.

Rab singled out a giant Sikh and introduced him. "Anil Singh, my head of security."

Singh was tall and proportionally broad, with shoulders like yokes and pectorals almost obscenely defined by his shrink-wrapped uniform.

He enclosed her hand in his, and she thought that the slightest pressure would crunch her metacarpal bones. He smiled and inclined his turbaned head, but his brown eyes lacked the slightest civility.

I don't like this man, she thought; and something told her that the sentiment was mutual. She wondered at his reserve, though it wasn't that difficult to work out. He suspected her, firstly, for her political affiliations and, secondly, for her intimacy with his boss: Chandrasakar had said on more than one occasion that Singh was his most loyal employee, who'd served the organisation for more than twenty years.

"I trust you won't have a lot on your hands during this mission, Mr Singh," she smiled.

He replied coldly, "We must be most vigilant at times when a civilian might think there is no call for vigilance, Miz Das."

She smiled at him. "That's Dr Das, Mr Singh. Well, I'm delighted that Rab will be more than adequately protected," she said, pointedly took her lover's arm and moved on.

They stood beside the floor-to-ceiling observation screen overlooking the busy port. Chandrasakar said, "Did I miss something there?"

His boyish puzzlement was endearing. She

squeezed his arm and whispered, "Singh is suspicious of me, not to say jealous. He doesn't like the idea of his boss slumming it with an Indian lowlife."

He stared at her. "You *read* that?"

She laughed. "I don't need to read him," she said. "It was obvious from his body language, and the little he did say."

"I'll have a word with him, tell him that you're a great friend and to be trusted."

"No," she said quickly, "that would only antagonise him even more. Just let him be."

He nodded. "If you say so, Parveen."

He pointed out the shuttle, surrounded by maintenance engineers and techs, and looked at his watch. "We should be boarding in little under thirty minutes. Will you excuse me one moment?"

She smiled as she watched him stride to the centre of the room; eyes followed him and a silence fell.

"Ladies and gentlemen..." he began. "First of all, my sincerest thanks that you consented to join me on this mission. It isn't every day I fly to the edge of the Expansion to explore a newly discovered planet, and I wanted only the very best scientists, technicians, and back-up staff to accompany me..." A patter of applause greeted his words, which he damped with a raised palm and a smile. "We'll be taking my best ship, *Kali's Revenge*..." He went on, detailing the ship's attributes for those who might be interested.

Das watched him, noted how he commanded the room with his presence, and not for the first time thanked her lucky stars.

She was still daydreaming when a figure loomed

at her side. She turned to see Anil Singh staring down at her.

"Mr Singh..." she said, edging away.

"I just thought I'd tell you, *Doctor* Das," he said, with sarcastic emphasis, "that despite the fact that you've gained Chandrasakar's... intimacy, shall we say... neither that nor your eminence cuts it with me. Do I make myself clear?"

She tried to outstare him. "But Mr Singh," she tried, "I have absolutely no idea–"

He took her elbow in a grip like a robotic claw. "Then I'll be plain. I don't trust communists as far as I can piss." He smiled, sweetly. "And you can tell the boss what I said in exactly those words, if you dare."

He unhanded her and strode away before she could marshal a reply.

Heart pounding, she turned to the viewscreen and stared out, hating herself for feeling so shaken.

Later, she told herself, she'd probe him. If his shield was cutting-edge, then she'd get round that by employing a virus. She wouldn't let the fascist prick treat her like shit...

She grabbed a beer from a passing waiter and drank quickly.

Chandrasakar wrapped up his address and rejoined her. "I saw Singh...?" he began.

She smiled easily. "He just came over to apologise for his coolness earlier, Rab."

He nodded. "Good man," he said. He indicated the shuttle; a fuel tanker was beetling from its flank. "Ten minutes and we'll be on our way."

Parveen looked around the room. She noticed someone standing alone further along the rail; he was staring out at the port, one foot lodged on the lower rail, holding a nearly empty bottle of Blue Mountain beer.

He was tall, dressed casually, with a thin face, close-cropped, receding hair and dark eyes. He was handsome in a paired-down, sinewy kind of way, and noticeable as the only person in the room not wearing a Chandrasakar Organisation uniform.

"Rab," she said, indicating the loner, "who's that?"

He looked. "Oh, the telepath. Jeff Vaughan. Come on, I'll introduce you."

"No," she said, surprised by her vehemence. The encounter with Singh had troubled her more than she'd first thought. There was something self-contained and coolly calculating about Vaughan. In her experience, male telepaths were arrogant, and she could do without another dose of macho posturing right now.

"No, but I'd like to scan him, if that's okay?"

Rab smiled. "Be my guest." He said, watching her with obvious curiosity.

She touched her handset. She was instantly aware of many points of mind-shield static in the room around her. She filtered them out and concentrated on Vaughan.

He was shielded, of course, and with an efficient system. She concentrated, but her probes slid uselessly around the static enclosing his mind.

Rab said, "Well?"

She shook her head. "He has a damned good shield."

He looked disappointed. "So you can't...?"

She smiled. "There is always a way, Rab." She

gestured to a waiter bearing a tray of drinks; at the same time she touched her handset. She felt an almost imperceptible tickle travel from her metacarpal hardware to her fingertips.

The waiter stopped before her. She touched the bottle of Blue Mountain beer on the tray, and the tickle ceased. "Would you take the beer across to Mr Vaughan," she told the waiter, "and say that Mr Chandrasakar sent it?"

The waiter snapped a bow and hurried over to Vaughan.

"What was all that about?" Rab asked, non-plussed.

"A virus," she explained. "You'd be surprised at the number of aliens who use shields, even though we can't read their thoughts, as such."

She glanced at him. He nodded, oblivious of her lie.

Vaughan listened to the waiter, took the beer, and lofted it at Chandrasakar with what looked to Parveen like a sardonic salute.

The telepath tipped the beer into his mouth and resumed his inspection of the tarmac.

Rab murmured, "But won't his system alert him to the breach?"

"It doesn't cause catastrophic failure; just enough to let me through."

She tried another probe, and a minute later she broke through his compromised defences.

She closed her eyes, leaned against the rail, and was swamped by his psyche.

She was rocked by the strength of his personality, by the love he felt for his wife, Sukara, a small, plain Thai woman... except to Vaughan she wasn't plain at all, but radiant... Parveen accessed his memories, the person he was years ago, before Sukara, and she experienced pain at the despair he'd felt then, his nihilism, as the world he inhabited was a world without hope, and his job as a telepath brought him into contact with the worst that world had to offer... And then, over the course of a few weeks, as Sukara saved his life literally, he got to know her, to love her, and she saved his life again... only this time she'd saved his soul.

And then Parveen read about his sick daughter Li, and the pain he was feeling at having to leave behind Sukara and the girls, and his anxiety, despite all his reassurances to Sukara that everything would be okay... And she read his suspicion of Chandrasakar, and his fear at what lay ahead, at having to read the dead mind of the engineer – and that brought forth another slew of deeper, more unpleasant memories of when he'd read dead and dying minds more than twenty-five years ago for the Toronto Homicide department...

She withdrew quickly, pulled out her probe and shut down the program. She leaned against the rail, breathing hard and sweating.

Rab was all concern. He touched her hand. "Parveen–?"

"I'm fine. It's... I'm always like this when I've read..."

Except, she told herself, she...wasn't... Some people had the kind of personality that... swept you away; there was no other word for it. She suspected that Vaughan was personable in company, but to be privy to the inner workings of his mind was to be made aware of how good a man he was... and the love he felt for Sukara... Parveen reddened as she realised that she felt – what was it? Jealousy? To be the subject of such committed and constant devotion...

She looked across at Vaughan, and realised that his demeanour of aloof indifference was a charade he'd perfected over the years of practising his trade as an investigative telepath. The psychological truth was far more intriguing than the misleading physical appearance. She looked forward to getting to know the telepath over the course of the next few days.

"Well?" Rab asked.

"Well, I think he's good at his job, Rab. You've picked one of the best. You can trust him."

"But," Rab said, "does he trust me?"

She smiled. "Let's say that he has his suspicions."

"Anything definite?"

"I'll be able to get a better idea over the next few days," she told him.

A port official entered the room and signalled across to Chandrasakar. Minutes later he led the way from the lounge and across the tarmac towards the waiting shuttle. Parveen accompanied him to a private cabin at the front of the craft and strapped herself in for take-off.

Minutes later the main engines fired and she found herself thrust back into the padded seat as the shuttle attained escape velocity. She peered through the viewscreen at the diminishing scale model that was Bengal Station as the shuttle rose towards Chandrasakar Station high above.

SEVEN

PHASE OUT

Vaughan stared down at the Station as the shuttle climbed rapidly. He located Himachal Park and the tiny speck of the café where he, Sukara, and the girls went for coffee. His thoughts turned to Li and the treatment due to commence in the morning.

He touched the back of his neck. He'd arrived at the port at nine that morning and Chandrasakar's crimson-uniformed PA had introduced him to a Dr Pavelescu. The medic had examined Vaughan's occipital system, then inserted the necropath program – a simple data-pin – into his handset and instructed him in its use. All told, the procedure took fifteen minutes; the program would run parallel with his current tele-ability, so that his regular telepathic awareness would not be compromised. The pin would be ejected once Vaughan had read the dead engineer.

He was now a necropath, once again. He sat back in his seat and stared through the screen, wondering what the next two weeks might bring.

"Quite a view, isn't it?"

He turned at the sound of the voice. An Indian woman smiled down at him, outfitted in the bottle-green uniform of a Chandrasakar Organisation scientist. She gestured to the couch opposite. "Would you mind...?"

"No, of course not."

She folded herself elegantly into the seat and extended a cool hand. "Parveen Das. I'm a xenologist with Kolkata University, seconded to the team for the duration of this mission."

"Jeff Vaughan," he supplied. "Telepath. But I'm not reading."

She smiled. "We're all shielded, as a matter of course. It's something that Chandrasakar insists upon."

He suspected her ancestry was largely Dalit, or one of the other low-castes. She was slightly stooped, her round faced pockmarked, her chest concave: all of which could have been corrected by modern surgical and medical techniques. It was some indication of her personality, and perhaps even her political leanings, that she had elected to remain as nature intended.

Vaughan thought that her various individual physical defects should have made for a less than prepossessing whole, and yet something in her elegant poise, and her cultured accent – precise Indian English – made her oddly attractive.

He said, "A xenologist... Is Chandrasakar expecting to find alien natives?" Or has found them, he wondered. Was this one of the things that the tycoon had failed to mention at their original meeting?

"Chandrasakar likes to cover all eventualities, Mr Vaughan. The chances are that my specialism will be redundant on this trip, but he's asked me to act as your guide and nursemaid for the duration."

"In other words you've been paid to keep an eye on me, make sure I don't stray?"

Her brown eyes hardened. "I'm not Chandrasakar's dogsbody, Mr Vaughan."

"I'm sorry. I didn't mean to be flippant. And call me Jeff, okay?"

Her eyes relented and she smiled.

He looked around the cabin, ensuring that the scientists and techs were out of earshot. "What do you know about the mission?"

She slipped a rubber band from the top pocket of her uniform, gathered her long black hair, and cinched it in a ponytail. "Rab lost a ship on Delta Cephei VII, then sent another ship to investigate. I suspect they found something... interesting. You?"

He considered, then said, "No more than that."

Das slipped her gaze through the screen and gazed down. Bengal Station had vanished in the cerulean immensity of the ocean. The rucked swathes of India, Burma, and Thailand – all scorched khaki – were stark against the blue sea.

"I'm intrigued."

She cocked an eye. "Yes?"

"I saw you with Chandrasakar at the reception... I would have thought someone of your background, and a man like Chandrasakar, would mix about as well as oil and water."

She nodded, tight-lipped. "I can keep what he stands for, and the man himself, in separate compartments."

He refrained from making a snide comment. Instead he said, "So you agree that he's just another capitalist who makes millions for his shareholders, and for himself, while he and his fellow capitalists keep millions of people in conditions of slavery?"

She regarded him neutrally. "He would argue that he does what he can for those in his employ."

He shrugged. "But what do you think, Parveen?"

She smiled, and refused to answer the question. "My politics lean towards an incremental reform of the present global system," she said, "moving towards old-fashioned late twenty-first-century socialism and arriving eventually at what we have achieved in India. And you?" she went on quickly. "Where do you stand?"

He looked at her, then shook her head. "I have an innate mistrust of any group of more than three people. Who was it who said that power corrupts?"

Das tried to keep the disdain from her face, but failed. "Political apathy never helped anyone, Jeff. Ah, here we are…"

He watched her as she gazed through the viewscreen, and he wondered at the complex loyalties she kept in check behind her shrewd, gimlet eyes.

They had passed into the deep blue of space while they'd chatted, and beyond the screen Chandrasakar Station was sliding into view.

What struck Vaughan first was its immensity, and then the complexity of its detail. It seemed to hang at an angle, a canted spinning top bristling with a thousand decks and ports and columnar living quarters, all of it scintillating gold and silver in the ceaseless sunlight. Second only to the startling fact of its dimensions was the sheer number of craft either making their way to or coming from the Station. He counted more than thirty – from shuttles to great voidships – before giving up.

Discreetly, he enabled his tele-ability and was amazed to find that not one mind of the many that teemed in the hive of the station was readable; his probes encountered thousands of static patches denoting mind-shields. He killed the program.

"Impressive, hm?" Das said.

He nodded. "And I thought the spaceport on Bengal Station was huge."

"Chandrasakar had this built when Bengal spaceport reached capacity. It's a small continent out there." She pointed. "And if I'm not mistaken, that's the voidship that will be taking us out to Delta Cephei VII."

She indicated a docked ship that more resembled something from the insect kingdom – a hybrid wasp and praying mantis, perhaps – than anything mechanical. "He calls it *Kali's Revenge*, Jeff. It's the latest in voidspace technology."

The shuttle docked, pressure equalised, and they filed down the long umbilical that snaked around the perimeter of the station. Zonia led the way, with the scientists and technicians, and Das and Vaughan, in her wake. Minutes later they came to a viewing platform metres away from the golden epidermis of *Kali's Revenge*, where they paused to take in the waspish liner.

"Any other ship would take at least five or six days to get to Delta Cephei," Das said. "This thing will do it in about two days."

"Quite a boat."

"Cost fifteen billion euros to construct."

He looked at her. "That'd feed the starving of South America for a decade."

She glanced at him, then back to the ship. "Don't play me for a fool, Jeff. I'm not that crass."

He let it ride, and their guide escorted them through the entry iris and into *Kali's Revenge*. Their guide paused in a plush atrium more like the foyer of an expensive hotel.

"We will be phasing into the void in a little under two hours, ladies and gentlemen. If you would care to make yourselves comfortable in your respective quarters..." She indicated a corridor to their right. "You will find nameplates indicating your rooms. Mr Chandrasakar will be dining in the main observation lounge at phase-out, and you are invited to join him."

Vaughan left Das and made his way along the corridor to the individual berths. He found his name on a sliding door, which opened at his touch.

The room was surprisingly spacious, with a large bed, a shower unit, and a long viewscreen looking away from the Station. He crossed to it and stared out. Earth turned below; India was moving towards the dark side. He imagined Sukara getting Pham and Li settled for bed and he felt a quick welling of love for his family.

He sat on a chair beside the viewscreen and tapped a code into his handset, enabling the void-space program. He used it now, just to check that it was functioning, even though his regular communication program would have sufficed.

Seconds later the screen flared and Sukara beamed out at him. His heart kicked at the sight of her.

"Jeff!" she cried. "Where are you?"

"Aboard *Kali's Revenge*. We phase-out in a little under two hours. I'm missing you already."

"I'm missing you, too, Jeff, and so are the girls. They send their love. What's your room like?"

"Imagine the Hilton in space, only smaller." He stared at her, wishing he were there. "I'll soon be back, Su. And I'll call every day, okay?"

"I'll look forward to that. So... tell me about all the people you've met so far."

"A medic called Pavelescu and a woman called Das. I think she's been detailed to keep tabs on me."

"She pretty, Jeff?"

He smiled. "To be honest she looks like Mahatma Gandhi and I think she thinks I'm politically apathetic."

"Well, you are," she laughed.

He smiled. "God, Su. I wish I were with you now. I'm due to have dinner with Chandrasakar and the rest of his team, but I'd rather go with you to the Ruen Thai."

"When you get back, okay? We'll all go out to celebrate."

"Good idea."

They chatted about nothing in particular until a chime and a soft female voice announced dinner in the main observation lounge.

"Must go, Su. See you soon. I love you."

"Love you too, Jeff. Take care."

He signed off, then stared down at the Indian Ocean, at where he thought Bengal Station might be.

He left the room and made his way to the observation lounge.

One thing that puzzled him, as the door slid open to admit him into the oval-shaped chamber beneath a bell-jar dome, was that Chandrasakar should choose to entertain his team during phase-out, the transition period when the ride was far from smooth.

A dozen scientists stood beneath the dome, clutching wine glasses and chatting. A waiter approached with a tray bearing an ice-cold bottle of Blue Mountain beer. Vaughan smiled and accepted the drink.

Parveen Das came over to him. She had exchanged her severe uniform for an evening dress, and she looked almost feminine. She wore her hair long, and had even applied pale indigo eyeshadow.

"Ready for the transition?" she asked him.

"I'll keep tight hold of my beer," he said, hoisting it.

"No need. You won't notice a thing, unless you're looking out into space."

She introduced him to a couple of scientists – a biologist from Japan called Kiki Namura and an Australian geologist, David McIntosh. The latter was clutching a beer in a big fist and laughing at something Namura had whispered behind her small hand.

They exchanged polite small talk for a while, Namura excited about this, her first extra-solar trip, while McIntosh recounted his last voidship voyage to study the volcanic rock formations of Vega III.

Eyes turned to Vaughan, who told them he'd visited two colony worlds, and on the second had read the minds of elephant analogues. They thought he was joking and laughed politely.

"Parveen?" McIntosh asked.

"This will be my fifth field-trip off-world, and potentially the most interesting."

They were interrupted by Chandrasakar's clearing his throat and then ringing his sherry glass with a spoon. "Ladies and gentlemen," he announced. "Dinner is served."

The twelve diners seated themselves around an oval table, where nametags had been arranged on a table-top made from some black alien marble which scintillated with tiny silver lights like a starscape.

Vaughan found himself between Namura and McIntosh; Parveen Das was seated to Chandrasakar's right. To his left was a bulky Sikh, whom Chandrasakar introduced as Singh, head of security. He continued around the table, introducing his team one by one. When he came to Vaughan, he smiled and said, "Jeff Vaughan. Jeff is a telepath, and one of the best."

Vaughan lifted an ironic glass to the tycoon, aware of suspicious stares from some of those around the table.

Dinner was served by mechanically efficient waiters – vegetarian Gujarati fare with rice and naan – and Vaughan listened to McIntosh as he recounted his experiences on Vega III. Only Kiki Namura asked him about his telepathic ability, staring at him timidly with big eyes and saying, "But it must be terrible to be privy to the secret thoughts of others."

He nodded, pleased and surprised at her common sense; most people assumed that mind-readers were a privileged elite, eavesdroppers on secrets they'd use to their own advantage.

The tintinnabulation of silver on crystal rang out again, as Chandrasakar bombastically called for hush. When he had it, he made a show of consulting an old-fashioned pocket-watch. "Ten seconds to phase-out and counting. Ten, nine..."

Despite Das's reassurances, Vaughan made sure he was holding his beer as the scene outside the dome began to flicker: the Station vanished momentarily, like the picture on a faulty holovision, then returned briefly, vanished again to be replaced by a uniform grey backdrop streaked with marmoreal veins of white.

Vaughan glanced at his beer; not so much as a ripple disturbed its surface.

A polite patter of applause greeted the transition. Chandrasakar raised his glass. "To the success of the mission!" he said, and the words were echoed around the table.

Chandrasakar proceeded to hold forth; he was an able if single-minded raconteur, telling humorous stories about his travels around the Expansion and recounting some of the odder customs on the human colonies he'd visited.

At one point he reached for Parveen Das's hand and clutched it. Vaughan glanced at Das; she was laughing with him, more than comfortable with the tycoon's attention. Vaughan wanted nothing more, then, than to probe her mind.

Dinner broke up after coffee; some of the team excused themselves and made for their rooms, while others moved to the adjacent bar. A couple of Chandrasakar's crimson-uniformed staff moved among the travellers, asking if anyone would care for sedatives to put them under for the duration of the voyage. Vaughan thought about it, and elected to accept the offered drug.

Tired after a long day, he retired to his room and stared out at the streaked grey of voidspace. He fingered his handset, wanting to see Sukara's face, talk to her. It would be the early hours of the morning now, so he resisted the urge; instead he replayed the conversation they'd had earlier, and froze her face from time to time when he found her expression irresistible.

He lay on the bed, and on impulse enabled his tele-ability. He probed, sliding around the dozen or so mind-shields on the upper decks, and aware of perhaps thirty or more below, where other techs, scientists, and members of the security team were berthed.

He stood and made his way to the door, exited and moved down the corridor towards the bar with the intention of picking up a night-cap. He passed Parveen Das's room; her mind-shield static was absent from the room. He moved through the observation lounge. As he entered the bar he saw Chandrasakar and Parveen Das leave by the opposite exit, hand in hand, and take the elevator-plate to the next level.

He returned to his room, drank his beer, and probed. High overhead, two areas of static came together and melded into one.

EIGHT

A JOB OFFER

Sukara dropped Pham off at school at nine that morning and was strolling back through the Level Two park with Li when her handset chimed. A cheerful European woman smiled out at her. "Chintara Sukarapatam?"

"Yes?"

"I'm Louise Graham, Dr Grant's PA. Dr Grant will be working with you and Li over the next few weeks at St Theresa's. I'm calling to ask if you'd be able to bring Li in at some point this morning?"

"I don't need an appointment?"

The woman smiled. "Your daughter is a private patient. I understand that Mr Rabindranath Chandrasakar is underwriting her treatment. She will be receiving priority care from now on."

"Well... I'll bring her in straight away, if that's okay? Say, ten?"

"That's fine. Ask at reception for Dr Grant. We'll see you at ten."

Sukara thanked her and cut the connection.

"Nursery school!" Li cried, hanging on Sukara's hand.

"After we've been to the hospital, Li. A nice doctor's going to examine you again."

Li pulled a pantomime face of exaggerated forbearance. "Not *again*, Mum?"

"Not for long, and if you're a brave girl the nurse might give you another certificate."

This excited her. "Can I put it on my wall near the other one?"

Sukara nodded. "Anyway, how are you feeling today?"

Li stuck out her tongue and rolled her eyes. "Bit ill, Mum."

The trouble was, Li was an expert at feigning sickness for effect. She had Jeff wrapped around her little finger. Li's slightest cough had had him running to the medicine cabinet. He'd been surprised, the other day, when Sukara had told him that Li was no worse than usual and was just winding him up. He'd turned to Li, to find her grinning like a guilty imp.

They made a detour across the park towards St Theresa's.

Beyond the open end of Level Two, Sukara saw a voidship approaching the Station. The sight of its colossal bulk reminded her that Jeff was light years away and getting more distant every second. Soon, she thought, he would be a thousand light years away, as far as any human being had travelled from Earth.

It had been great talking to him last night, the line as good as if he were here on the Station. But later, when he'd cut the connection, a cold and vast loneliness had set in, depressing her. It was as if she were back to being the Sukara who'd arrived on the Station years ago, who'd met Jeff Vaughan for the first time, realised what a good man he was, and feared that the last thing he'd want was to get involved with her.

Those few days had been the loneliest of her life.

Then he'd called her from his hospital bed, to say he wanted to see her again, if she'd care to visit.

Sometimes she felt a terrible dread at the thought of what might have happened to her if he'd not bothered to call. She would never have known all the love and happiness she would have missed, of course, but the thought that it could have all been so different made her almost physically sick.

"Here we are!" Li carolled and dragged her through the hospital's revolving door to the reception desk.

Sukara gave Dr Grant's name and seconds later she was riding the elevator to the fifth floor. She was ten minutes early, but a nurse ushered her through a plush anteroom into the surgery.

Dr Grant was a tubby European in his sixties, with a mass of silver hair and a reassuring smile. He was good with Li, telling her that he was going to take a little of her blood but that he'd pay for it with tokens she could use in the hospital shop. Li liked the idea of this and proffered her arm willingly to the nurse.

The small Indian woman drew an ampoule of blood and hurried off into an adjacent room. Li spotted a box of toys in the corner of the room, skipped over to it and immersed herself in play-acting spacemen and monsters with the latest holo-movie tie-in action figures.

Dr Grant read Li's case notes from a big screen on his desk, then swivelled to face Sukara. She felt her pulse race.

He placed his fingertips together, looking at her like an uncle with bad news to impart.

"Now, Sukara. No doubt Dr Chang informed you of the gravity of the situation. Your daughter is seriously ill, but with the right treatment we should be able to have Li on her feet again in no time. Her condition is known technically as acute lymphoblastic leukaemia, which stated simply is when the body produces immature white blood cells instead of mature cells which fight off infection..." He went on in this fashion, mixing vague abstractions like "pull things round" with terms such as "blast cell anomaly" and "platelet regeneration"; Sukara felt out of her depth, understanding very little of what he was saying and wanting just the bald, uncategorical assurance that Li could be cured.

He finished and watched her. "Do you have any questions?"

Her throat felt dry, and she was twelve years old again, sitting tongue-tied before her teacher who was chastising her for poor results in English.

"Dr Chang... he told me that there was a seventy per cent chance that everything would be okay." She shrugged. "When you get the results from the blood test, will you be able to tell me any more?" She stumbled and stuttered with her words, and sounded like one of the illiterate street-girls she taught.

"Sixty, seventy, eighty… it varies from case to case. If Li were older, say in her teens, then the chances of a lasting cure would be much reduced. But she's…" He referred to the screen, "just over four. I'll be able to tell you more when I've had time to examine the blood tests."

"When that will be, please?" she asked, and knew she sounded impatient.

"I should have a better understanding of your daughter's condition a little later today. I'll have my PA call you with the results around five. In any case, I'd like you to bring Li in tomorrow for a day or two. Then we can begin the treatment."

She felt something rise in her chest, constricting her throat. "You mean… Li will be in hospital overnight?"

Dr Grant spread his hands. "I'm afraid it's unavoidable. Then we can run a few tests, initiate treatment and assess her reactions, and then if necessary adjust the treatment accordingly."

She nodded, trying to get her thoughts together. "I… will I be able to stay with her?"

"By all means." Dr Grant smiled. "We have rooms set aside for parents and guardians."

She smiled, knowing that she appeared pathetically thankful. She wondered why members of the medical profession, who after all were only doing their jobs, reduced her to such inarticulate gratitude.

"If you could bring Li in at midday tomorrow, we'll take it from there, yes?" he said, with an upward inflection in his tone, which diplomatically signalled the end of the consultation.

Sukara smiled and thanked him again, then dragged Li complaining from the toys. She took the elevator down to the foyer, considering what she'd learned from the appointment. A lot of big words and hot air, she thought, wondering how she'd spend the next few hours until the doctor's PA called with the test results at five.

They would be the longest few hours of her life, and she wished Jeff were around to share them with her.

"Nursery now?" Li asked, pulling her in the direction of the nursery school building on the far side of the park.

Sukara remembered her promise, despite a reluctance to leave Li now. She wanted to spend time with her daughter, spoil her with ices and Vitamilk... Three afternoons a week she taught basic English to the working-girls on Silom Road, but yesterday she'd arranged with the head of the language school for two weeks' vacation so that she could look after Li while Jeff was away.

Li normally attended nursery while Sukara taught, and Sukara was obscurely put out that her daughter would rather go to nursery than spend time with her now. She told herself that she was being clingy, walked Li across the park and dropped her off in the noisy playground.

She decided to try to forget about the call at five by doing some shopping in the food market on Level Three; she'd take the upchute to the top level and have a coffee in Himachal Park before picking up the girls.

Around five, she thought, she would be back at the hotel preparing dinner in the suite's well-equipped kitchen...

She'd bought a bag full of vegetables and was

moving through the bustling crowds towards the spice stall when her handset chimed. Her heart lurched and she thought: Li's blood test...

She stopped and stood with the bag between her ankles, buffeted by the crowd. She accepted the call. An aged, wrinkled face – like a grandfather turtle, she thought – stared out at her. "Oh, Dr Rao..." She wondered what the old rascal wanted now.

"Sukara, my dear, I trust that I have not called at an inopportune moment."

"Ah, no... No, of course not. How can I help?"

His lipless mouth widened in what on any other face might have been described as a smile; on Dr Rao it merely looked like just another, deeper wrinkle. "My dear, I wonder if I might have the pleasure of your company for a little while this afternoon? I... I am embarking upon a venture which I am sure you might find of some little interest."

"Well..." she said, guardedly. "What kind of venture, Dr Rao?"

"It is in the nature of education, my dear, the realm of learning whose benefits cannot be overstated. If perhaps I might have an hour of your time...?"

She smiled to herself, intrigued at the thought of what new scheme the old doctor might be cooking up now. "Okay, Dr Rao. Look, I'll be at the café in Himachal Park in about half an hour. I could meet you then."

"The pleasure will be mine entirely," Dr Rao said with impeccable grace, and signed off.

She finished her shopping, then took the upchute to the top level. She walked through Himachal Park, Jeff's absence all the more painful here; once a week they took time out to have a coffee with the kids, chat, and stare out across the ocean as the voidships came in.

After the artificial daylight of the lower levels, the sunlight dazzled. She found herself wondering when Jeff would land on Delta Cephei VII, and what the sun there would be like.

Later tonight, if he hadn't called by nine, she'd take the initiative and call him.

She dropped her bags with relief, sat down and ordered an iced tea. The weather on the top level was hot and humid; the monsoon had yet to bring its seasonal relief. She dug her sunglasses from her bag, slipped them on, and sat back in the sunlight.

Five minutes later the small, insect-like figure of Dr Rao, his cane tapping ahead like a lone antenna, probed across the concourse in her direction. He saw her, hoisted his stick and hobbled across to her.

"Sukara, how pleasant it is to see you again. I take it your husband is among the stars as we speak, and Li receiving the finest treatment money can buy?" He seated himself, his wide lips set in a curve suggesting self-satisfaction at his role in effectuating the aforementioned scenarios.

Sukara smiled to herself. There was something about the doctor's self-righteous demeanour that always struck her as comical.

"Jeff should be landing on Delta Cephei VII pretty soon," she said, "and Li starts her treatment tomorrow."

"A splendid state of affairs," Dr Rao said. He ordered a salted lassi and sat back with his arthritic fingers knotted around the knob of his cane. "And now, the small matter of my latest venture..."

Sukara sipped her iced tea and smiled. "I'm all ears, Dr Rao," she said, using the odd phrase that Jeff had introduced her to years ago.

"You are obviously cognizant of the fact that I am the... ah... shall we say benefactor of a number of indigent street children. It is a sad fact that, without my ministrations, they would find life on the Station well nigh impossible. I do my little bit to ease their burden."

Sukara nodded. "Jeff's told me all about your good works, Dr Rao," she said, straight-faced.

He beamed his reptilian smile. "But it came to me recently, in a blinding flash, that I might do more for the children in my care." He paused, so that Sukara might prompt him.

She obliged. "But what could that possibly be, Dr Rao?"

"My children," he declared, "need educating."

She blinked. "Educating?" She agreed, but she failed to see how educating the street-kids might be of any benefit to Dr Rao, who after all lived from the earnings of their beggary.

The old man nodded vigorously. "The situation is this; my children have gainful employment until approximately the ages of fifteen or sixteen, when they take it upon themselves to flee the nest, as it were, to leave the succour of my starship haven and try their luck in the real world. I lose contact with many of my children, and can only fear for their fates. A few I do manage to trace – and it is the plight of these few unfortunates which prompted the line of thought which culminated in my latest benevolent scheme."

Sukara nodded encouragingly and sipped her tea.

Dr Rao went on, "Many of my children, when they reach a certain age, fall foul of the lure of lucre, promiscuity, and villainy. In short, Sukara, they fall into the clutches of those less scrupulous than myself, and find themselves ensnared in lives of vice, thieving, prostitution, and such. Now this, I reasoned, was the result of their simply having no other choices, of being precluded from the many opportunities open to them if they were requisitely educated."

"So you intend to educate them away from lives of crime?" she said.

"You state the truth of my aims with admirable economy, my dear."

She nodded slowly. "That sounds like a very good idea," she said. "But how does that involve me?"

He thumped his cane upon the decking. "Now this is my suggestion, Sukara. I intend to open a small school, teaching my children the basics: English, mathematics, history, information technology, and the like. I have certain teachers in these fields interested in my proposals, and when it came to approaching a teacher of English certain acquaintances of mine suggested that I might do worse than consider your good self. Word of your good work on Silom Road has preceded you, my dear. Now," he hurried on, "before you remind me that you have teaching employment already, let me say that the post I am offering you would be for two days a week, so would fit in perfectly with your current situation. Besides which, I would offer you the monthly stipend of a thousand baht."

Sukara looked at Rao with surprise. The offer was twice what she was earning on Silom Road.

"Well, it's tempting…"

"But before you commit yourself, Sukara, perhaps you might care to come with me and visit your prospective pupils aboard their starship home?"

Jeff had told her all about the crashed starship, fixed between the decks of the Station like a fly in amber; it had crash-landed more than fifty years ago, when Level Thirteen had been the top deck, and rather than go to the considerable expense and engineering effort of removing it the authorities had, with characteristic Indian practicality, simply built up and around the stranded vessel.

"I think," Dr Rao went on with a twinkle in his eye, "that when you meet the children, your heart and head will open to the idea of giving them a comprehensive education."

The prospect appealed to something in her; she enjoyed teaching, and the money would be useful, but more than that there was something ultimately pleasing about the possibility of improving the lives of street-kids like her sister, Tiger.

Of course, she was curious as to how a scheming businessman like Dr Rao might profit from educating the children in his care, but for the time being she would take the rogue's professed altruism at face value.

"When would I come and see the children?" she asked.

His lips stretched in an alarming display of pleasure. "There is, as they say, no time like the present."

Sukara looked at her handset; she had four hours before picking up the girls, and said as much to Rao.

"Sufficient time and more in which to descend to the ship, make a tour of its environs, and meet my children."

"In that case, Dr Rao..." She drained her tea.

Rao beat his cane once upon the decking in manifest delight. "Then let us be off, my dear!"

NINE

CONFLICTING FORCES

Kali's Revenge powered silently through the void. They made love well into the early hours, then slept till late the following morning. They had breakfast in Rab's private suite high on the nose-cone of the ship, the arching dome above them showing the depthless opalescent grey of void-space.

After breakfast Rab excused himself and worked at his softscreen, and Parveen took the opportunity to wander around the ship. She activated her tele-ability and decided that now was the perfect time to probe the individuals she had earmarked for further investigation during the meet-and-greet session in the spaceport lounge. These included Jeff Vaughan, the scientists Kiki Namura and David McIntosh, and the surly Sikh security chief Anil Singh. She didn't relish the prospect of confronting Singh so soon after their last encounter, but she was determined not to let his threats get to her. She was pretty sure that his suspicion of her was based on prejudice rather than intelligence, but she wanted to make absolutely sure.

Perhaps half the team had elected to be sedated for the duration of the trip, while the rest opted to follow the day—night pattern of Indian standard time they had left back on Earth.

She learned from a steward that Vaughan was sedated for the duration of the voyage. She found an observation nacelle close to the individual team cabins, settled down, closed her eyes, and pushed out a probe towards the sleeping telepath.

She told herself that she was doing this for Rab, but wondered if she were deceiving herself. She had liked what she had read in Vaughan's mind back on Earth, and while Vaughan had his vices – a blanket prejudice against his fellow North Americans, for one thing, and a mistrust and resentment of intellectuals because of his own lack of education – these were more than counterbalanced by his attributes: he was honest and loyal and... this was what Parveen found most attractive about him... he loved his wife.

She swam through his dreams, a mixture of erotic visions of Sukara interspersed with his fear of reading the dead engineer, and immersed herself in a deeper strata of his unconscious mind. She dipped into his past, reliving the horrors of his time with the Toronto Homicide Department, and then the years spent running from the assassin called Osborne, right up to the point of his confrontation with the killer, and his acceptance of his death at Osborne's hands... And his salvation, when Sukara had shot Osborne dead, and Vaughan's subsequent slow turning away from a life of solitude as he came to place his trust in his wife-to-be.

She read his political apathy, which she found appalling. She was reassured that his mistrust of Rab was not so much based on anything he knew about the tycoon, but because it was in his nature to despise those with power and influence. It was the one aspect of his former cynicism that maintained in his current, more mature worldview.

She could tell Rab that Vaughan was to be trusted in the role he had been hired to carry out: he wanted nothing more than to get the reading of the dead engineer out of the way and return home to his wife and daughters.

Parveen withdrew her probe, slipping from his mind not without regret. A part of her, a guilty part, wanted to access his memories of his time with Sukara, and share in their love-making. She would have liked to meet his wife, to probe her and read what it was like to be the object of such affection... She told herself that she did not feel jealous: she had Rab, after all, and she knew what she felt for him. It would have been reassuring, however, to know for certain what Rab really felt for her.

She deactivated her tele-ability, left the observation nacelle and its hypnotic view of the swirling void, and moved to the bar.

This was where the majority of Rab's team had congregated, sipping beer and coffee and chatting about the forthcoming landfall.

She found Namura and McIntosh poring over a softscreen laid flat on a low coffee-table; they were paging through a set of moving images showing the Expansion's only other fungal world, Tourmaline,

Bellatrix III.

She fetched a beer from the bar and approached the table. "Do you mind if I join you?"

Namura smiled up at her. "Please..." She gestured, and Parveen knelt beside the tiny Japanese woman. McIntosh nodded his greeting.

"I'm showing David what to expect when we land," Namura said. "If you've never experienced a fungal landscape before... well, let's say that you have a treat in store."

McIntosh indicated a panorama of ochre bracket fungus growing from a mountainside. "Look at that..."

Namura smiled. "And Bellatrix III is only partially covered, David. According to the telemetry from the exploration vessel, eighty per cent of Delta Cephei VII is covered during its winter. It's fast-growing too, so the landscape will be ever-changing."

Parveen tried to envisage the idea of a perpetually mutating terrain, and failed.

Covertly, she touched her handset, enabling the psi-program. She expected the pair to be shielded, and they were – and not just with the standard-issue Chandrasakar Organisation mind-shield. Their minds were cloaked by far more sophisticated software.

A part of her wanted to leave well alone, but that was impossible. She owed it to her government to find out what she could about the embedded foreign agents. At the same time she owed it to Rab.

She was, she realised, trying to please two disparate parties, and at the same time attempting to unite the conflicting forces within her: her heart and her head.

She tapped her handset, summoning the virus, then laid a finger Namura's hand and exclaimed, "Look," pointing at a quick-growing fungus-analogue that sprouted in the foreground of the screen.

She would read Namura first, and if necessary move on to her lover. In the event, she learned all she needed from the Japanese biologist.

Namura was expounding at length on the type of fungus they were watching, oblivious of the viral infection already working to break down her mind-shield.

Parveen feigned interest and scanned Namura's revealed mind.

She cast aside the layers of trivial short-term memories, fleeting emotions, images of Namura and McIntosh making love in the shower that morning... and found what she'd been looking for.

She read that Namura's lover, Dr David McIntosh, had run up an increasingly large gambling debt, which threatened his tenure at Sydney University if its extent were revealed. Two years ago a mysterious benefactor had stepped in with an offer of cash – if the Australian were to report back on certain findings of the Chandrasakar Organisation on the colony world of Paradigm, Vega IV. McIntosh was a geologist, due to be posted to that colony, and someone wanted to know the extent of the planet's oil reserves. McIntosh didn't ask why, and reassured himself that the knowledge wouldn't, couldn't, hurt Chandrasakar... and the half a million dollars his benefactor promised to pay him would get him out of serious trouble.

Not long after that, McIntosh had met the doll-like Namura and they'd started a tempestuous affair. Just six months later the Australian's controller had exerted pressure to draw Namura into the sticky web of deceit. They – and McIntosh suspected the FNSA – wanted information relating to Namura's mission for Chandrasakar, on the world of Kallianka, Procyon II. If that information was were not forthcoming, then certain parties might get to know of McIntosh's gambling debts... For the sake of her lover, Namura had consented to provide it.

And now they were in it up to their necks, not spies who had turned coat for reasons of ideology or greed, but naïve innocents out of their depth in a world of intrigue they barely understood.

This time, the FNSA wanted all the information on Chandrasakar's mission to Delta Cephei VII, and the pair were in no position to refuse.

Parveen withdrew her probe, nodding at something Namura was telling her about the die-back rates of certain fungal species.

She had expected to loathe the pair, if they had indeed turned out to be plants of the FNSA. Instead, all she felt was an immense pity. They were mired in an impossible situation, and in the months and years to come their controller would exert ever more pressure, asking for more and more, risking their cover for greater gain until, as expendable units, they would be found out and eradicated... Parveen had no doubt that that is just what Rab, or rather his security team, would do if the truth were to get out.

She sat back with her beer, considering what she should do. She would have had no qualms at all about telling Rab about the pair if they had been committed FNSA spies, but they were like children caught in a mine-field.

She couldn't tell Rab, and so sentence them to death. The only alternative would be to keep a close eye on the pair, read them frequently and ensure that they sent nothing back to the FNSA that might prove injurious to Rab and his organisation.

At the same time, she knew that she should inform her controller of what she'd found out so that India might choose to influence events, even to the point of blackmailing Namura and McIntosh to its own ends.

She couldn't bring herself to do that, either.

Sickened, she made an excuse and left the pair to the softscreen, crossed to the bar, and ordered another beer.

She considered her next move. She should really seek out Singh, the head of security, and attempt to read him – but if she were honest with herself she had to admit that she'd had enough of slipping unawares into other people's minds.

Then she had second thoughts as she considered her encounter with Singh back on Earth, and wondered again if he knew something about her work for the party. The only way to reassure herself on that score would be to probe the bastard.

She was about to find a steward who might know of his whereabouts when Singh himself strode into the bar and moved among the scientists, chatting amiably. Parveen watched him cross to where Namura and McIntosh were still absorbed in the images of Bellatrix III. He joined them, looked at the scrolling images, and chatted for a while.

She touched her handset, sent out a probe, and came up against Singh's impenetrable mind-shield.

She had not, honestly, expected to be able to break down his shield; he was the head of security and had the latest cloaking software. If she were to read Singh, it would mean getting close to him, infecting his handset with a virus.

He was in conversation with the scientists for about ten minutes, before moving off and introducing himself to a grey-haired, stocky woman in her fifties drinking coffee and contemplating the void through the curving viewscreen. She wondered if he were systematically doing the rounds as a matter of duty, and if so whether he would come to her in due course.

For the next thirty minutes he moved around the bar, making a point of chatting to everyone. Parveen braced herself for the inevitable encounter.

He came to the bar, stood next to her and ordered a beer; just when she thought he was giving her the cold shoulder, he turned to her and nodded curtly.

"Mr Chandrasakar gave me orders to familiarise everyone with the routine once we land," he said.

"I'm surprised you decided to include me," she smiled. "That's uncommonly courteous."

"Mr Chandrasakar might have told you already–" Singh began.

She took a long swallow from her bottle. "We had other things with which to occupy our time, Mr Singh."

He compressed his lips, so that they formed a thin line hyphenating his fat cheeks. "That hadn't escaped my notice."

"Well, that's reassuring. You are head of security

after all. I suppose it's a priority to know who the boss is bedding."

Singh considered his reply. "To be honest, I'm surprised in his choice. Have you paused to consider what a multi-millionaire might see in you?"

She maintained her smile. "Have you asked Rab that, Mr Singh?"

"He has the pick of the most exclusive escort agencies on Earth, Dr Das. Perhaps... perhaps he's become involved with you because you represent a regime he finds odious and he's intrigued by the gullibility of a supposedly intelligent woman."

It was the way he laid emphasis on the word *represent* that gave her pause. Her smile felt rigid as she replied, "Well, that's something you will never know, Mr Singh."

He shrugged, the start of a smug smile turning his lips.

"But you said you're here to discuss the routine after landing..." As she said this, she reached out and casually turned Singh's beer bottle, ostensibly so that she could read the label.

"We'll be coming down close to the exploration vessel *The Pride of Mussoree*," Singh said. "Scientists will be allowed out once a security cordon has been erected. Part of my brief is to ensure the safety of everyone aboard the *Kali*, so I'd appreciate your co-operation when leaving the ship." He reached out, gripped his beer in a massive hand, and drank.

Below the level of the bar, Parveen activated her psi-program.

"As you might know, what happened to the crew of the *Mussoree* is not known. Until their fate is ascertained, then everyone aboard the *Kali*, with the exception of Mr Chandrasakar, will be under my command. I hope you don't find that an undue burden, Dr Das?"

She shrugged. "Why should I, Mr Singh? I don't intend to do any long long-distance trekking once we've touched down."

She probed, and again came up against the barrier of his mind-shield. It confronted her with a white-noise of static, through which not the slightest hint of Singh's mentation leaked. She was surprised that her virus had not broken down his defences to the point where she could at least detect stray surface emotions and short-term memories, but she scanned nothing.

"Well, I'm delighted that we know where we stand on that issue, at least," he said. He was moving away when he stopped suddenly, then turned and stared at her.

"And if you try that trick again," he said with deliberation, "I'll respond with a virus that'll not only scramble your hardware but give you serious brain-damage, ah-cha?"

He moved off before she had the chance to recover her composure. She watched him go, knowing that she had emerged from the encounter, once again, at a disadvantage. Her heart was thudding and she felt at once angry and embarrassed. Perhaps she should have held off the virus... but his behaviour towards her had suggested he knew something about her. She would do her best to avoid him in future.

She ordered another beer and for the next ten minutes considered what to do next. She left the bar and made her way to Rab's suite. She approached the sliding door and stepped through with assumed casualness.

Rab was still scanning his softscreen, his back to the door. She crossed to him, laid a hand on his shoulder and kissed the top of his head.

Something in his manner, as he remained staring at a list of figures on the screen, gave her a cold feeling in the pit of her stomach.

"Rab?"

He didn't look up at her. "Singh just called me. He reported what you did." He turned in his seat and looked up at her. "Parveen, he's my head of security and he doesn't take kindly to having his hardware messed up by third-rate viral programs."

She bridled at the *third-rate*, but didn't let it show. "Rab, I'm sorry. I thought…"

"What, you thought you'd read everyone aboard the ship? I wanted you to keep an eye on Vaughan. I said nothing about my security team."

"I'm sorry. It was just…" She considered telling his about their *tête-à-tête* back on Earth. "Look, he made it obvious he doesn't like me–"

He reached out and took her hand, and she almost melted with the relief. "Parveen, Singh is a brain-dead thug who also happens to be good at his job. I employ him as a security guard, not a conversationalist."

"Rab, if you'd heard what he said back on Earth–"

He interrupted, pulling her towards him and installing her on his lap. "Parveen, his father was a politician with the Khallistan Independence Party back in '34 when the communists staged the coup.

His father was interned and sentenced to hard labour. He died in custody when Singh was twenty. Of course he doesn't like anything your party stands for, and he sees you – in your relationship with me – as something of a threat."

She looked at him. "You aren't trying to say you suspect me..." she began, shamed by her own mock-indignation.

He shook his head, and his reaction seemed genuine enough. "Of course not." He stroked her cheek. "Look, we might be poles apart politically, but that doesn't alter what I feel for you."

She kissed him, relief flooding through her. "Thank you, Rab."

"I'll have a word with Singh," he said, "tell him to lay off. But no more attempted probes, promise me, Parveen."

She promised.

"Excellent. I thought we'd dine alone tonight, then have an early night. We make landfall first thing in the morning."

She slept well, that night, reassured by Rab's words, and woke just as the *Kali* was phasing from the void. She showered quickly, grabbed a coffee, then hand in hand with Rab took the elevator down to the observation lounge.

A dozen scientists were crowded around the viewscreen, staring out at the new world and exclaiming in surprise and delight. She joined them, while Rab excused himself and made his way to the bridge.

Far below, the world turned slowly as the *Kali* made spiraldown. They descended rapidly, and a world without seas came into view. Within minutes the terrain resolved itself into vast tracts of ochre vegetation, which, Namura explained, were the fungal-analogue rafts which covered much of the planet's surface.

The Japanese biologist was straining on tiptoe to stare out, and beside her the tall, red-headed McIntosh smiled tolerantly.

Parveen felt a quick stab of sympathy for the hapless couple, then turned her attention to the view of Delta Cephei VII.

TEN

ULTERIOR MOTIVES

Sukara and Dr Rao left the café, crossed Himachal Park, and eased their way through the surging crowds on Chandi Road. They passed Nazruddin's, the restaurant where she'd first met Jeff, and came to Dr Rao's favourite coffee house where he had informed her, what seemed like a lifetime ago now, of her sister's death.

They hurried inside, and Sukara passed the very table where she'd sat, a naïve and ignorant child herself, while the doctor had covered her hand with his own scaly claw and broken the news. The memory brought a sudden blockage to her throat.

Dr Rao led her through a bead curtain at the back of the coffee house, past a calamitous kitchen, and into a tiny white-tiled room on the facing wall of which was a steel door.

"My private access to the elevator to Level Twelve B," he explained.

Sukara watched as he tapped a code into a console beside the door. She blinked in surprise: by an

odd coincidence it was her own age and Pham's:
27-10.

The door slid open, revealing a tiny cubicle. Dr
Rao gallantly bid her enter, then eased himself in
beside her. He touched the controls and the door
slid shut; a second later the cubicle gave a stomach-
heaving lurch and Sukara felt as if she were falling.

Dr Rao rapped on the wall with his cane. "There
are other means of entry and egress to and from the
starship, through which my children make their
way, but in my old age I prefer the comfort of an
elevator."

Their descent seemed to take an age. Dr Rao
clicked his tongue to some complicated Hindu
drumming rhythm. In the confined space, Sukara
was very aware of his body odour: old man, rose-
water hair pomade, and garlic.

"One's first sight of the starship, Sukara, is one to
treasure: it is a sight to behold, to employ a cliché.
No one fails to be impressed."

She looked at him. "Do you get many visitors?"

"The ship's whereabouts is not widely known.
However, certain esteemed friends and acquaintances of mine, senior politicians, dignitaries, and
the like, have been known to seek an audience with
me."

He beamed at the steel door like a supremely self-
satisfied turtle.

Five minutes later the lift clanked, bobbed to a
halt, and the door ground open.

Sukara stared, blinked, and stared again.

Before her was a starship enmeshed in a complex
webwork of steel girders and struts, the whole over-
grown with what looked like the content of the

Amazon jungle. Lichen covered the ship's prognathous nose-cone and lianas garlanded the girders
that held the ship in place. The scene was bathed in
the dazzling light of a dozen halogens.

Dr Rao said, "The vegetation often baffles visitors, my dear, but the explanation is simple. When
the ship crash-landed, it was carrying a consign-
ment of seeds, among other things. The containers
burst and found their way into a myriad nooks and
crannies, and then came the monsoon... This was
the top deck, many years ago, of course."

They left the elevator and walked along a narrow
catwalk suspended over the riotous vegetation.

"How did you acquire the ship, Dr Rao?"

"I was at the time influential in certain governmental circles, shall we say, and when the building
of another level of the Station was proposed, I put
in a bid for the starship." He smiled. "And it was
accepted."

As they drew closer to the flora-embroidered
flank of the ship, Sukara saw a dozen children
squatting on fins and engine cowls like so many
monkeys. Behind viewscreens she saw more children in the ship's lighted interior, playing tag or
sitting cross-legged and eating from bowls.

They entered the ship, climbing a ramp into a cargo
hold crammed with bunks; she saw that the bunk-
beds were, in some places, stacked twenty high, and
to access them children swung from the ladders and
bars again like primates in shorts and T-shirts.

"How many kids live down here?" she asked.

Rao beamed as he gazed around at his kingdom.
"At the last count, perhaps two hundred, give or
take one or two. They work in shifts of six hours,

and all of them return here during the hours of darkness. I feed them all, and of course provide complete medical care."

She looked around at the staring kids, and only then noticed that all of them were in some way maimed or disfigured. She recalled that Tiger had allowed Dr Rao to remove her left leg, the better to facilitate her employment as a street beggar.

"And now, Sukara, a little tour of inspection, as it were..."

He led her from the dormitory and down a corridor to another vast room, this one fogged with steam and filled with the smell of cooking curry and rice. Twenty tiny figures, wearing nothing but ragged shorts or underpants, toiled in the kitchen.

"As you see, my charges never want for comestibles."

They moved to another, smaller chamber, where a dozen children sat at sewing machines. "And I must keep my children in clothing," he said. "As my eminent guests have been wont to say, I have created a veritable city in miniature down here."

Sukara smiled to herself, and thought of her little sister living out the last years of her life in this grim underworld.

She wondered if it were preferable than life on the streets of the levels above, and thought that all things considered perhaps it was.

"And down here we have some of the private bedrooms, given over to the kitchen and laundry workers."

They passed down a long corridor, off which were the narrow cabins which had originally berthed the ship's crew.

Dr Rao paused outside a closed door, and cleared his throat. "This room," he said, "belonged to your sister. Not a day goes by when I do not recall her smiling face. Please, if you would care to..."

He eased open the door, stood back to allow her entry, and had the tact to stand outside while she stepped inside and gazed around at the cramped, dirty room.

Her eyes filled up as she recalled the tiny girl she had known in Bangkok – not Tiger then, but Pakara, just fifteen when she had left the city for what she hoped would be a better life. The tragedy was that, compared to the life of prostitution she had led in Thailand, what she had found on Bengal Station probably had been an improvement.

Another girl had the room now, evidenced by posters of male holo-movie stars, dolls, and a threadbare teddy. These scant and pathetic possessions might as well have belonged to Tiger...

She thought of Jeff, who had knelt by this very bunk and held her sister's hand while she died.

She dried her eyes, turned and stepped from the room. Dr Rao laid a gentle, understanding hand on her shoulder and ushered her back down the corridor to the voluminous cargo hold.

They stood side by side at the top of the ramp and stared out over the confusion of girder-work and greenery.

"As you can see, Sukara, I provide as best I can a stable environment for my many charges, but once they reach adulthood and elect to leave my jurisdiction, then my ability to be of assistance is diminished. If they were educated, could find their way into professional positions... But I need not labour the point, my dear."

Sukara nodded. "Where would I teach the children?" she asked. "Down here?"

Dr Rao looked radiant. "I have a small schoolroom set aside on Level Two," he said, "which overlooks the ocean. It is a most amenable environment in which to learn."

She said, "I couldn't start for a few weeks, until Li is better and Jeff is back."

Rao bowed his head in complete understanding. "We will arrange a starting date in the fullness of time, my dear."

She glanced at the chronometer on her handset. "It's time I was getting back," she said.

"I will accompany you to the elevator, Sukara."

They crossed the catwalk, and Dr Rao entered the code. The door slid open. "I have various tasks awaiting my attention down here," he said. "If you simply press the upward arrow..."

Sukara smiled and said, "Thanks for showing me around, Dr Rao."

He patted her hand. "My dear, the pleasure has been mine entirely. It is thanks to you, and the other teachers I have employed, that these children and others will lead full and profitable lives when they leave my sanctuary. It is my fervent hope," he went on, "that when they do find gainful employment and positions of status, that they will remember the start in life I gave them; they might even, I dearly hope, remember their benefactor in his old age..." And he reached out and pressed a button. The door slid shut.

As the elevator rose, carrying her to the top deck,

Sukara laughed out loud. She had known that there had to be an ulterior motive for Rao's altruism, and now she had it: not satisfied with taking their earnings while children, Rao would exert pressure to relieve them of their gains when they were wage-earning adults, too.

She found her disgust at the rascal's wily methods warring with a contrary and oddly irrational liking of the man.

She was looking forward to telling Jeff all about her afternoon.

She hurried from the coffee house, pushed through the crowds on Chandi Road, and took a downchute to Level Two. Ten minutes later she collected Li from the nursery, then crossed the park to Pham's school.

If they hurried, they would be back at the hotel in time for five, and the results of Li's blood test.

The thought filled her with foreboding.

Pham ran from the school with a plastic ball she'd extruded during a manufacturing lesson that afternoon, and she and Li raced across the grass playing football.

Sukara smiled, watching their carefree antics.

The chime of her handset, when it came seconds later, froze her to the bone.

It was four-forty-five.

She accessed the call.

Dr Grant's smiling PA – Sukara couldn't recall her name – looked up at her.

"Yes?"

"Sukara? I am ringing about your daughter, Li…"

All Sukara could say, again, was, "Yes?"

"Dr Grant would like you to bring Li into his surgery at the soonest available opportunity, Sukara. Please don't be overly worried, but there are one or two anomalies in your daughter's blood test results."

Sukara sank to the grass. "What's wrong?" she asked.

"If you could bring Li into the surgery, Sukara, Dr Grant will be happy to discuss the matter with you."

Sukara just stared. "Shall... should I bring her now?"

The woman smiled. "That would be excellent, Sukara." And she cut the connection.

Sukara slumped down onto the grass, her legs too weak to support her. She was aware of a loud buzzing in her ears and her heart was racing. She looked across the park to where Li and Pham were tiny figures, the ball arcing through the air between them.

She wanted to call Jeff, to have the reassurance of his voice, but at the same time she couldn't bring herself to burden him with the worry that clutched her now.

She realised that she was crying. She stood, dried her eyes, and hurried smiling towards the girls.

ELEVEN

ABDUCTION

Vaughan was woken by the soft chimes of a bedside communicator. A soft female voice said, "Landing in thirty minutes. If you would care to gather in the observation lounge... I repeat–" He reached out and silenced the device.

The viewscreen in his room was opaqued, and he decided to treat himself to the first sight of the planet from the observation lounge.

He showered quickly, dressed, and made his way through the ship.

The sliding doors to the lounge parted, and the first thing that hit him was the sunlight. Delta Cephei was a yellow supergiant fulminating above the horizon, not so much yellow as burnt orange, and bristling with molten ejecta and fiery loops.

The ship was coming in low, down a valley between what Vaughan took to be mountains. The scientists were gathered excitedly before the curving glass, staring out and exclaiming from time to time. Parveen Das stood beside Kiki Namura and David

McIntosh. Namura saw him and waved. "Mr Vaughan! Mr Vaughan! You must see this!"

He crossed to the group and stared out. The ship was moving slowly, silently, down a long corridor between rearing land masses; they were not mountains, he saw now, but what looked like outcroppings of some vegetable growth.

A waiter was circulating with a tray of coffee. Vaughan grabbed a cup.

Namura gestured through the screen, smiling at Das and Vaughan. "The predominant vegetation on Delta Cephei VII," the biologist said, "is a fungus-like growth. It covers the planet during the temperate periods – that is, what we would call spring and autumn. During summer and winter, conditions are too severe for the fungus-analogue to survive, so it dies back and flourishes at the next clement period."

"Is it spring or autumn here now?" McIntosh asked.

"Spring," Namura said, "and as you can see, the fungus-growth is coming to life."

Coming to life, Vaughan thought, was a prosaic way of describing what was happening outside. He had expected a static landscape, even on learning that the supposed mountains were actually fungal growths; but as he stared through the curving glass he was startled to see movement amid the masses and rafts of cream-coloured vegetation. Stalks grew, snaking and twisting towards the sun as if seen via the medium of time-lapse photography; forests of tall trees, for want of a better expression, rose visibly, sending out side-shoots and fan-shaped shelves, and exploding in great bursts of waving cilia.

Das said, "Delta Cephei VII describes a highly elliptical orbit around its primary. It takes approximately twenty-five years to make an entire circuit. It has long harsh winters, and short, intense summers. Winter lasts in the region of ten years, and summer something like two."

"The fungus-analogue has adapted itself admirably to the severe conditions," Namura said.

McIntosh frowned. "I wonder if the conditions out there militate against finding sentient life?"

Namura shrugged. "Life, even sentient life, is amazing in its versatility. I've read about sentience coming about in even more adverse conditions than these."

"It would make things easier for Rab if there weren't a sentient native life form," Das said.

Vaughan wondered if he detected a note of criticism in her tone. He decided to be blunt. "And where would you stand on that, Parveen?"

She looked at him appraisingly. "What do you think? As a good socialist I would be opposed to the exploitation of a sentient race, and its planet, for mere financial gain."

"And as a... friend of Chandrasakar's?"

She looked away, staring through the screen at the panorama of twisted fungal growths. "I pity any sentient creature who finds itself standing between the organisation and its aims," she said. "It would be better in every respect if Delta Cephei VII harboured no intelligent life."

"Its elliptical orbit," McIntosh said, "with harsh summer and winters, wouldn't make it a prime candidate for colonisation."

Namura laid her head on one side and considered. "There are similar colony worlds. What about Janus, Epsilon Indi II? And Coney's World, Vega VI? They're extreme, and are successful."

"But as extreme as here?" the Australian persisted.

Namura shook her head. "You're right. No, not as extreme as Delta Cephei VII."

McIntosh said, "Delta Cephei VII. A bit of a mouthful. Doesn't it have a name?"

"Not as yet," Das said. "That will come later."

Vaughan sipped his coffee. "No doubt someone will want to call it Chandrasakar's World." He glanced at Das.

She nodded. "There have been precedents. Verkerk's World, for instance, named after the tycoon who funded the exploration."

"Chandrasakar's World," McIntosh mused. "It has a certain ring."

"Speaking of the man," Vaughan said, directing this at Das. "I don't see him around."

She chose not to respond.

Namura hid her mouth behind a small hand and laughed, "We come to a new world, and Mr Chandrasakar remains in his bed?"

"That's the rich and jaded for you," Das said, and Vaughan gained the impression that Das's criticism of her lover was for the benefit of those around her.

Not for the first time, he wondered where her true loyalties lay.

The thrumming of the main drive, an almost subliminal hum more felt than heard, fell an octave as the ship banked ponderously. Vaughan held on to the padded rail before the viewscreen and watched as it descended in a routine spiraldown. New vistas came into view, a forest of relatively small, silvery stalks ending in polyps which waved in the down-draft of the ship, and a range of what looked like upright fans, perhaps each the size of a house, sil-very-green on one plane and striated with gills on the other.

"That stuff looks thick," McIntosh said. "Won-der how far down it is to the bedrock?" He laughed. "You have it easy, Kiki. All you have to do is step out and grab a handful of mushrooms..."

Vaughan's concern was more practical. "I wonder how tough that stuff is? I mean, will it take the weight of the ship?"

Das said, "The rescue vessel didn't report any dif-ficulties."

"Fungus, despite what we might think, can be exceptionally tough and fibrous, Mr Vaughan," Namura said.

Kali's Revenge was hovering in situ and coming down with painful exactitude in a flat valley between two rearing fungal hills. Suddenly the descent ceased; Vaughan thought he sensed a slight give as the vegetation took the weight of the ship, a resistance which made the *Kali* slowly rise and then settle again.

"Look," Namura said.

"*The Pride of Mussoree*," Das said.

The exploration vessel was sitting on a plain of fungus level with the *Kali*, perhaps 500 metres away. It was probably half the size of their ship, a 100-metre long teardrop with shaped vanes and fins like some ugly deep-sea fish. It bore the green livery of the Chandrasakar Line, the little of it that could be seen through the growths that had moulded themselves around the alien invader. The far side of the ship was entirely cupped by an enfolding wall of fungus, and smaller, shelf-like growths protruded from the ship's curving flank.

The effect, Vaughan thought, was of a child's model starship lost in some weird alien garden.

"The exit hatch is open," McIntosh pointed out.

Vaughan saw the triangular opening in the flank, already invaded by snaking tendrils and spaghetti vines.

"Well, what do you think?" boomed a voice behind them.

They turned to see Chandrasakar beaming at them. Dressed in green multi-purpose EVA garb, and not his usual formal suit, his democratised appearance struck Vaughan as an attempt to come over as one of the team.

They turned and stared through the viewscreen at the *Mussoree*, the ochre fungal landscape and, above it all, the vast globe of the sun.

"It's..." McIntosh began. "It's weird... *alien*," he finished inadequately.

"I'm sending out the security team first of all," Chandrasakar informed them. "They'll cordon off the entire region for a couple of kilometres, taking in the *Kali*, the *Mussoree*, and much of the surrounding high ground. We don't know what happened to the original crew, so we're taking no chances. They'll make the area secure, and only then will we venture out."

Namura said, almost to herself, "I wonder if we're in danger, even here?"

Chandrasakar shook his head. "I assure you that we're quite safe, my dear."

"You mentioned that there was only one survivor of... of whatever happened," McIntosh said.

Chandrasakar nodded. "She managed to make it back to the ship. She's in cold sleep."

Namura indicated the open hatch. "But if whatever attacked them... then surely they might have entered the ship?"

"We don't know whether they were attacked," Chandrasakar said. "The rescue mission I sent out found no such evidence. The fact that the engineer made it to cryo suggests that even if they were the subject of an assault, then it wasn't followed up."

McIntosh said, "So when we unfreeze the engineer, we'll find out what happened."

"But," Namura put in, logically, "why didn't the rescue mission do that?"

Chandrasakar hesitated, and Vaughan hoped he wouldn't come out with the fact that the engineer was dead. As a telepath he risked suffering enough mistrust without the team knowing that he had the grisly ability to read the minds of the dead.

He glanced at Das, but she gave no indication that she was aware of his status as a necropath.

Chandrasakar said, "Let's just say that there were certain... complications. The ensuing investigation should provide all the answers."

McIntosh peered through the screen right and left. "Where's the rescue vessel that found the *Mussoree*?"

"Long gone," Chandrasakar informed him. "I can't have a starship sitting redundant for months now, can I?"

Vaughan was about to ask the tycoon about the *Mussoree's* security during that time, when there was a stirring of interest among those gathered before the viewscreen.

Something moved outside, below the viewscreen. They watched as a ramp extended from the flank of the *Kali*, digging into the fungal matter of the planet's surface and shaving up a curling bow-wave of the stuff.

Seconds elapsed, and then a figure came into view. It wore blue body armour and carried a bulky assault rifle. Vaughan recognised Singh. The head of security moved cautiously down the ramp, followed by his team of a dozen individuals. All were armed, and half of them carried backpacks; they split into pairs as they stepped onto the surface of the planet. Vaughan half expected them to bounce, as if on some fibrous trampoline, but the surface seemed solid underfoot.

Four guards made their way across to the *Mussoree*, led by Singh, while the rest of the team fanned out around the two ships.

Vaughan glanced at the gathered scientists. There was an air of expectancy among them, almost a sense of anticipation, as if they half expected whatever had happened to the crew of the *Mussoree* to befall the security team now.

Singh and his men entered the starship, stepping over invasive rafts of fungus. They paused in the entrance, and then Vaughan saw something move beyond them. It was quick and silver, dancing nimbly towards them on six long legs. He felt his pulse quicken.

Namura had seen it too. She gave a shriek and reached out to grip McIntosh's arm.

Chandrasakar laughed. "Security drones," he

said. "I had the rescue mission leave them aboard the *Mussoree* when they departed."

The gathered watchers relaxed, Vaughan with them.

In the entrance of the *Mussoree*, Singh consulted with the drone; then he and his men followed the AI, turned right within the ship and disappeared from sight.

To either side of the *Mussoree*, other guards could be seen climbing the slopes, ever attentive and weapons readied. Vaughan watched as six guards to right and left vanished into the polyp forest, followed by a complement of the *Kali's* own spider drones.

Two hours later he was in the observation lounge with Namura and McIntosh; they had breakfasted and then moved with coffees to an area of padded seats before a curving viewscreen. While the scientists talked shop, Vaughan nursed his coffee and watched the play of light across the ever-changing landscape as the sun rose.

Two things conspired to give the surface of the planet the visually disconcerting effect of never quite remaining the same; the first and most obvious was the rate of growth of the ubiquitous fungus. Vaughan experimented. He stared at an area of land for a few minutes, then closed his eyes for a minute. When he opened them again and stared at where he had been looking, the land had shrugged new growths into being. It was like nothing he had ever seen before, and on some deep-seated psychological level he found it disturbing. The second aspect of the change was that as the day elapsed, then the fungus changed colour; from the cream of morning, through the yellow and burnt orange of midday, to its current hue of deep bronze. Vaughan wondered what sunset might bring, and whether during the period of darkness the growths might revert to their earlier, etiolated off-white.

His inspection was interrupted by the return of Parveen Das and Chandrasakar. "I've just heard from security," the tycoon reported. "They've secured the immediate vicinity with the aid of drones. It's safe to go out, though I counsel caution. There's a laser cordon that will stop anything from getting in, and likewise from getting out. Please don't attempt to stray beyond this. For the time being, too, the *Mussoree* is out of bounds until security has gone through it from top to bottom." He paused, then said, "I suggest you venture out in pairs, and stay within sight of the ship."

As the scientists trouped from the observation lounge, Vaughan caught Chandrasakar's attention and said, "When will you be needing me?"

"Not for a good few hours yet – maybe even not until tomorrow. We've got to secure the *Mussoree*, and then assess the situation with the engineer. I have a team of medics on standby to get in there. Take it easy for a while, go for a stroll. If you're going out there, Dr Das, could you accompany Mr Vaughan?"

She nodded. "Ready for a short hike, Jeff?"

"Lead the way."

Chandrasakar watched them as they took the elevator to the exit hatch.

They approached the exit and Vaughan stared

through the triangular opening at the copper-hued landscape. He slipped a hand under his jacket and touched the butt of his laser, as if for reassurance.

The *Kali* had come down on a great raft of fungus, and as they stepped out onto the ramp he saw that the growth had slowly ballooned around the edges of the ship. A dozen spidery drones were employed in burning the slow growth, flensing away great chunks of the stuff with mono-molecular filaments.

Vaughan inhaled.

Das laughed. "It's almost like fried mushroom. Almost, but there's something sick-making about the stench."

"I wonder if they're edible?" Vaughan mused.

"Dammit, I forgot to bring along my field-guide to edible fungi."

They paused at the end of the ramp. "Well," Vaughan said, "this is a first for me."

She looked at him. "I thought you said you'd been to a couple of other worlds?"

"They were settled colonies. This is *terra incognita*. A truly alien planet. Here goes."

He stepped from the gunmetal steel of the ramp and onto a swelling of sun-baked fungus. He had expected it to give, to be spongy underfoot, but it was just like stepping onto hard, roughened timber. He knelt and attempted to push his fingers into the ground; he might as well have tried to make an impression in solid oak.

McIntosh and Namura had wandered away from the ship and were standing side by side, staring around them in wonder. Vaughan crossed to them, followed by Das.

"When I read the survey reports from the rescue mission," Namura said, "I never dreamed it would be so... so un-earthlike. Nor, I must admit, did I dream that the entire surface would be covered with the stuff." She laughed. "This is a biologist's dream."

McIntosh said, "And a geologist's nightmare. I wonder how far we'll need to drill through the mushrooms to get at the really interesting stuff?"

Namura knelt, taking a knife and paring a sliver of fungus from the ground. She placed the sample in a plastic container and stowed it in her backpack, speaking quietly into her handset.

They moved on, past the *Mussoree*, and climbed the rise that had grown beyond the ship. Vaughan noted that the security drones left by the rescue mission had been busy cutting away the fungal growth from around the exploration ship. He wondered if, without their attention, the planet would have consumed the starship and left no trace of its whereabouts.

He shielded his eyes and looked up at the sun. It was a little duller than Sol, he thought, though much, much larger; seen from here it seemed to mass at least ten times as large as their home star. The slow ejection of fiery whips from its circumference, and the gelid progression of sunspots across its vast surface, was a mesmerising spectacle.

"Do you know how long a day lasts here?" he asked Das as they climbed.

"Approximately thirty hours," she said. "Sixteen of daylight and fourteen of night. We're about..." She consulted her handset, "two-thirds of the way through the day."

McIntosh peered at the chronometer on her handset. "You've customised it for the planet's diurnal cycle? Clever."

"When in Rome..."

If it took security the rest of the day to ensure the *Mussoree* was safe, then he had a long wait before he was required to read the dead mind of the engineer. Part of him wanted nothing more than to get it over with, while another part was relieved by the delay. He tried to forget about the dead engineer and appreciate the amazing landscape.

They reached the crest of the rise and halted, gazing back the way they had come. From this elevation, level with the curving upper superstructure of the *Mussoree*, they had a clear view of the valley's extent; the two ships were situated on either side of the valley bottom between the two hills; further down the valley opened out towards a distant plane, shimmering a dull copper in the heat.

He heard a sudden, loud buzzing sound coming from high above, and as he looked up he saw a vast, ever-changing cloud of what looked like insects; the amorphous swarm swept overhead, turned as one and rolled above the *Mussoree*, blotting out a third of the sun.

"Look at that," Namura said, pointing. She stared at the polyp forest that extended away from the rise towards the distant 'mountain' range. The stalks were swaying in the slight breeze, tall, fettuccini-like lengths. Vaughan smiled as he anticipated telling Sukara all about Delta Cephei VII.

"I must go and grab a sample," Namura said. McIntosh shrugged and said, "Mushroom hunters..." following her as she moved towards the swaying forest.

Vaughan and Das watched them go. The distance was deceptive; it took the couple perhaps five minutes before they reached the forest and slipped between its moving boles.

"I wonder if I'll be redundant here," Das said.

"I haven't seen any little green men," Vaughan said. He enabled his tele-ability again and scanned; but for the mind-shields of the *Kali's* crew, he came up with nothing.

"I've just scanned."

"And?" Das raised an eyebrow.

"You'd expect to pick up something if there were sentients within range. It's often impossible to actually read an alien mind, but I'd pick up signatures."

"And there's nothing?"

He nodded, switching off the program. "Not a thing. Of course, that doesn't mean to say that Delta Cephei VII doesn't have sentient life. If there were aliens, then they might be beyond range, or so alien it'd be impossible to recognise their signatures if they were under our noses."

Das laughed and tried to dig the heel of her boot into the surface. "Sentient fungus, hm? That'd be a first."

They were silent for a while, watching the landscape as it gradually, very gradually, changed colour; from the bronze of minutes ago to a deep, burnished mahogany. Here and there, high in the sky, he made out the dark silhouettes of what looked like birds, but giant examples more like pterosaurs.

Vaughan considered his words, then said, "Do

you mind me asking how you and Chandrasakar came to…?"

She bridled. Something flared in her eyes. "If you think I'm merely attracted to his wealth, his power–"

"I never said that," he defended himself. "But… now that you've mentioned it, some people are attracted to those very attributes."

She stared at him. "Are you?" she asked.

He smiled. "No. No, quite the opposite."

She squinted at him. "You mean… for you, powerlessness has a certain allure?"

He wondered if she had purposefully misconstrued his words. He thought about it. "Well, probably, yes. Men often…" He stopped, then went on, "But what I really meant was that I find power repulsive – and those in power repulsive too."

She looked at him, still with one eye closed. "Very interesting, Jeff. Whichever way you look at it."

He shrugged. "For all Chandrasakar's altruism – his charitable acts and the like – I can't bring myself to trust him." He was trying to draw her, and he wondered if she was aware of it.

She was silent, so he said, "What do you think?"

She shook her head, dismissive. "I think you should be less suspicious," she said. "Rab, despite all he stands for, is a good man, ah-cha?" And her tone suggested that she wanted to end that topic of conversation.

He was about to say, "I'll take your word for it…" when he heard a cry from the polyp forest.

They turned in time to see McIntosh come sprinting out from between the giant fronds.

Vaughan felt as if someone had punched him in

the chest. He moved towards the Australian, then broke into a run to meet him. Namura, he thought; something's happened to the girl. He experienced a sickening sense of dread at the prospect.

He caught McIntosh, held his shoulders and shook him. "What the hell?"

The Australian was panting hard, sucking in painful breaths. "Kiki," he managed. "They've got Kiki!"

"Who, for Chrissake?"

"Didn't… didn't see them. I saw something move, a quick shadow. Then Kiki screamed and she was gone."

Later, Vaughan was surprised by what he did then. Perhaps, had he not been armed with the laser, he might have been more circumspect. Before he could give his actions a thought, he left McIntosh with Das and sprinted towards the polyp forest.

He drew his laser and slowed as he came to the thigh-thick trunks, each one sprouting from the ground at intervals of perhaps a metre. They were a sickly off-white, and the way they swayed back and forth fostered in Vaughan a certain queasiness.

He ran through the forest, aware of the sudden coolness in the shadow of the high umbrella polyps, and the odd stench that filled the air. It smelled like rotten meat, and seconds later he saw the cause: the plant's whip-like tendrils had snared on a number of small, furred animals the size of rats, but many-legged, which were bound against the boles in various stages of decomposition.

He wondered if this was what had taken Namura – and then he saw the footprints.

The fungus in the shadow of the polyps was soft

and easily bruised, and he made out two sets of footprints leading further into the forest. He followed at a run, wondering when he'd come up against the blue laser cordon.

The two sets of footprints parted company; the larger, McIntosh's, moved to the right as he'd evidently paused to examine a captured rat-analogue; Namura's continued ahead. Vaughan studied McIntosh's prints. They continued round the bole, advanced, and then were scuffed as the Australian had turned and run back through the forest, taking a different route to that of his entrance.

Vaughan rejoined Namura's prints and followed them for ten metres.

He stopped, knelt, and examined the ground.

A pair of skid-marks replaced the neat footprints; evidently Namura had been grabbed here and dragged off. He looked around the forest floor and made out more indentations in the fungus, prints around the same size as Namura's. He judged that her abductors had numbered around a dozen.

He stood and ran, following the prints through the forest.

Seconds later he heard the muffled cry. "David!" Namura yelled.

It was impossible to tell how far away she might have been. He dodged round the slalom course of close-packed boles. He wanted to yell reassurance to the Japanese woman, but thought twice about alerting her attackers to his presence. He wondered at the terror she would be experiencing now – the field trip of a lifetime having turned into a nightmare.

He hoped Das had alerted security: he would feel

better if he were to be backed up by Singh and his team.

He looked ahead through the serried boles, thought he saw a flicker of movement – slivers of green between the magnolia stalks. He increased his pace, his breathing coming easily, powered by adrenalin and the desire to save Namura.

There – again he made out glimpses through the forest: at first he thought the green was Namura's uniform, but then he reassessed the assumption. This green was a shade lighter.

Namura screamed. He was perhaps five metres from the woman and her abductors now, and he levelled his laser, set to stun, and chanced a shot.

The blast sliced through half a dozen trunks, and they not so much toppled as slid to the ground and lodged diagonally, impeding his progress. He struggled through the trunks, jumping some and ducking under others. Ahead, he made out running legs, sleek green backs: humanoids, then.

He reckoned he'd be upon them in seconds – but he reckoned without the terrain. One second he was upright and sprinting and the next he'd slipped and went sprawling head-first into a trunk, narrowly missing the decomposing remains of a rat-creature.

He picked himself up and looked ahead. There was no sign of Namura and the aliens. He called out her name. He examined the fungus underfoot, made out multiple footprints, and followed them. Five metres further on they split, taking different routes through the forest.

He paused and stared ahead. In the distance, perhaps ten metres before him, he saw an odd blue light. He was puzzled for a second, until he recognised the laser cordon. He approached its four parallel bars that spanned the generation posts planted at ten-metre intervals in the fungus.

He stared around him, wondering where the hell the aliens and Namura had vanished. He retraced his footsteps to the point where the aliens had split up, and looked for the heaviest set of prints working on the assumption that those must belong to the creature or creatures carrying Namura. At last he came upon slightly deeper indentations in the ground, made by what appeared to be two or three individuals – with frequent scuff marks, which suggested Namura had been dragged along.

He followed these until they stopped. He stood and stared, wondering how the aliens had managed such a vanishing trick. There were no trunks nearby up which they might have climbed... He knelt and examined the ground. He made out an opening, about the width of a hand, and as he watched the slow growth of the fungal floor sealed the gap even further. It looked, he thought, like a pair of slowly closing lips, humorously mocking his impotence to rescue the biologist.

He heard a sound behind him and jumped up, levelling his laser.

Singh appeared through the forest, backed by half a dozen of his men and a couple of spider drones. "What happened?"

"They took Namura."

"They?" The Sikh looked around, alarmed.

He glanced at Singh. "Who the hell do you think? Aliens."

His words had the effect of alerting the rest of the

guards, who looked about nervously, weapons aimed into the surrounding forest.

Belatedly Vaughan enabled his tele-ability and directed his scan underground. He read nothing – not even the static of Namura's mind-shield – as evidently they had already passed beyond the limit of his probe.

He told himself that even if he'd probed earlier, he would have read only the obscure signatures of extraterrestrial minds: it would have done nothing to help him save Namura.

"How did they get through the barrier?" Singh snapped.

Vaughan indicated the seam in the fungus. "They didn't. They went through there. The hole closed after them."

Singh pushed forwards. "Stand back." He aimed his laser at the seam and fired, excavating a small, blackened crater in the ground.

Vaughan peered; there was no sign or any tunnel or corridor beyond. "We need to get back," he said. "See if Chandrasakar has any digging equipment…" Even as he said it, he was aware of the futility of attempting to find Namura now.

Singh detailed two of his men to remain beside the charred pit, then led the way back to the ship. As Vaughan emerged with the security team from the forest and came to the crest of the hill, he looked down and saw that scientists and crew had left the *Kali* and gathered by the ship's ramp. He hurried past Singh and down the incline. An air of fear, a miasma almost palpable, hung about the gathering.

Chandrasakar, Das, and McIntosh came to meet

him. "Kiki?" McIntosh said; he was white, wide-eyed.

"She's alive. I don't think whoever took her intended to harm her–"

Das stared at him. "Jeff, what happened?"

"She was taken by perhaps a dozen aliens. Small, green – your standard comic-book Ee-tees." He described how they'd utilised tunnels through the fungus to get around the laser cordon.

Chandrasakar said, "You scanned them?"

Vaughan thought about telling the truth – that in the heat of the chase it hadn't entered his mind to scan – but decided against it. "Of course. But I didn't pick up a thing."

Chandrasakar looked at him, almost suspiciously, and Vaughan wondered if he'd seen through the lie. The tycoon turned and spoke to Singh in lowered tones.

"So…" Das said. "What do we do now?"

"We've got to go after Kiki!"

"Is the ship equipped with digging equipment?" Vaughan asked. "We could always…"

Chandrasakar shook his head impatiently. "No, but even if we had diggers, I'd counsel caution—"

"But the bastards have got Kiki!" McIntosh cried.

"Rushing after them might not be the best way to get her back," Chandrasakar said. "The fact that they didn't kill her immediately–"

Vaughan said, "Presumably the aliens were responsible for what happened to the crew of the *Mussoree*?"

Chandrasakar shrugged. "That's a possibility, but debatable. We'll find out in time."

Das said, "Do you know if the aliens were armed,

Jeff?"

He shook his head. "I... something suggests to me that they weren't. They appeared to be naked, as far as I could make out."

"But what do they want with Namura?" Das said.

Vaughan looked at the swaying polyp forest. "The same as they wanted with the crew of the *Mussoree*?" he said. "Perhaps *they* might still be alive."

"We could speculate until the sun turns blue, Vaughan," Chandrasakar said impatiently. "Let's get McIntosh to the sick-bay, then meet in the observation lounge and take it from there."

That evening, as Delta Cephei went down behind the high fungal horizon in an effulgent blaze of ruddy light, Vaughan sat before the viewscreen in the observation lounge and drank a beer.

Immediately after Namura's abduction Chandrasakar had called a meeting in the observation lounge. Present were the tycoon himself, Das, Singh and his deputy in security, and a couple of head scientists. They had gone over and over what had happened to the biologist, and Vaughan had again recounted what he'd seen.

The meeting broke up with little achieved, other than a total ban on crew venturing further than fifty metres from the ship for an indefinite period. Security were patrolling the perimeter, aided by a dozen spider drones.

The atmosphere at dinner that evening had been tense, with long silences and brittle conversation. Vaughan had been glad to escape to the nacelle with his beer.

He calculated that it would be in the early hours of the morning now on Bengal Station, so he couldn't call Sukara. Instead he summoned her blurred image on the screen and stared at it for a long time, wishing for the end of the mission and longing for the journey home.

He was on his second beer when McIntosh joined him. The big Australian seemed jumpy, harried, continually running a hand through the red mop of his hair.

"You don't mind?" He indicated the opposite foam-form with his bottle.

"Of course not. Sit down." Vaughan hesitated, then said, "I think she's going to be fine, David. I know it's a hell of a thing…" He shrugged. "We'll find her, okay?"

McIntosh managed a smile. "Thanks. It's just… we're close, Jeff. We've been together over a year…"

Vaughan went to the bar and came back with a pair of beers.

They were joined by Parveen Das, and Vaughan was pleased that she didn't have Chandrasakar in tow.

McIntosh asked, "What went down at the meeting? We're not going to just sit here while Kiki…"

Das said, "Of course not, David." She looked at Vaughan, then went on, "Look, this is between us, okay? There was a survivor from the crew of the *Mussoree*. She's in coldsleep as we speak. Tomorrow, Jeff will meet her, read her, and find out exactly what happened back then."

Vaughan stared at her, more than a little surprised

that she knew about the engineer.

McIntosh said, "Read her? Why not just get her out of suspension and question her?"

"The medics say she's traumatised," Das said, "that it's safer if she doesn't relive the incident. It'll be better for her if Jeff just reads her mind. Then," she went on, "we might be able to work out exactly what's happening here."

"Cheers to that," McIntosh said bitterly, raising his bottle.

The Australian turned in a while later, but not before making a detour to the bar for a couple of beers.

When he'd gone, Vaughan looked across at Das and said, "You said earlier that you didn't know what I was doing here?"

She looked at him speculatively. "Rab told me just now."

"One of the advantages of sleeping with the enemy." He watched for her reaction.

Her expression remained neutral. "That all depends on whether you consider Rab the enemy, Jeff."

He laughed, and decided to be blunt. Three beers had loosened his circumspection. "For Chrissake, Das, who are you working for?"

She pursed her lips. "Would you believe me if I said I'm working for myself?"

He considered this. "Pass," he said. Then, "So he told you that the engineer's traumatised?"

She had been staring through the viewscreen as the land around the ship darkened. Now she turned quickly and said, "She isn't?"

Vaughan smiled to himself, pleased that Chandrasakar evidently hadn't told her everything. "Something like that," he said.

A minute later – a long, silent minute – Das pushed herself from her seat and said, "I'm going to turn in. Night, Jeff."

"Sleep well," he said, and he hoped she picked up on the note of irony.

He fetched another beer from the bar, sat in the nacelle, drank, and stared out into the darkness. Night was not absolutely pitch black on Delta Cephei VII. The fungus glowed in the darkness, giving off a low, lambent light. Occasionally he made out the silvery twinkle of a patrolling spider drone.

He brought up Sukara's image on his handset and stared at it. As the night wore on he became steadily more inebriated, and only later, in the early hours of the morning, did he admit to himself that more than what had happened that afternoon, more than the fear of the aliens and what might have befallen Kiki Namura, he dreaded reading the engineer's dead mind later that day.

TWELVE

A TURN FOR THE WORSE

Sukara woke suddenly, snatched from a terrible dream in which she was falling.

She sat up, crying out, and found herself in a strange bedroom. It was not the hotel, but smaller, more minimally furnished... Then she had it. She was in the guest room at St Theresa's.

Li...

She rolled out of bed and dressed quickly. She grabbed a bulb of coffee from a dispenser, decided against having a shower, and hurried into the corridor.

Last night on the way to the hospital she'd made a detour to drop Pham off at a friend's on Level Three. Kath took Pham in without a second thought and said she could stay as long as Sukara was at the hospital. They had hugged for a long time after Pham had run off to play with Kath's daughter, and Sukara thanked the gods she had such a good friend.

Then she'd hurried to St Theresa's and the consultation with Dr Grant.

Now she moved along the corridor to Li's room and slipped inside.

The bed was empty, and something lurched sickeningly within Sukara. She felt a solicitous hand on her arm. "It's okay –" a nurse was smiling at her, "– Li's in the examination room. If you'd care to follow me…"

They moved down a corridor, and then another. The nurse ushered her into a small room, without a bed or other furniture. She turned in query to the nurse, who pointed at a viewscreen in the far wall.

Sukara approached the viewscreen slowly, her heart in her mouth, and stared through. Li, wearing only a pair of white underpants, looking incredibly thin and vulnerable, was stretched out on a metal table, a dozen silver tubes inserted into her small body. She was unconscious. Dr Grant was reading something from a big screen behind Li's head, and another doctor was talking to him. Two spider drones, looking alien and inimical, were poised over Li, from time to time adjusting catheters, taking out tubes and replacing them with others.

Sukara turned to the nurse. "What's happening?"

"It's okay. It's a routine examination. Nothing to worry about."

It didn't look routine, but then what did she know? With the drones and the silver tubes bulging into her daughter's arms, legs, and torso, the procedure looked invasive and painful.

Last night Dr Grant had examined Li for over an hour and then, while her daughter slept, had sat Sukara down with a cup of coffee and explained the situation.

Li's healthy white blood cell count was low, very

low. Dr Grant had explained, as if she were a child, that white blood cells were what helped the body fight off infection. In the morning, he said, they would attempt to clone healthy white cells from Li's body. Later, they would introduce them into her system and so start the process of treating her disease.

She felt tears welling as she stared at Li. She wanted to hug her daughter, repeat over and over that she loved her and that she would be okay. She wished Jeff were here now, beside her, to hold her hand and reassure *her* that everything would be okay.

Last night Sukara had asked Dr Grant if Li would be okay, hardly able to ask the question in little more than a whisper, and stared at the man's big, ruddy face for any give-away signs before he spoke.

"Li is very ill," he'd said, "but I am confident she'll pull through. The next two days will be critical. If the cloning works as it should, then she'll be over the worst–"

"And if it doesn't?"

A terrible hesitation as Dr Grant had looked her in the eye. "Then we'll try the process again, and if that doesn't work we'll attempt a transfusion of manufactured cells. That will be a short-term measure only, until we've successfully cloned her own blood."

Then Sukara had asked, in a voice little more than a whisper, "What are her chances?"

"At the moment, they're in the region of fifty-fifty. They might rise tomorrow if the cloning takes."

His words had slammed into her solar plexus like

an ice-cold axe, and that night she had hardly slept.

Now she turned to the nurse. "Do you know how it's going?"

The woman looked apologetic. "I'm afraid I don't. Dr Grant will be out presently. He'll see you then."

The drones danced around Li, removing the tubes and catheters. Two nurses eased Li's limp body onto a trolley and whisked her from the room. Dr Grant pointed to the screen, indicated something to the other doctor; both men looked grim-faced, serious. Sukara wanted to hammer on the glass and ask what the hell was going on.

The nurse touched her arm again and indicated a door. Sukara passed into a snug consulting room and took a seat. The nurse eased the door shut behind her, and she felt suddenly very lonely. She waited, her pulse loud in her ears. She wanted to be with Li now, and hold her hand.

She knew that soon Dr Grant would step into the room, stern-faced and silent; he would sit down behind his desk and steeple his fingers and tell her the bad news.

Sukara knew it.

When the door opened, she jumped and gasped aloud, the feeling of foolishness soon replaced by a terrible apprehension.

Dr Grant perched on the edge of the desk, hands on knees, and smiled at her. She wondered if this was his way of breaking bad news.

Sukara just stared at him, mute. At last she managed, "How is she?"

"The good news is that the cloning took one hundred per cent. Her white blood cell count is back in the normal range. What we're doing now is placing your daughter in the treatment chamber and beginning the chemical process that should eradicate all trace of the disease."

Sukara felt light-headed with relief. She wondered if it were too early yet to think that Li would survive.

"If you'd like to come with me..."

Dr Grant slid from the desk and ushered her through the door. They entered another room in the centre of which was a huge white, tubular device with a door at one end. It reminded Sukara of a giant washing machine.

A technician hauled open the door and pulled out a slide-bed.

Dr Grant said, "Li will be placed in here for a couple of hours, and the treatment will begin. She'll be unconscious all the time, and for the rest of the day. We'll bring her round again at six. You might care to go home for the rest of the day and come back later."

She nodded. "Can I watch this part of the treatment?"

Dr Grant smiled. "Of course, but there isn't much to see."

Li was wheeled into the room. She was wearing a white gown now, contrasting with her tanned limbs and jet hair. Two technicians lifted her onto the slide-bed. Dr Grant smiled at Sukara and gestured towards Li.

She stepped forwards and took Li's small, warm hand. Her fingers were limp, unresponsive. She kissed her cheek and stood back as Li was inserted into the machine and the door eased shut behind her. Something hard and painful blocked Sukara's throat and her eyes swam with tears.

Through an access hatch in the side of the machine, the techs hooked up tubes to the catheters in Li's arms, then crossed the room to a bank of monitors and stationed themselves before the consoles. Seconds later a bright blue light filled the machine, and Sukara stared in at her daughter.

Dr Grant touched her arm. "There's little we can do now. If you'd like to take a break, get something to eat…?"

"Can I come back later?"

"Of course. Li will be conscious again at six."

Sukara nodded and followed Dr Grant out of the treatment chamber.

She returned to the bedroom, showered, and changed. There was a café in the grounds of the hospital, overlooking the park. She'd get something to drink, buy a book, and try to read for an hour or so.

She took the elevator to the ground floor and left the hospital. She sat in the ersatz sunlight and ordered an iced tea, then decided to call Jeff.

She wouldn't mention the latest scare. She'd simply say that Li had begun the treatment and that the doctor was confident of her making a full recovery… It wasn't really a lie, and anyway she didn't want to worry him.

She tapped the code Jeff had given her into her handset and waited, heart thudding. Seconds later the screen flared, flashed with static, then resolved.

Jeff's lean, dark face looked out at her. He smiled. "Su…"

"Jeff." She choked on a sob. "Great to see you."

"How's Li?"

She nodded. "She began treatment this morning. She's in a big machine – like an industrial washing machine. You wouldn't believe it. Dr Grant's happy with how things are going. It's after eleven now. She'll be unconscious until six."

"Where are you?"

"In the hospital café, grabbing a drink. I think I'll go and fetch Pham from school, take her out for lunch." She smiled. "Anyway, what's the planet like?"

He returned her smile. "Christ, Su, I love you," he said. "Can't wait to get back. But Delta Cephei VII... It's like a big fungus farm. Look." The image on her metacarpal screen swayed as Jeff moved to a viewscreen and positioned his handset so that she could see out.

"Weird!" she said, staring at a rolling landscape of orange fungus and strange, sprouting mushrooms.

Jeff said, "It's early. I've just got up. Today's the day..."

"Oh...!" She felt suddenly guilty that she'd forgotten all about the reason for Jeff's being on Delta Cephei VII. "You're reading the dead engineer..."

He nodded. "In a few hours."

"Does anyone know what happened to the crew?"

"Not yet, Su."

"But you aren't in danger, are you, Jeff?"

He smiled. "No, of course not."

She felt a quick stab of relief. "I'll be thinking of you."

"Thanks. It'll be fine, once it's over. I'll call you

tonight, okay?"

She nodded. "I'm missing you, Jeff. Wish you were here. I want to hold you."

"Missing you too, but I'll soon be back."

"Oh – by the way, I saw Dr Rao yesterday, and guess what?"

She spent the next ten minutes telling him about Rao's job offer, and discussing whether she should take it. Jeff said why not, which pleased her, and said they'd talk it over when he got back.

They chatted on, Sukara reluctant to break the link and be alone again. Ten minutes later, listening to Jeff describe the sunsets and the quick-growing fungus, she felt herself welling up. She wanted to tell him how horrible it was here without him, and how the last few hours had been hell... but the last thing she wanted was to set him worrying. Instead she sighed, told Jeff she loved him, and said she'd better say goodbye now and go for Pham.

He blew her a kiss and cut the connection.

She sat for a while, gazing at his still image, then turned off her handset. She finished her tea without tasting it, staring across the park to the open-ended west side of the Station: the sea scintillated, and a warm wind blew in across the grass, laden with the scent of jasmine and bougainvillaea.

She quit the café and took the long, curving path through the park. She had hardly left the shadow of the hospital when she heard a shout from behind her.

A young Chinese orderly in a white tunic was chasing after her. "Miz Sukara!" he cried again.

She stared at him. "What is it?"

He caught up with her, panting, and pointed at

her handset. "You were talking, so we couldn't get through. But I saw you in the café…"

She felt dizzy. "What's wrong?"

He looked straight into her eyes. "It's your daughter, Li. I'm afraid she's taken a turn for the worse. Dr Grant wants to see you."

Bile rose in her throat. She swallowed, tasting the acidic liquid. Her vision misted, but she managed to follow the orderly back through the grounds of the hospital.

"This way," he said, taking her arm and hurrying her past the entrance towards a service lift on the outside of the building. "It's quicker."

He palmed a sensor and the door opened. She stepped inside, resisting the urge to break down and cry out loud; it was ridiculous, but she felt that she had to maintain her composure before this complete stranger.

He thumbed a panel and the lift jerked into motion.

Too late, she realised that something was wrong. The lift was going *down*…

"But…?" she said, turning to the orderly.

He smiled at her, raised something, and sprayed it in her face.

And a second later Sukara lost consciousness.

THIRTEEN

REVELATION

Vaughan was woken early by Sukara's call. He chatted to her, cheered by the illusion that she was close by, then cut the connection, slipped from his cabin and left the ship.

Delta Cephei rose at his back, sending his long shadow sprawling before him across the fungal valley floor. His earlier curiosity about the coloration of the fungus at night-time was now answered: by some effect of photochemical synthesis it had reverted to its default cream hue during darkness. Now, with the appearance of the sun, it began the slow change, turning chartreuse as he watched.

The landscape had undergone a transformation while he'd slept, too. The valley floor had hunched itself, so that, instead of providing a flat plane between the *Kali* and the *Mussoree*, a slight hillock had appeared. A thousand smaller growths had sprouted across the plane; these resembled conventional Terran mushrooms, but knee high, with thick boles and gaudy crimson parasols. The drones had been busy during the night, cropping the fungus from around the ships to create two deep, waterless moats.

Vaughan walked up the hillock between the ships. A mushroom, much taller than the others, had sprouted on the crest, and he sat down with his back against its sturdy trunk, sick at the thought of what the day would bring.

He thought of Namura's abduction, and wondered if he were in danger here. The aliens had used their knowledge of the fungal terrain to snatch her and escape. They could do the same now, he thought, create an opening, take him, and vanish down the aperture before it closed up. He slipped a hand inside his shirt and gripped the butt of his laser.

As he sat, a tall hatch in the side of the *Kali* opened, and seconds later a flier hovered out. Six security guards sat in the open-topped vehicle, each one gripping a rifle. The flier settled on the ground and from the ship trooped a procession of drones. One by one the silver spiders crawled over the flier, retracted their telescopic limbs and clamped themselves to its flank like so many metallic barnacles. The flier rose ten metres and set off away from the ship; it made a circuit of the cordoned area, then headed towards a distant range of what might have been mountains or just another fungal outcropping. Vaughan watched as it dwindled to a dot in the distance and was lost to sight.

He saw movement behind the viewscreens along the flank of the *Kali*: the tiny figures of the crew going about their business. A team of scientists came down the ramp, accompanied by armed guards, and set up a spindly drilling rig. McIntosh was with them, though he stood off to one side and cast a long glance around the area as if searching for clues to his lover's whereabouts.

Vaughan watched as the scientists bored through the fungal mantle, reading from softscreens and making hushed comments to their handsets as the experiment progressed.

He wondered about the dead – or, technically, the dying – engineer aboard the *Mussoree*. He'd lain awake during the long night thinking about reading her mind. The thing to do, to preserve his sanity, would be to skim her most recent memories as her consciousness dwindled away to the terrible end-point of oblivion. Her last recollections of her time on Delta Cephei VII were what Chandrasakar was eager to know about anyway; Vaughan would avoid delving too deep, miring himself in her personality, her memories of family and loved ones, her joys and regrets.

He closed his eyes as the sun warmed him, and after a sleepless night he must have dozed. He lucid dreamed of Sukara and the girls, and was startled, some time later, by a voice calling his name.

"Jeff? When you're ready…"

He shook his head, waking to find himself on the weird surface of an alien world, the images of Sukara receding rapidly.

Chandrasakar was standing at the foot of the incline, flanked by the medic, Pavelescu, and the head of security, Singh.

The tycoon waved. "If you'd care to accompany us across to the *Mussoree*…" Like a condemned man he stood and joined the trio. Chandrasakar nodded a greeting. "The engineer will come out of suspension in approximately fifteen minutes." He hesitated. "I don't envy you what you have to do, Jeff. I know it must be hell, but I hope you realise its importance, especially in light of Namura's abduction?"

Vaughan nodded. "It's what I signed up to do, isn't it?" He sounded needlessly petulant, even to his own ears, and regretted it.

"Well, let's get it over with." They approached the ramp of the *Mussoree* and entered the ship. A complement of guards snapped to attention as Chandrasakar passed, and Vaughan caught sight of perhaps half a dozen security drones lurking in corners, scurrying across walls and ceilings.

The *Mussoree* was a small ship, and it wasn't long before they reached the cryo-suspension chamber. Singh remained outside the sliding door, and Chandrasakar and Vaughan stepped into a v-shaped room with pods built into the sloping walls to left and right. Three of the pods were vacant but the fourth held the dim shape of the engineer behind a frosted crystal cover.

Three technicians sat around the pod, consulting softscreens jacked into the suspension unit. One of them looked up and nodded to Chandrasakar as they entered the chamber.

The others eyed Vaughan with expressions which combined pity and distaste, as if he were being led to the gallows.

Two of the techs stood and slipped from the room, leaving Pavelescu and the head technician to deal with the job of decanting the dying engineer.

Chandrasakar stood by the door, his expression

neutral.

The tech tapped a code on his softscreen and the crystal cover cracked with a loud hiss. A cloud of escaping cold air filled the chamber, as if it were the woman's premature ghost. The rack on which the engineer was lying slid forwards and levelled out.

The first thing that Vaughan noticed was the wound that disfigured the side of the woman's head: something had removed a section of her skull above her temple. The second thing he saw, with a jolting shock, was that she was Asian, small, slim, and serene-featured. A sudden involuntary sadness rose in him.

Pavelescu inserted a catheter into her jugular, tapped something into a softscreen, and nodded to Vaughan. "She's all yours."

Then he and the technician backed off and stood respectfully like morticians in the presence of a grieving loved one. A monitor on the tech's softscreen bleeped faintly as it recorded the woman's fading consciousness.

Vaughan slipped onto a seat beside the rack. He tried not to look at the woman's face – she looked ridiculously young, perhaps twenty, too young for her life to have ended like this – and he considered, fleetingly, duping Chandrasakar. He could always simulate the reading, concoct some story about her being too far gone for her memories to be accessible, and the tycoon would be none the wiser. He thought about it, then tapped the enable code into his handset. To abdicate the responsibility merely to save his own pain would be a dereliction of duty. He owed it to the engineer to find out who or what had killed her – and perhaps along the way learn what had happened to her colleagues and to Kiki Namura.

He closed his eyes and found himself, involuntarily, reaching for the woman's cold hand. He gripped it as he sent out a probe towards her shattered sensorium.

He ceased, for a terrible few seconds, to be wholly Jeff Vaughan. Despite his best intentions he was unable to shield himself from the fact of the woman's identity. She invaded him, her awareness of herself overcame him in a great wave, taking his breath away and flooding him with unwanted thoughts and memories, fears and regrets.

He struggled to gain purchase on her most recent thoughts, while battling to ignore who and what she was, which was impossible.

Patti Yuan... twenty-three... on her third mission for the Chandrasakar Line; she had a lover...

Oh, sweet Jesus Christ.

Her lover was a woman called Jenny Grendle, the pilot-geologist aboard the *Mussoree*.

Vaughan was rocked by a blast of grief, and the sudden image of what had happened to Jenny Grendle.

He gripped the woman's hand all the tighter, his other hand grasping the edge of the slide-bed. Eyes still closed, he cried out. He felt someone's hand on his shoulder.

He wanted to pull back, retreat from the dark and terrible vortex that was Patti's dying psyche. But he knew he had to continue. He battled to order her thoughts, to cast about through the shattered and fragmenting images and piece together the crew's last few hours on Delta Cephei VII.

He caught an image, followed it, despite the woman's pain, and experienced reality through the eyes, the mind, of Patti Yuan.

As per regulations, the crew had monitored the area around the ship before two of them – a biologist and mineralogist – donned atmosphere suits as a precaution and ventured out.

Patti and her lover Jenny remained aboard the ship, in radio contact with the others.

Vaughan concentrated; visually it was like watching an image on a defective holo-screen which kept breaking up, fragmenting; Patti Yuan's emotions underwent a similar dysfunction, both the result of her injuries and the fact that she was gradually, inevitably, dying.

Skip to: a cry in Patti's earpiece. The biologist, Gonzalez, had seen something: movement, a scurrying figure behind a sprouting fungal stalk.

Skip to: another cry. They were under attack, Gonzalez yelled, being fired upon by green humanoids. Henderson was down, shot through the chest.

Gonzalez was returning to the ship.

Vaughan, via Patti's eyes, watched through the viewscreen as the Mexican came into view, running towards the ship pursued by the humanoids. Before Patti could stop her, Grendle leapt from her seat, snatched a rifle and ran to the exit. Patti followed, yelling.

By the time Patti came to the exit, Grendle was kneeling at the top of the ramp, laying down a barrage of covering fire as Gonzalez zigzagged towards the ship through an obstacle course of fungal trunks. Patti thought he was going to make it, and realised she was screaming at him to hurry. Then her yells turned to sobs as a shot ripped through the Mexican's lower back, exploding his entrails across the ground before him.

Skip to: Patti beside Grendle, firing a rifle as the green men attacked. She called out a command to the ship's core to break out the complement of combat AIs, and seconds later six silver spider-drones leaped over the two women and joined battle.

Skip to: something hitting Jenny Grendle in the chest; Jenny turning to her lover with an almost beatific expression on her face as blood pulsed through her shattered ribs.

Vaughan fought the tidal wave of the woman's emotion, the pain of losing a lover...

Then something knocked Patti off her feet; a projectile had slammed into her head. She felt a dull pain, out of all proportion to what she should be feeling as a piece of her skull, hinged on flesh, flapped forward, and obscured her vision as she toppled backwards.

She was being carried rapidly, and she thought for a second that the green humanoids had got her. She saw a flash of silver, a scissoring glint of legs, as two spider drones hauled her back through the ship.

And...

A stray memory, evanescent... Vaughan strained to capture it.

A voice. She'd heard a voice as she was dragged from the exit.

A human voice...

"*We've got the ship!*"

And Patti's last thought, on the threshold of

death, as the combat drones reached the suspension chamber and eased her into the cold-sleep unit, was: *The green creatures speak English...*

Vaughan cried out in pain. Patti Yuan slid towards oblivion, her mind full of grief at the death of the only person she had ever loved, at the terrible realisation of her own approaching end. It was as if he were being dragged down with her, sucked into the vortex of nothingness towards which the woman, seconds ago so full of life and vitality, was heading.

He cried out again and forced himself upwards, a swimmer fighting the pull of a terrible tidal rip; he pulled away from her as blackness encroached, as everything she had ever known was reduced to absolute nothingness and Patti Yuan died.

He released her hand and pushed himself from the slide-bed, fell to the floor on all fours and vomited as relief flooded through him, blessed gratitude that he was who he was, Jeff Vaughan and alive, and yet carrying within him the last memories of Patti's death, memories that would haunt him until the day of his own inevitable end.

He felt someone turning him over so that he lay on his back, and a cold sensation on his inner arm, and then a warm smothering sensation as the sedative took hold.

Two hours later he slumped in the padded nacelle of the observation lounge. Chandrasakar perched opposite him, flanked by Singh and Pavelescu. Vaughan sipped his coffee and stared out at the slowly shifting terrain, biding his time until he was good and ready to recount what had happened to the crew of the *Mussoree*.

Like depression or an insistent migraine, Patti Yuan's death had lodged itself in his head and would not depart. He had known it would be like this, though he had forgotten the severity, the degree of his identification with the dead subject. It was as if a part of him had died, and he knew that this feeling was a reminder of how it would be to face his own death, one day.

And in the forefront of his mind was what he had discovered about the *Mussoree's* attackers: they had spoken English. They had been human.

Chandrasakar said, "I can appreciate how traumatic it must have been..."

Vaughan interrupted, dragging his gaze away from the landscape and focusing on the tycoon. "You can't. You might have an inkling, an intellectual hunch. But unless you've gone through it, you've absolutely no idea."

At least Chandrasakar was man enough not to argue the point. He merely spread his hands in a gesture of concession.

"Were you able to...?"

"Find out what happened? Of course. I was with her through it all, right up to her death."

He stopped there and gazed through the viewscreen again. Perhaps it was petty of him, but he was relishing having this power over Chandrasakar. Until now he had been in the tycoon's control, at his beck and call; it was refreshing to be able to call the shots.

He finished his coffee and called the waiter for another. He took three or four sips, paused, then began outlining the final hour aboard the *Mus-*

soree.

He recounted the initial exploration made by Henderson and Gonzalez. He described the attack on the pair, the subsequent raid on the ship, and Grendle and Yuan's futile defence. He stripped the account of all the pain he'd experienced, and omitted to mention that the pair had been lovers. He kept it as factual as possible, not wanting to trigger the woman's memories that rode alongside his own.

He paused when he'd recounted the drone's actions in getting the engineer into coldsleep. Singh said to Chandrasakar, "That ties in with the drones' limited report, sir. Grendle was beyond their aid, but they stowed Yuan in the mortuary."

Pavelescu said, "But we're none the wiser why they attacked in the first place–"

Vaughan sipped his coffee and said, "They wanted the *Mussoree.*"

"What makes you think...?" Singh began.

"The last thing Patti Yuan heard before she lost consciousness was a cry from one of the attackers. It was in English." He repeated the phrase. "*We've got the ship!*"

Pavelescu stared at him. "Are you sure about this?"

"I'm as sure about it as Patti Yuan was," Vaughan said.

Pavelescu said, "But if they wanted the ship, and killed the crew, then why didn't they–"

Singh interrupted, "Why didn't they take the ship? Think about it, Pavelescu. They might have killed the crew, thought they'd got the ship, but the combat drones fought them off."

Chandrasakar questioned Vaughan, going over

his account and asking for details. Vaughan found himself repeating what he'd said, going over the same old ground and growing resentful.

The tycoon picked up on this and said, "I appreciate what you've been able to tell me, Jeff. I know I cannot hope to understand the pain, but you have my gratitude."

He gestured at Pavelescu and Singh. The three men stood.

Vaughan looked up. "And the green men? The humans...?"

Chandrasakar seemed to hesitate before saying, "That remains the big mystery, Jeff. I don't know."

You lying bastard, Vaughan thought.

The tycoon made to leave the lounge.

"I think you've forgotten something," Vaughan said.

He ejected the necropath program from his handset and held it out to Chandrasakar. The tycoon nodded, accepted the pin, and strode from the observation lounge with Singh and Pavelescu.

Vaughan sat and a stared at the dregs in his cup. He realised that what he had feared for some time was over, and the relief was immense. But now, along with the residual pain of Patti Yuan's passing, was the mystery of the green men – and a suspicion was beginning to form in his mind.

He recalled how, earlier, Chandrasakar had quizzed him about whether he'd read the minds of the green men while searching for Namura. Vaughan had claimed he'd probed and read nothing. The look Chandrasakar had given him then – either doubtful or suspicious – now made sense.

Chandrasakar had known all along that the green

men were not aliens.

He looked through the viewscreen. Chandrasakar had exited the ship and stood on the plain, deep in conversation with Singh. As Vaughan watched, he dismissed the head of security and walked over to the drilling rig where a team of scientists, David McIntosh among them, were still working.

On impulse Vaughan pushed himself from the seat and strode from the lounge. He took the elevator and hurried down the ramp and across to where Chandrasakar was in conversation with the scientists.

He stopped by the group, and his brooding presence must have made itself apparent to Chandrasakar. The tycoon turned impatiently and said, "Can I help you, Jeff?"

"We need to talk. About who killed Yuan."

Chandrasakar opened his mouth, as if to remonstrate, then nodded. "Okay, Jeff…" He moved from the scientists and gestured up the incline, to the tall mushroom under which Vaughan had sat first thing that morning. They climbed towards it.

As soon as they were out of earshot, Vaughan said, "How long have you known the green men were human?"

Chandrasakar looked at him as they walked. "My team briefed me about your perspicacity before we hired you, Jeff. They told me that half a life-time of reading minds had given you acute perceptions, that you could tell when someone was lying, or telling the truth, even when you weren't reading."

Vaughan dismissed this with an impatient wave. "What the hell's going on here?"

They reached the tall mushroom, and Chandrasakar gestured in invitation for Vaughan to be seated, as if he owned the planet.

Chandrasakar hunkered down beside Vaughan, the pose oddly democratic and out of keeping with the paunchy tycoon. "I'll come clean with you, Jeff. I'll tell you what the situation is here if you'll keep it to yourself, okay? No one knows why we're here other than my head of security, Singh. I want to keep it that way. Deal?"

Vaughan nodded, wary. "Go ahead."

"Twenty-five years ago, just as voidspace was opening up, the Federated Northern States of America sent out a colony ship on a long haul to what was then beyond the edge of the Expansion in search of a habitable planet; I think they wanted to set up a far-flung frontier, a kind of marker as to their vaunted ambitions. Anyway, the ship, the *Cincinnati*, made landfall here on Delta Cephei VII."

Chandrasakar paused, and Vaughan thought of the early colonists and the difficulty of existing on such an inimical planet with its long, harsh winter and short, fiery summers.

"And then?"

"And then, earlier this year, one of my exploration ships flying about a hundred light years from here picked up a weak signal from the colonists, meant for Earth."

Vaughan looked at the tycoon. "Earlier *this* year? They didn't try to communicate with Earth before now?"

Chandrasakar shrugged. "They might have done; it's impossible to tell—"

"Do you know if the FNSA sent out a follow-up

mission?"

The tycoon shook his head. "The FNSA was undergoing something of a recession around that time, remember – the last thing they wanted to spend money on was expensive follow-up missions."

"So..." Vaughan said, "this communiqué?"

"The colonists reported that they'd established a settlement here, despite the conditions. They also reported that they'd found something of a... revelation beneath the surface of the planet."

Vaughan eyed the tycoon. "A revelation?"

"That was the word they used–"

"What was it?"

Chandrasakar smiled. "That's what we came here to find out, Jeff. The message was so scrambled it was hard to decipher – and my scientists suspected that it was cut off purposefully before it was completed, as if there were two competing opinions among the colonists about whether to broadcast what they'd found."

"Do you think the communiqué made it through to the FNSA?"

"We suspect that either the communiqué did get through, or my security was compromised and factions on Earth found out that I was equipping a mission to Delta Cephei VII."

"What makes you think...?"

"Forces opposed to what I was doing were determined to stop me. They disabled the original ship I had ready for the mission – with a pretty effective bit of industrial sabotage – and then targeted the telepaths I'd shortlisted to accompany me."

"The assassin..." Vaughan said.

"I think it was their little game to let me know that I wasn't alone in my knowledge of the importance of Delta Cephei VII, that they were onto me. And to slow me down." Chandrasakar paused. "I pride myself on the high levels of security in my organisation, Jeff, but there was clearly a breach. And the fact that either the FNSA or some other organisation or government knows about Delta Cephei VII makes it even more vital that we get to the bottom of the mystery, sooner rather than later."

Vaughan wondered what else Chandrasakar was failing to tell him.

The nature of the revelation the colonists had discovered?

The identity of those who had hired the Korth assassin?

Not for the first time, he wished he could probe the tycoon's wily mind for just five seconds.

Then he considered Parveen Das, and wondered if the Indian government had its sticky fingers in the affair... Was it possible, even, that Das's paymasters had been behind the assassination of the telepaths?

He wanted suddenly to be a thousand light years from Delta Cephei VII and everything it represented about the tawdry affairs of humankind.

His thoughts were interrupted by a cry from down below.

McIntosh had left the drilling rig and the other scientists and was running up the incline towards Vaughan and Chandrasakar. He was accessing his handset as he ran, and then looking up and waving madly. "Jeez, it's Kiki!" he called out.

He came to them panting and held out his handset. Kiki Namura's high, shrill tones filled the air. "David! I'm okay; they're treating me well. I have a message. They wish to negotiate. But first, they want the telepath – Vaughan – to come out into the open with his hands in their air."

Vaughan stared at McIntosh's handset, hardly believing what he'd heard.

Chandrasakar accessed the signal on his own handset and said, "How do they know about Jeff, Kiki?"

Namura sobbed. "They asked me. I had to tell them."

"Why do they want him?"

"They... They want him separated. Down there in the hollow, beside the *Kali*."

"And then?" Chandrasakar wanted to know.

"And then they want to negotiate for the use of the *Mussoree*," Namura said.

Chandrasakar looked at Vaughan. "You were right, again, Jeff."

McIntosh spoke into his own handset. "Negotiate?" he asked, his expression grim.

Her reply must have confirmed his fears. "For me, David."

Vaughan said, "Tell them I'm going–"

Namura said, "They say you must walk to the side of the *Kali* with your hands in the air. If you try to enable your psi-ability, they say they'll kill me. They're watching you. They're out of probing range now, but when they come for the ship..."

"I'm on my way," Vaughan said, glancing at Chandrasakar.

As he raised his hands into the air and strode down the incline towards the flank of the Kali, he looked about him for some sign of where the green men – the colonists – might be secreted. At least, now, he knew why they had signalled him out. Not to be shot, as he'd first feared – though that was still a distinct possibility – but so that he'd be out of probing range if and when they boarded the *Mussoree*.

He came to the ship, turned, and stood with his hands in the air, feeling like a bull's eye on a firing range.

He considered what it might be that the colonists didn't want him to read, and wondered if it could be what they'd discovered beneath the surface of Delta Cephei VII.

FOURTEEN

SLAUGHTER

He stood at the foot of the *Kali's* ramp, hands in the air. Delta Cephei was climbing into the bright blue sky, a fulminating fireball. Sweat trickled from his hairline and dribbled down his neck.

Five minutes had elapsed since the communiqué from the colonists. A stasis had overtaken the scene, with the drilling halted and the scientists and techs standing beside the rig like a redundant Greek chorus. Chandrasakar and McIntosh stood beneath the wide parasol of the mushroom high on the incline. As Vaughan watched, looking for the first sign of the colonists, Chandrasakar moved off down the incline towards the *Kali*, followed by McIntosh. The former was speaking surreptitiously into his handset.

They came to a halt five metres from Vaughan, and Chandrasakar lowered his handset and stared across the plain towards the *Mussoree*. From the ship emerged half a dozen drones, mincing on silver scissoring legs across the fungal terrain to take up positions on the perimeter of the cordoned area. Next came a scientist and a technician, who crossed to the *Kali* and climbed the ramp.

Vaughan looked at Chandrasakar. "You're not going to give them the ship?" he asked incredulously.

Chandrasakar kept his gaze on the surrounding fungal outgrowths. "What do you think? Of course I'm not."

McIntosh was watching Chandrasakar, concern etched on his face. "We can't do anything to endanger Kiki."

"The welfare of all my staff is a priority," the tycoon answered shortly.

Vaughan saw movement to his left. He turned his head in time to see a quicksilver glint: a spider drone taking cover behind a stand of fungus. Once he'd seen the first, he quickly saw others, perhaps a dozen taking up positions on the perimeter of the valley where the two ships lay.

Then he saw members of Chandrasakar's security team; they were moving through the fungal stands like snipers, then settling themselves so that they had the area covered.

He wondered where the colonists might emerge; they had, after all, twenty-five years to familiarise themselves with the nature of the metamorphosing landscape. They had taken Namura and disappeared with stealth and cunning: he wondered if they would be equal to the tactics of Chandrasakar's security team and drones.

Chandrasakar's handset chimed. He answered with a barked, "Yes?"

It wasn't Namura this time, but a man's voice, high and accentless. "We're coming out. If any of you make a move – and that includes your drones – the girl is dead, understood?"

"Perfectly."

"We want free passage to the *Mussoree*–"

"And then…?" Chandrasakar said.

"We have technical experts, scientists and pilots. We're taking it back to Earth."

"Where you'll sell your secret to the FNSA?"

A hesitation. Then, "We *are* the FNSA. We're only doing what anyone else would do in the circumstances – consolidating our power."

Chandrasakar said, "The *Cincinnati*, I take it, is no longer spaceworthy?"

The colonist hesitated. "If it were, why the hell do you think we'd want the *Mussoree*?"

Vaughan thought the tycoon was stringing the colonist along, playing for time. No doubt security, or the drones, were pinpointing the source of the call.

"You were supposed to be a self-sufficient colony," Chandrasakar said. "Why couldn't you repair your ship? Let me guess… You're not the main body of colonists, right? You're a breakaway group, rebels. The others are opposed to what you're…"

"Chandrasakar," the colonist said with a threat in his voice, "shut it. We're coming out. We're well armed, and we've got the girl. If you try anything, she dies and a lot of your people with her."

"The *Mussoree* is yours," Chandrasakar said with apparent equanimity.

Vaughan stared around the plain, looking for movement; other than for the swaying polyp forest on the distant incline, all was still.

Movement, when it came, was sudden and all the more shocking for it. Half a dozen green men emerged as if by magic from the ground on the incline below the tall mushroom; their leader had an arm locked about Kiki Namura's neck, and a pistol lodged in the small of her back. His colleagues, all armed, surrounded him in a protective cordon.

They were not alone, Vaughan saw. He made out perhaps a dozen others, singly and in pairs as they emerged from slits and fissures in the fungal ground and hurried towards the *Mussoree*.

They were green, Vaughan realised now, by dint of the fact that they were covered from head to foot in a fine verdant powder, which made them at once alien and inhuman. A ludicrous touch was the ragged garments some of them wore, tattered shirts, shorts and vests; others were naked.

They moved quickly across the plain towards the *Mussoree*, Namura stumbling along with them, wide-eyed with fright.

Vaughan wanted to lower his handset, access his tele-ability and read the secret in the minds of the colonists, but at the same time knew better than to move.

He wondered what plan Chandrasakar had concocted. He knew that the tycoon would not let the colonists get away with the ship, but at the same time it would be difficult to disable the colonists and effect Namura's escape.

He glanced at McIntosh. The Australian looked distraught.

The first colonists were almost at the ramp of the *Mussoree* when the firing began.

Vaughan was unsure who started it. There was a movement from behind a stand of fungus to the right of the ship, and then a colonist fired. In the same instant he saw a second colonist fall on the perimeter of the plain, sectioned by laser fire.

Then the air was alight with criss-crossing laser beams and the whine of projectile missiles. He heard screams and curses and dived to the ground a second before a laser sheared over his head and dinned into the side of the *Kali*. Prone, he looked up and witnessed a scene of chaos. The plain was strewn with body parts and smeared blood, and the few colonists left standing were not going down without a fight. Quicksilver spider drones, flashing lasers, came out of cover and advanced with mechanical indifference, losing legs and armour as they went but advancing nevertheless, firing all the time and reducing the outlying colonists to so much ripped meat.

In the melee, Vaughan saw Kiki Namura go down. Her captor took a laser shot in the head, and made good his promise to take the biologist with him.

To Vaughan's right, McIntosh let out a cry and broke into a run towards where Namura lay.

Vaughan cried out and launched himself at the Australian. He tried to tackle him to the ground, but McIntosh dodged him and ran – straight into the path of a solid projectile.

Vaughan looked away, and gagged as a hot spray of ejected body fluid smacked him full in the chest. He hit the ground and stayed there.

Then, after all the hellish noise, the zizz of lasers, the hiss of projectiles, the screams and cries of the dying and the wounded, a sudden and awful silence settled over the scene, and Vaughan lifted his head and stared.

The stillness was what struck him first, the absolute unmoving tableau that seconds ago had been a seething pit. Even the drones, upright among the dead, had come to an unnatural halt, their duty done. Perhaps two dozen bodies littered the plain, not one of them in one piece; most were colonists, with one or two security personnel – along with McIntosh and Namura.

Vaughan picked himself up, surveyed the scene for a second, then limped across to where Namura lay face down beside the colonist. He knelt, reached out and touched the side of her pretty face, her staring eyes no longer wide with fright. The colonist's projectile had opened a hole the size of his fist through her back, and in the confusion a stray laser bolt had drilled her forehead. He told himself that she would have died instantly.

He was aware of movement all around, as security personnel came out of hiding and moved among the dead.

Then he saw Chandrasakar, fastidiously picking his way through the charnel debris towards him.

He had a terrible presentiment, then: the tycoon was about to return the necropath program and ask him to probe the minds of the dead colonists. Then he knew better. Chandrasakar would want to keep that secret, if indeed he possessed it, to himself.

The tycoon looked about him, an expression of mild revulsion on his well-fed face. "We couldn't let them have the ship," he said quietly to Vaughan, as if seeking exculpation.

Vaughan said nothing, but stood and looked around at the carnage.

Chandrasakar turned to his security personnel. "Get rid of the colonists. Gather our dead and place them in the ship. We'll arrange suitable ceremonies when the time is right."

His men moved among the dead, acceding to his command.

Vaughan gathered his thoughts and said, "You could have let them enter the ship; they might have kept their word and released Namura."

Chandrasakar looked at him, almost as if he were beneath his contempt. "When you are in a position of power, I have learned from experience, you do your utmost to maximise that power and not allow your opponents the slightest opportunity of gaining the upper hand."

Vaughan opened his mouth to argue that that ploy had cost an innocent woman her life, but restrained himself. He turned and walked towards the *Kali*. He saw, behind the elongated viewscreens that dotted the ship's flank, a gallery of shocked spectators. He wondered if Parveen Das was among them, and if she'd witnessed the slaughter.

FIFTEEN

A TERRIBLE COINCIDENCE

Parveen Das woke late, found the bed beside her empty, and vaguely recalled Rab getting up a couple of hours earlier. She'd had too many beers the night before, in the aftermath of Kiki Namura's abduction, and her head pounded as she sat up. She moved to the bathroom, drank a lot of water, then showered and dressed.

She couldn't face breakfast, but decided she could manage a coffee. She took the elevator-plate to the observation lounge, considering Vaughan and his actions yesterday. She still couldn't decide whether his racing after Kiki had been brave or foolish. She'd scanned him after the event, and read that he didn't know either. She supposed it was just the impulsive, selfless action of someone who cared about other people. He had been armed, but even so... Had Parveen been in his situation, she would have left well alone.

She entered the lounge and saw a group of scientists and crew gathered before the viewscreen, staring aghast and exclaiming. She hurried across the room and eased her way through the press. Many of the scientists were turning away, retching, but all Parveen could do was stare out in shock.

The scene between the starships was a battlefield strewn with lasered body parts. She made out the corpses of what appeared to be humans daubed in green – and then saw the remains of McIntosh and Namura.

But who were the green men? The aliens Vaughan had seen earlier?

She touched her handset and sent out a probe.

She came across a guttering consciousness on the cusp of death. The green men were not aliens, but FNSA settlers. She concentrated, at first reading only intense physical pain and the terrible awareness of approaching death; beyond, deeper, she caught fleeting images, desires. The colonists had been attempting to board the *Mussoree*, to get back to Earth to tell the FNSA about something they'd discovered underground... She concentrated, chasing the secret as the man died: she saw the image of what must have been an alien city, and then no more.

She withdrew her probe and moved on. Another colonist lay near the *Mussoree*, at the very limit of her range. She scanned, but this one was even further gone than the first. She read dwindling memories of vast underground caverns, of a rebel contingent fighting other colonists in brief skirmishes.

The man died, and she moved around the plain, searching in vain.

She probed a couple of security personnel within her range, getting through their partial mind-shields but reading nothing of significance: they had had orders from Singh to take out the colonists if they approached the *Mussoree*, which is exactly what they had done.

Then she read Vaughan, directly below her, and his mind was filled with grief and regret at the deaths of Namura and McIntosh.

Parveen quickly withdrew her probe and braced her arms against the padded rail, head hanging.

Namura and McIntosh...

She went back to the security guards and read them: they had had no orders to kill the FNSA pair, as far as she could detect. But what about the spider drones? Had they been ordered to take out the pair?

The question she wanted answering, the question she knew she must ask, was whether Rab had known that they had been spies. As she pushed herself from the rail and hurried from the lounge, she knew the answer: it could not be a coincidence that the FNSA plants had died in the fire-fight; therefore Rab must have sanctioned their killings.

Sickened, she took the elevator and dropped to the exit ramp. Rab was striding into the ship, a grey pallor suffusing his mocha complexion.

"Rab, we have to—"

"Not now, Parveen..." and he gestured feebly to the carnage outside.

"That's what I want to talk to you about."

He stopped, staring at her, then nodded briefly. "Very well. Let's go to..." and he gestured to the elevator plate.

They rode up in silence, Rab staring impassively at the passing bulkhead, Parveen's mind a whirl of supposition and the questions she needed to ask.

They stepped from the plate and she followed him to his suite.

He hurried over to the bar and poured himself a stiff brandy. He gestured with the bottle, inviting her.

She shook her head. "You didn't tell me, Rab."

He looked genuinely confused. "Tell you what?" He stood with his back to the bar. He appeared to be shocked at what had taken place.

She gestured. "The colonists." She'd start there, and work around to Namura and McIntosh. "You said nothing about the fact that an FNSA colony ship had landed here."

"Parveen–"

She went on, "I would have thought you might have trusted me that much."

"Parveen, there's a time and place for everything."

"And this is it. I want to know–"

"I mean," he said patiently, "that there's a time and place that would be safe to tell you about the colonists. And I judged that it wasn't on Earth, or aboard the *Kali*."

"Then *where*?" she asked incredulously.

"I was going to tell you when we'd left most of the scientists here and gone underground."

She blinked. "You don't trust your own...?" She stopped. He'd known about Namura and McIntosh, then. Something turned cold in her gut.

"In my position, Parveen, it pays to be cautious. But rest assured, I would have told just as soon as I judged it wise to do so."

She hardly heard his reassurances. "You knew about Namura and McIntosh, didn't you?"

It was Rab's turn to look surprised. "Meaning?"

"You knew," she said, "that they were FNSA plants."

He hardly missed a beat. "How did you know about them?"

She could hardly admit that she'd read them earlier. She gestured outside. "When McIntosh lay dying, I read it in his mind. He was a plant, though an unwilling one. He was coerced into turning traitor, but you probably know all about that." She stopped, staring at him, then said, "You had them killed, didn't you, Rab?"

He held her gaze, considering his words before replying. "Would you believe me if I said that, honestly, I didn't give the order that led to their deaths? I... I'm as shocked as you and everyone else at what happened. It was an accident, a coincidence."

She opened her mouth, but no words came. She wanted to believe him; more than anything she wanted to believe that the man she loved couldn't have been so cold and calculating as to so ruthlessly sanction the killing of two naïve and innocent people.

Impasse... A silence filled the room. They stared at each other.

Rab made a move. He very precisely placed his brandy on the bar, crossed the room and stood before her. He reached out, stroked a strand of hair from her cheek, and drew her to him.

She felt his warmth, and hated herself for mistrusting him.

"Parveen, please... I know it's hard. I know what

all the evidence suggests... but I'm not a monster, despite what your colleagues in India might suppose. The deaths of Kiki and David were a terrible coincidence."

She wanted to believe him, more than anything... She found herself nodding and sniffing back her tears.

She said, "The colonists wanted to get back to Earth, tell the FNSA about something they found down there."

"And that's why we'll be going underground soon."

"You don't know what the colonists discovered?"

He smiled. "Honestly, I don't know."

She held him. "Rab..." She looked up, pulled away. "If you'd let me in, let me read you, just for a second..."

He dashed her hopes. "Parveen, I promise that soon, very soon, I'll do that, okay? Very soon I'll let you share everything I know."

She could have gone on, argued, told him that if he loved her, truly, then he should have nothing to hide... But she desisted. She took what small comfort she could from his promise, and nodded.

Rab said, "Good. Now, how about a drink?"

She shook her head. "I... no. I need a little time alone to think things through, okay?"

He squeezed her hand. "I understand, Parveen," he said, and let her go.

She left the suite and took the elevator down to the observation lounge.

SIXTEEN

DEVELOPMENTS

Vaughan found Das slouched on a foam-form, nursing a drink. He fetched a beer from the bar and crossed to her. She looked up. Her eyes were red, as if she'd been crying.

Outside, the mopping-up operations were still going on – conducted, ironically, by the spider drones with just the same level of clinical efficiency as they'd employed during the slaughter.

"Mind if I join you?"

She shook her head. He sat down and watched her. She didn't look up.

He drank his own beer, and at last said, "I wonder if you could tell me something?"

She looked up, enquiring.

"I'd like to know who you're working for."

"What makes you think—?" she began.

"Look, I know you know more than you've told me, and I want to know where you stand in all..." he gestured towards the clean-up, "...all this."

She touched a control on her handset, looked at

him appraisingly for a while, then nodded. "First, tell me what *you* know about what happened, Jeff."

He regarded her, considering how much to tell her. "Okay. Kiki's abductors weren't natives, as we first thought. Apparently a colony ship landed here twenty-five years ago, sent out by the FNSA. They found something underground. They – or rather a faction of the original colonists, Chandrasakar thinks – wanted to get back to Earth so they can inform their government." He watched her, but she showed no surprise. He went on, "Chandrasakar effectively stopped their little plan, even if it did mean sacrificing Namura, McIntosh, and a couple of security personnel... If you didn't know before now, you lover is a scheming son-of-a-bitch who'd stop at nothing to get what he wants."

He thought she might bridle at this, but she regarded him evenly.

"Anyway, that's what I know."

"You're a truthful man, Jeff. You're also a good man."

Her words surprised him. He lowered his beer and looked at her. He recalled her touching the controls of her handset and staring at him. He had a sudden, awful suspicion.

She confirmed it. "You're not the only telepath aboard the *Kali*," she said.

He thought: my mind-shield, but even as the thought formed, she was smiling. "I corrupted your shield back on Earth, in the spaceport lounge. It's useless."

It was odd to be on the receiving end of a probe, to know that everything within his head, his innermost secrets and most private memories, were private no longer, that Das was reading him as he had these very thoughts.

Despite himself, he said, "I don't believe it."

She smiled. "You miss Sukara, Jeff. You miss her like hell. Even after six years, you're very much in love. And the sex is still great–"

"Don't–"

"She likes it best on her back, with you kneeling before her, gripping her ankles and spreading her..."

It was petty of him, but he couldn't stop himself. He threw the remains of her beer in her face and watched her splutter.

"Turn it off!"

Slowly, glaring at him, she complied. "Happy now?" She mopped her face with a napkin, smiling to herself.

He said, "There is a thing called honour, even among telepaths."

"You said you didn't believe me."

"So you've made your point."

She pulled her hair back and knotted the tresses behind her head. He looked for the jacks and ports in her occipital region with which all telepaths were implanted; oddly, she wasn't.

She saw him looking. "It'd be too obvious if I had the usual rig." She indicated her handset. "So everything is in here, routed sub-dermally up to my cerebellum."

He took a mouthful of beer, thinking things through. "Will you reciprocate," he said, "and turn off your shield? I'll promise not to read what you and Chandrasakar get up to in the sack."

She shook her head. "I can't let you in. I can't compromise my security. However, I'll keep my side of the bargain. I know all you know, so I'll come clean with you, okay?"

He nodded, opened his second bottle and said, "Okay. You're working for the Indian government, right?"

She inclined her head. "They recruited me while I was a post-grad at Kolkata. I was a willing convert. I've travelled the Expansion, feeding things back to them for the past ten years. Then... well, believe it or not I got involved with Rab before this mission came up."

"Do you know what's going on down there?"

"As far as I know the original colonists have split into two factions. The majority were against the dissemination of what they discovered beneath the surface of the planet; the minority – the green men – wanted nothing more than to get word back to the FNSA government on Earth."

"How do you know this?"

"I've only just found out about the colonists. I probed one of them out there."

"But your government knew about Chandrasakar's mission, right?"

She smiled. "Why do you think I'm here, Jeff?"

He considered this, then asked, "Do you think Chandrasakar knows what the colonists found?"

"I suspect so, which is why he's so focused on getting down there. He doesn't know if any other power bloc intercepted the signal, but he's taking no chances. He wants to get at whatever it is before the opposition sends out a ship."

He looked at her, a thought forming. "But do *you*

think the FNSA are on to it? Did they ever receive the communiqué?"

"I suspect so, yes." She hesitated, then said, "I also suspect it was the FNSA who sent the assassins to kill the telepaths. The FNSA don't have ships anywhere near the capability of Chandrasakar's. They wanted to slow him down, and so hired the assassins."

"Why didn't they just do what your people did, and plant someone aboard the *Kali*?"

She gave a grim smile. "They did."

He stared at her. "Don't tell me..."

She nodded. "I corrupted Namura's shield. She and McIntosh were working for the FNSA."

"So you went and told Chandrasakar, and he took the opportunity to wipe them out?"

"Of course not." She glared at him. "I didn't say a word to Rab. I decided to keep an eye on Namura and McIntosh myself." She paused. "For what it's worth, Rab swore that he didn't have them killed. He claimed they were killed in the crossfire."

Vaughan recalled what Chandrasakar had told him immediately after the killing. "And you've read him, verified this?"

She shook her head. "No, Rab is shielded."

"So am I, but that didn't stop you."

"I..." She hesitated, then went on, "I've held off trying to probe him."

He watched her, wondering at her reluctance to read the tycoon. He tried to keep the sarcasm from his tone as he asked, "So... he told you he had nothing to do with the death of two enemy agents down there, and you believe him?"

She looked genuinely pained, as if battling with conflicting desires. "Jeff... I want to believe him. I can't accept that he's the kind of person who'd–"

He interrupted. "Get real. You're a telepath. You've read minds, you know how things work. You don't get where Chandrasakar is without being ruthless and looking after your own interests."

She avoided his eyes and stared down at her beer. She looked abject, slouched there with her raw eyes and bitter expression.

"There is one more thing I'd like to know," he said. "Why are you levelling with me like this?"

She considered the question, staring through the viewscreen. After perhaps a minute, during which he thought she wasn't going to reply, she looked up and said, "I've been reading you, Jeff, on and off during the journey here."

"And getting off on my sex-life?"

She ignored that. "I wanted to know who you were, who you were working for, what you knew... and where your allegiances lay."

"And you no doubt found out all about me," he said.

She shrugged. "I read what happened back in Toronto, how the FNSA cut you, made you a necropath, how you did a runner and have been running ever since. I know you've no love for the FNSA–"

"Or, for that matter, for any other big organisation, government, company, you name it. They're all corrupt."

"But some," she said, "are more corrupt than others."

"You don't say? And who might the relatively

squeaky-clean guys be? Let me guess. Your lot, by any chance?"

She smiled. "Jeff, don't try to deny it. If you were to come down on any side in this, it'd be with us. You have... let's say... *leanings*."

"So what if I think what's happening in India is a little less corrupt and self-serving than what the FNSA and the rest are doing?"

"I think, when it comes down to it, you'd rather the Indians got their hands on whatever's down there."

"There's another option," he pointed out. "I might think that the original colonists got it right – that whatever is down there should remain hidden, secret."

"That, Jeff, surely depends on the exact nature of the secret, doesn't it?"

"That remains to be seen." He shrugged. "But you haven't answered my question. Why so open with me all of a sudden?"

She stared through the viewscreen at the plain between the two starships. He followed her gaze. The spider drones, having taken part in the slaughter, had done their bit in clearing it up; all that remained on the fungal plain were stark slicks of crimson.

"I've been thinking things through... since what Rab told me, after what I saw down there. The fact is, I don't know who to trust. I... I love Rab. I thought at first he wanted me along as a..." She faltered and smiled. "I know this might sound naïve of me, but I thought he wanted me along as a companion, a lover."

"And now?"

"Well, I am a xenologist, after all."

"Meaning?"

She shrugged. "It would explain why he wanted me along on this trip, if the colonists had found an alien race down there."

"But he hasn't told you as much?"

"That's another thing he's keeping close to his chest." She looked up from her bottle. "Anyway, when I read you... Look, I read that I can trust you, okay? The fact is, I want to trust Rab as well, but... I must face the possibility that he's using me for no other reason than I'm his tame telepath."

He thought about it. He had to be cautious. He wasn't a hundred per cent sure he could trust the woman. "So... what do you suggest?"

"We stick together, look out for each other; pool information – and be very, very wary."

"Of Chandrasakar?"

Her expression was pained. "Perhaps. But also of his security personnel. Singh in particular has it in for me."

He regarded the dregs of his beer, lips pursed.

"Well, what do you say?"

He thought he had nothing to lose. He would play along with Das until he knew exactly where he stood with the woman. "Okay, but we've got to be careful. And you do hold one hell of an advantage over me. I'd trust you more if you'd drop your shield."

She shook her head. "Can't do that, Jeff."

Through the viewscreen he saw a flier bank in from the left and land between the two ships. He recognised the vehicle as the one that had set off earlier that morning, though now only one blue-uniformed security man occupied the vehicle. A single silver spider drone, like an old-fashioned hubcap, barnacled its flank.

Das's handset chimed and she accepted the call. Vaughan saw Chandrasakar's cherubic face fill the tiny screen.

He looked out, down onto the plain. Chandrasakar was standing beside the flier, speaking with the pilot.

"Parveen," Chandrasakar said. "There have been developments. My men have found an entrance leading underground, close by what's left of the *Cincinnati* in the mountains north of here. We're packing up and making our way there."

Das glanced at Vaughan and raised her eyebrows.

Chandrasakar continued, "Will you find Vaughan and tell him to gather his belongings? We'll be heading north in an hour."

Vaughan finished his beer, curious about why the tycoon might want him along.

Das cut the connection and looked across at him. "Well, you heard the man. I've got a feeling that the next few days might prove interesting."

SEVENTEEN

DESCENT

He sat in the rear of the flier and stared down at the land passing far below.

It was late in the day and the fungal landscape had taken on a burnt orange hue; as he watched, vast sections of land moved slowly, hunched itself, or sprouted new shoots and tendrils. It was, he thought, like looking down on a cooking pot full of some bizarre algae simmering in slow motion.

The colony ship, according to Chandrasakar, was a thousand kilometres north of where the *Kali* had come down, and Vaughan judged that they had flown most of that distance by now. They had passed actual mountain ranges on their flight, great ragged razors of grey rock cutting up through the ubiquitous fungus, and at one point they overflew a lake nestling in what looked like a high volcanic caldera, its neat circlet of crimson water a stark contrast to the surrounding grey rock formations.

He sat next to Das, while two security personnel occupied the front seats. In the leading flier, Chandrasakar was accompanied by Singh and Pavelescu. Three further fliers were following, carrying the scientists, more security men, and spider drones.

Das touched his arm. "There."

He looked down at where she was pointing and saw the remains of the *Cincinnati*. The ship had come to rest in a deep valley bottom, its superstructure patched by a voracious fungal growth and blackened by fire.

"Looks as if it crash-landed," he said.

"I don't think so. I suspect it was cannibalised in the early days."

"And the fire damage?"

She frowned. "Pass. Perhaps something to do with the conflict between the colonists and the rebels?"

He wondered at the thoughts of the colonists on first seeing this unique landscape; to think that this would be home, to be made the best of, for the rest of their lives... At journey's end, colonists desired something similar to what they had left behind on Earth, some Eden-analogue to help them forget how far away they were from home. This landscape was about as alien as it was possible to be, and yet still be habitable.

They flew on for about a kilometre to where the foothills of the mountain range rose above the encroaching fungus, buckling higher and higher. Minutes later they came down in a mesa free of fungal growth. A hundred metres away an angled crack, fifty metres high, split the mountainside.

Vaughan climbed from the flier, stretching tired limbs, and walked over to where Chandrasakar was addressing his security personnel and the half dozen scientists. The tycoon indicated the rent in the rock behind him.

"My team found steps chiselled into the cliff-face beneath the opening, and more inside," he was saying. "The colonists, we suspect, live underground. It's our mission to locate them and establish friendly relations. It's unfortunate that our initial meeting was with a group of – we suspect – rebels who wanted to get away from the planet." He looked around the gathering. "Any questions?"

A scientist asked, "If the FNSA has settled Delta Cephei VII, then where does the Chandrasakar Organisation stand in the scheme of things?"

"The precise status of the colony has yet to be determined, hence this sortie," Chandrasakar said. "It might be that the colonists wish for independence, in which case we might find ourselves with room for... negotiations."

The meeting broke up, and Chandrasakar crossed to Vaughan. "A word about why I wanted you to accompany us, Jeff."

Vaughan said, "As I recall, the agreement was that I'd read the engineer."

The Indian smiled and gestured with a placatory hand. "Rest assured that hers is the last dead mind I'll ask you to probe."

"But live minds is another question?"

"You will be invaluable in locating the colonists down there, Jeff. It's a big place, and the old needle in a haystack metaphor applies here. I'll ensure that your work is amply rewarded when we return to Earth."

Vaughan nodded, playing along with the tycoon. He suspected that Chandrasakar wanted him along so that he could keep an eye on him. He had one other telepath on his team, after all. Unless, of course, Chandrasakar didn't trust Das.

"And Das?" Vaughan asked.

Chandrasakar looked at him. "What about her?"

"She's a xenologist. What's her role in all of this?"

The tycoon gestured to the world at large. "This is an alien planet, Jeff. I need someone with us with her expertise on the off chance we happen across a sentient extraterrestrial species." He glanced up at Vaughan, as if wondering whether he'd buy it.

Vaughan nodded. "Do you think that likely?"

"In my experience, Jeff, it's wise to be ready for all eventualities, however unlikely."

The tycoon crossed to where the scientists were unloading their packs from the fliers. Vaughan found a rock and sat down. He would call Sukara and tell her about the starship, and that soon they would be venturing underground; he would omit mention of the slaughter and the sickening political intrigue.

He tapped in the code and anticipated seeing Sukara; he felt a tightness in his chest at the thought of Li and how her treatment might be progressing.

He judged the time on Bengal Station would be around eight in the evening, but Sukara failed to answer his call. He told himself not to worry; he'd try again later, when they were underground. The rock would provide no barrier to the voidspace communication program.

Despite himself, he worried.

He looked up and saw Das watching him, an expression of pity on her face. Ignoring her, he crossed to the fliers and collected his backpack containing food and water rations.

Chandrasakar and Singh set off up the hillside, followed by a dozen security personnel and the six scientists; Das and Vaughan brought up the rear. A dozen prancing spider drones, their foot-pads rattling on the stone, went fore and aft.

It was a short climb to the cliff-face, and then a longer one up the twisting flight of a hundred or so steps to the opening. Five minutes later they stepped under an over-arching cowl of grey rock, moving from the full glare of the sun to a disconcerting half-light. Vaughan blinked; it was ten seconds before his vision adjusted and he made out the enclosing walls. The opening widened out, becoming a high cave, which narrowed again into blackness. They were equipped with flashlights, which illuminated a narrow pathway leading, at the back of the cave, to a square opening, cut with geometric precision. Steps led down into the bowels of the planet.

With the absence of sunlight, the temperature plummeted. Vaughan was grateful for his insulated one-piece suit.

Chandrasakar sent a couple of drones ahead, then followed. A minute later, with everyone else having processed themselves through the narrow opening, Vaughan followed Das down a narrow flight of precarious steps. They descended for about ten minutes, and then the steps ended; Vaughan heard gasps from up ahead.

They were in a cavern, easily the size of the *Kali*, a chamber whose walls were adorned with glowing fungus. One by one they switched off their flashlights, and it was as if the natural illumination brightened in compensation: the cavern was filled with a pulsing verdant light. Vaughan moved off to one side, reached out and touched the wall. His fingers came away green, and he understood now the colouration of the colonists. He wondered whether the fungus was an adornment they had chosen themselves, or an infection – or infestation – they had had thrust upon them along with the troglodyte lifestyle they had been forced to adopt.

The party set off again, moving in single file along a path, which skirted the edge of the cavern.

Vaughan enabled his tele-ability and made out the mind-shield static before him. He caught up with Das and said, "Are you reading?" He was more than a little uncomfortable at the thought.

She nodded. "And have been since we landed."

They were walking side by side; her dark face was made sickly by the fungal light.

She said, "I know it's painful, being away from Sukara, with Li ill. You have my sympathy, for what it's worth."

Painful, he thought, doesn't describe it.

"I..." she said. "I don't often read true love, Jeff. I read people who kid themselves, or who think they've found it, but what you feel for Sukara..."

It was impossible to keep visions of his wife from his head; who she was now, the kid she had been when they first met.

"She saved my life," he said, "and needed someone."

"And is a good person," Das finished.

He nodded, and formed a question. Before he could articulate it, Das said, "No, I haven't. I haven't had a lover for years. And then Rab came along..."

"It's strange..." he began.

"... having someone read your every thought," she finished. "The tables are turned. The telepath is the subject. I can read your every thought, access your every emotion, your every memory, far, far back... I look into your head and I know you, Jeff."

Disturbing, he thought.

"You're a different person, did you know that?"

"To who I was years ago, before Sukara?"

She smiled. "You were one sad, cynical bastard back then. That said, you had every reason to be."

"I wish you'd turn that thing off," he said. If I probe any little green men, he thought, I'll let you know.

"Okay," she said, reached to her handset and killed the program.

They walked for a while in silence; they were approaching the end of the cavern, where it whittled down to form a tunnel still twice the height of a man. The green fungus followed the contours of the wall like the skin of a reptile, glowing eerily.

They entered the corridor behind the others, and the floor beneath their feet began a gradual downward slope. The nearest scientist was perhaps five metres ahead.

Vaughan said, "The others in Chandrasakar's team? Have you used your viral program on them, too?"

"Singh has protection I can't overcome," Das told him. "For obvious reasons. The others... what they know isn't considered priority by Chandrasakar."

"So you've read them? How much has he told them?"

She glanced across at him, her eyes unreadable dark pits in her lit face. "None of them know that the colonists have discovered something. I suspect he's let Singh in on it. He and Singh are like this." She crossed two fingers. "And it'd make sense to clue in your head of security."

"So as far as the others are concerned, this is all about contacting the colonists?"

She nodded. "There's a sociologist in the team, a psychologist, as well as the more obvious specialisms. Geologists and mineralogists, to assess the planet's potential worth."

They walked in silence for a while. He wondered how long the trek might take; how long before the colonists came into range, and along with them their secret?

A thought occurred to him. "What are the chances that Chandrasakar would have another telepath on his team?"

She pursed her lips. "It's a possibility."

"You said you couldn't read Singh," he said. "What if he's a telepath?"

She shook her head. "My people checked his history. He's a security expert, and nothing more." She grunted a humourless laugh. "If there was the slightest chance of his being Chandrasakar's pet telepath, Jeff, you don't think I'd've come clean with you, do you?"

"Of course not," he said.

Unless, he thought, she and Singh were *both* Indian spies...

He was glad she wasn't reading now, though it didn't really matter. When she next probed, she'd read his suspicion about her and Singh; she'd read that he trusted her about as much as he trusted Chandrasakar.

She had a massive advantage over him – and one that he could do nothing about.

The corridor descended more steeply now; in some places the descent was so steep that steps had been hewn in the rock. They descended, and the muscles in Vaughan's legs set up a painful ache in protest.

He said, "His team, the scientists and techs... they're all loyal to the Chandrasakar Organisation?"

She nodded. "All one hundred per cent Chandrasakar men and women. They've been with him years. He treats them well, and they respond. Almost Pavlovian," she said. Then, "Why do you ask?"

He shrugged. "Just wondering if we might have any allies when the crunch comes."

"Don't rely on anyone else. It's you and me against the universe."

He turned, wondering if a spider drone was behind them. The corridor was empty.

They walked on in silence for a while.

A few minutes later Das said, "Ganesh, but I thought life as a Saharan Bedouin was extreme."

He looked at her. "Meaning?"

"Human beings," she mused. "They adapt to anything. We live on ice caps, in deserts. There's a colony out Sigma Draconis way, they declared independence twenty years ago and don't like visitors. They live on islands of floating vegetation that's the sole food of a cetacean, which the humans in turn prey upon. They have no government as such, and in their society everyone is equal who can hunt for food. Those who can't are summarily and ceremonially drowned. They're post-industrial by now, of course. Been there a hundred years."

He glanced at her. "Sounds like they live some kind of egalitarian ideal. I'm surprised you haven't shacked up with them."

"Watch it, Vaughan," she said. "Anyway, I was just wondering what we'll find when we happen across the colonists. They must have adapted in many odd ways."

Vaughan scanned ahead, came across twenty areas of mind-shield static, and nothing more.

"No sign of anything yet," he reported.

They walked on.

Perhaps an hour later the corridor opened out again, sloped, and dropped into another vast cavern.

Ahead, he heard Chandrasakar give the order to set up camp for the night. It was late, by Vaughan's reckoning well past sunset, and for the first time he realised how tired and hungry he was.

He and Das entered the cavern and dropped their backpacks.

"Hey," a scientist called out. "Come and look at this!"

EIGHTEEN

LOYALTIES

Parveen joined the procession around the cavern walls, examining the bas-relief carvings, but she found it hard to summon the requisite measure of wonder which everyone else seemed to be exhibiting. Intellectually she knew what the panels meant – the sequence of frames showing stick-shaped humanoids with domed heads was the first indication that an alien race was, or had been, native to the planet – but she was more preoccupied with the course of recent events, and how they might impinge on her.

She still couldn't decide how she felt about Rab; her heart wanted nothing more than to abandon herself to him, to trust his reassurances, but she knew there was always the possibility that he might very well be using her to his own ends. Was this why she had so impulsively divulged what she knew to Vaughan? She knew she could trust him, and sooner or later she might very well be in need of an ally.

Now another thought assailed her. Something that Vaughan had asked on the way down: might Singh be a telepath?

According to the information on the data-pin compiled by her controller, Anil Singh was nothing more than what he appeared: a steroid-abusing thug with an over-developed pride in his ability to maim... But what if party intelligence had got it wrong, and he was a telepath? It would make sense for Rab to have an in-house telepath loyal to him.

What sickened her was the thought that if he were a telepath, then her shield might not be up to the task of baffling his probes. What if he'd read her every thought, her recent conversations with Vaughan, and reported back to his boss?

She glanced across the cavern. Singh had made the rounds of the frescoes like a bored visitor at a museum, and was now back with his team, setting up camp and breaking out rations around a heater; they had encamped together in a small group apart from the rest of the expedition.

She looked across the cavern at Rab. He was deep in discussion with a group of scientists. Later, she decided suddenly, she would do what she had been too scared of doing before now, and try to invade his shield, even though she suspected she'd fail.

"What do you make of them?"

She jumped, then laughed nervously. Vaughan stood beside her, gazing at the carvings.

"Well, they're certainly not the work of the colonists," she said, fatuously.

He smiled. "I came to that conclusion myself." He reached out, traced his fingers around the out-line of a stick figure. "I wonder how the first meeting between the colonists and the aliens went? I wonder if they're a friendly race?"

She smiled. "Most alien races that we've met are, Jeff. Gone are the days of the stereotypical idea of the alien as the hostile other. Only the Merth have been vaguely inimical, and that was because of an initial misunderstanding." She looked at the dome-headed, almost amphibian-seeming figures. "Of course, these carvings are old. They might be the work of a race now extinct. Conditions are harsh here, to say the least."

He nodded. "Anyway... I came over to see if you were hungry." He gestured to where the main group had deposited backpacks and bedrolls. He'd set up a heater and broken out the self-heating food trays.

"Famished. What's on the menu?"

They crossed to the camp and sat down, Vaughan handing her a tray. "Dal baht or lamb masala." He shook his head. "The Chandrasakar Organisation spares no expense."

They snapped the seals on the trays and ate the dhal.

She hoped the conversation wouldn't come round to the topic of security again: she didn't want him quizzing her about the status of Singh, and working out that she'd been less than tactful in seeking him as an ally – even though she'd been at a low ebb at the time.

Thankfully he asked her about herself. "I'm intrigued–" he began.

"By?" she asked.

"By people like you," he said.

"How many thirty-something commie xenologist

telepaths have you met, Mr Vaughan?"

He smiled and forked dal and rice into his mouth. "I mean, people consumed with an over-riding belief system."

"You make me sound like some religious fundamentalist–"

He gestured with his fork. "You said it, Parveen."

She looked at him. "You're serious, aren't you? Listen, religious belief is nothing more than superstition, though some might call it faith: it's the same thing. My set of beliefs are based on a rational analysis of the socio-economic state of the modern world."

He shrugged. "As far as I'm concerned, and I've read enough people to make a case, political beliefs and religious faith are the same in this respect: they make for an intolerant mind-set that doesn't allow the admission for the possibility of error, or that the other view might possibly have credence."

She shook her head, containing her anger. "But I know that the only way forwards for the human race–"

He shrugged. "Say no more, Parveen." He was smiling to himself.

She ate for a while in silence, then said, "Rather my certainties, and the possibility of good that might accrue for my fellow man, than your apathy. That's one thing I didn't like about you from what I read."

"Apathy. You're not the first person to have pointed that out."

She looked at him. "And how do you feel about that?"

"I couldn't give a damn one way or the other

what other people think about me," he said, but she saw that he had the grace to smile.

"Your anti-intellectual stance is as self-centred and insular as the intolerance you deplore in those with definite beliefs."

He cocked an eye at her. "You think so? That's interesting. But you see, I've read so many minds that I think I've learned something about my fellow man. And that is, they all think they're right on some deep, fundamental level, no matter how wrong they might be. I might give my trust to individuals, because their solipsism is manageable, but as far as organisations and political parties are concerned..."

"You think of yourself as an anarchist."

He laughed, without humour. "There you go again. Why the eagerness to label people? I think of myself as Jeff Vaughan, husband of Sukara and father to Pham and Li. My loyalties end there."

She looked at him. "I don't know whether to think of you as one deluded bastard, or supremely fortunate."

"Just think of me as Jeff Vaughan, husband and father, and leave it there, okay? You've read my mind. You know that's all that matters to me."

She continued eating. "You know, I'd like to meet Sukara someday. I'd like to read her, read the goodness you see in her." She looked up. "Have you read her?"

"You've been in here." He tapped his head. "Didn't you read it?"

"No, not that. There was so much..."

He shook his head. "When I first met her, I wasn't reading, but I picked up her goodness."

"And you've never been tempted to...?"

"No. I promised her. Anyway, I know her well enough not to need to pry. I know and love her."

She nodded. After a moment she murmured, "I... I wish I could read Rab."

"Well, it'd make things here a bit easier."

"No, I mean... for personal reasons. I'd like to read what he thinks about me."

He stopped eating and regarded her. "You really fell for him, didn't you?"

She smiled. "Who would have thought it? Card-carrying party member falls head-over-heels for filthy capitalist exploiter."

"I'm sorry. It must be painful. The conflict."

She looked up. "Anybody would have thought you'd read me."

"I don't need to probe to see that you were lonely before he came along, that part of you regrets letting your heart rule your head when you met him."

"Jeff, I've always lived up here, tried to rationalise my loneliness–"

"But we're all slaves to the tyranny of our biology," he said.

"You seem to have done okay by it."

He shrugged. "It takes time," he said. "I went through years of not letting myself get close to people, in my case for fear of getting hurt. Then, the big cliché, the right person came along."

He reached out and squeezed her hand. "But hey, who's to say we haven't got Rab wrong? He might by the altruist people think he is..."

"Yeah, and he might love me too, hm?"

They scraped their trays clean and Vaughan settled down on his bedroll, linking his fingers behind his head and gazing up at the green vault overhead.

She looked around the cavern. "I'm not at all tired. Too much going on up here... I'm going to see what Rab's found out from his scientists."

"See you in the morning," Vaughan said, yawning.

She stood. Rab had left the group of scientists who were examining the frescoes and moved off to stand by himself, gazing at the images.

She crossed the cavern, enabling her tele-ability, and joined him.

"Parveen... how are you and Vaughan getting along?"

She tried to judge his tone, detect jealousy. It seemed absent: he was enquiring with professional interest in mind. "Fine, Rab. He's just glad to have got reading the engineer out of the way."

"We can trust him?"

She smiled at the royal 'we'. "He has no political loyalties, no axes to grind."

He smiled and returned to the inspection of the frescoes. "Rab..." she hesitated, then went on, "You didn't tell me about the aliens. You knew, didn't you? I would have thought..." She tried not to sound like a hurt little girl.

"Parveen, I've said it before. Security."

"You did know?"

"The communiqué from the rebel colonists made some mention... but it was garbled. Let's just say that I suspected."

"I wish you could have trusted me enough to tell me that," she said. On impulse she reached out and touched his hand. A second later she felt the metacarpal itch as the virus made the transit.

She pulled away and looked at him. "Will you tell me this, at least," she murmured. "What do you feel about me?"

He smiled and took her hand. "How many more times do you want the reassurance, Parveen? Anything I don't tell you is because of reasons of security. Not because I don't trust you, but because I'm suspicious of betrayal by those close to me."

She looked at him, and surprised herself by saying, "Like Singh?"

"Anil? No, of course not. I have utmost faith in him."

She sent out a probe. She encountered the static of his shield, an abstract hiss where his mind should be. Then, minimally and fleetingly, she did read something: it was almost too tenuous to detect. The virus had broken through briefly, even though his defences were working hard to rebuild themselves.

She read a flash of impatience with her, as much as a father might feel towards a child – but did she also detect a father's love, she wondered? The contact was too transitory to tell; she probed deeper.

She was taking a chance, of course. If his defences alerted him to her viral attack, as Singh's had done, then she would merely claim that she was attempting to read what he felt for her.

She said, "Tell me, Rab. Is Singh a telepath?"

Not only did she want his verbal assurances that Singh was not telepathic, but she wanted an accompanying flash of mentation from the tycoon that would confirm it, and ease her fears.

"Anil? A telepath? No, of course not. Where on earth did you get that notion?"

She probed, and caught something, very deep and

very faint: Rab's ultimate trust in Singh, and his belief that his chief of security was not a telepath.

Of course, she thought – that didn't rule out the possibility that the security chief was telepathic.

She smiled and squeezed his hand. "Rab, I'm just looking out for you, okay?"

He reached out and touched her cheek. "Parveen, that's sweet. But I assure you that I can trust Anil, ah-cha?"

She withdrew her probe and, when Rab had turned back to the frescoes, disabled her psi-program.

She left Rab and crossed to the camp, frustrated that her probes had done nothing to allay her apprehension.

Not only that, but she had failed to detect if Rab felt the slightest affection for her.

She was assailed, then, by another disturbing thought: if Singh were a telepath, but hadn't reported her deception to his boss... then might he be keeping the knowledge to himself for ulterior reasons?

Vaughan was asleep. She considered trying to sleep herself, but her mind was too active. Instead she crossed to the scientists huddled around a heater and joined in their lively speculation.

NINETEEN

EXTRATERRESTRIALS

Vaughan woke suddenly.

He blinked up at the green, momentarily confused and wondering where he was. Then it came to him in a rush. He was a kilometre or more underground on Delta Cephei VII, and the green vaulting above him was the luminescent fungi. He sat up and accessed the chronometer on his handset: he had been asleep for just over six hours.

He struggled from his padded sleeping bag and stood up.

A group of scientists huddled before the wall-frescoes a few metres away, chatting; their voices must have woken him.

He joined them. "Definitely alien?"

Last night, dog-tired, Vaughan had given the frescoes a cursory inspection before eating and turning in. They'd certainly looked alien to his inexpert eye. The scientists, being scientists, considered that on balance the likelihood was that they were perhaps extraterrestrial in origin...

Now a stout grey-haired Thai woman in her fifties was certain. "Without a doubt. Look at this."

She indicated a line of engravings, set out after the fashion of a cartoon strip, showing a series of primitive, dome-headed stick figures going about their alien business; they were carrying what looked like amphorae and long sticks. Vaughan was not surprised that the figures accorded to default humanoid proportions: a head, two arms and two legs. Ninety-five per cent of the aliens discovered so far in humankind's expansion were similarly humanoid.

Other scientists were filming the frescoes and taking measurements with sophisticated com-apparatus.

"My guess is that these carvings are in the region of fifteen thousand years old, maybe more." She ran her fingertips lightly across their surface, smiling to herself.

He moved off, looking at the stick figures carved around the time humankind were painting the caves at Lascaux.

"So, Jeff, Delta Cephei VII does have sentient alien natives." Parveen Das stood next to him, yawning.

He said, "This puts a whole different perspective on Chandrasakar's plans for the planet. No more grabbing this alien real estate as part of the Expansion."

"Always assuming the natives aren't extinct," she pointed out.

"Assuming that, yes," he agreed.

"But the colony planet isn't what he wants to grab, is my guess. It's the secret – the alien secret? – he's after."

Vaughan nodded, wondering what the secret might be.

"While you were snoring last night, we got into a lively debate about the Ee-tees," Das said. "We didn't arrive at any firm conclusions, but the speculation was interesting."

"Speculation?"

"For instance, did the aliens achieve industrial, scientific, technological standards? Did they attain spaceflight? My guess is that they didn't. The nature of their world means they're a subterranean people, who venture to the surface – if at all – only for brief periods when the surface temperature is clement. So their scientific inquiry might not be directed towards the stars."

"They might not even have attained technology," he said.

She shrugged. "It's impossible to tell, until we go deeper, find out more. Who's to say they're still around? Look at all the extinct races we've discovered the remains of in our travels."

He thought about it. "To discover, maybe meet, an alien race for the first time..."

"Anyway," Das said, "How about some food?"

Back at the camp, the others were up and breakfasting. Vaughan and Das joined them and sat together, eating eggs and beans from pre-packed trays.

He wrapped his hands around a cup of self-heating coffee. For all his padded suit, he was still feeling the chill this far underground.

Chandrasakar moved across to them. "This is where the party splits," he said. "It's as good a place as any. The scientists, with the exception of

Parveen, are staying here to continue their research. Six security personnel and four drones will remain with them. The three of us, with Singh, six security men and six drones, will continue onwards."

Vaughan looked at the squat Indian as he spoke; he wondered what was going on behind those eyes; what plans, what greed.

"Do you think we'll find who carved those frescoes?"

Chandrasakar looked at him. "It would be a remarkable experience if we did."

"Even though it might rule out claiming the world as a potential colony?"

He could see that Chandrasakar was keeping tight control on his irritation. "There is more to our expansion than mere territorial claims," he said.

He watched the tycoon closely as he asked, "Did you know about the aliens when you set up the expedition?"

Chandrasakar considered the question, and Vaughan was surprised by his reply. "I'll be candid with you, Jeff. The communiqué we intercepted did mention them."

"Did the colonists say if they were still around?"

Chandrasakar shook his head. "They didn't. That's one of the reasons we're here," he went on. "The push for knowledge is an oddly nebulous pursuit, my friend. Who knows from where benefits to humanity might accrue?"

Vaughan looked away. There were times when he found the little Indian insufferably smug, and he didn't know whether the best reaction would be to laugh or to condemn.

"Right." Chandrasakar turned and addressed his

team. "Let's pack up and head off, everyone."

They set off five minutes later, leaving behind them the vast frescoed cavern and dropping through the rock by means of a narrow tunnel. Singh and a couple of drones led the way, followed by Chandrasakar and three security men. Two further security personnel, Vaughan noted, took up the rear this time. He wondered if this were an intentional ploy on Chandrasakar's part, to keep an eye, and perhaps an ear, on him and Das.

"Did you know Chandrasakar knew about the aliens?" he asked Das.

She considered his question, before nodding. "He admitted as much to me only last night."

Vaughan smiled and grunted a humourless laugh.

She looked at him. "And what does that mean?"

"It means, I wonder what else he's keeping from us?"

She shrugged and looked ahead.

He enabled his tele-ability and probed. Only the mind-shields were evident. He decided to keep the program running on the off chance that it might warn him of the approach of any extraterrestrials.

The corridor dropped, wending its way through a natural fissure in the rock, and the party dropped with it into the depths of the planet.

Three hours later the corridor levelled and opened out into a long chamber; a worn track ran the length of the wall to their left, and Vaughan thought of it being used over millennia by beings making forays to the surface of the planet.

Up ahead, one of the guards said, "What the hell...?"

He was a hundred metres ahead and kneeling beside a natural gully in the rock that crossed the cavern floor and veered to run parallel with the track. The gully was about three metres wide and brimming with a crimson, viscous substance, which flowed in a rapid, muscular torrent.

In the distance Vaughan watched as the guard dipped the tip of his laser into the steam; it came away dripping slow liquid globules.

It was then, shocking in its unexpectedness, that Vaughan felt the first odd stirrings of something other than the mind-shields in his head.

He looked at Das, touching his temple. "I'm getting something."

She stabbed her handset.

He probed, and he knew then that the aliens of this planet were not extinct. He made out, perhaps a hundred metres ahead, a dozen slithery signatures of minds not human. Their thoughts were unreadable, their emotions and memories mere abstractions.

"Rab!" Das yelled. "Aliens!"

The security personnel dashed ahead, followed by the drones. The two following guards eased past them and gave chase. Vaughan and Das followed along the path towards a narrow fissure in the rock. The aliens, by his reckoning, were beyond the fissure and moving rapidly away. He wondered if they had been disturbed by the unexpected arrival of Chandrasakar and his team, and were beating an alarmed retreat, or if they had been expecting the humans and were leading them towards...

He never finished the thought. He and Das were bringing up the rear of the group, separated by about twenty metres, when he sensed an alien mind-signature in his head and glimpsed sudden movement to his right. Two sleek green figures, moving fast, leapt from the crimson river, grabbed him and pulled him into the fluid before he could resist. He heard Das scream briefly as she too hit the river.

He expected the shock of water, and received instead another surprise. The warm, cloying sensation gripped him and dragged him beneath the surface and along at an alarming rate. Later he wondered how he was able to breath; he must have been submerged for minutes, and yet never once felt the panic of suffocation. It was as if his mouth and nose were covered by a permeable membrane which allowed the passage of air.ß

He felt what might have been hands on his body, pushing him here and there, as if steering him at speed downstream. All was darkness. The only sensation was the odd invasive pressure of the rubber-like medium that had captured him as he tumbled head over heel.

He tried to cry out, but either his mouth failed to make the sound, or any sound he did make was muted by the fluid. He wondered if Das were reading his frantic mind, and hoped that, wherever the aliens might be taking him, they would be taking her too.

He sent out a probe, but found nothing. He attempted to locate the alien minds. The bizarre thing was that, despite the fact that he could still feel the occasional proddings from his alien abductors, he was unable to make out their abstract signatures. It was as if the viscous medium of the fluid were acting as a barrier, which would explain how the aliens had been able to come alongside him and Das in the stream and leap out unnoticed until the very last second.

And this made him think that their abduction – however fantastical this notion might be – had been intentional.

It was hard to judge the passage of time; long minutes seemed to elapse, though it might have been seconds or even an hour. He was locked into a tumbling darkness, with only the warm envelopment of the fluid and the infrequent prods of the aliens to stimulate his senses. He entered into a kind of audio-visual deprivation; deaf and blind, he had only his tactile sense with which to order his impressions of what might be happening. At times he seemed to be tumbling, limbs flailing, while at others he was drilling through the fluid like a torpedo.

Then, with a sudden change in routine that came as a shock, he was falling. A moment later he fetched up painfully against what he assumed was a wall of rock. The fluid drained from around him, and he heard a grunt and felt Das's limbs fall across his body seconds later. He struggled upright, extricating himself from the Indian, and looked around.

They were in a natural sink-hole, with a circular opening at his feet through which the fluid had presumably drained. He looked up and made out a circle of green light high above. The walls of the natural prison extended two metres above his head, as effective as any purpose-built oubliette.

He touched his shoulder, realising that at some point he'd parted company with his backpack.

Das climbed to her feet, panting. She looked at him. "What?"

"My pack. It's gone."

She peered behind her. "Mine too."

Only then did Vaughan notice her right arm.

Her handset was covered by what looked like a splint of crimson rubber.

Alarmed, he looked at his own arm. His handset was similarly encased in the fluid – except, he found, it was no longer fluid but had hardened into a solid, impermeable cast.

Das was staring down at her arm, her expression horrified.

His tele-ability had been enabled, but when he probed now he came across nothing – neither the alien minds nor Das's mind-shield.

"Clever," he said. "Very clever. We're dealing with creatures who know what they're doing."

"They've deliberately disabled our tele-programs?"

"As effectively as chopping off our arms, only more humanely, if you can say that about aliens. They've also stopped us from communicating with the others." He paused. "And the way they singled us out…"

"What the hell do they want with us?" She stared up at the roof of arching green fungus high above.

He touched his jacket; he was still armed with his laser. Das saw him checking, and did the same. She pulled out a small laser. "Me too. They didn't disarm us. More fool them."

"My guess is that they didn't bother to take our weapons on purpose."

"What are you driving at?"

"I think they don't mean us harm. They're friendly." He paused, then said, "I think they took the two of us for a reason."

"What if you're wrong? What if they simply didn't know about our weapons? What if they're not friendly, but mean us harm?"

"I don't now why, but I don't get that impression."

"Well, I hope to hell you're right." She stared down at the crimson shell covering her handset. "Wish they'd left this operable. I feel like half a person without it." She paused, then said, "I wonder how they knew that these control our tele-ability?"

He shook his head and said, "Another mystery to add to all the others." He smiled to himself.

She looked at him. "What?" she snapped.

"It has its advantages," he said. "My thoughts are my own, for once."

She looked away, examining the walls of their prison, searching in vain for hand- and foot-holds.

For however long the handsets were disabled, he thought, he was on an equal footing with her. The knowledge was reassuring. More troubling was the fact that with his handset disabled he would be unable to contact Sukara.

She hunkered down across the well from him. "I wonder what happened to Rab and the others?"

"Probably still chasing shadows."

"I wish I knew where they were."

He nodded. He could imagine her frustration, and her fear. Their imprisonment would allow Chandrasakar a chance to discover whatever secret the colonists had found down here. Her pay-masters wouldn't be best pleased if his mission succeeded while Das languished in alien custody.

He said, "Don't worry, whatever the colonists came across, it more than likely had something to do with the aliens."

"Meaning?"

"Meaning, we're probably closer to the secret than Chandrasakar and company."

She considered this, then said, "Did you see the aliens?"

"A brief glimpse."

"More than I saw. What were they like?"

"Small, very small. Three feet high, at a guess. Slight and green... I don't know whether they were furred, scaled, or skinned." He recalled his fleeting impression of the two abductors. "And they had domed heads."

She said, "The creatures in the frescoes."

She pushed herself to her feet impatiently and paced the cell. She examined the shell encompassing her handset and tried to prise off the material with her fingers. Failing, she moved to the wall and struck her arm against the rock once, twice, and a futile third time.

Vaughan watched with mounting amusement – then discovered that he was not the only spectator to her frustration.

He looked up and saw, peering down at him over the rim of the rock, the domed head of a native.

Its eyes were bulbous and compound, dark purple against the slime-green of its skin. It was not alone; other creatures had joined it, perhaps ten or a dozen, looking down at the captive pair in silence.

"I think they're finding your antics very entertaining," he said, gesturing up at the alien audience.

Das looked up quickly, and was about to call out something when she was interrupted by a noise from the hole at her feet. Vaughan heard a gurgle, then a rush of something fluid.

The crimson liquid came up in a spurting rush, rising warm and cloying around his legs. In seconds it had reached his shoulders and lifted him off his feet. He spread his arms across its surface and was carried up towards the lip of the rocky well.

He scrambled to the edge and held on, then hauled himself out and lay gasping on the rock. When he looked up he saw that the aliens had retreated and were squatting on thin legs, for all the world like terrestrial frogs, and watching with dark, unblinking eyes. There were perhaps fifty of the creatures, occupying a great, green-illuminated cavern.

Vaughan stood slowly and raised his hands into the air. He stared at the aliens, disconcerted by their massed regard.

An alien rose, left the squatting assembly, and approached them.

It stopped before Vaughan and Das, and he was suddenly aware of his heartbeat. The creature stared up at him. It had no facial features other than those outsized eyes – or so he thought until it opened its mouth. Its lips unsealed in a long, thin hyphen, and it spoke.

"Come," said the alien.

TWENTY

THE TREK

Vaughan managed a smile, realising how meaningless the expression might be. The alien stood before him, frog-like but longer in the body, and stared at him with massive, compound eyes like sieves.

He said, "What do you want with us?"

Behind the lead alien, the others remained squatting, watching him with a disconcerting fixity of attention.

The alien made no reply, but its fellows moved as one. They seemed to vanish into fissures and cracks in the rock of the chamber, to drain away like the fleshy equivalent of the crimson fluid. Seconds later only their leader remained.

Beside Vaughan, Das stepped forward. "Why have you taken us?"

In lieu of a reply, the creature turned and moved rapidly towards the chamber's far wall. It walked with an oddly elastic, cushioned motion, giving at the knees so that its torso bobbed as if suspended on springs.

It slipped through a narrow fissure in the rock. Vaughan expected it to return, beckon them after it. When it failed to do so, he turned to Das and said, "What now?"

"Let's go after it."

They hurried towards the fissure and peered within. The alien was bobbing along a narrow corridor, giving no indication of being interested in its human charges.

Vaughan followed.

"Did you hear it back there?" he asked Das. "Or am I going mad?"

"Well... I did think it said 'come', but it might have been coincidence. It wasn't that distinct. Perhaps it said something in its own language."

He increased his pace to keep up with the elastic strides of the alien. "If it does speak English, then that means it's had contact with the colonists."

"Which might explain why they disabled these." She held up her arm, cocooned in its crimson shell. "They knew about them from the colonists, right?"

"And they don't want us to contact Chandrasakar and the others."

"Which begs the question, what do they want with us?"

He peered ahead as the alien disappeared around a corner. He hurried after it and found it bobbing along another natural tunnel, this one sloping downwards at a thirty-degree angle.

I'm following an unknown alien, he said to himself, and I feel not the slightest threat...

They caught up with the alien as it negotiated a flight of steps chiselled into the sloping path; something about the way it took the steps, with caution, as if it were dipping its toes into icy water, suggested unfamiliarity. Vaughan wondered if the steps were man-made.

In the green light of the walls, he examined the alien more closely. It was naked, and its skin ran with a sebaceous film, catching the fungal glow in swirling highlights. It gave off a pungent reek, too, not unlike smelling salts.

Vaughan breathed shallowly.

Behind him, Das said, "Perhaps the aliens are what the colonists tried to contact their government about? These are their discovery."

Vaughan thought about it. "Something about them must be pretty damned special to have Chandrasakar make the journey out here..."

She nodded. "You're right."

They looked primitive, with no apparent evidence of technology; but he knew that first impressions, especially when dealing with Ee-tees, were often deceiving. He'd reserve judgement until they came to journey's end.

"Wonder where Rab and his men are?" Das said.

"Did you get the impression that the others were led away from us? That the aliens deliberately separated us and pounced?" He half-turned to look at her; she nodded.

He gave his attention to the descent, and almost fetched up against the alien's slim back; it had paused before another constructed feature in the rock, this time an archway. It raised a long-fingered hand to its forehead – almost in a gesture of obeisance, Vaughan thought – then stepped into a small, square chamber.

He followed it. A smaller archway mirrored the first on the opposite wall, and through it shone dazzling light.

The alien stopped, turned, and stared at the humans.

Seconds elapsed. Its great eyes watched them.

The most alien thing about this, Vaughan thought, is the total absence of social protocol between our races; it was like looking into the eyes of a lizard and hoping for some kind of communication.

And then the creature confounded his assumptions by opening its slit mouth again.

"Fear, no..." it said, the words barely a whisper. "Trust... yes."

And without a further word of explanation, it turned and stepped through the second archway into the blinding golden light.

Vaughan followed the alien through the arch, then stopped and stared in wonder.

At first he thought that they had somehow come *through* the mountain and emerged into the open air again, though the landscape was unlike the fungal terrain they had left far behind them. They were standing on the threshold of a vast plain, which extended ahead and to either side for perhaps fifty kilometres and was encircled by a range of jagged mountains. The plain was flat and uniform, consisting of what appeared to be a savannah of golden grass laden with a heady, herbal scent.

He turned to Das. She was staring up, her neck craned at an awkward angle. "Shiva," she said under her breath.

He looked up, and knew that he was wrong about the geographical nature of where they were.

They had not emerged into daylight through the mountain. They were still deep, deep underground. They were in a cavern the like of which he would have thought impossible, until he saw it with his own eyes.

The cliff-face at their backs rose vertically for kilometres, and then arched overhead to form a gargantuan canopy, which covered the entirety of the plain before them. Embedded in the roof of this monstrous cavern were what appeared to be miniature suns, great nuggets of crystal which scintillated with ersatz daylight and filled the plain with a golden illumination.

Vaughan thought of the alien's words. It was almost fear he felt now, a heady feeling combining agoraphobia with a mistrust of the unknown.

But the alien had counselled them to trust in it, also...

He thought about the colonists. He had pitied them earlier, thinking of them leading a meagre troglodyte existence far underground in the green light. But if they had found this cavern – and he could think of no reason why they might not have – then they had discovered a paradise.

Das said, "I wish I had the use of my handset, Jeff."

He looked at her. "To scan for the colonists?"

She shook her head. "To do a few calculations." She smiled at him and explained. "I suspect this isn't a unique feature. It's either natural, or made; either way, imagine if the vast planet is pocked with them like... like a pomegranate. Imagine how much living space there'd be. Perhaps this was what the colonists discovered? A planet packed with sufficient living space for thousands of cities?"

"And Chandrasakar wants a part of the real estate down here," Vaughan said. "A ready-made, habitable, safe, and enclosed environment."

Das smiled. "Which comes, unfortunately for him, with its very own sentient natives."

The alien paused before them; it was moving rapidly down the incline towards the golden savannah. It looked up at them, and though it said nothing Vaughan knew that it wanted them to follow.

They hurried after the alien, which had come to a halt before the grassland. Vaughan and Das paused beside it, staring out across the expanse. It was not, he saw, grass of any kind, but thin wisps of yet another fungal variety, strands as thin as fibre-optic cable reaching to his hips.

The alien stared at them, the look in its dark eyes indecipherable, then lifted a long, thin hand and gestured out across the plain.

"Is it saying that we should cross it?" Das asked.

Vaughan squinted at the distant mountains. "Hell of a trek," he said.

He looked at the alien, and gestured. "To the far mountains?"

The alien said nothing, merely turned and stepped into the fungal grass, which reached up to its chest.

Seconds later an odd thing happened. As they watched the creature wade through the savannah, the fungal stalks around the creature changed from their default golden hue to a shade of deep orange. No sooner had the alien passed on, than the stalks resumed their original gold. Like this, the creature

moved in an accompanying nimbus of colour, perhaps two metres across, as if continually tracked by
a diligent searchlight.

"Well, we'll never lose him... or her," Das said,
stepping in after the alien.

Vaughan followed and looked around him as the
whipping cords instantly transformed themselves
from gold to pulsing tangerine.

He walked alongside Das, the bobbing alien leading the way. From time to time he called to it, "My
name's Jeff. Jeff Vaughan..." or, "Are you taking us
to the other humans? Do you understand me?" But
as expected the alien gave not the slightest acknowl-
edgement that it was being addressed.

"You're wasting your time, Jeff," Das whispered.

"Do you think it understands us?"

She frowned. "It's a possibility, but perhaps it
deems the questions irrelevant. How to work out
the mindset of an alien? You know what alien
minds are like from attempting to scan them, no?"

He nodded.

She laughed without humour. "Human beings are
enough of a riddle, much of the time."

He glanced across at her. "How long have you
been a telepath?"

"Just under five years."

"And you did it for the cause? You tested psi-positive and had the cut for the good of the party?"

"I believe what I'm doing is for the good of
humanity, Jeff. It was a small sacrifice to make."

"So you do consider it a sacrifice?"

She gave him an appraising look. "Yes, I do.
I've... I've read things in some minds that I'd rather
not have read. I've been tainted by thoughts I'd

never have myself. But I'm telling you nothing you don't already know. And you do it day in, day out, for a living – and read *criminal* minds."

"Well…" He shrugged. "I suppose it makes me appreciate good people. And it does pay the bills."

He turned as he walked, looking back the way they had come. They had already covered perhaps half a kilometre, and the cliff-face they had left behind loomed above them, riven with cracks and fissures. It was impossible to see the opening through which they had emerged. He realised that they would be terribly exposed, out here in the open, if Chandrasakar and his party were to stumble across the cavern.

He looked ahead to the distant mountain range – if mountains they were. It was impossible to see if their peaks joined the overarching ceiling kilometres above, as a fine mist cloaked the upper reaches of the range.

The alien was perhaps five metres ahead of them, out of earshot. Vaughan said, "So where would the Indian government stand on what we've found down here?"

She glanced at him. "What do you mean?"

"If this was what the colonists wanted to tell the FNSA about, this 'revelation' as Chandrasakar called it – the ultimate real estate bonanza – would India be in on the land-grab?"

"You judge my government by your knowledge of Western powers, Jeff."

"Come on! It isn't as if your people are whiter than white! What you did in Bangladesh wasn't exactly an act of altruism."

She stared at the alien. "We invaded to protect

our border cities from insurgents," she whispered.

"Whatever," he said. "Well?"

"Okay." She nodded. "We'd first assess the position of the alien natives. It might be that they would willingly cede portions of their land. I mean, it isn't as if this place appears overly populated. If there are thousands of subterranean pockets like this..." She shrugged. "Discovering and terraforming, or adapting, extra-solar planets is an expensive business. This would be a treasure trove."

"And the slight matter of the FNSA having got here before you?"

"Well, according to Chandrasakar the colonists were split as to whether to tell their government what they'd discovered. Technically, the FNSA haven't planted their flag."

"So Delta Cephei VII is fair game?" he said.

"Think of how opening this world up would benefit the masses of humankind on overcrowded Earth."

He laughed at this. "Or rather, think how opening the world would benefit the high-ups and apparatchiks of the Indian Communist Party."

She glared at him. "No, Vaughan, the ultimate winner would be the proletariat."

Bullshit, he thought. But he knew how futile it would be to argue the point.

More to himself, he mused, "I feel sorry for the damned aliens, caught between the fascist FNSA and your scheming crowd."

"What's the lesser of the two evils, Jeff?"

He wasn't going to admit that she had him there. "How about a third alternative? We leave well alone? Let the aliens keep their planet. It's bad enough that they have a bunch of American colonists here anyway."

She shook her head. "A massive waste of resource potential, Jeff, especially if these pockets aren't utilised by the natives."

"We'll never agree," he said. "Let's just wait and see what we find, okay?"

She smiled to herself. "Let's do that, Jeff," she said.

But the communiqué *had* been sent, he thought; the scavengers were circling round the prey, hungry for the kill.

Ahead, the alien had come to a halt. It knelt, disappearing from sight, marked only by the circle of orange strands. Vaughan approached and peered at what it was doing, Das at his side. The alien was rooting through the fine soil, gently pushing away rootlets with its long fingers and digging deeper. It found something, eased it from the ground, and set it to one side, then resumed its digging. Vaughan saw that it had unearthed a red object the size of a grapefruit, and seconds later it had another, then a third.

It stood, bearing the fruit, and passed one each to Vaughan and Das. As if in instruction, it peeled its own and slipped the pulpy, apple-coloured flesh into its lipless mouth.

Das hesitated. "Do you think we should?"

He thumbed open the thin peel and tore off a chunk of flesh from the globe. It tasted sweet and then pungently spicy, with the consistency of banana.

"It's not bad," he said. "Go ahead, try it."

She peeled her fruit and tentatively nibbled at the flesh.

"I've tasted worse," she said as they set off again.

Vaughan finished the fruit and looked about him. The lack of geographical features made it difficult to judge the distance travelled; the cliff-face they had left seemed kilometres away, but the range towards which they were travelling seemed no closer than when they had set off.

The ceaseless routine of the walk soon became monotonous.

He thought of Sukara, Pham, and Li. He wanted nothing more than to be able to talk to Su, reassure her that all was well, and receive similar reassurances that Li's recovery was progressing. The longer he went without contacting her, the more she would worry.

When I get back from here, he thought, that's it; no more leaving Earth without Sukara and the girls.

Das looked at him. "What's wrong?"

"Nothing. I'm fine."

She said, "Missing wifey and the kids?"

"What do you think?"

"Ah, the palliative of domesticity," Das sighed.

He glared at her. "It's what matters to me," he said. "But as you've never experienced that..."

She opened her mouth to say something, but evidently thought better of it.

They continued in silence.

They had been walking for two or three hours – without the use of his handset, he was unable to tell exactly how long – when he thought he saw an irregularity in the savannah a few hundred metres ahead. He stopped, stared, and knew he wasn't seeing things.

"What is it?"

He pointed. "There, eleven o'clock."

"I see it. Looks like an old flier to me, Jeff."

The alien had evidently seen it too, as it veered off course and headed towards the vehicle. Two minutes later they came to a clearing in the savannah, and Vaughan stopped and looked upon the remains of the burnt-out flier. Beside it, planted in the soil at regular intervals, were half a dozen crosses lashed together from metal spars and struts.

"Graves," Das murmured.

The flier was a bulky, old-fashioned model, its paintwork blackened and bubbled with the ravages of fire. It looked incongruous in so alien a landscape.

Vaughan turned to the alien. The creature was standing to one side, staring at the flier and the crosses with its massive, unmoving eyes; it gave the impression of suitable reverence, but then it gave the same impression no matter what it did.

"What happened here?" Vaughan asked the alien. "Do you know?"

The alien didn't so much as turn in his direction.

Das said, "My guess is it has something to do with the rebels. Either it was their flier, or the colonists, and it was caught in the fight. If there was a battle of some kind... then that would explain the fire-damage to the *Cincinnati* back there."

He moved along the line of graves. There were no inscriptions scratched into the metal crosspieces to signify who was buried, not even so much as an RIP.

He crossed to the flier and peered inside. It was gutted, with a great hole punched through the passenger door. Whoever had been inside the vehicle had stood no chance of surviving the impact of the missile.

"I wonder what the natives thought of this?" Vaughan said. "Strangers drop from the stars, and the first thing they do is start killing each other."

Das grunted, "What makes you think they don't get up to similar things, Jeff?"

He shrugged. "In my experience, humans seem to have a peculiar propensity for internecine violence. Think about it. With the exception of the Korth, have we come across a race as aggressive as ourselves?"

"Maybe that's because most of the races we've discovered have been older than us; they've... matured."

"I rest my case," he said.

Das moved around the wreck. "I just hope the humans we came across weren't the only survivors of the conflict."

"I wonder if the natives are aware of the slaughter up there?" Vaughan shook his head. "Christ, the poor bastards don't know what they're in for."

Das looked at the alien, who had moved to the edge of the clearing and appeared to be waiting for them to continue. "Well, it doesn't seem to make our guide any more reluctant to have anything to do with us," she said.

They left the clearing and followed the alien.

Perhaps two hours later, Vaughan looked back. There was no sign of the clearing and the burned-out flier; the savannah stretched seamlessly to the right and left. Ahead, the mountain range seemed just as far away.

A while later he asked, "How long do you think

we've been walking?"

She paused and looked back at the distant cliff-face. "We aren't even halfway there, Jeff. I don't know. Four hours or so?"

"Seems like more. I'm bushed."

"I wonder if our friend intends to let us rest?"

He laughed. "I could always ask him, for all the good it'd do."

They walked on, and it was perhaps an hour later when the alien paused, turned to look at them, and then moved off sideways into the savannah. It bobbed down, vanishing from sight. Vaughan stepped forward and peered at what it was doing.

He smiled to himself. The alien was standing now, having rolled flat a section of savannah, creating in the process a deep mattress of flattened fungal strands.

"Do you think it was aware we were tired?" he asked Das.

She looked up at the bright, ersatz suns embedded in the ceiling far overhead. "Thing is, will we be able to sleep with the lights on?"

The alien had moved off as Vaughan and Das sat down on the surprisingly spongy bed of flattened strands. He watched the creature pluck something from several fungal stalks nearby and return to where they sat.

It passed them what looked like buds, the size of a thumb. The alien inserted the third one into its mouth, chewed, then lay down and curled into a foetal ball.

Vaughan shrugged. "Here goes…"

The bud certainly wasn't as pleasant as the earlier fruit, but then he suspected it wasn't meant to be.

It was hard and bitter, and left a sharp aftertaste on the palate. A minute later he began to feel woozy.

"And?" Das said, watching him, the bud halfway to her lips.

"Nice," he slurred, slumping onto the wonderfully comfortable fungal bed.

"Jeff, this might be dangerous!"

He heard her, but he was past caring, and seconds later oblivion claimed him.

TWENTY-ONE

ESCAPE

Sukara came awake quickly and found herself in the back of a flier, dazzled by sunlight.

Despite her fear, she knew better than to move. She was alone on the back seat, slumped behind the driver with her head against the side window. There was no one else in the car other than the Chinese orderly... or rather the impostor orderly. Either he had misjudged the dose of sedative he'd sprayed in her face, or had taken longer than planned to get her to the flier... At any rate, the fact was that she was awake – and could move her arms and legs – and he was unaware of the fact.

The question was: who was he and what did he want?

The bastard wasn't an orderly and had nothing to do with Dr Grant. He wouldn't have sent an orderly running after her, and she swore at herself for being taken in so easily. But at the same time she felt a stunning relief: the bastard had used Li as a pretext, knowing that it would have the desired effect of making her biddable to his suggestion of taking the outer lift, down to the under-level car-park...

So Li was still okay.

She felt a welling of anger, the quick urge to do the bastard permanent damage.

She ruled out the possibility that the Chink was a rapist or related sadist. He knew about Li; had planned the abduction to the point of posing as an orderly. Which might not preclude the possibility that he merely wanted to hurt her, but she thought not. There was another reason behind the abduction.

She thought of the assassin who had tried to kill Jeff, and had succeeded in murdering the other telepaths. Could this have something to so with those attacks?

She put the question aside. Her priority was to find some means of getting away from her captor.

She turned her head minimally and peered through the window.

They were on the top level, flying low. She saw Chandi Road flash by, with the expanse of the spaceport beyond. They were flying north-east. At some point they would land – and then Sukara would make her move.

The Chink turned in his seat and she closed her eyes, feigning unconsciousness. She counted twenty long seconds, then slit her eyes open fractionally.

Slowly, she moved her right hand towards her handset. She pressed a release code on the console. A second later the communications pin Jeff had given her ejected itself. She gripped it in her right hand – a silver needle almost five centimetres long, slippery in her sweat-soaked palm. For the rest of the ride she fantasised about the amount of damage she could inflict with the needle and a lot of righteous rage.

The flier slowed. They were at the northern end of Chandi Road, where the ethnic make-up phased from Indian to Thai. The flier dropped suddenly and eased itself down a narrow alley, with barely six inches between its bodywork and the walls of warehouses and industrial storage depots.

Sukara knew she had to be fast and decisive when the time came. If she messed up... she didn't like to consider the possibility. The bastard was probably armed, so she had to make the first blow a telling one.

The flier came to a halt and settled in the alley, and her heartbeat raced.

To the right of the vehicle was a compound, its wire-mesh gate open as if awaiting her delivery.

The Chink jumped from the flier and opened the back door. Sukara closed her eyes and gripped the needle. Her captor opened the door, against which she was leaning, and she half-fell from the vehicle. This made his task easier. He gripped her under the arms and tugged her from the flier. Her heels banged painfully on the concrete as he dragged her into the compound.

She hoped that he didn't have an accomplice at this end of the operation. One bastard she might be able to deal with. Two would be a little more difficult.

He laid her on the ground, easing her head onto the concrete with incongruous care. She heard footsteps as he walked away from her, then the sound of a door being unlocked.

She opened her eyes, but all she could see was sky and a margin of guttering overhead.

She had to act now, while his back was turned.

She leapt to her feet and sprang towards the bastard.

He turned, obligingly, and she leapt at him screaming and stabbed the needle into his face. She would remember the bastard's expression for a long time after that: the wide-eyed look of shocked fright, the toothy rictus like some Chinese carnival dragon. She would remember his scream, too, as she stabbed.

She was surprised by the rubbery resistance of his eyeball. The bastard fell to his knees, yelling, a hand to his right eye and blood spurting between splayed fingers. Sukara turned and took off, gripping the needle as she careered out of the compound, turned left and sprinted down the alleyway.

She felt a surge of elation, a mix of adrenalised flight reflex and the delight of revenge. She replayed the stabbing and told herself that he deserved it not so much for the abduction, but for the lie about her daughter.

She heard a shout from back down the alley. She turned. The bastard was staggering from the compound, waving something. She judged she was a hundred metres away. He pointed at her and a split second later she saw the foreshortened streak of a laser vector lance her way. She dived, scraping her knees and palms, and the vector raced over her by about half a metre. Then she was up and running again, zigzagging between the alley's walls. She heard another screech of ripped air as he fired again, and she dived. This one missed her by centimetres. She looked up as she took off like a sprinter from the blocks. She was about ten metres from the bustle of Chandi Road. The third vector lasered a neat, stinking hole in the flapping material of her jacket and gouged concrete from the wall to her right.

She came to the road and turned left, instinctively. Only later did she wonder if her unconscious mind knew where it was taking her. She barrelled into pedestrians, earning curses in Hindi and Thai. She fell, scattering a gaggle of old men, picked herself up and elbowed a passage through the throng. She slowed, not wanting to give her pursuer the advantage of tracing her by the commotion she might cause.

She eased herself into the press, her breathing returning to normal, and hurried down the road. She glanced behind her. If the bastard were still chasing her, there was no sign of him. She told herself not to be complacent. He'd overcome a skewered eyeball to give chase, and he'd be out for vengeance. A wounded animal.

Then her heart jumped as she heard aggrieved cries behind her. She looked over her shoulder. Perhaps twenty metres further back she made out a disruption as someone fought their way through the crowd towards her.

She yelled in fright and sprinted, taking a slalom course between ambling citizens. She wondered where to go, where she might be safe from the berserker.

The she saw Dr Rao's coffee house twenty metres away on the left of the road, and thanked her intuition.

Just as she was approaching the building, the press around her seemed to congeal, slowing her progress. She abandoned all pedestrian etiquette now and thumped her way through the mass of bodies, crying out and tearing aside startled citizens. She heard another cry in her wake, a plea to stop the bitch who'd attacked him, and a second later the crowd loosened and she stumbled up the steps of the coffee house and into its cool interior.

She was aware of shocked faces as she tore down the central aisle. A waiter laden with a full tray neatly sidestepped her and she raced past, through the beaded curtain and turned left into the storeroom. She almost collided with the elevator door in the far wall, found the command console and stabbed the code. Her age and Pham's: 27-10.

She wondered if the lift would be at the bottom of the shaft. In that case she would be cornered. All her efforts to escape would be for nothing. She turned, looked around the room for something heavy to throw at her pursuer. A crate of stacked mineral water to her left, a broom to her right. She almost laughed at the thought of attacking the bastard with a broom handle.

A cry from the coffee house, followed by a crash of trays and crockery. The waiter hadn't been so nimble, this time.

She gripped the needle and was about to reach out for the brush when she heard a scraping sound behind her. She turned. The lift door was slowly opening. She dived inside, hit the descend command. The doors eased shut just as a blur of colour appeared outside. She heard his cry, the zizz of his laser. The door clanked shut and the lift plummeted.

Sukara collapsed against the far wall and choked on a sob. Relief coursed through her like a drug. She was safe, for the time being. She'd call Dr Rao. He had contacts, people who might be able to help her.

She tried to recall the duration of the descent when she'd made it with Rao yesterday. Five minutes, at least.

She heard the distant crump of an explosion, far above. That could only be the doors, blasted by a laser. A second later the carriage swayed, and for a terrible second she thought that the bastard had lasered the pulley cables, that she'd fall to her death half a kilometre below.

But the elevator continued its descent. From time to time it bucked, and she wondered what her pursuer was doing.

Then she had it. He'd launched himself at the cables, was sliding down their length. Soon he'd hit the carriage roof. He had a laser – but it would take time to cut through the steel of the ceiling. Perhaps she'd make it down to the starship before he cut his way through.

She heard a resonating thump as the Chink landed on the roof, and the carriage juddered with the impact.

She cowered in the corner of the lift, as if trying to put as much distance as possible between herself and the Chinese bastard. She looked up. She heard the regular pulse of a laser. He was trying to slice through the ceiling...

She turned on her handset and entered the code Dr Rao had given her the day before. She'd explain the situation, tell him that a lunatic was after her. If Rao were down in the starship, perhaps he could help her, conceal her in his ship.

A second later his wizened face peered out at her. "Sukara, this is a welcome surprise. How is…?"

She said, "Dr Rao! I'm in the lift, coming down. Listen, someone is chasing me." Then, unaccountably, the tears started and she sobbed, "He's on top of the lift. He has a laser. He's cutting his way through. Please, help me!"

Rao was silent for five seconds, assessing the situation. "Sukara, listen to me. Do exactly as I say. When the lift doors open, run out and turn right. There is a girder immediately to the right of the door. Hide behind this, crouch down, and do nothing else. Do you understand?"

"But—"

"Do as I say! I will attend to the matter from there. Do you understand?"

She nodded. "But if he cuts through the ceiling before—"

Dr Rao shook his head. "That will take time, I think. More time than the lift will take to arrive here. Don't worry, Sukara. I will help you."

Sukara looked up. She saw a black, smoking line appear on the underside of the steel ceiling, and she gave a mewling cry.

Rao said, "Do you know who is following you, Sukara? Do you know what they want?"

She shook her head, screwing herself further into the corner. "No. I've no idea. He's Chinese. He sprayed something in my face, took me somewhere off Chandi Road in a flier. I stabbed him in the eye and got away. He followed me to the coffee house—"

Dr Rao smiled. She could see that he was moving. His head bobbed as he held his handset up to his face. "You are a brave and amazing woman, Sukara. But then I have always known that."

"He's cutting through the ceiling, Dr Rao!"

He looked away from the screen. "You are almost here. Remember, run from the lift and turn right, hide behind the girder. Keep your head low, ah-cha?"

She nodded.

Dr Rao cut the connection and Sukara felt terribly alone.

She looked around the interior of the carriage. There was no lit indicator to tell her how far she had dropped. The blackened line on the ceiling was about half a metre long now. She hoped Rao was right in his assessment of the time it'd take the bastard to cut through the ceiling... But what if he intended only to cut a gap wide enough to insert the barrel of his laser and shoot her?

But why, then, had he not killed her earlier, in the hospital lift? He'd abducted her, and therefore wanted her alive. Even when he'd fired at her in the alley, she guessed that he'd aimed to clip her, stop her flight, rather than kill her.

The descent seemed to take an age. She was convinced that it was slower than the first time. She wondered if her pursuer had done something to retard the elevator's speed. She looked up. The scorched line was almost a metre long now, and as she watched it turned at right angles, describing a letter L.

It would be only a matter of minutes before he cut the steel enough to bend it down and squirm through...

She counted the seconds, willing the lift to arrive

at the starship. She reached two minutes and looked at the ceiling. The second scorched line was as long as the first now. As she watched, the bastard began the third, creating a neat hatch...

She took ragged breaths, telling herself to be calm. Soon she would reach the starship. She'd do exactly as Dr Rao had told her, and hoped he'd be equal to the threat.

A thud resounded in the carriage, Startled, she looked up. The bastard had cut a neat U-shape in the ceiling, and now he was stamping on the metal, bending it inwards. With each thump of his boot the steel flange gave a couple of centimetres. Soon he'd drop through. She sobbed, gripping the needle and vowing not to give in without a fight.

Then the lift clanked, bobbed, and halted. She jumped to her feet with a cry and stabbed the door button. It eased open with agonising slowness and she squeezed out, stumbled free and staggered to the right. She saw the girder, a vast diagonal beam twice her width. She dived behind it, ducked and clamped her mouth shut to stifle her sobs.

She heard the desperate thudding from within the carriage, then a cry and a thump as the bastard landed. Sukara saw movement to her right. Someone was crouching behind the girder across the catwalk from her. Before she could work out who it was, she saw the Chinese bastard as he sprang from the elevator.

She heard the shots, six of them one after the other, echoing in the cavern. Sukara closed her eyes. The Chinaman gave an abbreviated cry. She opened her eyes. Her pursuer was writhing on the catwalk, his torso a pulpy mass of blood and disorganised bone. Another shot, and something seemed to erupt from his head, skull shrapnel and a beautifully parabolic spurt of blood.

Then silence...

Sukara crouched where she was, unable to move.

The figure across from her stood up and shuffled out from behind the girder. Dr Rao was holding an antique pistol. She looked down at the Chinaman's body and nodded in satisfaction. Wobbly, Sukara climbed to her feet and hurried across to him, avoiding the mess on the catwalk.

She found herself in the old man's arms, sobbing.

"Sukara, all will be well. Do not fear."

She turned her head, stared at the bloodied body. "How...?" she began.

Dr Rao smiled and held up the pistol. "It might be old, Sukara, but there is much to commend the simple projectile weapon." He frowned. "Though bullets are a rare commodity these days. I wonder if I should have been more sparing..."

Sukara couldn't help laughing, almost hysterically, as it entered her head that she might get the bill for the bullets when all this was over. She wouldn't put it past the mercenary doctor.

She was still gripping the communications pin. She wiped the congealing liquid on her sleeve and inserted the pin into her handset.

"Come," Rao said, taking her arm. He eased her along the catwalk.

"What about...?" she said, gesturing at the corpse.

"I will deal with the disposal," he said. "One less thug on Bengal Station will not be missed."

They came to the starship and he sat her down on

an engine cowling. "I will arrange protection, Sukara. I think it best if you leave here. I will assign a boy to take you to Level Three, where I have a safe house. You will take a posterior exit."

"But what about Pham, Li...?"

He nodded. "Worry not. I will contact a security company I have used before. These people are impeccable. They will escort you to and from the hospital, and ensure your safety at all times." He looked at her. "Do you have any idea what this was all about?"

She shook her head. "They knew about Li." She told him of the bastard's deception, how she guessed that he wanted her alive. "It might have something to do with the murder of the telepaths... or maybe Jeff's mission."

Rao licked his reptilian lips. "That is a possibility, but one that need not concern us overly at this juncture. One moment." He moved into the starship, and emerged a minute later with a tiny one-armed Indian boy.

"Ajay will take you to Level Three. Do you know Bhindi Road?"

She nodded.

"Take the first right turn after the park. There you will find apartment number 10 on Nehru Street. The security code on the door is..." She activated her handset and took down the code and the safe haven's address.

"And as soon as you go, I will arrange for your continued security. Please do not worry, ah-cha?"

She embraced him, kissed his leathery cheek, and whispered, "Thank you, Dr Rao."

"Now go. *Chalo!*"

The boy trotted off and she followed him on a tortuous course through a forest of girders and across a walkway to the far bulkhead. Here he undogged a hatch and revealed a dark access column, with staple-shaped rungs welded to its interior. The boy ducked inside and climbed, and Sukara followed.

If the descent in the elevator had seemed to take aeons, then the climb to Level Three took even longer. It became a repetition of identical movements, which soon had her arms and legs throbbing with pain. Mentally, too, she was undergoing torture. She might have fled the bastard, but she knew she was far from safe. They knew who she was, knew about Li, and presumably knew about Pham, too. She decided that, when Dr Rao's security men ferried her from the safe house, she would pick up Pham from school and go to the hospital, where she would stay without venturing out until Jeff got back.

The thought helped to settle her nerves.

They came to a hatch, which Ajay opened and squeezed through. It was an even tighter squeeze for Sukara. Then they were in a service conduit between the levels. Ajay pointed to another set of welded rungs.

"Nearly there now, ah-cha? This Level Four. Short climb only now."

He led the way and Sukara followed. They emerged minutes later inside a small room full of electrical generators and fuse boxes. Ajay moved to a door, cracked it an inch, and peered out. "You go, now, ah-cha? This Level Three!"

She smiled at him and slipped through the door.

It banged shut behind her.

She recognised where she was – a wide corridor not far from the food market. The address Rao had given her was perhaps half a kilometre away.

She eased herself into the crowds flowing towards the market, feeling safe within the faceless anonymity of the thousand busy citizens. She turned down Bhindi Road and hurried past the park.

As soon as the security team arrived, she told herself, she would go for Pham. That was her priority now.

She turned right, off the busy avenue, and almost ran down the quiet street. Not far to go now. The crowds and the noise were far behind her. This area was affluent, a series of plush apartments overlooking a central reservation of palm trees.

She found number ten and was about to enter the code when a voice behind her said, "Sukara?"

She turned, disbelieving. A Chinese face – for all she knew the brother of the bastard she'd stabbed – grinned at her. She wondered how he'd found her, and even had time to consider the possibility that the first Chink had tagged her with something.

"This time, bitch, you won't get away so easily."

He jabbed her viciously in the belly and she gasped with the pain and dropped to her knees. Then he punched her face. She fell, the back of her head striking the ground. He stood over her, smiling, enjoying himself.

Sukara lay on her back, and the last thing she saw before passing out was the close-up view of a spray-can.

TWENTY-TWO

THE UNDERLANDS

They walked on.

Vaughan judged they'd been travelling for perhaps three hours since waking that 'morning'. How long he'd slept, after eating the soporific bud, was another guess, but he felt refreshed and relaxed as if he'd managed a full night's sleep. They'd breakfasted on the same grapefruit-sized fruit as earlier, and drunk the watery contents of a horn-shaped gourd the alien had dug up too. The alien, as was its wont, had uttered not a sound all day.

Vaughan reckoned that approximately twenty-four hours had elapsed since they'd started underground, way past the time he should have called Sukara. She would be expecting to hear from him imminently, and would only worry when he failed to call. He tried to push the thought to the back of his mind.

At least now the mountain range they were approaching was closer than the cliff-face they had left. To their rear, the wall of rock they'd passed through was a hazy grey curtain, indistinct where it phased into the cavern ceiling. Ahead, the range had resolved itself, and Vaughan saw that it was indeed an enfilade of jagged mountains. Each one terminated in a peak, like so many lofted scimitars, and there was a space between their summits and the crystal-encrusted ceiling far above. The sheer enormity of the subterranean cavern system was beyond his comprehension; perhaps Das was right in speculating that there might be thousands of such pockets within the planet.

They'd come across more wildlife down here: not just the insects and birds they'd seen on the surface, but hopping rodent-like creatures, green-scaled and darting, and larger, long-nosed quadrupeds like hybrid tapir-pigs. All had been docile, running off into the savannah when they'd happened upon the unlikely trio.

Das said, "I reckon another couple of hours and we'll reach the foothills."

"And then?"

"What then?" Das called to their alien guide. "Where are you taking us? It'd make things easier if you'd communicate."

"You're wasting your time."

The creature didn't deviate one iota from its steady bobbing gait.

Beside him, Das turned and squinted back the way they'd come. "Hey, am I seeing things?"

"What?"

She had stopped and was pointing at the cliff-face far behind them.

Vaughan joined her and peered. A third of the way up the cliff-face, on the threshold of a diagonal rip in the rock, Vaughan made out eight tiny figures: Chandrasakar, Singh, and the six security personnel; they were accompanied by half a dozen glinting points of light, the spider drones. As he watched, the party made their tortuous way down the cliff-face towards the savannah.

Vaughan said, "I don't see any aliens with them."

She fitted a hand to her brow and watched the distant humans. "They're alone. Come on. Let's not hang around."

They hurried after the bobbing alien.

"They'll think it strange that we haven't tried to contact them," Vaughan said. "They don't know our handsets have been disabled."

She nodded. "You're right. Rab would think it suspicious."

"As far as he's concerned, we're running away from him."

She glanced at him. "That presupposes he can see us."

He gestured to the give-away circles of orange discoloration that kept pace with them through the savannah. "I think the chances are that he has."

She increased her pace. "The sooner we get to the foothills," she pointed out, "the safer we'll be."

"You don't think...?"

"If he assumes we're running away, trying to reach the colonists before him..." She shook her head. "I don't know..."

He hurried after her. A grim possibility occurred to him. Technically, he was in the pay of Chandrasakar. He'd signed a contract, for which he'd not only receive payment, but more importantly Li would get the latest treatment for her illness.

If he was seen by Chandrasakar to be running away with Das... How might Chandrasakar react then? Surely even the tycoon wouldn't stoop to contacting his people on Earth and halting Li's treatment?

It was a slim possibility, but a frightening one.

Ten minutes later, the first laser vector scythed down a swathe of savannah three metres to their left.

The first that Vaughan was aware of the attack was a cry from Das followed, instantly, by the blinding flash of the laser vector and the sizzle of the fungus as it burned.

He dived, dragging down the alien with him. As he fell, he thought how repulsive the creature's cold, slick skin felt. Only then did the fear kick in.

The sickening reek of charred fungus filled the air.

Das was beside him, breathing hard. "Okay, I think it's best to split. Put a couple of metres between us and head for that outcropping in the foothills, okay?"

He nodded.

"Okay, let's go!"

Vaughan half-stood and sprinted, hauling the alien to its feet as he went. The creature seemed aware of the danger and ran at a nimble crouch on a zigzag course through the fungus.

The second laser vector fried a stretch of fungus in their wake. Vaughan felt the heat of the blast on his back. He kept on running, rather than obey his impulse and go to ground. Better to present the bastards with a moving target rather than a sitting duck.

He chanced a backward glance in time to see the

third vector lance out from the cliff-face. It was not a member of the security team firing, he saw, but a spider drone. That struck him as ominous. Drones were mechanical, things of precision, not prone to human error.

The dazzling blue laser beam lanced over his head by a matter of centimetres and set the savannah afire before them. They dodged the incineration, using the pall of smoke as cover as they sprinted for the foothills. Vaughan judged the tumble of rocks were perhaps half a kay away now; refuge was in sight. Once they'd made the outcropping it would be easy to remain hidden. He wondered if Chandrasakar would chance crossing the savannah, putting himself at risk of return fire. Then he wondered where the alien might be taking them: through the mountain to relative safety, hopefully.

It struck him, as he panted towards the first of the jutting rocks, that only one spider drone was firing, and he wondered why Chandrasakar was conserving the shots of the other two drones he had with him. Perhaps the tycoon was confident of picking them off without having to unleash his full firepower. He flung himself behind a stand of silver-grey rock, hauling the alien in beside him. A second later Das thumped down a metre away and rolled into the cover of the rock.

The fourth vector struck the rock formation above them, sending shrapnel shards shooting through the air.

The alien was squatting on its haunches, impassive. It stared up the hillside as if plotting the next leg of their flight.

Das said, "Okay, so far so good." She squinted up

the incline, then glanced at the alien. "Where are you taking us? We need to know. Do you understand that?"

The alien responded, not with words, but by extending a long, thin arm and pointing up the hillside.

Vaughan made out a jagged slit in the rock, perhaps half a kilometre away. The terrain in between was littered with rocks and boulders, which would provide adequate cover.

Das nodded. "Great. Okay... How do you want to do this, Jeff?"

He thought about it. "If we go one by one, from rock to rock, then we're signalling exactly where each of us will be coming from. Let's go together, okay?"

She nodded. "Sounds good to me. Got that?" she said to the alien.

It failed to respond. Vaughan found himself gripping its thin, boneless hand.

"Okay," Das said. "After three. One, two, three! Go!"

They half-stood and sprinted to the next bulging rock up the hillside, twenty metres away. They made its custody without attracting any further laser fire.

"Right, again! See that spur right ahead? Let's get there, rest up, and see if we can see what they're doing, okay?"

Vaughan nodded. Das gave the count and they ran. Vaughan gripped the alien's hand, almost dragging the creature in his wake.

This time, two vectors homed in on them almost simultaneously. The first one exploded rock at

Vaughan's feet, while the second missed him by centimetres. He yelled as a searing heat scorched his
upper right arm.

He was still a few metres from the spur, and all
the drone had to do was take its time, sight him,
and fire.

He hauled the alien into his arms and sprinted.
Seconds later, a laser vector exploding behind him,
he dived painfully behind the spur, dropped the
alien, and lay gasping for breath.

Das crouched over him. "They almost got you,
Jeff."

He sat up and looked at his upper arm. The material of his jacket was melted; he pulled it away from
his raw shoulder, gasping at the pain, then ripped
the sleeve to access the wound.

Das examined it. "Dammit, I had salve and synthi-flesh in my backpack."

"Not as bad as I expected," he said. "I'll live."

The alien squatted next to him, taking in the raw
patch of flesh with its outsize eyes.

Das turned and looked through a split in the
rock. Vaughan stood and joined her.

He searched the plain. As far as he could make
out, Chandrasakar and his team were still somewhere on the cliff-face, though at this distance it
was impossible to see them. He did see, however,
the spider drones – and he knew why Chandrasakar
had ordered only one of them to attack.

While the first drone had remained on the cliff-
face, using its elevation to target them, the other
two were making their way at great speed across
the savannah. Their progress showed not as a nimbus of discolouration, but as a dark chevron ripple

that swept through the fungal strands like the wake of a motorboat.

Das looked at him. "Shiva, look at them move! How long before they get here?"

They were covering hundreds of metres in a few seconds. "Not long. Ten minutes?"

"They'll be in contact with the first drone, so they'll know where we are." She thought about it. "We wouldn't be giving our position away if we fired at the bastards."

"We've got to do it. If we let them come after us…" He looked up the incline; the opening was perhaps a hundred metres away. "We'll probably never be in a better strategic position to strike at them." He hesitated. "You think you can hit a target moving that fast?"

"I can give it a try. You?"

He nodded. "I've had training. Let's just hope it proves worthwhile."

She drew her laser pistol, and Vaughan pulled his laser from its shoulder-holster. He knelt beside the crack, below the standing Das, and tracked the advance of the spider drones.

"I'll take the one on the left, Jeff, okay?"

"Let's do it." He eased his laser into position and took aim.

"After three. One, two, three… Fire!"

He touched the firing stud and a pulse blasted from his pistol. A second later he was amazed to see the drone spin into the air, all spinning silver limbs. It crashed to earth and was hidden in the savannah.

Das's shot missed the target by a hand's-breadth. Instantly it charted their position and a laser vector flashed out like a spoke, clipping the rock.

"You okay?" he shouted.

"I'm… I'm fine. Just got caught by debris." She crouched, a gash across her forehead leaking blood.

He moved to the fissure, looked down at the savannah. He was shocked to see that the surviving drone had made rapid progress; it danced through the fungus, eating up the kilometres and coming at them like a speeding flier.

Das joined him. "Shiva, it's close!"

She took aim and fired. The vector zizzed out from between the rock, ringing in Vaughan's ears. He peered down at the savannah. A second later the laser vector connected with the drone's domed cowl and it exploded in a spectacular burst of flame and silver casing.

She fell back against the rock, wiping blood from her face with the sleeve of her jacket.

"Sharp shooting, Parveen."

She nodded. "It'll buy us a bit of time… Okay, let's get out of here."

They stood. The alien was already hopping from foot to foot up the hillside, almost comical in its unconscious imitation of a bipedal frog. Vaughan followed at a sprint, Das on his heels

They had almost reached the opening when the laser beam lanced past them and slagged a wall of rock. They fell on their faces, Vaughan rolling and sliding down the hillside.

At first he thought the third remaining drone, on the far cliff-face, had fired at them; then he saw the drone he'd hit: it was dragging itself through the savannah on three legs, trailing shattered limbs.

Das knelt beside him, took aim and fired.

Her beam hit the drone's dome dead centre, spinning the spider off its remaining feet in a dervish whirl of limbs and ejected hardware.

"Persistent critters," Das said. "Let that be a lesson. We can't underestimate the bastards. And remember, there's still one of them with Rab and his security team."

"And three back with the scientists in the first cavern," Vaughan pointed out. "Chandrasakar could always call them in as reinforcements."

"Wish you hadn't reminded me..." she said.

They stood and hurried up the hillside towards the protective cover of the opening, the alien leading the way.

The opening turned out to be a cutting, open to the light, which passed between two rearing peaks. They entered the cutting and climbed a slope scattered with scree, the alien dancing ahead on its quick bandy legs.

She looked at him. "We've got to think about what we're going to do..." she said at last.

"Go on."

"It's my guess that the alien is taking us to the colonists."

He looked ahead. The alien was out of earshot. "It's a possibility," he said. "So...?"

"As I see it, we have the advantage here. We're a few hours ahead of Rab and his goons. We're that much closer to finding the colonists, maybe negotiating with them. At least, establishing friendly relations."

"We?" he asked. "You make it sound as if I'm suddenly a fully paid-up member."

She looked away from him. "Very well, absent yourself from the equation, Jeff. *I'm* half a day ahead.

That's to my advantage."

"One slight problem," he said, "is that the only means off the planet is aboard the *Kali*."

She shook her head, summarily dismissing the objection. "I'll put a call out for the Indian ship, which should be in the region, just as soon as I need to get away from here."

"Via your handset?" He held his own aloft. "If you haven't noticed…"

She shook her head. "I'm sure, once we've found the colonists, they'll have the means to unlock it."

He considered what she'd said so far. "Okay. So what's to think about?"

"This: when we find the colonists, what do we tell them about Rab and the others? The truth, that he's a businessman out for what he can get?"

"What's the alternative?"

"A story that'd buy us time – time to get my government in here. A story along the lines that Rab fronts a multicolonial organisation that treats its subjects as little more than slaves…"

Vaughan squinted at her. "A lie, in other words?"

She shrugged. "That depends on one's political philosophy, Jeff."

"I might not like the man, but from what I've heard about his colonial interests he treats his people relatively well."

She was shaking her head. "I think you'd rather the colonists, and the aliens, dealt with me and my government than the Chandrasakar Organisation."

"I'd rather the poor bastards were left to themselves."

"But that," she said, "is an impossibility. Live in the real world, Jeff."

They walked on, the alien leading the way tirelessly. Vaughan considered Chandrasakar and his motives.

"I've had a thought," he said.

"Let's hear it."

"I'm not sure that these caverns – no matter how vast they are, and how many thousands of them there might be – are what Chandrasakar's so interested in."

She glanced at him. "How so?"

"Consider this: why was he shooting at us? What reason might he have for trying to stop us?"

"Like I said – he wants to get to the colonists before we do."

He shook his head. "I can't buy that, Parveen. So we reach the colonists before him, and tell them that Chandrasakar's the devil incarnate... and all he does then is come along with all his business PR and soft-sells the colonists whatever they want. He simply buys them. Christ, Parveen, the man's a multi-billionaire. His organisation owns half the Expansion. He's not going to let the two of us get in the way of whatever it is he wants down here."

"Which, Jeff, is why he tried to fry us."

He shook his head. "No way. There's something else. Something big. He's trying to stop us before we reach the colonists, learn their secret, and report back to Earth." He indicated their scabbed handsets. "He doesn't know what's happened to these, after all."

Das paused and looked at him. "It's worth considering, I suppose."

"Mark my word," Vaughan said, and trekked on. Thirty minutes later the cutting opened out;

before them was a short rise. The alien had come to rest on the brow, staring down into another valley cavern. This one was without the crystal suns set into the high ceiling; it was meagrely illuminated by the ubiquitous green fungus.

Vaughan came alongside the alien and stared.

The alien squatted, interlacing its long fingers over its knees, and contemplated what lay before them.

The valley was smaller than the one they had left, perhaps half its size, and it was not covered in a fungal savannah. Instead, streets and buildings formed an extraordinary alien city.

"It can't be the colonists' settlement," Das said, her voice low.

He shook his head. "It's definitely alien."

It was in no way a modern city, similar to the kind he was accustomed to; it more resembled the pictures he'd seen of ancient, primitive cities, with two- and three-storey buildings laid out in a radial pattern, of a uniform sand colour and crumbling. The buildings were broad of base and tapering, terminating in flat roofs perhaps thirty feet high. Slit windows were their only feature.

As he stared, he made out a pattern to the city's development. It had been built, he thought, in exactly the opposite way to the development of terrestrial cities. Older, crumbling buildings occupied the outer precincts, while the further towards the centre the buildings appeared more modern and of cleaner lines. He supposed that was to be expected, if aliens had come upon the cavern from the savannah cavern, and settled its perimeter first.

There was another odd thing about the city: it was as still and silent as a graveyard.

"There's not the slightest movement," Das said. "It's dead, deserted."

Vaughan tuned to the alien and gestured down at the moribund metropolis. "Was this your city?" he asked.

As if in reply, the alien rose to its feet and stepped nimbly down the hillside.

Vaughan and Das followed.

"What I'd like to know, Jeff, is where are the colonists?"

They approached the sandy, featureless walls of the outer suburbs and walked along wide boulevards. The alien trotted on ahead, as if intent on leading them through the centre of the city and out the other side.

"I wonder why the colonists didn't make this their base?" he said. "I mean, it looks habitable enough."

"But... *monolithic*," Das said. "Forbidding. And the green lighting doesn't help."

Vaughan looked about him at the uniform façades. "Maybe that's because it's empty. Full of people and life... it might be different."

She remained to be convinced. "I think the colonists had more sense," she said, "and moved on to a better place. After all, who'd want to live in a city deserted by its alien builders?"

"I wish our guide would talk," he said. "I'd ask him why it was deserted, what happened to bring about the exodus."

They turned a corner, then headed towards the centre of the city on a long, radial avenue. At Das's suggestion they hugged the shadows, lest Chandrasakar send in his remaining drones.

The reached the city's hub, a raised circular plinth on which stood the carved stone figures of perhaps a hundred statues of beings identical to their guide. They described a great circle, their arms outstretched and fingertips touching, in a tableau Vaughan found oddly moving.

They walked slowly around the great circle of aliens, staring up at the carved figures, until they reached the other side and their guide hurried them onwards.

They passed through the city, reaching the outer perimeter of older buildings, and climbed the sloping ramparts of the cavern wall. This was not part of a mountain range, but an enclosing bulwark of rock, which curved high overhead to form the cavern's ceiling.

Vaughan paused and looked back. They had already climbed higher than the city's tallest building, and their elevation gave them a clear view across the rooftops to the pass through which they had entered the cavern. There was no sign of Chandrasakar, his men, or the drones.

The alien slipped into a cave-mouth, which proved to be the entrance of a wide, sloping tunnel, and Vaughan and Das hurried after it.

They descended for what might have been a couple of hours. At last, the tunnel levelled out and ahead Vaughan saw a slash of artificial sunlight cutting through the green gloaming. They approached a jagged opening in the rock and followed their guide through into another cavern.

This one was more like the savannah cavern,

though even vaster. A myriad crystal suns created a good imitation of daylight, and what they shone upon had Vaughan and Das staring in amazement.

The great valley, perhaps fifty kilometres by fifty, was divided into a series of arable patchwork squares, each given over to a different crop. A thousand farmhouses constructed from timber – or this world's equivalent – dotted the plain, and long, winding lanes connected the farms to hamlets and villages.

And here, in stark contract to the deserted city, there was life in abundance.

Vaughan saw figures working in the fields, and steering carts along the lanes – carts piled with produce and hauled by close relations of the tapir-pig analogues, though much larger. There was an air of bucolic industry about the scene that Vaughan, never having lived anywhere other than a city, found almost alien.

Which was strange, he reflected, because the figures at work in the valley were human.

He heard a sudden whistle off to his right. He saw a crude shack, lashed together from boles of fungus, and standing beside it a cart drawn by one of the tapir-pigs. Only then did he see the man, or rather boy, standing beside the animal and staring across at them. He was dressed in shorts fashioned from some crudely stitched un-dyed material, and a sleeveless shirt of the same fabric.

Their guide hurried across to the human, and Vaughan and Das followed.

The alien and the boy spoke in a high, fluid tongue; the alien turned and gestured to Vaughan and Das.

All the time the boy had been talking to the alien in its own language, his eyes had darted from Vaughan to the Indian woman and back again. He was perhaps sixteen – and therefore was born here, never having known Earth – with a shock of blond hair and a pale, open face. His skin, unlike the first colonists Vaughan had seen, bore no trace of green colouration.

The alien stepped nimbly onto the cart's front wheel and slipped over its side. It sat in the cart, peering ahead.

The boy said, "You should join him, quickly. He says others are following you. I'm Tom, by the way. I'll be taking you to Connor." He had a curiously flat accent, not at all the American twang Vaughan had been expecting.

Das stepped onto the wheel and hauled herself onto the cart's flatbed, bouncing on stacks of some yellow, flaxen stalks. Vaughan joined her and they sat side by side as Tom mounted a forward seat, snapped the reigns and steered the cart slowly down the hillside.

"I'm Jeff, and this is Parveen," Vaughan said. The boy just grinned and shouted at the draft animal to watch its step as the cart jolted over a pot-hole.

Beside them, their guide curled into a ball and slept.

Tom glanced over his shoulder, grinning. "It's true, then? You came all the way from Earth, aboard a starship?"

Das said, "Did the alien tell you this?"

The boy laughed. "No. He just told me about the others, those chasing you, and said we need to move fast."

"Then how do you know?" Vaughan asked.

Tom looked over his shoulder. "The Taoth told Connor to expect you. Connor told my father, who told me to be ready today with my cart."

"The Taoth?"

Tom jabbed his thumb towards the alien.

"And who's Connor?"

"Captain Connor. He's old, but he's still in command. I'm taking you there now, a little under a day's ride away, across the valley."

"And Captain Connor," Das said, "wants to see us?"

Tom repeated, "The Taoth told Connor to expect you."

"Specifically the two of us?" Vaughan asked

The boy smiled. "That's right. Two humans, a man and a woman."

Vaughan looked at Das, then said to Tom, "Do you know when the Taoth told Connor about us?"

Tom nodded. "That'd be a couple of days ago, when they reported you'd seen off the Greens."

Das turned to Vaughan and said in a whisper, "They knew, even *then*?"

Vaughan said to the boy, "How did the Taoth know that we – Parveen and me – would be coming here? I mean, we didn't even know ourselves."

Tom shrugged. "The Taoth… they're a strange and wonderful race." He tapped his head. "Some people think they can read our minds."

Das stared at Vaughan. "But aliens can't read human minds, and vice versa."

"Until we came across the Taoth, maybe," he said.

They had left the hillside behind them and were

pulling along a narrow lane between fields high with what looked like corn.

"Okay," Das said, "just supposing they can read our minds. Why did they take us, and not Rab or his security team?"

Vaughan shrugged. "They read his intentions. They knew what he wanted, and they didn't like that."

"And what about me? I want the same thing as Chandrasakar, after all."

He smiled. "But you don't know what that *thing* is…" he said. "So maybe you're no threat. Maybe the Taoth like your commie leanings, and want to show you their secret."

Das turned to the boy. "Tom, when your people landed here, what was it you found?"

Tom smiled. "These," he said, "the Underlands."

"And anything else?"

The boy frowned, doing his best to accommodate the stranger's odd question. "Well, we found the Taoth, of course."

Vaughan tried another tack. "What was it the Greens – the rebel colonists – wanted to tell Earth? We understand they sent a message about something they discovered here."

Comprehension flooded the boy's open features. "Ah… you mean Vluta?"

"Vluta?" Das echoed. "What's Vluta?"

The boy frowned again. "It's… it's where the Taoth live," he said.

Vaughan and Das exchanged a glance. "Where they *live*?"

Tom nodded. "It's where they went when they left their cities here."

"And when was that?"

"I think many cycles ago, perhaps as many as a hundred."

"A cycle being the duration the planet takes to orbit Delta Cephei, right?" Vaughan guessed.

The boy nodded. "My father told me that that's around twenty-five Earth years."

So the aliens had left the cities more than two thousand five hundred years ago, Vaughan estimated.

Das shook her head, exasperated. "But where did they *go*, Tom?"

He smiled, unsurely. "They went to Vluta," he explained, as if speaking to an idiot.

Das nodded, and raised her eyebrows at Vaughan.

Tom shouted as the tapir-pig decided to root for food in the lane. He prodded the animal with a stick and seconds later the cart was jolting on its way.

Vaughan stared out at a farmhouse, a rickety construction of fungal boles, something almost fairy-tale in its rude construction. A family sat on the porch, a man and a woman watching two little girls, absorbed in a game with their dolls. Vaughan smiled to himself.

Das went on, "But the aliens come back from Vluta from time to time?"

"There are always a few Taoth round about," Tom said. "I don't know if the same ones stay a while, then go, or if different ones come and go. They're a mystery, but we get on well." He frowned. "It's hard to put into words. The Taoth are just there, and we're here, and that's how it's been, long as I recall."

"Do you know how many of them are here?" Vaughan asked.

The boy shrugged easily and laughed, "Well, that could be around ten or so, or a hundred... It's really hard to say."

They passed another farmhouse, and fields worked by human farmers. Some of the workers hailed Tom, and he waved in greeting.

Vaughan lay back, lulled by the motion of the cart. He felt tired. He was aware of Das and Tom talking, but their words flowed over him, became a background noise, as he stared up at the spread of sparkling crystals and slowly slipped into sleep.

TWENTY-THREE

QUESTIONS

Parveen lay back on the tubers, watching the farmland pass by. Vaughan was asleep, and at the rear of the flatbed the alien was curled as if dozing too. She gazed back at the mountain range they had left behind, looking for the first sign of their pursuers.

She could be under no illusions, now, about just what Rab's sentiments were towards her. He had her down as the traitor she had been all along, and wanted her dead – and Vaughan along with her. She had tried to kid herself, when the firing began, that the spider drone had been under Singh's command – but the fact was that Rab was right there alongside the security chief and the drones. She had no doubt that he had given the command to fire.

She supposed it made her dilemma easier, now. She knew where she stood as regards her feelings towards the tycoon, though when she considered the weeks when she thought she'd loved him... the pain still bit deep.

She looked ahead. She had a goal, no longer

clouded by the stirrings of her heart. She would find out what the colonists had found, this Vluta place, if Tom's word was to be taken at face value, and then try to get through to her country's starship.

And Vaughan? He was a bit part player in the scenario now; she'd do her best to make sure he wasn't harmed, and try to get him off the planet with her. But only if he was willing to play the game according to her rules.

Tom glanced at her, shyly. He seemed intrigued by the colour of her skin. She smiled and held up her right hand. "You've never seen anyone from India before, Tom?"

He shook his head. "No, M'am. I heard about Indians, but..." he shrugged and smiled, "it was hard to picture what you looked like."

She laughed. "And yet there you are, living alongside green aliens?"

"Kinda strange, huh?"

She smiled and said, "Tell me about the rebel colonists, Tom."

"They're hard-liners, M'am. Connor calls them the Right Wing. Back on Earth, he said, they wanted supremacy for the FNSA."

"And Connor... he sounds an enlightened leader."

The boy shrugged. "He doesn't like the rebels. He said if they got what they want, they'll bring ruin to the world. Things are just fine here as they are here in Landfall. Or Kalluta, as the Taoth call this world." He smiled. "We don't want outsiders here, even the FNSA, messing things up."

"And then *we* arrive..."

He smiled self-consciously. "Connor told my

father... he said, the Taoth would help us when you came."

She sat up. "Help you? What did he mean by that?"

Tom gave his characteristic shrug again. "I don't fully know, M'am. My father didn't say, just told me not to worry about the future."

Parveen stared out at the passing land, the arable idyll that the colonists had eked out of this alien landscape.

She asked, "Did the rebels agree with the way of life you're living now?"

His reply didn't surprise her in the least. "They wanted to get away from living off the land. They said they wanted to build cities, manufacture machines, mine the planet. They said that was the only way to progress..." He shrugged. "But we seem to be doing pretty well, all things considered."

She smiled. That really depended, she thought, on the political system they'd adopted here. She had no great hopes that it was an egalitarian utopia where land was divided equally among the citizens, and wealth distributed to those who worked the land and supplied the meagre goods they must produce.

"Tom, who runs Landfall?"

He squinted at her. "Well, Connor runs the Assembly."

"You mean, he has total control?"

He shook his head. "Well, not really. There are regional councils, made up of elected members. They meet at Assembly every thirty days, and Connor runs the meetings."

"So he's more of a chairman?"

He nodded. "Something like that."

"But he doesn't tell the councils what to do?"

He frowned. "I don't think so. He advises them, and they make the laws. But if we have any problems, we just take them to Connor and he gives us good advice."

Parveen smiled to herself. And to think that a colony of the good old FNSA had come to this...

She asked, "And everyone has enough to eat on Landfall? No one starves?"

Tom laughed. "Starves? M'am, you throw seed into the ground and ten days later you're eating produce."

She wondered what the party would make of this. If there were indeed many thousands of caverns like this one... But there had to be a catch, she thought. They worship a god that demands ritual human sacrifice, or the Taoth take every fifth child...

She settled back into the tubers, rocked by the motion of the cart.

They chatted a little more; Tom asked her about Earth, and if it were true that people lived in cities ten times larger than the Taoth's old cities, and flew around the globe in air-carts, and didn't farm the land but had robots to do all the work for them on farms as vast as ten caverns?

She smiled and nodded and told him that, yes, it was all true.

He fell silent after that, lost in contemplation of the incomprehensible world that was Earth.

A while later she lifted her left arm and showed Tom the crimson encrustation that covered her handset. "Tom, do you know how to get rid of this stuff?"

He shook his head. "That's Taoth doing, right?

You had a device on your arm? I know that because some of the old colonists had them too. But the Taoth, they told Connor they were bad."

She looked at him. "The Taoth said this?"

"Yes, M'am. They put the scabs on some of the old colonists – that was another thing the rebels didn't like."

"Tom, what else won't the Taoth let you do?"

He pushed out his lips. "Nothing else, as far as I know. Just that."

"What about other machinery? Do you have holo-screens, audio-pins, scanners?"

He looked at her as if she were speaking a foreign language. "Don't know anything about any of those things, M'am."

She nodded and settled back, thinking through what she'd learned.

Minutes later she glanced at the alien, and realised that it was watching her with its bulging insect eyes.

She moved to the back of the cart so that she was sitting before the creature. "What are you doing to these people?" she hissed.

It continued its unremitting, inscrutable stare.

"You won't allow them handsets. And this..." She gestured around at the land on all sides. "All very quaint and rural, but they're living like peasants. When these people came here they had all the latest technology. Where has all that gone, that expertise? Why don't you want these people to... to progress?"

She stopped in exasperation as the alien deigned not to reply.

She stared at the creature; it was, she thought, the

second cousin to a tree frog, a lot larger and darker green, but similar nevertheless; and they had managed to reduce a colony of twenty-second-century human beings to the status of agrarian land-workers.

The Taoth had left their cities – abandoning their technology with them? – and retreated... somewhere. Vluta, whatever that was. And why had the rebels so eagerly wanted to communicate the fact of Vluta to the FNSA, and why had the Taoth and the colonists done everything to stop them?

She tapped the shell that covered her handset. "And when are you going to let us use these again? Why did you...?" She stopped as something occurred to her. Perhaps the reason the Taoth had disabled their handsets was to prevent her communicating with the Indian ship, when the time came? If Tom was right, and the aliens did possess a telepathic capability, then they were a more formidable opposition than they appeared at first sight.

She smiled at the irony of the situation; she knew now how uneasy Vaughan had felt, on having her read his every thought. The idea that the alien beside her might be telepathic made her more than a little uneasy. It would know what she planned, once she had the use of her handset again – calling in the Indian ship to lay claim to Landfall and to get her out of here... so what chance was there of the Taoth allowing that to happen?

She decided, suddenly, that when she did eventually get off the damned planet and return to Kolkata, then she would go to Anish Lahore and tell him that her days of working for the Party were over. She wanted her tele-ability taken away. From then on she would devote herself to her academic studies.

On discovering the secret of Landfall, she would tell him, she had discharged her obligation to Mother India.

TWENTY-FOUR

ULUTA

Vaughan came awake and struggled into a sitting position.

Das sat opposite him, head lolling with the motion of the cart. "Welcome back to the land of the living." She tossed him a grapefruit-analogue.

"How long have I slept?" He peeled the fruit and ate.

"Around six hours, maybe more. I've been quizzing Tom."

"Learn much?"

"The colonists down here occupy three caverns similar to this one, and number some ten thousand citizens in all. They farm the land, raise crops, and breed animals. They call the planet Landfall, unoriginally. The Taoth know it as Kalluta."

Vaughan glanced at the alien. Their guide was awake, seated at the rear of the cart and gazing back the way they had come.

Das hesitated, and he knew she was contemplating the wisdom of telling him something.

"What is it?"

"Just that... they live a pretty egalitarian system here. They seem to want for nothing..."

"I sense a 'but' coming."

"But, Jeff, the Taoth don't allow the colonists any form of technology. This was another thing that prompted the rift between the colonists and the rebels. The rebels were what you'd call progressive – but they were also politically right of centre, according to what Connor told Tom's father. The Taoth didn't want other humans coming here, and so influenced the colonists."

"Interesting."

"And they fixed these scabs to the colonists who had handsets."

"If they don't want us getting our hands on their planet," he said, "then they're not likely to let us use our coms, are they?"

She nodded. "They're... they're a primitive people, Jeff. My guess is that they were once technological, but since then they've devolved."

"And yet they have us... and the colonists... just where they want us."

He looked around at the limitless expanse of fields, the scattered farmsteads, the people working the land. "Did Tom say anything more about Vluta?"

She shook her head. "I didn't ask him, but I don't think he knows anything more than he told us."

Vaughan turned and looked back towards the jagged range of mountains they had crossed. "No sign of Chandrasakar?"

"I've been keeping an eye out," she replied. "They'd have taken a while to cross the savannah.

It'll be hours yet before they show themselves."

"We should warn Connor about them when we arrive."

She considered this. "I'll tell them who and what Rab is. I'll tell him that they should trust him about as much as they trusted the rebels."

Vaughan couldn't suppress a smile. "And how will you describe yourself, and who you represent?"

She shook her head, testily. "I'll see how things pan out. Whatever happens, my government wouldn't exploit these people as the Chandrasakar Organisation would." She stared across at him. "And I'd appreciate it if you keep quiet and let me do the talking."

He smiled, then made a sardonic mime of locking his lips and tossing away the key.

"But," he said, gesturing to the back of the alien in the cart, "I wonder if our friends here will be as co-operative? If Tom's right and they are telepathic..." He smiled. "Then they know all about us."

She muttered something to herself, lay back and closed her eyes.

Five minutes later Tom turned in his seat, holding the reins with one hand and pointing with the other. "See the farm over there? That's my father's. We raise tams and grow beet. Biggest farm in the area."

Vaughan squinted at a ramshackle construction comprising a central two-storey section and two sprawling wings, with attached outbuildings and barns. "Some place," he said.

Tom beamed proudly. "I'll be running the farm when my father retires," he said.

Vaughan considered Tom's simple life, contrasting it with that of a farm boy in the US or Canada two centuries ago. Take away the aliens, and the enclosed subterranean environment, then the two would have been pretty similar.

"How far are we from Connor's place?" he asked.

Tom indicated a range of hills a few kilometres ahead. "Connor's manse is on Overlook Hill. Another hour away."

The hills folded and buckled and became, in the distance, a range of mountains, which enclosed the cavern on three sides.

Das asked Tom, "Do you know how many caverns there are down here?"

Tom thought about it. "My people have explored at least a dozen," he said. "One beyond the other, all linked." He shrugged. "The world's vast, according to my father."

Das said, "Ten times the size of Earth, Tom."

The boy laughed. "Well then, how many caverns would fit into a planet ten times bigger than Earth? Thousands!"

He envisaged this place in twenty years from now, if the FNSA or the Chandrasakar Organisation, or whoever else, were given free rein: the way of life of these people would be gone for ever, replaced by bustling cities servicing vast mining concerns and other industries.

An hour later the cart began climbing a winding lane through the foothills, and soon an odd building came into view. It resembled many of the farms on the plain, with the addition of a barn door constructed from panels of the ship that had brought the colonists to Delta Cephei VII. Faded red, white, and blue letters, FNSA, adorned the door above the

Federated flag: a field of red stripes with a big white on blue star in the top left corner.

Tom saw Vaughan looking at the door. "Connor raised the best gurs in the land, before he retired. He kept them in there."

Vaughan smiled to himself.

Tom brought the cart to a halt. "Connor's always at home. He'll be expecting you. Just knock on the door."

Vaughan and Das jumped down, followed by the Taoth. Tom took up the reigns and clucked at the draught animal. He glanced down at Vaughan. "This is as far as I go. It was good talking."

Vaughan reached up and took the boy's hand in a firm shake. "Good talking to you too, Tom."

Das, he noticed, was striding towards the front veranda of the farmhouse, the alien beside her.

The boy watched Das walk away, then frowned down at Vaughan. He clearly wanted to say something, but found the words difficult. "I wonder–"

Vaughan said, "You're afraid that because we're outsiders, from Earth, we'll bring others here, change your way of life?"

"My father did say that if the rebels got what they wanted…"

"Tom," Vaughan reassured him, "I'll do my best to make sure that whatever happens my people won't spoil things down here, okay?"

The boy brightened and tugged the reins. As Vaughan lifted a hand and waved a farewell, he wondered at the wisdom of making such a rash promise.

He hurried after Das and stepped onto the porch just as the front door opened and a tall, balding man – combining the gravitas of a starship captain with the down-at-home appearance of a subsistence farmer, garbed in home-made dungarees, straw hat and all – smiled out at them.

He shook their hands and introduced himself, then bent to touch fingertips with the alien: they exchanged high, fluting words, during which Connor nodded and glanced at the strangers.

"Come in. I've been expecting you, but I suspect young Tom's told you all about that." He led the way into the house, up a flight of rickety steps to a long veranda overlooking the vale.

Connor spread an arm in a gesture encompassing the cavern. "Welcome to Landfall. Will you join me in a meal, and then we'll proceed with the journey?"

Das opened her mouth to say something, then had second thoughts.

They sat at a table, and a young woman brought out a selection of breads, cheeses and a bowl of salad. Jugs of amber juice already stood upon the table. The Taoth absented itself from the meal and moved along the veranda; it dropped into a squat and stared out across the valley.

Connor gestured at the laden table. "Please, join me."

They ate, Vaughan taking bread and cheese and a beaker of sharp, sweet juice.

Das said, "What exactly has the Taoth told you about us?"

Connor smiled. Vaughan guessed the captain was in his eighties, thin and sinewy; he gave the impression of someone happy with the life of a smallholder, the nominal head of a thriving colony.

"The Taoth," he said, "are economical with their words. They say the bare minimum in order to convey their meaning, and sometimes one must... interpret. Three days ago Rath here informed me that a starship had landed from Earth, and that two people would be coming soon to the valley."

"That's very interesting, Mr Connor," Das said, "because we didn't even know we'd be making the journey here."

Connor smiled, gesturing at the alien with a chunk of bread. "The Taoth are wise beyond our understanding," he said.

"Tom mentioned that they might be telepathic," Vaughan said.

Connor gave a phlegmatic gesture. "That might go some way to explaining their perspicacity."

Das leaned forward, impatiently pushing her plate to one side. "Mr Connor, what have the Taoth done to you people?"

Connor looked perplexed. "Done?"

"They disabled your handsets and proscribed technology. They've reduced you to living like... like peasants."

Connor smiled. "We are living the lives entirely suited to the environment in which we find ourselves. The old ways of Earth would not work here. The Taoth suggested this lifestyle, and we agreed to abide by it."

Das sat back, chewing on a crust of bread as she considered his words.

Vaughan said, "Mr Connor, can you tell us what the Taoth want with us? Rath wasn't exactly chatty on the way here."

"As I said, Rath came to me three days ago and

mentioned your starship, and the imminence of your arrival. He counselled me and my people not to worry; that all would be well here, in time. He asked if I might assist him in transporting you through the caverns, to which I agreed."

Das said, "With all respect, that doesn't answer the question."

Connor gave a nod of absolute understanding. "Parveen, I have learned over the course of more than two decades that the ways of the Taoth are often mysterious. They will impart only that which they wish you to know. I suggest patience, and reassure you that the Taoth are an honest and honourable people."

Vaughan raised his beaker to cover his smile at Das's visible frustration.

Connor ate with deliberation, and looked up at Das's next question.

"What can you tell us about the conflict with the rebel colonists, Mr Connor?"

His aged face showed pain at the question. "It was a most unfortunate time in the founding of the colony," he said. "We found that we were split into two factions, those who followed myself – the majority, I might add – and a minority who sided with Flannery, my ex-chief of security. Flannery and his men appropriated a telemetry rig and proceeded to send forth a message, intended for the FNSA. We managed, after the event and with the help of the Taoth, to track them down and destroy the apparatus. Since then the Greens have lived a life separate from the mainstream, one could say."

Das leaned forward. "The split was about what you'd found down here?" she said. "Tom mentioned Vluta…"

Connor frowned, stroking a sunken cheek with a weathered forefinger, and Vaughan thought the man resembled a veteran Shakespearean actor playing a role. "Vluta, as no doubt Tom told you, is where the Taoth make their home."

Das sat back, exasperated. "He did say that. But I don't understand why you wanted to suppress the knowledge of whatever it is you discovered. Why did Flannery want to communicate the finding to the FNSA?"

Connor pantomimed an expression of exquisite forbearing. "My dear, for the very reason that I proscribed Flannery's disseminating the information, cannot you comprehend my reluctance to tell you now?" He spread his hands. "What assurances do we have that you will not return to your ship and inform the Expansion of Landfall and Vluta?"

Vaughan said, "Parveen, Mr Connor does have a valid point."

Das glared across at Vaughan, as if willing him dead.

"If I gave you such a reassurance," Das said, "that I will not return to the ship, that I will not inform the FNSA, of what was discovered here…"

"Parveen," Connor said with infinite charm, "how do I know that you are a representative of the FNSA? You might work for any one of a dozen Terran organisations, in which case of course you wouldn't inform the FNSA. I might wear dungarees and breed gurs in my spare time, my dear, but I also captained a colonisation starship." Behind the man's charm, Vaughan saw, was a shrewd and calculating mind.

"Very well, you have my reassurance that I will inform no one on Earth of what you so obviously wish to keep secret."

Vaughan looked at Das, wondering whether he should intervene to foil her obvious lie.

Connor smiled. "In that case, I think you should ask Rath; he is, after all, a representative of the people to whom Vluta belongs."

Connor called across to the alien in a series of high, mellifluous notes.

The alien raised itself from its squatting position and bobbed across the veranda. It paused before the table, then climbed onto a chair. Clearly not accustomed to such furniture, it dropped into a squat and regarded Das with its massive eyes.

Then it turned to Connor and spoke briefly.

Connor smiled, then translated, "Rath says that he will gladly take you to Vluta, so that you might see it for yourselves."

Das blinked. "And we have his assurance of our safety afterwards? He'll show us, and we'll be free to go?"

Connor spoke to Rath, who replied with a single fluted word.

"You have his assurance," Connor said.

The alien spoke again, then slipped from the table.

Connor reported, "Rath says that, if you have quite finished, then we should be on our way."

Rath left the verandah and moved down the stairs, Das hurrying to catch up. On the veranda, Vaughan touched Connor's arm as the old man was about to step into the house. "But if Rath shows us what you expressly want to keep a secret—"

Connor halted him with a smile. "Jeff, I trust implicitly the judgement of the Taoth. Come," and he led the way from the farmhouse to the makeshift barn door.

He scraped open the starship panel to reveal a yawning dusty chamber. A bulky flier, similar to the burnt-out wreck they had come across on the plain, sat in pride of position.

"I rarely use it these days," Connor told them. "No need, you see. But it will be taking you on the last leg of the journey. Please, climb aboard."

Connor slipped into the driver's seat, caressing the controls with a smile. Rath sat beside him as Das and Vaughan settled themselves in the rear. Connor started the engine, the roar throbbing in the confines of the barn. The vehicle rose, bobbed, and wobbled out into the crystal-light.

Outside, Connor turned the flier on its axis and accelerated towards the mountains. They gained height and Vaughan looked back the way they had come. A pastoral patchwork stretched for kilometres towards the enclosing mountains. He made out Tom's farm-cart, tiny in the distance.

There was no sign of Chandrasakar and his team.

The flier approached the mountains and slipped through a v-shaped notch between two jagged peaks. Vaughan had expected to see another cavern bearing farmland, or perhaps savannah. He was not prepared for the sight that awaited them: a great alien city, perhaps ten times the size of the one they had passed through earlier, extended for as far as the eye could see. Indeed, Vaughan was unable to make out the far side of the cavern. Like the first city, this one was laid out on a radial pattern, and it comprised of identical two- and three-storey khaki-coloured buildings. Again an air of decrepitude hung over the place; it was more a mausoleum than a metropolis where, thousands of years ago, an alien race had made its home.

Connor brought the flier down so that they skimmed at head height along a wide avenue.

Das said, "Why did the Taoth desert their cities, Mr Connor?"

The old starship captain said over his shoulder, "They found a better place."

Das sighed. "Vluta, right?"

Connor smiled and nodded. Rath touched his arm, and the pair fell into muted conversation.

Vaughan murmured to Das, "How do you hope to keep your side of the bargain? When we know what the colonists found, you'll get back to your paymasters, right? So much for your good word."

Das looked at him. "The end justifies the means. I'll do what I'll do for the greater good."

"Hasn't that been the watchword of dictators and tyrants throughout human history?"

Das chose to ignore him.

Vaughan studied the buildings passing on either side. He had taken them, at first glance, to be no more than simple constructions of mud and timber – similar to the cities of many pre-industrial peoples on Earth. But when he looked closer, he made out evidence to the contrary. In places the brickwork had crumbled, revealing internal structural supports that resembled steel girders. That suggested a degree of technology he had thought beyond the

Taoth.

He leaned forward and addressed Connor. "What level of technology did the Taoth possess when they left the cities?"

"They were – they are – an advanced industrial race, Jeff. They mined their planet for ores and metals, and refined oils; they had advanced chemical processes."

"And yet they choose to keep you mired in the past," Das snapped. She stared at the passing buildings. "The city appears... basic," she went on. "I don't see any signs of industry."

"This is where they lived," Connor said. "Their industrial-manufacturing complexes are far deeper than this level of caverns."

Das said, "How far do the cavern systems extend?" Vaughan could see a calculating light in her eyes.

Connor replied, "They ring the world and extend down for at least five levels."

"*Shiva*..." Das breathed.

"And yet the Taoth just up and left," Vaughan said.

Connor glanced over his shoulder. "But not before exploring the planets of stars in the vicinity of Delta Cephei," he said with a smile.

"They had spaceflight?" Das said, wide-eyed.

"Sub-light, and they hadn't discovered the void, but yes, they had achieved spaceflight. You sound shocked."

"To be honest, I thought the race... primitive... despite their obvious talents. How wrong can you be?"

"You said they explored nearby suns," Vaughan

said. "Did they stay, set up colonies?"

Connor shook his head. "They found no habitable systems, and withdrew back to Kalluta."

"Strange," Das said.

Connor smiled. "Yes, that word does go a long way to describing the Taoth."

Conversation lapsed and Vaughan stared about him at the passing city. He estimated they were still not halfway across the metropolis, though the bulwark of the distant enclosure had resolved itself; not mountains this time, but a wall or rock curving far overhead to form the city's 'sky'. Like the last city, this one was illuminated only by the fungal growth.

Vaughan asked Connor about this.

"The Taoth preferred the green light for their cities. The crystal light they reserved for the caverns which they gave over to food production."

"The crystals are artificial?" he asked.

Connor nodded. "They store light and energy during the planet's short summer transit of Delta Cephei, and it lasts the long winters until summer comes round again. The Taoth that remained promised that they would instruct our engineers on the maintenance of the crystals, though they need servicing only every hundred or so Earth years."

They flew on for a while in silence, and Vaughan wondered at the mystery of the Taoth.

Connor said, "Imagine our excitement when we discovered these deserted cities."

"Which did you locate first?" Das asked. "The Taoth, or the cities?"

Connor smiled at the memory. "Oh, the cities," he said. "I think the Taoth were keeping their distance until they'd worked us out. We came down not far from the planet's equator and explored the area. We set up surface settlements, domes and such, but the extremes of summer and winter made the surface uninhabitable for much of the time. We needed to look underground if there was any possibility of founding a colony on the planet."

"How did you find the caverns?" Vaughan asked.

"Simplicity itself. We landed at the end of a winter cycle, with a year to go before summer came round again. When things started hotting up, we simply followed the native fauna – they led us underground to the first of the caverns. After that it was a case of following our noses."

Vaughan shook his head. "It must have been some day when you came across a Taoth city."

"You cannot begin to imagine, Jeff. I was leading an exploratory team with Flannery when we came upon the first city, two chambers back. We considered settling there, but decided that the crystal lighted planes were better suited to our purposes. We set up farms in the second cavern – it was already cleared of fungus, you see, by the Taoth, millennia ago. From there we ranged far and wide, up and down."

"When did you come across the Taoth?" Das asked.

Connor laughed. "When they wanted to be found," he said. "Or, to be truthful, when they found us. They'd left a skeleton crew, as it were, back here to maintain things. We'd been here perhaps a year when a deputation of Taoth approached us. I think they'd worked out we were relatively peaceable–"

"But the conflict with Flannery...?" Vaughan began.

"Didn't happen until we came across Vluta," Connor explained.

"When was this?" Das asked.

"A couple of years ago, Terran. We had a debate amongst our citizens – should we or should we not inform Earth, or rather the FNSA. The vote was overwhelmingly against the idea. Flannery of course was pro-dissemination. He let his anger fester for months, before taking violent action and appropriating the com-rig. That would be... what, a year ago? We've been expecting – dreading – a deputation from Earth ever since."

Vaughan grunted a humourless laugh. "And now you have it," he said.

Connor lifted the flier so that they were skimming over the rooftops. Vaughan looked down, imagining a city teeming with a population of aliens.

Why had they left the cities, he wondered, and retreated to Vluta... wherever and whatever that might be?

"How did you discover Vluta?" Das asked. "Did the Taoth show you?"

Connor shook his head. "We discovered it. I... I have the impression that the Taoth might never have let on, but for the fact that one of my foraging teams stumbled upon it by chance. You see, we'd come across so many alien cities occupying the caverns that this one seemed just like all the others."

"This one?" Vaughan asked.

"My team went through the city, salvaging what they could – metals, a timber-analogue. Then they came to the far cavern wall, and saw... that–" And he pointed ahead to the ramparts of the far cavern wall.

Vaughan stared. The wall must have been two kilometres away, but even so he made out, climbing its slope, the unmistakable sight of a vast sweep of steps, easily a kilometre wide, rising in a fan-shaped sweep towards an arched opening in the vertical wall of the cavern.

Even at this distance it possessed a majesty that merely hinted at the wonders that might lie beyond.

"What the hell...?" Das breathed.

"All will be revealed," Connor said, and accelerated towards the sweeping steps.

Rath touched Connor's arm and spoke, and Connor nodded.

He said over his shoulder, "Rath thinks it appropriate that we should alight at the foot of the steps and ascend on foot."

Vaughan nodded, aware that his heart was thudding in anticipation.

They came to the steps, like the semicircular sweep of an amphitheatre, and Connor settled the flier and sat staring up as if with reverence. Rath was the first to alight; Vaughan followed, then Das. Connor joined them and they stood side by side, staring up the incline in wonder.

Rath took the first step, then turned and gestured for the others to follow.

They climbed.

The stairway was made for smaller feet, and shorter legs, than humans possessed; Vaughan found himself making a series of small, quick steps, which soon tired him. They adjusted their pace to that of Connor, while the alien bobbed ahead, pausing from time to time in order for the laggardly humans to catch up.

"Okay," Das said to Vaughan at one point. "Three guesses. What will we find?"

Vaughan shook his head. "Beats me." He smiled. "But whatever it is, something tells me it'll be a disappointment."

She nodded. "Me too."

He paused, then said, "Some industrial process, a technological wonder?"

He stopped climbing and looked down the way they had come. They were barely a third of the way up the fanned stairway, but already they were above the level of the city rooftops.

He began walking again, head down, so as not to be daunted by the fact that the distant archway seemed never to draw any closer.

"I recall my first approach," Connor said a while later. "Just two years ago... but it seems just like yesterday. It is truly one of the wonders of the known universe."

Das looked at Vaughan. "Still prepared to be disappointed?"

He murmured, "Even more so," and looked up to see that they had climbed almost two-thirds of the way to the top.

A further ten minutes of measured ascent brought them to the entrance. They rested, sitting on the very highest step and looking down across the city. The flier, parked below, was reduced to the apparent size of a child's toy.

Behind them, Rath spoke.

Connor translated, "He says it is time to proceed."

Vaughan nodded and climbed to his feet, his chest tight with anticipation.

Connor followed Rath through the arch. Vaughan gestured Das before him, and he brought up the rear.

They were in a narrow corridor, at the end of which was another arched opening, and through it fell a shaft of bright blue light.

Rath stepped into the light and became a spindly silhouette, followed by Connor. Das hesitated, but only for a second, before she too stepped through. Vaughan took a breath and followed.

He found himself in a chamber perhaps as long and wide as a cathedral, though far taller. The chamber itself was unspectacular, merely a natural feature in the rock... but the wonder of it stood at the chamber's far end.

It was, he guessed, perhaps twenty metres wide and fifty high.

"What the...?" Das began.

Vaughan stepped forward, then began walking, until he stood before the wonder, his mouth open. He sensed the others beside him.

He turned to Connor, and then looked at Rath. "But what is it?"

Through the natural arch he looked down on a vast city, a series of tall, thin buildings stretching for as far as the eye could see and laid out on a series of canals; air-cars flitted through what looked like a night-time indigo sky – but how could that be, he asked himself – and he saw, disbelievingly, three huge moons hanging in the sky. Then he made out, beyond them, what looked like a spread of packed stars.

Beside him, Rath had dropped into a squat, staring up with its emotionless insect eyes. He wondered what thoughts were passing through its alien mind.

"What is it?" he asked Connor.

"Vluta," said the oldster.

Rath stood and raised both its hands in the air, as if in alien celebration. "Vluta," it piped.

"It's another chamber?" Das said, but she sounded unconvinced.

Connor shook his head. "Vluta is a city on a world circling a star over thirty thousand light years away, towards the hub of the galaxy."

Das shook her head. "But what...?" She gestured towards the city.

Connor smiled. "This," he said, gesturing at the great archway, "is a space-time portal, for want of a better word, connecting this world to that one."

TWENTY-FIVE

THROUGH THE PORTAL

Vaughan stepped forward until he was a metre from the membrane of the portal, still struggling to comprehend the consequences of Connor's statement. This busy metropolis before him – if he reached out, he might touch it – was light years distant, an alien city somehow made reachable by a technology so far in advance of human understanding that it made the science of voidspace travel seem like stone-age tool making.

He made out the tiny figures of aliens going about their business on the distant planet. They promenaded beside canals, crossed squares, and passed down boulevards lined with crimson, shock-haired trees. Three vast moons hung in the sky, and beyond them were the hub stars, an array so compacted it seemed to glow like a chandelier.

Das was beside him. "So this is what Chandrasakar wanted," she said.

"If he got his hands on this technology…" Vaughan began.

"He'd be invincible, Jeff. No one would stand a chance."

He looked at her. "You mean, your government wouldn't stand a chance?"

"I mean no one would. It'd be a disaster—"

He could only smile at that. "And if your paymasters got their grubby communist claws on it, it would be any better?"

She didn't even deign to glance at him. "We'd use it for the good of humanity," she said.

"I think I've heard that line before."

Now she did look at him, and her expression shocked him. He saw contempt in her eyes. "The fact is that I've got here before Rab."

"You know something?" he said. "Your attitude strikes me as familiar – like that of the old colonialists your party so despises. They discovered new lands, fabulous wealth, and claimed it as theirs as by God-given decree. Don't you think the Taoth might have something to say about that?"

"We won't take the technology, Vaughan. We'll negotiate. We'll put the case for our rights to use the technology for humankind's benefit."

Something close to despair opened up in Vaughan, then. He foresaw the fight that would ensue to claim the rights to utilise the alien technology, and there could only be one loser: he wondered if the Taoth were aware of what they had let themselves in for when they revealed their secret to humanity.

He laughed, but without the slightest humour.

Das looked at him. "What?"

"You might have got here first, Das," he said. "But Chandrasakar's not far behind. How do you fancy your chances against him?"

Instinctively she raised her right arm.

Vaughan shook his head. "I think the Taoth thought of that," he said. It gave him small comfort that she was unable to get through to her country's starship.

Das was staring through the portal. She pointed. "Look."

On Vluta, the portal stood at the top of a long flight of steps leading down to the canal-crossed city. As he stared, a dozen robed Taoth were making their way slowly up the wide stairway. Something lurched in his gut, for he knew that this delegation was meant for Das and himself.

A tall alien led the party, and when they reached the top of the steps the others paused and it approached. It seemed in every particular identical to Rath, except for the iridescent robe that clothed its bulbous torso and spindly limbs.

For five seconds it stared through the membrane at Vaughan and Das. Its bulbous eyes were unblinking, its expression unreadable. Then it stepped casually through the membrane, as if moving from one room to the next – a single step taking it 30,000 light years across space.

It spoke with Rath in their high, piccolo language.

Seconds later it turned to Vaughan and Das.

An age seemed to elapse. Vaughan counted his heartbeats. Ten, fifteen… He felt that the alien was about to say something, the significance of which he couldn't begin to guess at.

"Vaughan," the creature said at last in halting English, "will you please accompany me through the portal to Vluta?"

He felt suddenly dizzy. As if in reaction to the situation, he craved familiarity: he wanted Sukara, her embrace.

"To Vluta?" he echoed.

"There, we would like to speak to you of the way of things…"

He could not help himself smile at the alien's quaint phraseology.

Das stepped forward. "And me?" she asked.

The robed alien turned its impassive gaze to the Indian. "My Council…" and here the alien turned and gestured to the assembly of aliens beyond the portal, "have assessed your suitability and found you wanting."

Instead of being gratified at Das's summary dismissal by the Taoth, Vaughan felt a cold apprehension at the corollary of the alien's words: if Das had been found wanting, then he had not. He was, therefore, *suitable*… but for what?

Das waved a hand. "Wanting?" she said. "But I represent the Communist Government of India. If you know anything about my people, you'll know that we stand for the egalitarian principles."

The robed alien cut her short. "Please," it said with an air of courteous forbearance. "We know all about you people. We have made our decision." It turned to Vaughan. "If you would care to accompany me…"

It turned and walked towards the membrane, paused before the interface and awaited him.

Vaughan hesitated. Something more than the impossible fact of stepping across light years halted his progress. What, beyond the portal on Vluta, might await him?

Das said, "I'd be careful, Vaughan. You can't trust these people."

That, oddly enough, decided him. He turned to her and said, "For some reason, Das, I think I can."

He looked at the robed alien and nodded. The alien passed through the membrane and, heart racing, Vaughan stepped after it.

He was aware of a split second of dizziness, a rush of heat passing across his body, and then he was on a planet near the centre of the galaxy, bathed in the light of three alien moons. It was warm, sultry, and the air was spiced with a mixture of sweet and indescribable scents. The gravity was less than that of Delta Cephei VII and Earth: he felt buoyant, as if he might jump and leave the ground for seconds at a time.

He turned. Through the portal he made out the cavern, and the figures of Rath, Connor, and Das, staring at him. Das stepped forward, her mouth moving, though no sound travelled the light years. She was clearly remonstrating with Connor, who stepped forward and tried to restrain her as she reached out to touch the membrane.

Her hand seemed to halt in the air halfway towards Vaughan, as if brought up short by a pane of glass. She frowned, applied more pressure and grimaced in frustration. She turned to Rath and spoke angrily to him, but the alien heard her out and decided against gracing her tirade with a reply.

Instead, it turned from her and moved through the membrane, walking on past Vaughan and the robed alien and moving away down the steps. This had the effect of renewing Das's attempts to break through; she applied her shoulder and pushed, to no avail. Vaughan felt a touch on his arm. It was the robed alien, suggesting they leave her to her futile attempts.

"Please," it said, "this way."

The council of aliens was making its way down the steps, and the robed alien and Vaughan followed. At one point he turned back. Das had ceased her shoulder charges and had drawn her laser. For a terrible second he thought she was about to use it on the portal, but evidently she had second thoughts. She slipped the weapon into her jacket, moved away from the membrane and hurried across the chamber towards the far entrance. He wondered if she had decided to confront Chandrasakar when and if he arrived.

Taking a deep breath, Vaughan followed the robed alien down the steps.

TWENTY-SIX

END GAME

Parveen hurried from the portal towards the cavern's exit, paused, and looked back through the membrane to Vluta. Vaughan had disappeared with the aliens down the broad stairway, gone to learn whatever the Taoth required of him. The knowledge burned within her. If only she could have had more time with the Taoth – or at least more time with an alien willing actually to communicate with her – then she was sure she could have persuaded them to give the secret of their portals to her government.

It was ironic that they had chosen someone as politically apathetic as Vaughan to go with them to their world. She wondered what they wanted with him, and if he would be back to tell her. She very much doubted that.

Beside her, Connor cleared his throat. "I'm returning to the vale. Would you care to accompany me?"

She thought about what she should do next, then shook her head. "No. I should stay here. My... my acquaintances should be here pretty soon now."

He bowed his head in understanding. "If you need anything…" he began.

She raised her left arm. "Do you know how I might get rid of this?"

He smiled. "I'm afraid not. It's a phenomenon beyond our understanding. My guess is that the Taoth will remove it when they see fit."

He moved to step through the exit and descend the stairs to his air-car. "One thing," she said, stepping forward.

He paused. "Yes?"

She gestured back at the portal. "What do you think about… about *that*, about what the Taoth did to you, their proscription on technology, progress…?"

He smiled, placidly. "The Taoth helped us, Parveen. Without them, we would very likely have perished on this planet."

"But they could have allowed you to contact Earth, tell them about–"

He was shaking his head. "They discouraged our use of technology because we do not need it down here. And they didn't want Earth to know of the portal for obvious reasons."

That was it, she thought. The Taoth feared humanity. They feared what the spread of humankind might mean for the stability of their future – and perhaps, she acknowledged, they were right to do so.

She said, "But not allowing you to develop, to retain and use your technology… isn't that unacceptable social engineering?"

He smiled at this. "We accepted it," Connor said,

"and anyway, are not your people guilty – if that's the word – of similar social engineering?"

Before she could reply, he smiled his farewell and moved down the stairs. He eased himself into the air-car, started it up, and moved off down the long boulevard. She stood and watched him go, and soon the vehicle was a small speck flying low over the deserted city.

She sat down in the entrance of the cavern, staring out across the alien city, and considered her options.

Soon Rab would be here, eager to claim the secret of the Taoth. She smiled to herself. What the tycoon didn't know was that the alien race, outwardly so unprepossessing – they looked like nothing more than tree frogs, after all – were advanced in many ways beyond human comprehension. Even if they allowed the portal to remain *in situ*, which she doubted, Rab and his team would be unable to fathom how it worked. They would be as frustrated as she was, which was the only satisfying aspect of the situation.

But what to do now?

She couldn't contact her ship because of the damned crimson scab, and she couldn't rely on Rab's charity for a ride back home aboard the *Kali*.

She could always claim that she had left the party under duress – that Vaughan had forced her away at gunpoint. Or, better, what about the simple truth? That she'd been taken by the alien... Would he believe her, though?

She considered her feelings for the tycoon, and smiled at her naivety in thinking, not so long ago, that she had loved him.

What she had loved, she realised, was the thought of being loved. Rab had used her as he had used everyone else with whom he came into contact. Or had he, she wondered. He had used her to monitor Vaughan... but that did not preclude the possibility that Rab might, at the same time, have felt something for her.

She stood. She could not rely on the Taoth to allow her the use of her handset again, and therefore her only means of escape from the planet was aboard the *Kali*. When Rab appeared, she would play the innocent, claim abduction, even lead him to the wonder of the portal...

She was about to move down the steps when she saw a flash of movement to her left. She turned, and stopped dead in alarm.

Three metres from her, a scintillating spider drone appeared from behind a flange of rock. It regarded her with its swivelling optics. It raised a leg – one of its forward limbs, she saw – and aimed a laser at her.

She remained very still, then glanced towards the deserted city. There was no sign of Rab and his men. She knew she couldn't outgun the drone, but she wondered why it hadn't killed her immediately. Perhaps, she thought, for the same reason the drones had not killed her and Vaughan earlier...

They wanted her alive.

She said, "What do you want?" She was surprised at how calm her voice sounded.

From a grille on its underside, a transistorised voice said, "You will remove your weapon, place it on the ground, and kick it across to me."

She nodded. Very carefully she eased the laser from inside her jacket, laid it before her, and with the toe of her boot prodded it towards the drone.

It reached out with a dainty limb, picked up the weapon in a claw and squeezed. The laser buckled, twisted, and snapped. The drone dropped the debris to the ground.

"And now?" she asked.

"Now you will follow me."

She nodded. "Ah-cha, fine. Where are we going?"

"Follow me."

She nodded again. "Ah-cha. Lead the way."

The spider drone kept its weapon trained on her midriff. Its bottom half swivelled, and seven long, silver legs negotiated the steps. It tapped down the stairway and Parveen followed at a distance. She controlled her breathing. Rab wanted her alive. She would tell him about the alien abduction and just hope he believed her.

The spider drone came to the arching outer boulevard, crossed it, and moved down a long, wide avenue. Parveen followed, going through the words she would use to convince Rab, and more importantly trying to work out how she would play the reunion.

They came to a T-junction and turned right. The drone clicked ahead, something about its nimble tiptoe gait almost balletic. Its laser sighted her every centimetre of the way.

She looked past the drone. They were approaching a central plaza of some kind, a circular arrangement of stone which years ago might have been a fountain. The water was long gone, though, and the statue of a robed alien at its raised centre appeared helplessly isolated. It looked, she thought, exactly how she felt.

Then she saw Rab, and the sight at him, despite herself, sent a stab of pain through her chest.

He was standing with his back to her, one foot lodged on the edge of the fountain, gazing up at the alien statue. Beyond him, standing around the central statue, she made out his security team, Singh among them.

At the ticking arrival of the spider drone, Rab turned and stared at her. His expression remained steadfastly neutral, giving nothing away.

She smiled, attempting to flood her face with relief. "Rab! You don't know how relieved–"

She stopped. His face was unmoving, stone-like. "So you thought you'd leave us stranded, try to find out whatever was down here before us? Why, Parveen? Who are you working for?"

She blustered a laugh. "Rab? It wasn't like that... Listen, we were taken by the aliens, the Taoth. They–" she raised her left arm, as evidence, "–they disabled my handset. They brought us here–"

"Why just the two of you?"

She shrugged. "I don't know... I thought, maybe because we were telepathic. Listen, I didn't want to go with them, please believe that. And as for..." she shook her head, getting into her role... "How could you believe I'm working for anyone but you, Rab?"

Someone moved at the edge of her vision. Singh stepped towards Rab, spoke quietly to him in Punjabi.

Rab said to her, "What did the aliens want with you? Where's Vaughan?"

She licked her lips, nodded. "They took him, Rab. They showed us their secret and then they took him."

Singh said, staring at her with eyes as cold as ice,

"Took him where?"

She remained smiling at Rab. It was him she had to convince, win over to her side. "That's the secret of the Taoth, Rab. They have... portals, gateways through space. They don't need starships."

A light came on in Chandrasakar's brown eyes. "Where is it, Parveen?" he said.

"I'll take you, Rab. If..." She was taking a risk, she knew, but it might get him on her side.

"Yes?"

"If only you'll believe me. That I didn't cut out and try to find the secret myself–"

He nodded. He even smiled, and something of the old Rab brought back a slew of memories. Perhaps, she allowed, she was wrong to mistrust him. Her actions must have appeared more than a little suspicious, after all; he was quite within his rights to suspect her.

"Where is the portal, Parveen?" he asked.

Relief swamped her. She was going to get away from this with her life; she had almost won her passage back to home and safety.

She pointed beyond Rab and the buildings at his back, towards the distant rockface. Across it, like a splash of midnight ink, was the crack that gave access to the chamber housing the portal.

"It's through there," she said. "I'll take you."

She stepped forward, reaching out, and Rab smiled. She found herself wanting to touch him again, to feel his skin...

She knew, then, that she still felt something for the tycoon.

At that second, when she had allowed herself to think that everything would work out fine, Singh moved.

He raised his laser, and Parveen knew that he was going to shoot her.

Instead, the Sikh turned and blasted Rab.

She screamed and backed away as her lover slipped to the floor, his hand still outstretched, his head and a diagonal section of his shoulder slid from his torso and hit the marble slabs with a horrible, bloody slap.

The back of her legs came up against the edge of the fountain and she almost tripped. She sat down quickly, her back against the cold stone, fingers to her lips in shock.

A split second after Singh killed Rab, confirming all her worst fears, he turned and lasered the shocked security personnel behind him. She heard the hiss of his laser, then the incredulous, pained screams of the security men as they attempted to flee.

The spider drone stood before her, three metres away, weapon still levelled. She looked at Singh. The Sikh spoke to the drone in Punjabi, then turned to regard her.

She said, "Who... who are you working for?"

Singh smiled. "That hardly matters, Das."

"The Europeans, right?" If she could keep him talking, perhaps promise to lead him to the portal...

Singh said to the drone, "Ah-cha," and Parveen knew she was dead.

The drone fired. She saw a bright flash and felt a sudden, leaden blow to her stomach. Singh moved away, out of sight around the fountain. The drone remained watching her, mocking her with its mechanical dispassion.

She looked across at Rab's body, and wept. She wondered if he had really, truly loved her.

Perhaps, after all, he had.

It was her very last cogent thought.

She looked down in disbelief at the slippery warm mass she was cupping in her hands. The drone's laser had opened a wide slit in her abdomen, and the pain was becoming unbearable.

COSMOPATH

Vaughan followed the twelve robed aliens down the flight of sweeping steps. They came to a piazza paved in what looked like marble, which scintillated with a million tiny, multicoloured lights. A round table of the same substance, surrounded by similar chairs, stood beside a wide canal. The water was mirror-flat and reflected something vast and banded – and only then did Vaughan look up and notice, behind the arching portal through which he had just passed, a huge gas giant filling half the night sky, encircled by a series of rings canted towards Vluta.

Vaughan felt like laughing at the magnificence of it all.

The council had seated itself, and the tall, robed alien likewise. The latter gestured to the only vacant seat, and Vaughan fell into it as if in a daze.

He felt the combined attention of a dozen pairs of dark, insectile eyes on him. I should, he thought, feel something like trepidation. The fact was that he

experienced only a sense of calm, a feeling of
inevitability as if the events of the preceding few
days had been somehow pre-ordained.

"You must," said the tall alien, whom Vaughan
took to be the council's leader, or at least their
spokesperson, "have many questions."

He stared at the great metropolis surrounding
the portal. There was much familiar in the vista;
that was, his senses recognised those features
which had analogues with Earth: towering
obelisk-like buildings, and the lighted wedges of
air-cars flitting through the indigo night sky like
so many polychromatic tropical fish, and the reticulation of shimmering canals... But there was
much that, though registered by his senses, he was
unable to decode: filaments of golden light, so
faint and fast, that flashed between the strolling
citizens of the city across the canal; balls of light
like corposants, which hovered ten metres from
the ground; and an odd sound which repeated
itself with regularity: something like the boom of
a distant and sonorous gong which sounded in
mystifying syncopation with a swelling, heady
scent that swept across the piazza, like juniper-
scented incense, he thought.

But the chief wonder of all was the rearing portal,
which dominated this part of the city, magnificent
in both its architectural aesthetics and in what it
represented: the annihilation of the space-time con-
tinuum for the purpose of instantaneous travel.

Where to begin?

He gestured towards the portal and said, addressing the tall alien, "On first coming upon your race,
in my ignorance I thought you to be a simple peo-

ple... My apologies. This is beyond anything my race might create."

Instantly, a dozen quick golden filaments shot between the council, connecting their heads. The leader said, "But, Vaughan, we like to think of ourselves as a simple people. That is, uncomplicated, honest, sincere. And the portal..." it raised a thin-fingered hand to the membrane, "is not the work of the Taoth."

A silence followed these words, and Vaughan could only stare. "It isn't?" he said at last.

"It is the creation of a race of beings known as the Krevala. They are ancient. They attained sentience – that is, true sentience, the way of peace and non-conflict – more than a million of your years ago. They originated on a planet of one of the hub stars, and now occupy half the galaxy. They are, individually, vast beings, not unlike the creatures you call cetaceans. From time to time we are lucky enough to meet a travelling Krevalan, though it is a rare event indeed."

"And they created the portals," Vaughan said, "and gave them to the Taoth?"

The alien turned its hand. "Not so much gave," it said, "but granted, as the Krevala has granted eleven other races down the years the secret of the portals."

Vaughan looked up at the stars. "A dozen?" he said. "But there must be countless races out there?"

"Thousands," the leader agreed. "But only the Krevala, ourselves, and ten others make up the Krevalan Concordance."

Vaughan shook his head. "And these races?"

"Are those which the Krevala, in their wisdom,

deem have attributes worthy of their being admitted to the Concordance."

Another series of lightning-fast filaments connected the council, and before Vaughan could ask what these 'attributes' might be, the leader said, "They are old races, and very different in type – humanoids, avian, piscine, and some which have no Terran equivalents. But they have several things in common: they have all outgrown the petty, factional disputes which destroy most races before they attain the stars; they are philosophical races, peaceloving, bent on understanding the ways of the universe."

The alien was silent for a time, and Vaughan said at last, "In other words, very much unlike the human race."

More golden lights connected the gathered assembly.

Vaughan said, "I thought, when you mentioned the Concordance, that you might be considering the admittance of the human race..."

The alien said, "You mean, Vaughan, a part of you feared the idea."

He stared at the alien. "So you are telepathic?"

The leader gestured with its hand, turning it delicately palm-upwards. "Some of us possess the limited ability to apprehend the minds of alien races, yes."

Vaughan said softly, "Then you must know how unsuited we humans are to the aspirations of the Concordance."

A silence followed his words. A golden nexus connected all the Taoth then, including the leader. At last it said, "We were first made aware of the human race twenty-five of your years ago, when the starship landed on our planet – though the Krevala have known of you for aeons. When human colonists came to Kalluta, and found the caverns, we studied them from afar at first, watched their disputes, read their complex motivations. After a period we contacted the colonists, helped the more peaceful elements in their society gain ascendance, showed them how to farm and maintain the caverns – for without our knowledge they would have perished. Kalluta is a harsh world, as you know."

"But you were taking a risk," Vaughan said, "in allowing humans knowledge of your existence."

He felt, then, that if the alien could have smiled, it would have done.

"But Vaughan," it said, "we made contact only with the approval of the Krevala, after we had apprised them of the situation, that the colonists needed our help in order to survive. We made contact, and awaited your arrival."

Vaughan opened his mouth. "Our arrival...?" he echoed.

"The Krevala," said the alien, "are wise beyond our comprehension. It was they who... suggested, shall I say... the strategic withdrawal of the Taoth from Kalluta. They foresaw the arrival of the human race. It would be only a matter of time, they said, before more humans followed the first wave, intent on taking what they could from the planet, and from us."

Vaughan nodded. "A wise move," he murmured, more to himself.

"It is a sad fact," the leader went on, "that *Homo sapiens* must be contained. The slow diaspora of your people through the void to the near stars can be tolerated, but you cannot be allowed to learn the secret of the space-time portals. That would be a calamity beyond imagining. I can see into your mind, Vaughan, and read your contempt for your own race. Your experiences have left you with no love for what your people are capable of... though paradoxically you bear great love for certain of your kind, which," it went on with what Vaughan thought of as fatherly amusement, "is to be condoned. Many people in your situation would have turned to hate."

A frenzied reticulation of golden threads connected every alien then, and another Taoth leaned towards Vaughan and spoke.

"It cannot be stressed too forcefully, Vaughan," it piped in a tone higher and more urgent than the leader's, "how immature is the human race. You have barely evolved. You are still at that stage of your growth where the dictates of your historical survival govern your motivations on personal, societal, and governmental levels. You are a venal, untrustworthy race – which, it has to be said, all races are at certain times of their evolution. The Taoth are no exception, and nor are the Krevala, hard though that is to believe."

The leader resumed, "All of which is to say that for the foreseeable future, for millennia, even more, there will be no contact between the Concordance and your race."

Vaughan indicated the portal. "And that?" he asked.

"Will be closed down soon," the leader said. "The procedure is already under way. There will be nothing left for Chandrasakar, or others of his ilk, to discover and attempt to emulate."

Vaughan nodded. He understood the reasoning behind the Krevalan injunction. A part of him even revelled in the fact that the likes of Chandrasakar and Das's government would be denied the opportunity to exploit and plunder, but a part of him also felt shame.

At last he looked up and said, "But why did you bring me here? Why tell me this?"

He recalled the alien's words in the cavern, its dismissal of Das as unsuitable.

So why was *he* suitable?

Then he thought he knew why. He had no vested interests; he belonged to no regime, no government. "I'm a messenger?" he said. "You want me to return to Earth, to tell my people of the Krevala and the Concordance. To warn them off seeking contact...?"

Something about the silence that greeted his words told him he was wrong.

The alien said at last, "We wish you to tell no one about these things, Vaughan."

"Then why...?" he said.

"Vaughan..." the alien said. "There are many races like your own in the galaxy, races which show potential and promise but which at the moment are immature. Among these races we have... let's say that we have people who we can trust, people who like you possess a telepathic ability. These people, these aliens, are the subjects through whom we monitor the state of the respective race—"

"You mean... you're in telepathic contact with them?"

"That is so. They are... allies in our bid to monitor the races who one day we might see fit to admit to the Concordance. We might not be in contact with them for many of your years at a time; then again, we might contact them several times in a year."

Vaughan considered the implications of the Taoth's words. He, among the tens of thousands of telepaths on Earth and across the Expansion, was being singled out as the representative of his race. The idea was almost too much to contemplate.

"And you want me to be your human contact?"

The alien turned its thin hand. "Vaughan, you are loyal to no one but yourself and your family. We find your suspicions, your dispassion, an admirable trait. You have risen above the petty divisions that render your race so untrustworthy. You will be an ideal contact. We call the trusted ones, of the various races across the galaxy, Cosmopath."

Cosmopaths. Vaughan smiled to himself. He was to become a Cosmopath...

"How will this work?" he asked. "What do you require from me?"

Instead of speaking, the alien merely looked at Vaughan with its great eyes. A second later he heard a voice in his head. >>>*We will give you a code, and a program, which will allow you to contact us. More often, we will contact you. We will require information about the expansion of the human race, and developments in your sciences. We will also require information about the political situations which prevail upon Earth and across the Expansion. With this information, we can assess your race, its ambitions, its trustworthiness. It is a task not to be taken lightly, and of course you will be free to relinquish it at any time.*

Vaughan considered what he was being asked. He wondered if someone more suspicious than himself might question the motivations of the Taoth, their need for this information.

The alien reached out, touched the crimson scab that sheathed his handset. Instantly the scab dissolved, deliquesced, and ran in globules like mercury from his arm and to the ground where it seemed to soak into the glittering marble slabs.

>>>*Vaughan*, said the voice in his head. >>>*Access your tele-ability; send forth a probe. We are open to you...*

Hesitantly, Vaughan tapped the enable code into his handset, wondering what he might encounter in the minds of the assembled Taoth.

He sent a probe towards the alien leader.

He expected to read, if anything, mere abstract emotions and memories from the alien, incomprehensible to the human mind. What he encountered, instead, was not one mind but a million, a gestalt ocean of thought and sensibility.

>>>*This*, said a voice in his head, *is the collective unconscious of the Taoth. We are not a hive mind as such, though we do have a pooled cerebral cache which underpins and gives meaning to our individual identities. Revel in this, Vaughan, and behold the sincerity of my race...*

Vaughan found himself sinking into a great ocean of pacific sensibility. Much of it was abstract to him, merest sensations of mentation and emotion, as comprehensible to him as a complex abstract hologram might be to a child... and yet he did sense

the sincerity the alien mentioned, the underlying...
he almost thought of it as the *humanity* of the alien
race... but rather the underlying sense that its individuals had outgrown such material concerns as
personal gain, had banished the demon of the ego.

He knew, after just minutes of bathing in this
alien ocean, that the Taoth could be trusted.

He rose, emerged from the alien collective unconscious and took possession once again of his own
identity. He disabled his tele-ability and felt suddenly, oddly, very alone.

The alien said, "You will consent to be our
human contact?"

Vaughan saw that the head of every council member was turned his way; he felt the regard of a
dozen pairs of great, black eyes.

"I would be honoured to be your contact," he
said.

Instantly a frenzy of golden filaments connected
the heads of the aliens in a visually dizzying permu-
tation, and Vaughan sensed delight in the air.

"This is the code," said the alien, and relayed a
six-digit number to Vaughan.

"But..." He looked at the alien. "There are
telepaths on Earth who use viral programs... What
about the danger that I'll be read, my status as a
Cosmopath compromised?"

The alien said, "Do not concern yourself on that
account. The harn – what you called the crimson
scab – secured your program with a shield which
cannot be bypassed. Any knowledge you possess
will not be read."

Vaughan nodded, reassured. A thought occurred
to him.

The alien said, forestalling his question, "Yes, you can tell Sukara. If you connect your handsets, the harn will access her program and provide an unreadable shield."

Vaughan smiled and looked around the gathered Taoth. "Thank you," he said.

"We will return you directly to Earth, to Bengal Station," the alien said, "as your standing with Chandrasakar might now be... shall we say, problematical."

He stared at the alien. "You can do that?" he asked, then smiled at the stupidity of the question.

He thought of Sukara, and her delight at having him back so soon.

Then he considered Parveen Das, back on Delta Cephei VII and facing Chandrasakar and his henchmen alone.

He said, "I need to go back to Delta Cephei VII, briefly. Parveen Das, the telepath you found unsuitable, is still there. With your permission I'd like to fetch her so that–"

The leader reached out his hand and touched Vaughan's arm. "We understand. She is in danger. By all means bring her to this sanctuary, and we will transfer you both to Earth."

The council stood as one, and eleven members moved off along the canal while the twelfth, the leader, gestured Vaughan to accompany him up the plinth of steps to the arching portal.

Vaughan climbed the steps, wondering what he might find on Delta Cephei VII. Would Das believe him when he told her that they would soon be transferred to Earth? He wondered, also, what story he might concoct to explain why the Taoth had required his presence on Vluta.

They approached the membrane of the portal side by side and Vaughan stared through.

The chamber on the other side was empty; there was no sign of Das or Connor.

He turned to the alien. "One thing..." He considered Chandrasakar's discovery of the colonists, the underground caverns, and what this might mean to their way of life.

The alien pre-empted his question. "Do not worry yourself on that score," it said. "We have the matter in hand. Now go, and return soon."

Vaughan nodded, turned to face the portal, and stepped through. He felt a second of light-headedness, a rush of heat. Then he was on the other side, his step unbroken, walking away from the portal towards the cavern's entrance.

He paused and looked back through the membrane. The alien raised its hand in an oddly human gesture.

He turned and hurried towards the exit.

TWENTY-EIGHT

THE CODE

Sukara came to her senses in a bare apartment.

She looked through the window, saw the open sky as grey as pewter with the unshed monsoon rains. So she wasn't in Dr Rao's safe house on Level Two...

The only furnishings in the small room were the sofa on which she sat and a kitchen chair by the window. The heat was merciless. She was sweating freely, slick rivulets greasing her torso.

She tried to move, but her ankles were bound together and tied to the feet of the sofa. She tried to stand, but almost fell forwards. She slumped down into the cushions and looked around. Her cheek throbbed where the bastard had hit her, but more than the pain she felt an overwhelming sense of dread. They wanted something from her, obviously – but she had no idea what. She recalled the Chink who'd followed her, and wondered if her captors were aware of his death. If they were, then they might not be so careful with her.

She lifted her left arm and began tapping the police code into her handset.

Shockingly, someone hit her across the back of her head. She fell forward, yelling. She heard someone snicker, behind her, and at the same time someone else moved around the sofa and came into view.

It was not the Chink who'd caught her, but someone else – a grinning fish-faced bastard with a pudding-bowl haircut, the latest fashion among the Chinese on the Station.

The guy hunkered down before her, just out of arm's reach. He was holding a small enabling pin in his right hand. "You don't think we'd let you get away with that, do you, Sukara?"

He was sweating, and gave off an overwhelming stench of body-odour almost animal in its intensity. "Now, I hope you're going to be reasonable."

She took a few shallow breaths, trying not to inhale his stink. "About what?"

"About," said Fish-face, "giving us what we want."

This was more than just an abduction and possible rape by a bunch of psychopaths, she thought. "What do you want?"

"The code," Fish-face said, "that'll connect your handset to Jeff Vaughan."

So they wanted, for some reason, to contact Jeff. She guessed they'd tried using her handset while she was unconscious, but she'd erased the code on Jeff's instructions before he left, and committed it to memory.

"What do you want with Jeff?" she asked.

She felt another ringing blow on the back of her

head. She pitched forward, crying out. The second Chink moved around the sofa and sat on the chair before the window, staring out. It was the bastard who'd abducted her in the street.

Fish-face said, "We're asking the questions."

She rubbed the back of her head, staring past Fish-face at the door.

"Now, the code..."

She thought about it, then said, "I don't have a code. I don't contact Jeff. He contacts me."

The blow was all the more painful for being unexpected and lightning fast. Fish-face struck out, his fist connecting with her jaw, sending a blaze of pain through her skull. She rocked back, eyes wide.

"We can play this little game all day, but it'll get a little tiresome. We ask the question, you lie, and then we hurt you. Eventually we'll get tired of playing the game, and things will get serious." Fish-face paused and looked across at his accomplice who, well rehearsed, took up the line.

"Sukara," he said without taking his gaze from outside, "there is a bed in the next room, and we've brought enough cord with us to tie your arms and legs."

"And we have a knife," Fish-face went on. "Snick-snick, and off with your clothes..."

"And after that, we hurt you again."

"But," said Fish-face, "we hope it won't come to that. We hope you're going to be reasonable about this. Now, the code."

She knew the bastards would carry out the threat, and enjoy doing so, if she didn't give them the code. But they'd probably rape her anyway, code given or not... Thing was, would giving them the code compromise Jeff in any way?

She said, "I'll give you the code."

Fish-face smiled. He was truly ugly, and even more so when he smiled, with his underslung jaw and his small, jutting rows of teeth. "Good girl."

He reached out, took her arm, and drew it to him. He laid her wrist on his knee, inserted the enabling pin into her handset and held a finger above the keypad.

She repeated the code, preceded by the password. Fish-face entered them and waited.

Sukara stared at the screen, waiting for Jeff's face to fill it. She just wanted to see his face again...

The screen remained blank, then flashed up the barred circle sign denoting either access denied or unavailable status.

The guy by the window stood and moved across to the sofa. He stared down at the screen. He sounded disappointed when he said, "And I thought you were going to be reasonable..." He moved, purposefully, towards the bedroom door.

"That's the code! I swear! Please, try it again..."

The second guy stopped outside the bedroom door and watched as Fish-face re-entered the code.

Sukara's heart pounded, counting down the seconds.

She stared at the screen, willing Jeff to answer.

A second later the barred logo came up again.

Fish-face stood abruptly.

The second guy said, grinning, "A little fun, heh?"

Fish-face contemplated, fingering his out-thrust jaw. He smiled. "I have a better idea." He moved across to his accomplice and they conferred in whispers.

The result was that the second guy hurried across the room, opened the apartment door, and slipped out. Sukara briefly saw a flash of carpeted landing before the door closed: she thought of yelling for help, decided against it.

"We think," Fish-face said softly, "that there might be a better way of persuading you to give us the correct code."

"But it was!" she wailed.

"After all," he went on, "how persuasive can rape be, to someone who was raped a dozen times a day for baht?"

He moved out of sight, and Sukara heard an interior door snick shut.

She sat back and closed her eyes. Who were these people, she wondered, that they knew so much about her past?

She opened her eyes and sat forward, sickened. They said they had a better way of persuading her…

A thought occurred.

No, she thought. Please, no.

She reached for the jacket pocket in which she kept the security pin for Pham's school gate.

It wasn't there.

A pit of despair opened within her, excavating a grieving hollow in her chest.

She closed her eyes and sobbed. At least Fish-face wasn't here to see her distress.

She had no idea how long she sat there, eyes shut, fearing what would happen very soon now. She existed in a limbo of fear, consumed by the desire for revenge and the knowledge of the futility of her situation.

She heard a toilet flush, a door open. She opened her eyes.

Fish-face moved into sight and paused by the window, looking out.

A few minutes later he said, "Ah... here they are now."

It was all Sukara could do to stop herself yelling out loud in despair.

Two minutes later she heard a quick knock. Fish-face crossed the room and unlatched the door.

Pham moved into the room, wide-eyed. "Mum..." She shook her head. "But he said that Li was..." She stopped, staring at Sukara's bound ankles.

She spun and yelled at the second guy. "Who are you? Why–"

Fish-face lashed out, backhanding Pham across the face. She yelled and fell to the floor.

Sukara bent double, reaching out and pulling Pham towards her. Fish-face took Pham's arm and yanked her away. Pham struggled, kicking her legs and lashing out. The second guy grabbed her legs and between them they carried her, kicking and screaming, to the bedroom. The door banged shut.

Sukara sobbed and heard her daughter's screams, soon cut off. Silence.

A minute later the door opened again and Fish-face walked out. A minute... Surely they couldn't have had time to...?

She said, "Listen. I was telling you the truth. That was the code. Try again, okay?" She took a breath, then had an idea. "Listen, I kept all the other calls to Jeff, stored in here. Maybe if you access them, there'll be some way you can see that the code I used was the one I gave you, okay?"

Fish-face listened. Without a word he approached her, knelt, and took her arm. He accessed her handset and she told him how to enable the memory. He tapped at the keypad, then nodded.

"Hey, Sukara, it's your lucky day..."

He stood and walked around the sofa. The bedroom door opened and he spoke in low tones to his accomplice. Minutes later Pham appeared, moved around the sofa, and dropped into the cushions beside Sukara. She was silently sobbing. "They said... They said they'd..."

Sukara hugged Pham to her while Fish-face bent and shackled her ankles to the feet of the sofa.

"We'll be okay, Pham," Sukara said, over and over. "Keep quiet. Do as they say, okay?"

"But what do they want?" Pham whispered.

Fish-face said, "Okay. We'll try again."

He took Sukara's arm, accessed her handset and entered Jeff's code. Once again the barred sigil appeared. Fish-face nodded. "We'll give it an hour, okay, and after that..." He removed the enabling pin from the handset.

The two men moved out of sight around the sofa, and Sukara hugged Pham to her and closed her eyes, murmuring reassurances into her daughter's ear.

TWENTY-NINE

A NECESSARY EXECUTION

Vaughan came to the top of the steps leading down to the deserted alien city.

He paused, then moved to where the rocks on his left offered some cover. He crouched, enabled his tele-ability, and probed.

Nothing. Absolute silence. He had expected to pick up the static of Das's mind-shield, but he read nothing.

He stood and scanned the streets. They appeared empty, eerily silent. He wondered where Das had ßgone. Had she been picked up by Chandrasakar and taken somewhere...? His tele-ability had a range of a little over 500 metres. They could be anywhere beyond that.

He decided to head for the cover of the city and move systematically through the streets. He would search for thirty minutes, then return to the membrane. The thought of being reunited with Sukara filled him with joy.

He stood and hurried down the steps, coming at

last to the boulevard that encircled the city. He moved into the shadow of a crumbling, brown-walled building and probed. He reckoned he had travelled 300 metres from the top of the steps – but there was still no static from the mind-shields of Das or Chandrasakar and his men.

He moved from the building and hurried down the wide street towards the centre of the city, keeping in the shadows of the walls. Part of him wanted to return now, leave Das to her fate and get back to the safety of the chamber. Another part wanted to find Das, save her from Chandrasakar. He wondered if his motivations in wanting this were no more than the desire to show her that he had overcome the combined powers of her government and the Chandrasakar Organisation.

He reckoned he had walked a couple of hundred metres from the edge of the city when he detected the first faint signal of the mind-shield. It was a patch of static, very faint, on the edges of his perception.

He concentrated. It was around 500 metres away, to his right. He came to a turning and slipped along it, and as he did so the static of the mind-shield became stronger.

The static was unmoving, and he rapidly covered the distance towards it.

Then he stopped, panting, and pressed himself against the rough wall of a windowless building. He detected another eight mind-shields, a little way beyond the first. He calculated that they were all within 400 metres of his present position. They, like the first, were unmoving.

He moved forward with greater care, keeping to the cover of walls and buildings.

When he judged that the mind-shields were no more than fifty metres away, he stopped and considered his next move.

He was in the recessed doorway of a building that occupied the end of a row. The door was made of some toughened fungal material. He applied pressure, then a little more, and it gave under his weight. The room was small and gloomy. He ran through it to another, larger room, and found what he was looking for. A narrow staircase, with tiny steps, rose to the second floor. He climbed carefully so as not to put his feet through the ancient material.

The room on the upper floor was spacious and overlooked what once might have been a fountain. He moved to the shuttered window, reached out, and carefully eased open the shutter.

Light filled the room, momentarily dazzling him. When his eyes adjusted, he peered out – then pulled back quickly, hardly able to believe what he'd seen.

He took a breath, looked again.

He saw Das first. She was sitting against a low wall, very still, her legs outstretched before her and her hands holding something in her lap. Vaughan saw, with incredulity, that she was embracing the mess of her entrails that had slopped from the wound in her abdomen. Her eyes were still open, staring sightlessly at some point far beyond the confines of the cavern.

Only then did he see Chandrasakar.

His body was lying on its back five metres to Das's right. His head and shoulders, detached, were a metre away, connected by a long smear of blood.

Vaughan pulled back again, heart throbbing, and considered what might have happened. When he looked again he knew what he was looking for.

He saw no sign of a weapon near Das. He reckoned that she must have been shot where she sat, as there was an absence of blood anywhere around her. Similarly, there was no evidence of a weapon near the tycoon's body. They couldn't have killed each other.

He looked beyond their bodies, then, and saw the carnage. He counted the static of six further mind-shields, made out chunks of meat wrapped in blue material. They had been lasered, messily, and their sectioned remains were spread over the wide, sunken area of the empty fountain. He guessed that the security personnel had been running when the lasers struck, their momentum careening limbs, heads and torsos in every direction. He looked among the remains for Singh's turbaned head. It wasn't there.

So had Singh killed Chandrasakar, Das, and the security personnel who had been loyal to the tycoon?

Was he now somewhere in the city...?

Vaughan stared down at the carnage and considered what it represented: a messy Rorschach blot denoting the psychology of greed and the lust for power which rendered humankind so treacherous. No wonder the Taoth and the other aliens had fled before humanity's terrible expansion.

He was brought to his senses by the amplified voice of a drone. "We know you are there, Vaughan. Drop your laser and you might live."

He scanned, caught the faint signal of a mind-shield on the periphery of his perception, directly ahead of him across the square.

Either the bastard was a telepath with a range greater than his own, or Singh had seen him as he made his way through the city.

He slipped his weapon from inside his jacket, but he had no intention of dropping it as requested. He rolled from the window. A split second later a blinding laser vector lanced through the opening and crumbled the far wall. He stood and ran, not for the stairs but towards the gaping hole the laser had obligingly opened in the thin mud wall.

In the next room he continued sprinting, turned and used his shoulder against the wall. It gave and he staggered through into the next building. He hardly paused, but launched himself at the next wall. He crashed through, snagged by fibres and choked by dust. His escape might have been unconventional, but it might confuse Singh and buy him time.

The next wall, however, refused to buckle and he tried again, then gave up. He took the stairs four at a time and found himself in a small room fronting the street. Rather than risk Singh's lasers in the open air, he barged through a downstairs wall into the adjacent building. A door was situated on the far wall; he reckoned he could exit through this and keep the buildings between himself and Singh.

He scanned. Singh was perhaps 400 metres behind him, racing down the street in his direction.

He crashed through the door, turned left, and sprinted. Ahead, at the end of the avenue, he made out the rise of steps towards the triangular opening to the chamber.

He wondered if he could make it to the top of the steps before Singh reached the corner of the avenue and had him in his sights.

But what of the drones, he thought. He expected to be confronted by one of the mincing, mechanical spiders at any second...

He sprinted, lungs bursting and a shooting pain lancing through his right knee. He tried to recall the code the alien leader had given him in order to initiate mind-contact; he'd entered it into his handset, but he couldn't access the code while fleeing – and anyway, he couldn't rely on the Taoth to save him now.

He came to the boulevard encircling the city, sprinted out into the open and expected to earn a laser in his back at any second. He scanned. Singh was on the edge of his range, 500 metres away, but he was unable to tell whether or not he'd turned the corner.

There was still no sign of the drones, and he wondered how Singh might have deployed them. Why hadn't they shown themselves before now?

Seconds later a blinding laser vector missed him by a metre and turned the steps before him to rubble. He turned quickly, laying down a random pattern of laser fire that would hopefully buy him time.

He leapt the steaming debris and raced up the steps, dodging right and left. Another vector burned the air half a metre away and slammed into the marble with a deafening explosion. Shrapnel shards of stone tore into his flank and he cried out in pain. He was about ten metres from the top of the steps, with the same distance again to the rent in the rock-face.

He heard a distant cry and wondered whether

Singh was resorting to bargaining with him. Perhaps the fire so far had been warning shots only. It made sense: Singh, whoever he was working for, would want Vaughan alive in order to prise from him that alien's secret...

The next vector missed his leg by inches, and he guessed he was right. Singh was aiming to maim him, now.

He came to the top of the steps and launched himself towards the gash in the rock. He made it a second later, laser fire bringing slabs of rock down in his wake.

He dived through, falling on his face in the narrow corridor, then pushing himself to his feet and sprinting into the chamber.

He stopped dead. Now he knew why Singh had held off using the drones.

Two glinting silver spiders stood before the membrane, their weapons trained on him.

"Vaughan," a drone said, "drop your weapon. Now."

He did as instructed and raised his arms, looking beyond the drones. There was no sign of the Taoth through the membrane of the portal.

He heard a sound behind him and turned.

Singh appeared through the slitted entrance to the chamber. He stared at Vaughan, then beyond to the rearing magnificence of the portal and the spread of Vluta. He gripped a laser, directed at Vaughan.

He nodded. "They spoke of a wonder in the communiqué," he said. His gaze turned to Vaughan. "Why did the aliens take you?"

Vaughan licked his lips. "You wouldn't believe me if I told you."

Singh snapped a command in Punjabi. Behind him, Vaughan heard the quick ring of metal feet on stone. He turned. A drone was before him, its laser in his midriff.

Singh said, "If you don't tell me what this is, what the aliens wanted with you... then I'll give the order for your execution."

Vaughan turned to the Indian and managed a smile. "And do you think that'll bring you any closer to finding out what that is, Singh?"

The Indian spoke to the drone, and it raised its laser to Vaughan's head.

"Tell me," Singh said.

He nodded, and was considering what he might tell Singh when a voice spoke in his head.

>>>*We have the situation under control, Vaughan.*

He started, then thought: *What do you want me to do?*

>>>*Tell Singh to get the drone away from you; tell him that then you might tell him what he wants to know.*

Vaughan glanced at the Indian, wondering what the Taoth intended. "Okay, I'll tell you. But first, get this bastard away from me, okay?"

Singh spoke to the drone. Seconds later the spider lowered its laser, then retreated nimbly to where its companion stood before the membrane.

"Right," Singh said. "What the hell's happening here, Vaughan?"

>>>*We are a compassionate people, Vaughan,* the voice spoke in his head. *Do not judge us too harshly for what we are about to do. Singh would have no compunction about killing you, once he had*

removed your shield and read your mind.

So he was a telepath, Vaughan thought.

A second later three silver spokes of light lanced from beyond the membrane. They struck the drones and Singh simultaneously, reducing the spiders to slag and drilling the Indian neatly through the forehead. He remained upright for several seconds, his expression almost incredulous, then crumpled to the ground.

>>>*Please, Vaughan. Join us...*

Vaughan turned from the corpse, considering the Taoth's words, and their actions. He retrieved his laser, then stepped around the shattered drones and hurried towards the arching membrane of the portal.

A robed alien – he was unsure whether it was the same one which had spoken to him – approached the membrane and raised a hand in greeting.

He passed through the membrane, feeling a surge of heat race across his flesh, and staggered towards the Taoth.

The alien raised an arm, and seconds later the membrane flickered. The scene in the cavern wavered like the image on a faulty holo-set. Then it vanished, and in its place stood a giant, empty frame through which Vaughan saw the distant orb of the gas giant.

He was 30,000 light years from Earth – and safe.

Then his handset chimed.

THIRTY

THE JOY OF REUNION

He accessed the call and stared at the screen.

His surge of delight at seeing Sukara was instantly quenched when he looked closely at her face. She was tearful, and his first thought was Li.

"Su...?"

"Jeff! They have me and Pham! They want–"

The image on the screen vanished; the screen wobbled, and another face came into shot. This one was broad, pop-eyed, and prognathous. Chinese, he thought, made ugly with urgent intent.

Dread settled over him. "What do you want?"

"Vaughan? Jeff Vaughan?"

"I said what do you want?" His heart pounded. The Chinaman grinned, revealing small, sharp teeth. He looked, Vaughan thought, like a particularly predatory carp.

"The girl wasn't lying," he said. "We've got her and the kid."

"What," said Vaughan for the third time, with deliberation, "do you want?"

"First I'll tell you what'll happen to the girl and the kid if we don't get it, okay?" The Chinaman's mugshot vanished, replaced on the tiny screen by Sukara and Pham, their faces pressed together as they hugged each other tearfully.

"If you don't give us what we want, Vaughan, we'll kill the kid first. Got that? Right in front of Mummy. We'll drill the little cunt in the gut and let her die slowly. Then, if you're still playing hardball, we'll do the same with Mummy. Okay? Only we'll have a little fun, first."

Vaughan felt his legs give under him. He slumped to the marble floor, staring at the grinning face on his handset.

He nodded. "Okay," he said. "I'm listening. What do you want?"

In his head a voice made itself heard, soothing, calming. >>>*Do not worry, Vaughan. We can help you.*

"One, we want Chandrasakar dead. Got that? Kill the tycoon."

Vaughan nodded, wondering how to play this. It would be a mistake to tell them that the Indian was already dead, he knew. "Okay. And then?"

"We know there's something big down there, Vaughan. We intercepted the colonists' message. And we want to know what it is, got that?"

"What if–?" Vaughan began.

The Chinaman's piscine mug shot was whipped away, replaced by Pham's terrified face. Someone – the bastard's accomplice – hit her, hard. Her head whiplashed, her expression wide-eyed with pain and fright. Pham screamed.

Vaughan heard his wife's terrified sobs. Then the

first Chinaman was back, grinning out at him.

"No 'what ifs', Vaughan. We want to know what's down there."

>>>*Agree to their demands, Vaughan. Play for time.*

Vaughan nodded. "That might take a while. We're still moving through the caverns..."

The Chinaman grinned. "That's fine by us, Vaughan. We have all the time in the world. When you find out what all the fuss is about, get back to us. In detail. We want to know what's down there, and exactly where it is. How it's protected, how many colonists are down there with it... Then you kill Chandrasakar and his security team, okay?" The bastard showed his teeth again. "And we want to see their heads, Vaughan. Get back to the surface, tell the crew of the *Kali* that you met resistance, whatever. We'll be waiting for you when you get back to Earth."

He worked to maintain his even breathing. "And if I do this? What about Su and Pham? You'll let them go, okay?"

"Only when you're back here. Until then they're staying put."

Vaughan felt something rip within him, despair and hopelessness, and a maniacal desire for revenge.

He said evenly, "That's a lot to ask. What makes you think the crew of the *Kali* will buy my story?"

The Chinaman laughed. "It's up to you to convince them, isn't it? And it's not as if you don't have the incentive. When you're spinning them the lie, just think of what'll happen to your girls if you blow it."

Vaughan nodded. "Okay, okay. I'll do it–"

"We'll be in contact in an hour, and every hour after that, for progress reports."

Vaughan heard a scream – Pham's – and a second later he saw her tiny fist strike the Chinaman on the cheek. "You bastard!" she cried.

The screen yawed, then the Chinaman cut the connection.

What was happening now, thousands of light years away on Earth? He knew that the bastards had to keep Su and Pham alive if he were to deliver what they wanted – but it was what they might do to the girls in the interim the filled him with despair.

The alien was squatting beside him. It reached out, placed a thin hand on his shoulder. >>>*Do not fear, Vaughan. As I said, we can help you.*

He looked up. "How the hell–?"

"Come," it verbalised. "I alerted my colleagues when I understood your dilemma. We will open a portal to where your loved ones are being held. We will send you through. The rest, I am afraid, will be up to you."

Hardly daring to believe the alien's words, he climbed to his feet and followed it across the marble piazza towards a white-walled building. Several aliens emerged from the low doorway, exchanging bursts of golden light with the leader.

"The portal is prepared, Vaughan. Come."

Vaughan ducked into the building and saw, as if set flush with the far wall, a shimmering blue portal the approximate size of a coffin. The blue membrane flickered, and a second later he made out a darkened room in what looked like the basement of a tenement block. Pipes filled the room, an old boiler and stacked cartons.

"We were able to locate the approximate source of the call from the signal to your handset, Vaughan. This is two floors below where they are holding your loved ones." The alien paused, then said, "We know you will succeed."

Vaughan stepped forward, feeling light-headed. He turned and looked at the alien, then beyond it to the others watching him.

"And then?"

The alien made its calm, turning-palm gesture. "And then, in due course, we will be in touch. Farewell, Vaughan. Good luck."

He reached out, and the alien realised his intent and matched the gesture. They clasped hands. Then Vaughan turned quickly and stepped through the portal.

A dizzy sensation, a rush of heat, and then he was standing in a grubby tenement basement on Bengal Station, Earth.

It took him a few seconds to realise the full import of what had just happened, and then attempt to forget that and concentrate on saving Su and Pham.

He would have the advantage of surprise. The last thing the bastards would be expecting was for him to come bursting in through the door. At the same time, he knew there would be no room for the slightest error of judgement. He had one chance only to save Su and Pham, and he had to concentrate on the best way of going about the rescue. One thing in his favour was that he had plenty of time.

He enabled his tele-ability and probed. He caught the mind-noise of half a dozen individuals in the building above him. It was midday, he gleaned from the thoughts of an old woman on the first floor. Most of the tenement's occupants were at work. He filtered out the extraneous mind-noise and concentrated on finding Pham. Su had a mind-shield implanted in her handset, and no doubt the Chinese pair would be shielded – but Pham was not.

Seconds later he found Pham's cerebral signature, latching on to it with relief and at the same time pain. Pham was huddled on a sofa, clutching Su and crying quietly to herself. The side of her face still smarted from the Chinaman's blow, and she knew they were capable of killing her and Su without a second thought. Su's embrace was a source of comfort and reassurance. They were both shackled at the ankles, their feet tied together and the cord knotted to the legs of the sofa. Pham was bursting to go to the loo, but was determined not to wet herself in front of the Chinaman.

He read, on a deeper level, how much she missed him, how much she wanted to hold him... He felt tears sting his eyes as he saw himself through her perceptions: a powerful figure she wholly loved and trusted, the father she thought she'd never have.

He put aside his stepdaughter's emotions and concentrated on what she was experiencing, what she was seeing. Pham's perceptions of what was happening in the apartment would be his only guide from now on.

The last thing he wanted, he thought, was her to fall asleep: he probed and found that she was far from tired. Relieved, he closed his eyes and saw, in his head, the apartment from Pham's point of view.

One of their captors sat directly before them –

the fish-faced bastard who'd communicated with Vaughan – while the second was seated on a chair to their left, positioned by the window and looking out on to the street below.

Vaughan saw with relief that neither of the pair was holding a weapon. They both had laser pistols, he knew from Pham's memories, but Fish-face had slipped his into a holster beneath his jacket, and the other had taken his weapon from his holster and placed it on the window-sill before him. The danger would be that the second bastard would be able to reach his pistol in a second, if alerted: Vaughan would have to take him out first.

Still watching the apartment through Pham's eyes, he climbed the three concrete steps to a door and tried it. As he'd expected, it was locked. He withdrew his probe from Pham's mind and scanned the immediate vicinity. There was no one near the door; the closest anyone was to the basement was the old woman on the first floor, and she was bed-ridden.

He pulled out his laser, set it to low, and burned the lock. He allowed a couple of minutes for the slag to cool, then pulled open the door and stepped out. He was in a dark corridor leading to the lobby. He found Pham's signature again, checked that the Chinamen were still where they had been, and headed for the staircase.

He was half-way up the short flight when Pham looked at Fish-face as he stood up, stretched, and glanced at his handset. Vaughan stopped dead in his tracks, closed his eyes, and concentrated.

Fish-face spoke to his accomplice, "Hungry?"

The guy at the window said, "I'll get something.

Pork satay?"

"And coffee."

Pham watched as the guy near the window stood up and checked his wallet. He vicariously felt her hunger pangs. She said, "I want something to eat."

Fish-face grinned. "Tough."

Pham looked up at Su, who said, "Please. You can't keep us here without food and drink."

Fish-face laughed at this. "Oh, can't we? Watch us."

He gestured at his accomplice to get going.

Pham began to cry again, but she noticed that the second guy had left his pistol on the window-sill. Vaughan read her mind as, for a brief second, she contemplated how she might free herself and reach the gun... She tried to pull and twist her foot without being noticed, but the knots were too tight and she gave up.

Vaughan was at once thankful for this, and proud that she had even contemplated escaping.

She watched as the second Chinaman walked to the door and opened it. The door eased shut behind him with a loud snick.

Vaughan turned and moved from the foot of the stairs, across the lobby to the basement door as the guy's mind-shield static dropped towards him. He eased himself inside and closed the door, but for a fraction. From here he could see the tenement's entrance. He sniffed. The reek of molten plastic and metal filled the air. He hoped the bastard wouldn't notice it and decide to investigate.

Seconds later the Chinaman crossed the lobby, pulled open the door, and stepped out into the street. If he'd noticed the stink, he hadn't given it a second thought.

Vaughan thought through his options and decided how he was going to play it.

He concentrated on what Pham was seeing. Fish-face had remained standing, and now he moved across to the window and stared down at the street.

Pham said, "When are you going to let us go?"

Vaughan felt Su's quick squeeze, warning her.

Fish-face looked round and glared at Pham. "You heard what I told Daddy."

Pham felt despair. "But that's a long time away!"

The guy shrugged. "Tough."

Now Su said, "Jeff said he'd get the information you want. Why not let us go then?"

"Do I look like a fool?" And at this, Pham thought to herself: You do, actually, a fish-faced fool – and Vaughan found himself laughing. The guy went on, "What if he feeds us rubbish, eh? We want to get him back, debrief him. Then we'll let you go."

Pham stared at the man. Four years ago she'd faced similar danger, crossed the path of a ruthless killer, and she knew that Fish-face was likely to kill her and Su once he, Jeff, was back on the Station and the Chinks got what they wanted. He felt a wave of despair and terror sweep through her and she fought to control her tears. He wanted to reach out, console her, and relished the prospect of doing so very soon now.

He glanced at his handset. The other guy had been gone ten minutes. He withdrew his concentration from Pham's mind and stared through the gap at the tenement's front door.

He set his laser on stun, gripped it before his

chest, and waited.

Five minutes later a patch of mind-shield static approached the building. The door opened and the guy, laden with Chinese take-out, stepped through and crossed to the stairs. Vaughan eased himself from the basement and moved across the lobby. The guy was on the fourth step, his back to the lobby. Without ceremony, Vaughan lifted his laser and gave the guy a quick pulse in the small of the back. He spasmed, gave a short cry, and fell to the floor, tumbling down the steps and mashing the contents of the silver trays beneath his body. He'd be out for thirty minutes, at least: more than enough time for Vaughan to do what he needed to do.

He stepped over the guy and rushed up the steps, onto the landing and up the second flight. At the top he paused, concentrating. Pham's cerebral signature came from the second door along. Vaughan crossed to it, stopped, and gathered himself.

This time, he decided, he'd let the bastard see him; Vaughan wanted revenge, wanted the bastard to know that he, Vaughan, had come back to save his family.

He probed. He ignored Pham's despair and saw the room through her eyes. Fish-face was still near the window. If he'd seen his accomplice coming, then he'd be expecting him at any second.

Vaughan slipped his laser into his trouser belt, took a breath, and knocked on the door.

Through Pham's eyes he watched Fish-face move from the window, leaving his gun on the sill. He crossed the room, reached out for the door handle, and pulled it open...

Vaughan acted before the bastard could register

surprise. He grabbed Fish-face by the throat and dragged him from the room. With his right hand he punched him in the face, twice, and very hard. Fish-face grunted, eyes wide with shock and disbelief. Vaughan thrust him to the ground, smacked him in the face again, breaking his nose. He stopped, then, staring down at the guy's terrified face.

"Vaughan?" Fish-face mouthed in disbelief.

"How does it feel?" Vaughan said. "How does it feel to be helpless and on the wrong end of violence? You enjoyed hitting my daughter..."

The guy shook his head, either in denial or incredulity at Vaughan's return. "How...?"

Vaughan grabbed a handful of the guy's shirt, lifted him to the stairs, and pitched him down the steps. He fell head over heels, something breaking with a moist crunch as he hit the concrete landing below. He stared up at Vaughan, panting in pain, his face smeared with blood. Vaughan moved down a couple of steps, standing over the bastard, and drew his pistol.

The guy's eyes widened and he gabbled something at Vaughan, reverting to Mandarin in his terror.

"I'm going to kill you, just like you would have killed my wife and daughter..."

He saw the light in the Chinaman's eyes; the intent to deny, followed quickly by the realisation that denial would be futile.

Vaughan aimed the pistol at the man's head.

"No, please! Please!"

It was all he could do to stop himself from flipping the gauge from stun, but he thought of Su and Pham back in the room, knew what Su would want.

You lucky bastard, he thought, and fired at the

guy's chest.

Fish-face jerked, squealed, and lay very still.

Vaughan replaced his weapon and took deep breaths. He scanned. Pham had heard the commotion. She was wondering if the cops had arrived.

He turned and walked slowly up the steps. He wanted to savour this moment. He moved towards the door. He stepped into the room.

Su and Pham were staring at the door...

Su yelled his name and he felt the blast of Pham's emotion: relief and disbelief and joy. It was a flood too great to withstand; he killed the program and rushed across the room.

They stood, still shackled by the ankles, and a second later they were in his arms, sobbing and crying his name.

He held them both, feeling their weight, their solidity, knowing that nothing, nothing at all, even communication with an alien race 30,000 light years away, could compare to the joy of this moment.

"But how?" Su said, her face streaming with tears.

"I'll tell you all about it when we get out of here." He smiled. "But I don't know if you'll believe me..."

He unknotted the cords binding Su and Pham, then got through to Lin Kapinsky and told her to get her security team to the source of his signal. She blinked and started asking questions, but he cut the connection.

Pham was in his arms, touching his face as if to assure herself that he was real.

Christ, he thought, something bursting within his

chest. How could he begin to express the love he felt for his family?

"Li?" he asked Su.

She nodded, sniffing, "She's going to be fine, Jeff," she said, and broke down again.

Later, when the security team arrived, Vaughan hitched Pham onto his hip and gripped Su by the hand. They left the building, emerging into sunlight, and caught a taxi-flier to St Theresa's hospital.

DR RAO

Vaughan woke to dazzling sunlight.

He was disoriented for a second, his head still full of dreams. He was deep underground, in a weirdly lighted cavern, and spider drones were chasing him... He sat up quickly, then smiled when he saw Sukara sleeping beside him.

The events of the dream had happened more than a month back, though it seemed paradoxically both an age ago and incredibly immediate. He slipped quietly out of bed and showered; he was dressing when his handset chimed.

Lin Kapinsky looked up at him. "Hey, Jeff. I've just had the report back from security, about the bastards who kidnapped Su and Pham."

"And?" He moved to the lounge and stood beside the floor-to-ceiling window, gazing out across the sea.

"Security stripped the bastards down to their subconscious," she reported, pulling a face, "and as we suspected: they were in the pay of the Chinese – though of course the Chinks are denying any responsibility. The three were hired by a middleman known to have links with Beijing, the same go-between responsible for hiring the assassin who went after Parveen Das."

"Good work, Lin. The thing is... am I safe here? Will they send more goons after me?" It was a possibility that had worried him since returning to the Station. Playing safe, he had moved apartments a week ago, using some of the money Chandrasakar had deposited in his account to put a down-payment on a bigger place on Level One. The girls had been ecstatic at the move.

Kapinsky looked at him. "You're safe. You see, you never left the Station."

He stared at her. "What?" To account for his sudden arrival back at the Station, he'd told her he'd returned to Earth aboard a Chandrasakar exploration voidship – and she'd seemed to buy the lie.

"I've just had a communiqué from the port authorities," Lin went on. "They said that an identity anomaly occurred six weeks ago, when their records showed someone using your identity had left Bengal Station aboard a Chandrasakar Line voidship. Get this: they said that according to Station intelligence you never left Earth, and that they were investigating the matter." She shook her head. "Don't ask me to explain that, Jeff."

"Odd," he said.

"Anyway, I'll see you back here next week, okay? Take it easy."

He told her he would, and signed off.

He stared out at a passing voidship, wondering about the communiqué from the port authorities about his never having left the Station.

Minutes later, all was explained.

>>>*Vaughan*, said a voice in his head, as clear as if the alien were in the same room. *We arranged matters so that, to all intents and purposes, you were never away from Bengal Station: records there indicate your continued presence; the authorities assume someone used your identity to facilitate their departure from the port.*

That is appreciated, Vaughan thought, wondering at the omnipotence of the Taoth.

>>>*We are delighted that Li has made a full recovery, Vaughan. We will be in contact...*

He asked about the status of the colony on Landfall, and whether it would now be opened up to extensive colonisation and exploitation. His question was met with silence.

In the event, he found out later that day.

He moved from the lounge and crossed to the girls' room, standing in the doorway and watching Li and Pham in their pyjamas, playing with their doll's house. Pham saw him and smiled; Li was too intent on her game.

He just stood and watched them for a while, then fixed breakfast. Sukara crept into the kitchen and hugged him. "It's Saturday, Jeff. Let's go to the café in the park, okay?"

"Let's do that."

After breakfast they left the apartment and strolled through the quiet park hand in hand. Pham and Li raced ahead, inexpertly kicking a football.

The air was fresh; the sun dazzled. Yesterday, weeks late, the monsoon season had begun, drenching the Station in a refreshing torrent that lasted almost thirty minutes. They'd watched the deluge through the apartment viewscreen. It seemed symbolic, Vaughan had thought; an end to all the events that had begun six weeks ago, the day the Korth assassin had come after him and Sukara had told him about Li's illness.

Yesterday, an hour before the monsoon rains began, Sukara had heard from Dr Grant that Li was to be signed off from the physician's care, the cure achieved.

They strolled across the greensward towards the café. Sukara tugged his hand. "And how's my Cosmopath this morning?"

He laughed. "I've never been happier in all my life," he told her.

He should have known that she'd take the story of his time on Landfall, and the honour the Taoth had conferred upon him, in her stride. She was a remarkable woman. Her only worry was that he might be called upon to leave Earth again, at some point in the future.

He'd reassured her on that matter. "Su, while I was out there I made a resolution: I'm never going to leave the planet again without you all, okay? If I have to go, you're all three coming with me."

Sukara had just smiled and stroked his cheek.

Now his handset chimed. It was a feed, relaying to him a news subject he'd subscribed to after his return.

"What is it?" Sukara asked.

He read the text on the screen and smiled.

"News from Delta Cephei VII," he said. "And guess what?"

She pulled a face. "Surprise me."

"Reports are full of the follow-up mission to Landfall." He laughed as he read from the screen. "They've discovered an indigenous extraterrestrial race on the planet, living in a vast subterranean chamber."

Sukara looked up at him. "So that means…?"

He nodded. He recalled what he'd been about to ask the Taoth as he was leaving Vluta: what would the discovery of the colonists, and the underground caverns, mean to the colonists' way of life? The alien had said, before he could voice the question, "Do not worry yourself on that score. We have the matter in hand…"

He told Sukara, "The Taoth left behind a contingent of their fellows. That means, technically, Delta Cephei is a restricted-access world. The report says that further colonisation, and any industrialisation, is now prohibited." He thought of Young Tom and Connor; their bucolic existence was safe now, thanks to the Taoth.

"That's great, Jeff!" She peered ahead. "Hey, isn't that Dr Rao?"

Vaughan looked across the park, towards the café. The reptilian Indian was seated under the canopy, clutching his cane, a salted lassi on the table before him.

He raised his cane when he saw Vaughan and Sukara, and called out, "My friends! Please, join me. How provident a meeting."

Sukara said, "I ought to tell the old rascal that I'd like to work for him."

Vaughan kissed her. "And I ought to thank him for saving your life."

Hand in hand, with the girls racing ahead, Vaughan and Sukara made their way towards the café.

ABOUT THE AUTHOR

Eric Brown's first short story was published in *Interzone* in 1987, and he sold his first novel, *Meridian Days*, in 1992. He has won the British Science Fiction Award twice for his short stories and has published thirty-five books: SF novels, collections, books for teenagers and younger children, and he writes a monthly SF review column for *The Guardian*. His latest books include the novella, *Starship Fall*, and the novel *Xenopath*. He is married to the writer and mediaevalist Finn Sinclair and they have a daughter, Freya.

His website can be found at:
www.ericbrown.co.uk

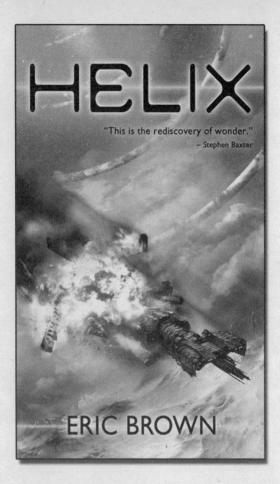

www.solarisbooks.com ISBN: 978-1-84416-472-1

Helix follows the plight of a group of humans who discover a vast system of planets arranged in a spiral wound around a central sun. The group set off to find a more habitable Earth-like world, encountering bizarre alien races on the way. But they must also find a means to stay alive...

 SOLARIS SCIENCE FICTION